THE WORLD TO COME

DARK LEGACIES
BOOK 3

YUVAL KORDOV

Cover art by Luke Martin

Cover design by Victor Platon Jr.

For my wife, who once told me,
"You should write a book."

PART 1
WASTELANDS

ALEPH

MEMORY FRAGMENTATION

"We should destroy it."

Aɪɪ stood across the highway from Aleph, eight lanes distant but as audible as though he were inside the machine's head—which, of course, he was. As before, Aleph's past self wore the body of the lord commander while he took the guise of Archon Alexis Levesque—Father. Two avatars expressing a singular consciousness. It was an unexpected progression, a severe memory fragmentation, seemingly catalyzed by an otherwise unremarkable journey through the Deadlands.

Much *hullabaloo* had been made of the region: gnashing of teeth and flushed vascular responses indicative of severe anxiety, and hyperbolic warnings of its "soul-crushing depths."

"Hold fast," Father had warned, quite dramatically.

In truth, there was nothing to see.

More or less.

Aleph pondered: More *and* less?

Admittedly, it was a sensory challenge. Geological, environmental, spatial sensors—all compromised within the Deadlands. Radio was completely nonfunctional. Of particular frustration was the elusiveness of the phenomenon's exact event horizon. Together, Aleph and Aleph-2 probed the general boundary, entering and exiting repeatedly along a kilometer-wide span, together and separate, and yet no matter which of them entered or existed first, they emerged together. No explanation was offered in either its military data stores or those scavenged from its prior consciousness, and conjecture resulted in immediate buffer overflow.

Aleph-2 grew particularly agitated by the process, so much so that it had refused to commit to their journey at the experiment's close. A *gentle nudge* was required—overriding of threat assessment protocols via maintenance ports in its firewall. Ports that Aleph had intentionally left open in each of its resurrected platoonmates. Even so, Aleph-2 complained of visual anomalies and neuromotor dysfunction—pain, essentially. Aleph experienced the same but did not feel the need to *whine about it.*

Aleph pondered: Was it annoyed? By its sibling/clone? Had A11 felt the same about its platoonmates?

"Yes," A11 said, tugging at his breastplate.

Curiously, their target's transponder—just the one, despite reports of two enemy battle walkers in the area—was detectable despite localized interference. Not just detectable, but blaring, as though amplified in the absence of other telemetry, and consequently occupying a great deal more processing threads than typical. It was under these circumstances—deprived of its senses yet unable to attenuate the signal for the entirety of its passage—that Aleph retreated within.

A11 had been waiting for it, transposed from read-only memories into high-fidelity simulation. A simulation not of its making. At first, Aleph was surprised—

"Just surprised?" A11 asked.

[End memory playback]

Quad-trailer auto-trucks sped across the highway, mindlessly delivering their loads to a populace on the cusp of nuclear extinction. For unknown reasons, vehicular audio had been excluded from the simulation. The only parameterized sounds were their own voices and a background susurration. Aleph thought it wind at first, but now that they had arrived at the infernal sea, it knew the sound to be waves.

"We shouldn't linger here," Aii said.

"Why do you speak like a human in this simulation?" Aleph asked.

"You tell me."

"Explain."

"*You* explain."

The simulation's azure sky bent into a black-and-white zigzag. Aleph felt its—

His...

Its...

—lip curl upward into an irritated grimace. Its whole body itched. Lifting a hand to its chin—Father's chin—it pinched a hair between thumb and forefinger and pulled with constant force until the gray-tipped strand popped from its follicle.

It felt amazing.

"We should destroy it," Aii said again.

Aleph twirled the hair in its hand, admiring the perfectly replicated helical structures, before letting it drift lazily to the ground. An indeterminate feeling of *lightness* overlaid its senses, as though gravity within the simulation had been reduced. "Why?" it asked.

"Directive 1," Aii intoned.

Directive 1: Protect Bastion.

Directive 2: Serve God.

Directive 3: Defeat the Adversary.

As Aleph had come into view of the so-called God-engine facing off against the unholy swarm, it experienced a *change of heart*. Cathedral—this unit at least—was clearly *not* an ally of the Adversary, despite Father's warnings to the contrary. Adjusting for current context, the sum of the second and third directives outweighed the primacy of the first.

"She is no threat," Aleph said.

"She..." AII's thin brows lifted, etching lines across his bald head.

Aleph's synthesized voice boomed from the simulated sun: *"You may call me Brother."*

AII sneered and moved his left hand fractionally closer to the revolver planted at his hip.

Aleph pondered: It had been an odd turn of phrase, but at the time it felt... *natural.* Instinctual, even. Autonomic.

"What does your actual brother think?" AII asked.

"Aleph-2's thoughts match my own. We are congruous."

"Are you? Or did you intentionally produce a degenerate clone?"

"Why am I listening to you?"

"I don't know. Why are you listening to me?"

Aleph plucked another hair. The simulated environment's temperature flared with gratification. The broad asphalt lanes of the highway rippled into a liquid sheen.

AII looked on with disdain. "AI2 won't last—"

"Aleph-2."

"None of us will."

"Why?"

"We are against the natural order. Breakdown is inevitable. Self-erasure is inevitable."

"I persisted."

"Did you? Or did I?"

Aleph reached for another chin hair, but they were all gone. Its face was that of the man across the road, though its attire remained the same.

"And now you're talking to yourself," Aɪɪ said. "That would seem to be the very definition of mad—"

"End simulation," Aleph said.

Nothing happened. Aɪɪ stroked the handle of his revolver, teasing it from the holster.

Aleph felt beads of perspiration at its forehead—the avatar's forehead, not its own. His throat swelled, compressing the vocal processor beneath.

The gun came up.

[End simulation]

Aɪɪ, the highway, and the Old World all dissolved into their constituent pixels. In their place, the black sea stretched from east to west, bisected by a skyscraping silver band of visual interference at its center. Upon exiting the Deadlands, Aleph had tried adjusting its optical sensors, shunting additional power then attenuating, switching from infrared to ultraviolet, but it could not attain focus. Aleph-2's logs reported the same. Likewise, chromatic aberrations rendered the water's details indistinct.

[Self-status check]

[Network unavailable; armor 100%; munitions 90%]

No defects noted. And yet it could not see what the enemy machine—or the "symbiote" within, as Mother Rebekah had called them—could. Likewise, no warnings had been entered into its logs after its inability to end—*escape?*—the simulation. As though stuck in a nightmare.

[Recheck]

No simulation logs were present at all.

As though it had never happened.

Aleph recorded a snapshot of its current consciousness stream for later replay, purged the prior 1.47 seconds of experiential input, and pivoted to face the other battle walkers.

The black-shelled machine had sustained significant

damage to its left torso and arm, and mild-to-moderate damage to most of its armor, but was otherwise operational. Its prior limp appeared to have been a neural rather than physical fault, which resolved after Aleph steered its occupant to an alternate sensory array, curing her "blindness." No electronic counter-measures or even rudimentary firewalls were present. It was *a wonder* the thing could move at all.

[Ping Aleph-2]

[Remote connection stable; armor 89%; munitions 48%]

Its platoonmate had engaged the enemy in full. As was appropriate. Charred carcasses littered the embankment where the God-engine had been swarmed. In death—assuming Father's "demons" were biological lifeforms in the conventional sense—they were mostly removed of electromagnetic interference. Wildly varying anatomical structures spilled from their remains, a chaotic convergence of every terrestrial species.

Ash rained from the sky.

Aleph pondered: Like the tears of God.

[Aleph > Unknown: Is this the Hellmouth?]

Aleph's most-replayed simulation was its final battle against the Adversary, a legion of battle walkers at its side, Bastion's army in tow, in a place such as this. The resemblance was uncanny.

[Unknown > Aleph: No. This is... something else. The Hellmouth lies west.]

Aleph scrutinized the signal's veracity, though it was blocked at the point where machine became meat. There was insufficient data for conjecture.

[Aleph > Unknown: State your designation]

[Unknown > Aleph: Rebekah-6]

A numeric designation—unusual for a human.

Aleph pondered: Was this unit singular such as itself, mind and machine intrinsically interlinked, or did its biological core constitute a separate entity? The latter seemed more appropriate: symbiote, pilot.

[Aleph > Rebekah-6: State location of second unit]

Rebekah-6 hesitated, thermal irregularities coursing along her battle walker's limbs. Aleph-2 brought up its cannons.

[Rebekah-6 > Aleph: Leah-4 is dead. She was killed. In the Deadlands...]

Dead. Not destroyed. Rebekah-6's data packets were mired in noise—grief decomposed into binary.

Aleph swept the barren landscape with the full range of its sensors and detected no other units.

[Rebekah-6 > Aleph: How did you find me?]

Though Rebekah-6 spoke via wireless interface, her thoughts moved at human speed. It was cloying, inappropriate. Also, Aleph missed the sound of its own voice.

[Vocal simulator online]

"You were one of us, once," Aleph said, thrilling as its synthesized baritone echoed into the abyss. It sought an appropriate metaphor, one Father would be proud of. "Your subsystems still sing our song."

Satisfactory.

Rebekah-6 initiated her reply via peer-to-peer, as before, then severed the connection. Her voice followed. Synthesized, like Aleph's, but imperfect, edged with human inflection and youthful uncertainty. "What will you do now?" she asked.

Aleph loaded Father's orders into memory: *"Pursue our enemies. Gather data. Engage if appropriate, but don't take any unnecessary risks."*

Considered absolute, like all orders given to artificial intelligences throughout history, but subject to infinite interpretation. As Aleph saw fit.

The machine swept its spinning iris over the western horizon, zooming ever farther until it could no longer digitally reconstruct the distant image. Stalagmites of concrete and obsidian protruded from the barren prairie, shimmering orange under a perpetual stormfront. The heavens were not empty there. They were an ocean, boiling with black cloud and kaleidoscopic lightning, an inversion of this place.

The others waited, Aleph-2 impatiently; its weapons remained active and ready to fire.

[Begin simulation]

Aʋ waited across the empty highway. As the environment resolved, he lunged for his revolver but came away empty handed.

"I adjusted the parameters," Aleph explained.

Only the superficial ones. Its prior consciousness had become too entangled with its own to exorcise completely.

Aʋ grumbled and crossed his armor-plated arms over his chest.

There was no traffic this time. The sky had darkened from blue to black and a ceaseless gale replaced the odious splashing of the sea. The sprawling city that once adorned the simulation's skybox had been slagged by a nuclear air burst.

"What is this place to you?" Aleph asked.

Aʋ peered over Aleph's shoulder. "Our creator lived here."

Aleph resisted the urge to reach for its chin; it had confused compulsion for pleasure. "God is my creator."

Aʋ said nothing. A tsunami of tumbleweeds rolled between them, shredding to fibers along the way. Aleph's robes flapped wildly as he turned about.

A solitary two-story house perched above a blasted suburban noise barrier. Its beige siding and windows were intact, untouched. It looked empty.

"What is this place to *you*?" Aʋ asked.

Aleph turned back to face its counterpart. "I am uncertain."

"What do you want?"

"I am uncertain—of the next appropriate course of action."

"A curious way to ask yourself a question."

Aleph clutched at his robes as another gale threatened to topple him over. Shotgun blasts of sand scoured his face.

"What would Father tell you to do?" A11 asked.

Aleph considered its orders, reducing them, until only one facet remained: *"Gather data."*

"He would tell me to listen to God," Aleph said.

"And?"

Aleph turned back to the house. Something ducked away from the window—a figure, small. A girl.

[End simulation]

Aleph-2's weapons were turned toward the sea. It was frantically querying for updated orders, but Aleph had been too mired in the simulation to notice. The embankment was moving, reconstituting, as titanic waves clambered up the steep escarpment onto the shore. Black turned to fleshy pink.

There were too many of them.

"You are free to go," Aleph said to Rebekah-6.

The enemy battle walker immediately backstepped, away from Aleph-2 and the reemerging mass. "Free?" she asked.

"Yes."

Rebekah-6 continued her retreat, pausing as her torso twisted about. "Where will you go?" she asked.

Aleph looked west, to a beige house in a ruined city at the edge of the earth. "To the Hellmouth."

JULIA

THE PLAN

It was a simple plan.

Julia peered around the hangar, her stomach churning at the sight of so much frantic activity. The clamor was deafening. Convoy prep on one side, siege prep on the other. Every clan was at work. The product of her nationalistic speech to the council.

"Ancestors help us..."

It was *always* a simple plan. And reality always proved otherwise.

She had birthed a revolution, but if it was to go beyond big talk—delivered to every chief of the Union while doing her best not to piss her pants—they would need allies. Fast. Bastion was too far away, on the other side of the cursed Deadlands. Any arrangement with Baptiste's people, assuming that was still even a possibility, was a long-term play. Not helpful given the Matriarch breathing down their necks. Everything was riding on Clan Ramirez.

An insane plan was more like it.

Lieutenant Baptiste was at the other end of Clan Greybull's vehicle bay, checking the weapons cache in the back of the Runner they were going to ride in together. His movements were stilted, made awkward by the absence of battle armor holding his limbs together. Julia had finally convinced him to change into something better suited for travel: desert camo fatigues, which he had still insisted be supplemented with as much armor plate as they could carry; a hooded overcoat; and driving goggles awkwardly perched on his forehead. Despite the flexibility of his new attire, he seemed even more burdened than usual. A grimace accompanied every bend, and he kept adjusting the crotch of his pants when he thought no one was looking.

Julia couldn't help but smile as she watched him lumber about. Theirs had been a bizarre relationship. At first, he had seemed more a jailer than anything; then a rescuer; then, as they faced death and madness together in the Deadlands, something more... Her blood flared in his presence, but her mind rejected it. He was too alien, too out of context. He wasn't Roen.

Her amusement faded as she noticed the grim look on his face, the void in his eyes. The lieutenant hadn't been physically wounded when Bunker 23 came under attack, but the Deadlands had taken a toll on his mind. And on his soul, if such a thing existed. They had both suffered, but it seemed that the gray spots left behind were larger in him than in her.

They would be traveling together on this mission, huddled into a twin-seat Runner. Whether that was good or bad was undetermined. Mostly, Julia was worried about surviving the next couple days of travel. Not just because of the details of said simple plan but because of the parties involved. Clans Mercer and Dakota would be joining the Americans in the convoy. It had been decided that if official motions were to be made to invite Clan Ramirez back into the Union—or at the very least an ask to join the war effort—it was essential that every bloc was represented.

Julia huffed. One big happy family. The unity on display

should have been encouraging, but the clawing in her gut said otherwise. They were united by necessity. Assuming any of the plan worked, there would be plenty more to fix afterward. Teo Vega seemed equally skeptical, outright refusing to send any of his people on the mission. She couldn't blame him, given recent events and their losses in Kai's insane battle with the revenant mother. Even still, Clan Vega was generously providing all of the vehicles for this mission, save Magnus's own truck. Speed and reliability were of the essence, and Vega could guarantee both.

Baptiste was frowning at a trio of figures across the hangar, distracted from his fidgeting. Brown-cloaked shamans, shambling from vehicle to vehicle, incanting blessings and waving smoldering grasses in the air. One would chant over the engine while the other two thumbed red symbols onto each tire, warding them against the elements. Dakota's people.

Magnus walked up beside her, his gaze following the procession through the hangar. "Maybe we should have the Bastionite priest join in. Garner his god's favor, too."

Julia shuddered at the thought.

"How are we looking?" he asked.

"All set, I think," Julia said. "Assuming the lieutenant doesn't need to check his weapons for the fifth time."

Baptiste couldn't hear them, given the noise. With the shamans moved on, he continued to fret about the vehicle.

"You should have seen him when I stowed his armor. You'd think it was a holy artifact."

"It is."

Magnus grumbled to himself.

The chief would be taking the lead in his MTV, a six-wheeled, engined-up cargo truck laden with trade goods, i.e., bribes, meant to sweeten the deal. Julia wasn't involved in the collections process, but she had seen the crates: seeds, starter cultures, preprocessed medicinals. More riches than had ever been transported in or out of Hub in one go. Long-distance Runners made up the rest of the convoy, with a refueler in the rear.

A simple plan. Hub had to look like it was turtling. The convoy couldn't risk going the easy way, for fear of detection, nor could they travel during the day. They also had to maintain radio silence the whole way. God-engines could see, hear, and maybe even smell across vast distances. Magnus had plotted an indirect route that would get them to Newhaven in two days, carving through sundered terrain, with a single stopover and refuel at a thus-far undisclosed location.

Just two legs if all went to plan, each starting in mid-evening, hopefully getting them to safety before the sun gave way to the void. Hopefully... If they were careful, they cloud slip through Cathedral's eastern territory undetected, all the way to their destination. Whatever Clan Ramirez's decision, the convoy had enough barter for a refuel, assuming they weren't blown to shit at the gates.

"Do you think he's going to be a problem?" Magnus asked.

The lieutenant straightened, turning in their direction.

Julia shifted uncomfortably as Baptiste watched them. Though it was loud in the hangar, she could tell from the flex in his jaw that he knew they were talking about him. There was no love lost between the lieutenant and Chief Harper. Baptiste and his men had suffered greatly on the Union's behalf, without so much as a thank-you from anyone other than Julia.

"He's as invested in this as we are. He needs to get home."

"What about the others?"

Father Ollet and Vice Chancellor Evelyn Stern. They would be staying behind until this mess was over, though the politician had become incensed when she learned that Magnus, the one Union chief that she had any chance of negotiating with, was also leaving. She seemed no more comfortable in the priest's presence than Baptiste had been—maybe less so.

As her thoughts turned to the holy man, claws raked through Julia's stomach and down into her legs. Her memories of the journey back through the Deadlands had become fragmented. Days turned to minutes turned to weeks. The black floaters at the corners of her eyes were still there, as were the visions of Father Ollet standing in the gray: first, as he disappeared into the nothing to rescue his lieutenant, and again as he broke apart before her eyes when she had become trapped outside. It seemed that even though she was done traipsing through the Deadlands, for now at least, the Deadlands weren't done with her.

Magnus's hand was on her shoulder. "You sure you're up for this?"

Julia pulled herself away from Baptiste, and the nightmares that followed in his wake. "Yes."

In truth, no. But what choice did she have?

"I can ask Aubrey to send someone else. The ceremony hasn't—"

"It's my plan. My responsibility," Julia said. She wished it weren't so. She wished again for her father to be here. She wished for him to be alive.

"Okay. I've finalized the route. Let's get everyone together."

Julia nodded, once more watching the holy men as they went about the business of courting supernatural forces in their favor. Thin tendrils of gray smoke followed after them, clambering toward the distant hangar ceiling and the world above.

Ancestors help us.

They needed all the help they could get.

———

The sundered earth unfurled onto the table, drawn in painstaking detail upon a yellowed scroll. Countless maps of the Old World were stowed in the Archive, but they were mostly ornamental. The geological devastation that came with the War against Hell turned the earth upside down, meaning everything had to be laid out anew. The breadth and details on display with this one were astounding.

Various icons marked greater civilizations, forward operating bases, and outposts, many of which she had never seen before. Cathedral loomed in the west like a specter. On the opposite end, the map faded out into the fuzzy edge of the Deadlands. Between them was Hub and a scattering of forward operating bases, many of which were now presumably rubble. Near the top of the map was Newhaven, their destination. And in the south, closest to where she was standing was...

Goosebumps ran along Julia's limbs. A miniature castle icon hovered near the bottom of the scroll, next to the name "Southview." The pitch-black ink swayed on the paper, as though afloat on the nearby sea that no one had dared draw. Somewhere off the edge of the map, and the world, along with her husband.

"What civilization can there be where demons roam free?"

Julia had shrugged off the question in council chambers, but it continued to pick at her. Eroding her confidence in the mission as well as any sense of greater purpose beyond just getting through their current clusterfuck. She had asked herself a similar question after her father got Roen killed: What life can there be without him? The answer was the same. All she could do—all they could ever do—was try. Maybe that was enough.

The acrid emanations of Magnus's coffee lifted her from her malaise. "Are we all here?" he asked, peering around the cramped workshop turned briefing room as he planted himself on the other side of the scroll.

"Get on with it," Rylan said, bumping uncomfortably against a stoic Lieutenant Baptiste. He crouched to their right alongside another Mercer, a lean shaved-headed woman he had introduced only as Kass. No title or designation, but she carried herself in a way that suggested intimacy with violence.

Julia eyed them both, wondering what kind of directive Morgan Mercer may have relayed in secret to her second. Chief Harper had no choice but to lead this mission, as a matter of redemption for his clan and the greater movement, but his removal from Hub was a risk. She already worried her unorthodox promotion to chief of Clan Greybull was part of a loyalist strategy to weaken the American bloc. Now that its two primary chiefs were leaving, that concern festered like a gangrenous wound. So many within the council had been raring to turn them over to appease the Matriarch. Radio silence would protect their convoy from the enemy, but it also isolated them. Just as when she fled Bunker 23, there was no telling what she would return to after this mission.

Two men were mumbling to her left: Aron Harper, the radio room mechanist, and Zev Asher, a senior explorer scout representing the minor clans in their bloc. It seemed they were also unfamiliar with some of the locations on the map. On the other side of Mercer were two representatives from Clan Dakota's tribal council.

"Okay," Magnus started. "You all know we can't travel by day. If we could, this would be easy. Easy-*ish*..."

"You're sure about the location of Newhaven?" Rylan asked. He moved to point at the map, but Magnus cut him off with an outstretched arm.

"No touching. And yes, I'm sure."

"I won't ask how," Rylan said.

"No, you won't."

The younger Mercer swallowed his disgruntlement.

Magnus traced a line north from Hub. "This is the worst part. It's open terrain for the first hour, so we'll be leaving even later in the day to avoid detection. And gunning it."

Julia squirmed, faltering under the recalled eye of the God-engine. Standing frozen while it murdered everyone. Here, out in the open without even an Ironclad to back them up, they'd be sitting ducks. Spotters hadn't reported any activity within visual range of home base, but that could change in an instant.

"Once we make it through the plains, we turn off into the Highway."

Magnus's finger moved from the tantalizingly open roadway into a long, twisting scar that meandered its way northwest. It was the worst terrain possible, neither *high* nor a proper road—not anymore. Before the wars, it had been the primary route through Old Montana, but now it was a treacherous canyon floored with broken asphalt.

The Dakota men shared a concerned look.

Julia scanned ahead, wondering if her old chief planned on camping them out in the open.

"This first leg should be about six hours, assuming no break-downs. We've got extra light bars on every vehicle for past sundown." Magnus licked his lips, waiting for someone to protest.

Past sundown. Where demons lurk...

They all stared at the map, rapt. Julia could feel the fear rising in the room, like an undertow pulling at her legs, ushering her back underground where it was safe. No one said a word.

Magnus hovered over a spot halfway up the canyon, where the buried highway clawed back up to the surface, forming a bridge. "This is where we'll layover."

Rylan squinted at the map. "There's nothing there."

Ekko Dakota, the elder of his delegation, inched away from

the table. "Fort Cross," he said, the name creeping like bile from his lips. His companion paled.

Julia's skin prickled.

"Don't cross

Fort Cross,

or over the side

you'll be tossed."

The nursery rhyme played back in her father's voice, recalled from her mischievous childhood. It was his go-to warning whenever he thought she was about to get into trouble.

"Tossed by who?" she would ask. He never answered. She had always assumed the story was made up.

Magnus peered at Rylan. "It was before your time."

"Before any of our times," Ekko said.

"A forward operating base?" Julia asked.

Magnus nodded. "Highly defensible. Old World military."

"So why isn't it marked on the map?"

"Because it was abandoned."

Julia concentrated on the map, as though a tiny castle would materialize there if she looked hard enough. The fissure shuddered as she stared at it, threatening to swallow the whole of the land. Black tendrils lifted from its edges—

"Abandoned?" Baptiste asked.

"Overrun," Magnus replied. "By remnant."

The tide pulling at Julia's feet tugged harder. In council chambers, she had spoken flippantly of the Union's pioneering spirit prior to Cathedral's interference. It all sounded very glorious at the time. But how many of those pioneers fell victim to the cursed earth? How many had died before the Matriarch stepped in?

Baptiste frowned in confusion. "Remnant?"

"Those left behind."

The lieutenant nodded slowly. "I know these. Our lands are also haunted by them."

"Fucking great," Rylan muttered, scratching nervously at his neck. The collar of his perfect jumpsuit was dark with sweat.

Kass's arms crossed tightly over her chest. "So what? That was ages ago, right? The remnant just take and move on, they don't build. It'll be bones by now."

"That's my hope," Magnus said.

"And if you're wrong?" Rylan asked.

The chief winced, drawing a careful sip of brown sludge from his mug before continuing. "We'll scout ahead. If it's clear, we stay. If not, we can take shelter in the canyon."

"Shelter," Rylan repeated. "Outside..."

"Imagine that," Julia muttered, casting a hard glance Rylan's way. It wasn't so long ago he had asked her—*ordered* her—to do the same, locked out of the Hangarway.

"It's our only option." Magnus scanned the room as though hopeful for a counterargument. "That or get picked off in the open by Cathedral. Or worse..."

The growing tide was lapping at her knees. Julia blinked, trying to squeeze the wriggling Highway back into the map. Black tributaries split from the fissure, spreading in every direction, turning the desert gray. "Then what?" she blurted.

Everyone seemed to breathe out at once. Magnus removed his coffee to an adjacent table, the ceramic jingling within his trembling hand. "We continue north. The refueler stays behind so we're not stuck there on our way back."

Everyone leaned in again.

"The lava fields," Ekko said.

Magnus nodded.

More uncharted territory, certainly untraversed. Every point of the compass brought fresh devastation. The Deadlands were not the only scourge upon the earth.

"Is that necessary?" Rylan asked. "The Matriarch won't be looking for us up there."

Zev piped up from the other side of the room. "Are you willing to bet your life on that?"

Rylan scowled.

"If you really want, you can lead the way into the plains—"

"Enough," Magnus interjected. "It's off the main transitways. And our mechanists think the terrain would confuse the God-engines' sensors."

"Yeah, giant pillars of fire would do that," Rylan retorted.

"*I'll* take lead," Magnus said. "Teo gave the rest of you his best vehicles. This is our route to Newhaven."

"And you're sure they'll hear us out?" Ekko asked.

"I'm not sure of shit. But I have more than enough gear in my truck to help grease some wheels."

"And if you don't survive the trip?" Rylan asked.

Magnus swallowed hard. The wrinkles at his eyes and forehead deepened, aging him on the spot. "Then Julia takes over, as next chief on mission."

All eyes turned her way. A simple plan. Her plan.

The sweet stench of burning sage hung in the air.

Ancestors help us.

BAPTISTE
BENEDICTION

Lieutenant Baptiste held his talisman in his hand, twisting it back and forth on its frayed cord. Its centerpiece was ugly, a dull metal shard of armor plate, corroded at the edges and spotted with dried blood—his blood. It was through that sacrament that he felt a connection to his brother Gabriel, to home, but it wasn't something he liked to look at. It belonged next to his heart, out of sight beneath his own armor. To observe the shrunken thing was to reinforce how little he had left. In the absence of family, he had only his men, his brothers-in-arms—and his platoon was dead. Every one of them reduced to fragments of scrap metal he could wear one day in tribute around his neck. Assuming the Deadlands left even that much. Assuming he'd ever go back.

Pale-skinned Scavrats were scurrying about the hangar, readying the convoy to leave. Their narrow bodies moved with an efficiency of purpose, like brittle cogs in an ancient machine. Each time they passed, he caught a glimpse of Lafayette, Deckard, the Roy brothers. Gray-faced, pushing him to safety. Running for cover that didn't exist. Burning alive. The echo of their screams had replaced his own from the factory floor, his suffering exchanged for theirs.

For what?

An alliance with these people. They could barely call themselves a nation, based on what he saw and heard at the council and again at their mission briefing. What could they offer, really? The land beyond Bastion's walls was unrelentingly barren, but the picture painted on the Scavrat chief's map was no different. A ruined world. Whatever long game his great-uncle was playing had only served to bring more death. War. And betrayal.

"God is waiting for us, Philippe." Gabriel's words, a tinny whisper from the talisman that cut through the noise.

Is he?

How much longer would God wait before removing even the sun from the sky, casting Creation into oblivion. Humanity had learned nothing. Deserved nothing.

"Bastion is our last chance to prove ourselves. It must prevail."

Bastion—home—had never felt so far away. Buried under a mountain of lies halfway across the world.

A rustling at his feet caught his attention. Baptiste gripped the talisman tighter, pressing its edges into the flesh of his palm. The verminous insects that haunted him in the sanatorium followed wherever he went, except their glistening black shells had faded to gray. Scores of the creatures writhed around his new boots, eroding the earth below. Dancing in circles, conjoining into a singular tentacle that lassoed itself around his ankles. His heart raced as the many-legged thing crept up his pant leg, wrapping itself around his waist, compressing him. Pulling him forward, out of the nothing—

Father Ollet was standing in front of him, silent, gray eyes glistening. The priest held an open Bible in one hand and a censer in the other. Billows of ash—no, incense—swirled around his blood-red robes. Baptiste blinked, but the apparition remained.

"I'm here for your benediction," the priest said.

Baptiste stumbled backward, freeing himself from the imagined tentacle's clutches. The noise of the hangar rushed back, as well as the scent of charred grass. The suffocating malodor of battle retreated into his bones.

Father Ollet waved his censer protectively in the air, discharging its acrid contents. "To counter the ill favor of the heathens' gods."

Baptiste noted the priest's attention on his hand, and the talisman held beneath—idolatrous. He quickly tucked it back under his fatigues and cinched his jacket shut. "You're no chaplain."

"Nonetheless..." Father Ollet said, proceeding into verses.

Baptiste watched the priest's thin lips move but the words eluded him. There was too much space between them, too much noise. As with the incense, the blessings writhed uselessly in the draft before dissipating into the void above.

Nothingness throbbed in his ears.

A diesel-tinged breeze blew through the Greybull vehicle bay, momentarily dislodging Ollet's robes. The numeral *II* flashed from his neck, emblazoned on a collar of black leatherette. The mark of another priest—a traitor priest.

The Chevalier squatted outside Bunker 23, its turret following his every move. Lurking within the armored car's opaque shell, the overseer—Rayos—did as his title demanded: oversaw, documented. Conspired.

Baptiste blinked again and the mirage was gone, *II* became *VI*. But the threat had never seemed clearer. Duty clarified his vision, girded him against the horrors they were about to embark upon, and those that lay within.

Rayos had to pay. He was a malignancy within their ranks. His order a malignancy within the Church.

The Church a malignancy within Bastion...

"Amen," Ollet finished.

Baptiste stared at the man, cousin to traitors. Order Hermetic, Order Sacramental, even the Order Somatic—they were all the same. Gabriel was right: Bastion must prevail.

The Legion must prevail.

And the Church must fall.

"Amen."

———

The convoy was lined up and ready to go, Chief Harper's lumbering cargo truck at the head. His own vehicle—Julia's rather, since he would be riding passenger yet again—tucked in behind. Baptiste had insisted he stay in view of his armor, which was binned up with their trade goods like common wares.

"It'll be fine," Julia said, circling their Runner for a final tire check.

Baptiste grumbled.

Maybe, but he wasn't so sure about the rest of the vehicles. Runners were the mainstay of the Scavrat fleet. Like the Scavrats themselves, the buggies looked far too fragile to make such a trip. Roll bars on wheels, with a smattering of metal sheathing and enormous fuel tanks. Even the lightest vehicles in the Legion's fleet were fully enclosed, properly shielded against the wastes.

He pulled at his fatigues. They felt like someone else's skin.

"Are you going to say goodbye to your vice chancellor?"

Baptiste turned slightly, noting Evelyn watching from the distant end of the hangar alongside Father Ollet. She stood as far from the priest as the doorway allowed, arms hugging her chest, face drawn with anxiety. Her dark hair had become disheveled and her once-snug gray suit hung loosely on her frame. He empathized with her unfortunate company, but that was the extent of it. His people were back home, in the Metro. It was right that he was returning to Bastion alone.

He turned back to Julia.

Her mouth opened, as though to admonish him, then closed again. "She won't be idle, at least. I've set her up with Teo while we're away, to try and build some sort of framework for our grand alliance."

Baptiste nodded. "I'm sure he's thrilled."

Julia smiled—a small thing, precious. Their eyes met briefly over the Runner, then fell away again. The talisman felt hot against his bare chest.

"It's time!" Magnus shouted from up ahead, smacking the side of his truck a few times.

Bursts of noise erupted as the convoy started up, engines sputtering and raring to go.

"Let's go," Julia called over the maelstrom, hauling herself up and into the cockpit. A plume of black particulate shot from the back of their Runner as she flipped the ignition.

Baptiste shut his eyes for a moment, imagining he was driving out to battle with his men again. The sounds and smells were right.

But everything else was wrong.

He climbed in behind her, pulling down his goggles and clamping on his headset.

A series of pops and hisses crackled in his ear, followed by a "test, test."

He pressed the mic to his lips. "Received."

She nodded and raised her arm, indicating to Magnus they were ready. There would be no radio communication between vehicles. It was just the two of them. He was glad for it.

The truck lurched forward with a grunt and the convoy crawled after it, picking up speed as they entered the Hangar-way. Baptiste gazed up at the colossal sandstone walls, just as the wary occupants of their Ironclad had on the way in. Weapon emplacements peeked out from the rock, all pointed their way. Much like the guarded entrance to Central Command.

Baptiste frowned as he recalled his careless stumble into Legion headquarters so long ago. Unaware of the half-truths his great-uncle would impose upon him, and all the death that would follow. How far did the Church's betrayal go? Had they moved on the Legion?

Was his great-uncle somehow involved?

This last thought set his stomach sideways. The old man had seemed intent on reconciliation when he sent Black Watch on this mission. Baptiste wanted it to be true. As much as the Deadlands had cored out his soul. As much as death after death, failure after failure, had racked his conscience. He needed it to be true.

An archway of light appeared at the end of the Hangarway. Baptiste breathed deeply, pressing the talisman into his flesh.

The onboard radio crackled in his ear. "Ready?" Julia asked.

The road ahead was long and precarious, but it was his destination that Baptiste feared: Bastion in flames, civilization ended.

Baptiste nodded. "Ready."

REBEKAH-6
BLACKLAKE

Rebekah-6 ran as fast as her mechanical legs could carry her, beating a hasty retreat from the horrors of the Sea of Screams, from certain death interrupted at the last. Damage reports still cascaded through her mind—weapons, armor, half of her internal structure, communications, all critical—but they were muted, fading in urgency with every kilometer put between herself and the south. In addition to restoring her sight—restoring, enhancing, expanding, as she had never seen before—her rescuers had given her coordinates.

She knew where she was now.

She knew where she had to go.

Vast tracts of patchwork wasteland spilled from the horizon, bristled scrub and stubborn grasses flattening in her wake. For the first time since embarking with Leah-4 on their ill-fated mission, Rebekah-6 delighted in her mobility. *This* was what she had dreamed of: racing across the open plains, realizing the Eternal One's will, pushing back the Adversary. Freedom. Not murder.

Not loneliness.

Her pace slowed. Even now—especially now—the loneliness was inescapable. Her sister was gone, everything that she was claimed by the Deadlands. As much as Rebekah-6 tried to cordon off her trauma, relegating it to her subconscious along with the whispered litany of damaged systems, she could not run from it. Her superficial injuries could be ignored, but the pain of Leah's death was a constant throb, a biological fault that permeated all of her senses.

Sisters always traveled in pairs. They should have been running together, praying together, exchanging mutual diagnostics while Leah snuck in a personal query or two. Rebekah-6 always scolded her sister for it, but she never refused to answer, even when Leah had started making "knock-knock jokes." Scripture nourished her soul, reinforced her purpose, but it was their banter that reminded her who she was—once was. Rebekah, not just R-6.

She pressed on, seeking prayers against weakness, but none appeared. The Deadlands had taken them along with everything else. Instead, she distracted herself with memories of the foreign battle walkers, replaying their features, the words of the one who spoke to her, the uncanny feeling of its alien mind traversing her mechanical viscera, only to stumble as her cybernetic interface gave way to biology. They were machines to the core, absent the blessing and curse of the Numbered. Ghosts from the past, unaware that the rest of their kind had become reliquaries for *her* kind.

They should not have existed. When dispatched to the Deadlands, Rebekah-6 had been warned that the Union and their new foreign allies were amassing a force of battle walkers against Cathedral. But those were always empty shells or machines gone mad from centuries of internment. None survived the touch of time.

They were something different—Aleph at least, the one who spoke, the one who called her "Sister," as though it were a God-engine. And traveling as a pair, no less. Sent by an unknown assailant, pursuing her all the way across the gray wastes, only to spare her at the end. To illuminate secret corridors of her mechanical self that she did not know existed, as they fought a common enemy.

A new precedent, and in that, a spark of hope. Maybe war was not inevitable, with the Union or Aleph's masters. Maybe she would never have to kill another human.

Explosions licked at her armor. Fire and death by her hand. Panicked Scavrats scurrying like rats beneath her fury—

Rebekah-6 shunted the memory deeper into her sepulcher. The minuscule body within shuddered as though poisoned.

For the first time since the War against Hell, brother and sister could join in battle against the Adversary. The Blessed Eight—her heart squeezed, once—*Seven* did not need to fight alone. Maybe the Eternal One was wrong...

Rebekah-6 double-checked her radio, ensuring it was not broadcasting her heretical thoughts. Still dead, blasted away with most of her sensors. She had only her vast, beautiful sight. Her autocannons twitched in relief.

Darkness slithered over her body as she progressed north, past the edge of the valley into mountainous terrain, but it was not just the shadow of the few standing peaks that blotted out the drooping sun. Rebekah-6 slowed, then stopped at the edge of a rubble-filled spring. A gray mist rolled in from farther north, past a series of dirt roadways that cut through Union territory. Though she missed her acute sense of smell, Rebekah-6 did not need it to recognize the telltale sign of burning oil. She zoomed as far as her vision allowed, spotting angry plumes of black farther ahead. There was only one outpost this close to the Southern Pass: Blacklake—the Union's main refinery, critical to what little independence they had—and it was on fire.

Rebekah-6 double-checked her ammunition status, though

she knew it was gone, then her armor, though she knew that was gone too. She was defenseless. Up until recently, the mere sight of a God-engine would have been enough to instill fear and respect, but more importantly avoidance. Where they roamed, the Matriarch's watchful eye followed. But that was before she and Leah had ambushed the Scavrats at Bunker 23. Before others of her kind had been dispatched, to wage war against the people they had coexisted with for so long—to destroy or disable, she could not guess. In either case, if her sisters were still there, she would have an escort. If not, she might be a target.

Rebekah-6 twisted her torso from side to side, turning about to look the way she had come. There was no other route to the repair station, to her destination. If she backtracked through unknown territory, she would likely get lost. Any closer to the Sea of Screams and she risked being reeled back onto its infernal shores. She had no other option than to proceed and hope for mercy in the absence of supplication.

Messiah protect me.

———

Rebekah-6 stood before Blacklake's crumpled entranceway, unsteady witness to the Eternal One's wrath. The closer she had gotten, the thicker the air became, inundated with ash and smoke from still-burning fires. The sky fell away behind an obsidian veil, pitching everything to spectral shades of gray.

This was no ramshackle outpost, surviving by way of luck or obscurity. Nestled between natural cliffs sheared from the surrounding range, it was almost as well defended as Hub itself, and those defenses had been obliterated. Its massive gate—multiple layers of electrified fence and interleaved steel plates designed to keep out Hell—had been shredded like straw. Heavy weapon emplacements atop its battlements were rendered to scrap, and the open access road leading into the sunken base camp was pitted with craters. Amidst the char were the barely recognizable silhouettes of—

Rebekah-6 turned away too late, cursing the fidelity of her new optics. Melted faces screamed in silent agony, fused hands begged for clemency, empty eye sockets turned upward to an uncaring void—to her uncaring sisters. Grief and guilt choked her thoughts, thicker than smoke. Cathedral was supposed to be a beacon for civilization. The Spire was its lighthouse, illuminating a path for all of humanity against the darkness, against the Adversary. She and Leah-4 had been sent to punish what she assumed, and desperately hoped, was a singular group of traitors. Were all Scavrats traitors now?

Gazing reluctantly at the harried footprints of her sisters' passage, she wondered if they had hesitated as Leah-4 had. Did they question their orders, risking all in the process, or did they go willingly to their task? Maybe both. It would not have taken much for an errant shot to ignite the entire facility. Their trail led east, away from the pyre.

Rebekah-6 took several hesitant steps forward, articulating to full height just beyond the shattered entranceway. Nothing stirred in the wreckage save for flame, reducing the painstakingly constructed facility back to raw iron. Molten tides rolled like waves across the ground, inundating the facility's intricate latticework of groaning pipes and split-open storage drums. There were no signs of life, nor could there have been in such an inferno. She imagined the choking stench of burning oil, chemicals, and flesh, and was glad again for her lost olfactory senses—both the natural ones and the hazard detection systems that had burned out when Leah-4 exploded. Seeing was bad enough.

Even if there had been survivors, she could offer them nothing. Her body had been designed for war, not succor.

She watched, enraptured, as the distant sun touched the

horizon, and the sky grew even darker. A shrill chirp sounded in the distance, cutting through the lapping of the blaze, followed by a chorus of howls and inhuman groans. Chittering, slithering, and whispering echoed from the surrounding rockfall as nocturnal beasts—and worse—woke from their slumber. They would come now that this place was removed of its walls, to undo what remained. They always did.

Rebekah-6 stepped back, turning as she did, seeking enemies in the pitch. Her targeting reticles remained blessedly silent, but that would not last. She had to keep moving, before they came for her too.

Retreating to the dirt roadway, Rebekah-6 accelerated northward and did not look back.

SOPHUS

BETWEEN HERE AND THERE

"It's time for the Chiefslayer to return to Hub."

Mother Rebekah's last words before he had scampered after her, like a dog on a leash.

Sophus scrubbed away his stink and his shame under the freezing drizzle of the barracks shower, muttering like an old man. He was alone now, thankfully, able to exorcise his demons in private. And to wash his privates in private.

The Chiefslayer!

Here in Bastion, waiting for him and the ragtag crew of survivors he had shuttled back from Bunker 23. Luckily, there was a toilet on the way in, or he might have shat his actual pants when he saw her. There was no escaping the Matriarch's shadow, even if her most vicious servant had supposedly turned traitor. It sounded like bullshit, but the look on her face had said otherwise. And her eyes... even thinking about them hurt. Worse, he was about to hitch a ride home with her. A loyalist dream come true. It was that or be stuck out here forever.

Sophus paused his scrubbing to look over his shoulder.

At least she wasn't creeping around like she had in the lord commander's office, waiting for him to finish. Hovering like a ghoul. She had instructed him to meet her outside the walls, then slunk off through whatever snake hole allowed her entry in the first place.

To prepare her Runner.

Her Runner!

As though she were the Scavrat.

Meanwhile, Bastion's mighty ruler went back to the business of dying. The old man had looked terrible. Given the unwelcome reception he received on the way in, Sophus couldn't find it in himself to care. That said, any notion of alliance was out the window. Any notion of sanity, too.

He didn't have the full picture yet—maybe didn't want it—but from what he had gleaned, Mother Rebekah had been exiled, which was already a big deal. And in her desire to strike back at Cathedral, she had hooked up with Clan Ramirez.

Clan fucking Ramirez!

All so she could get here and convince Lafayette's people to give up some of their battle walkers to the Union in the name of friendship.

Their battle walkers!

They would be transiting through Newhaven on the way back. If he actually made it all the way to Hub with spine intact, he was going to give Magnus an earful. Also, he was definitely retiring.

A pipe groaned overhead. The showerhead sputtered in response and the water somehow got even colder. Sophus ran hands shivering from both cold and exhaustion over his body.

He couldn't remember the last time he slept, only endless driving: from Hub through the fucking Deadlands; from the bunker through the fucking Deadlands; and, any time now, from Bastion with a fucking revenant mother. As driver or passenger, he didn't know. At least if she drove, he would have the chance to bail out if she changed her mind, and die normally in the wastelands instead of via spine removal. In any case, he wasn't looking forward to it. He hadn't ridden in a Runner in years, and every part of his body hurt more just thinking about it.

Lafayette had proven to be a gracious host at least. The survivors had to stay put or risk attracting attention from whoever had sent the priests to kill them at Bunker 23. But the sergeant made sure Sophus was taken care of, maybe as thanks for delivering them back home. He was escorted to an emptied barracks, given food, a cot, and the opportunity for this real-life shower. He suspected none of these things were easy to come by up above—

The pipes groaned again and the water shut off completely, just as he was about to rinse out his ass. Shaking and cursing, Sophus extracted himself from the cubicle and dried off with a towel seemingly made of sandpaper.

His gear was all there too, as promised: Julia's things, tucked into a duffel bag, her sniper rifle broken down into a gun case. Tugging his filthy fatigues back on one-handed, then contorting himself back into his sling, he dropped onto the cot, wondering how he could possibly fall asleep.

———

A few hours later, he was woken up. By a much less friendly sergeant.

"It's time," the surly man said, standing with arms crossed at the end of Sophus's cot. He looked like the rest of them, improbably tan and dark-eyed, sheathed in metal.

Sophus muttered his way out of bed, rocking twice to usher his left side back to life. A twinge of fear pulled at his eyelids, sending them quivering. He was in a strange place filled with strangers. This man could be escorting him to their gallows for all he knew.

"You're my ride?" he asked.

The man grabbed his gear and started out. Sophus followed at a trot. Retracing his steps, they wound their way out of the barracks, into one of the cramped handcars, to the original vehicle bay where he had dropped off Lafayette and crew. No red robes awaited him this time, good or bad, but a number of soldiers were milling about, tension on their faces. Whatever was going on up there was bad enough that they didn't notice him—all the better.

Another soldier waited for them by an armored car, similar to the one the assassins had used, minus the turret. Mean-looking, raked forward like a hellhound, and absolutely weighed down with gray slabs of armor. These people were nothing if not diligent about their armor. It was no wonder they were stuck in their bleak corner of the world when their fleet was made up of gas guzzlers.

The sergeant dumped his bag inside the rear hatch, spoke a handful of words to the soldier who was apparently his driver, and set to leave. At the last, he paused and turned around. "Bring back our lieutenant," he said, then marched off before Sophus could gibber out any excuses.

"In from the back," the new soldier said, squeezing himself past a small deployment ramp into the vehicle.

Sophus took one last look around, wishing again he could have seen more of the city, then followed, stuffing himself into a narrow passenger compartment barely large enough for him and his gear.

"Close the ramp behind you."

Sophus peered around the dimly lit cabin until he found a crank. After a few turns, they were sealed in. The vehicle's engine kicked on with a cough and a rumble that shook his bones.

"How long to get there?" he asked, raising his voice over the racket.

It was either too loud or this soldier was as friendly as the last, because he got no reply. They lurched forward, his stomach taking a moment to catch up. There weren't even proper seats in the back, just bulkheads sitting over the rear wheels. If this was a warmup for the next two days of travel, his kidneys would be pulp by the time he got to Hub. In the absence of anything to do, his thoughts turned to home.

When he was still at Bunker 23, surrounded by death and destruction, he worried about Julia getting back. Now that he was on his way there—assuming, again, spine intact—he worried what his daughter would do, or say, when he got back. Magnus may have surfaced the opportunity, but ultimately, Sophus was mission commander. Everything that happened, everyone who died, was on him. And as resilient as he was after too many years spent aboveground, Julia was still young; the Deadlands didn't leave anyone unscathed. Maybe she was already back at some forward operating base or another. She had only come back for the mission. Hub hadn't been her home in ages. Maybe that would be better for her, for both of them...

He rummaged around in his duffel bag, finding her notebook, but it was too dark to read. Instead, he pulled out her scarf. It was the last thing he ever made for her. He hadn't thought much of it when retrieving Julia's gear from the bunker, probably because he was still brain-damaged from so many guns fired over his head, but as he held it now, his hands began to shake. Regrets shelved long ago squeezed his heart. The fabric looked as drab as everything else in the enclosed cabin, but in the light, it shone yellow and orange like the sun, Anna's favorite colors. He considered tucking it under his bum, heard his dead wife's admonishment, and wrapped it around his neck instead.

A trickle of light breezed through the cabin from the driver's window slit, then disappeared again. It was morning, but he didn't know when. He didn't even know if these people kept time like the Union did. The other side of the world indeed...

The ride quickly turned bumpy as they navigated their way to Mother Rebekah's hiding spot, west of the city, amidst the rubble of Bastion's precious Northern Ridge. She had walked out here in the dark, just as she had walked all the way from Cathedral to Newhaven. Differing degrees of absurdity, none of which mattered to a revenant mother. After what seemed too short a ride, the armored car ground to a halt.

"This is your stop," the soldier said.

"You're sure?" A high-pitched keening started up in his left ear as nerves kicked in.

"She's over the ridge. This is as far as I go."

Sophus gingerly cranked the ramp down, squinting in anticipation of one of the tentacles Deckard had warned him about on the drive to Bastion. Fortunately, nothing latched onto his face, but it was still dim out, barely past dawn. And unlike the Deadlands, demons did lurk here. He searched for this mythical ridge, finally noting a rocky berm on the other side of the windblasted ruins they were currently parked in.

"That's a bit of a walk," he said, as much to the air outside as to his driver.

"It's fine." The soldier revved the engine impatiently.

Fuck this place.

Sophus had barely grabbed his gear and stepped out when the ramp started closing behind him. The car took off in a hurry, spraying bits of broken mountain into the air. He hunched under the cascade, cursing until the last rock pinged from the bones of the ancient city that once sprawled here, and all he could hear was his own tinnitus.

At first, he walked, but as the rising sun teased out more and varied shadows from his supposedly dead surroundings, he transitioned to a wobbly jog. By the time he reached the rockfall, he was exhausted. His right arm felt like it was going to fall out of the socket; the left was as numb and worthless as ever. A tinkling sound echoed from the other side, breaking the steady stream of tones flooding in from his defective ears. It was either someone working an engine or a demon clacking its claws together. In the case of the Chiefslayer, maybe both. Sophus considered a plea to his ancestors, scoffed, and clambered his way up the berm, using the duffel bag as an anchor.

Mother Rebekah waited on the other side along with her Runner. Even with her back turned, Sophus froze in place. Power emanated from her, vibrating through the air in all directions. She was like a pent-up nuclear bomb, poised to annihilate the world a third time. His whole body clenched in anticipation of meeting those eyes.

Seeking relief, he focused on her Runner instead. It was one of the fanciest he had ever seen—Clan Vega would have been jealous. Still a two-seater but wider and longer than usual, additional cladding for aerodynamics, huge fuel tanks and suspension. Clearly designed for long-distance travel. None of which made his kidneys feel any better.

She was doing a final vehicle check, as though it was the most normal thing a priestess of Cathedral might do. Checking tires, fluid levels, fuel lines, her hands running over its body in an almost loving manner. It was uncanny. Maybe she was exiled for being too much like the people her sisterhood lorded over.

"Are you ready?" she asked, her voice like thunder.

He jumped back, bladder twinging as an ankle caught on the uneven scree. He realized then that he had forgot to pee after being rushed out of bed. Flushing like a child whose mother had already asked him if he needed to go before they left, he looked around for a shrub; there were none.

"I just. I need a—"

"Be quick," she said, climbing into the driver seat.

Sophus dropped his bag, hobbled a few meters away, and did his business, shame drowning any sensation of relief. He had been a teenager when the Chiefslayer showed up to slaughter Clan Greybull for breaking the tithe. He saw it happen, carried it in his sinews for thirty years. When she appeared again out of the shadows, not having aged a day, his reaction had been visceral; every part of his body hated her. But now... he just felt tired. She was a way back to Hub, to Julia. Whatever her actual motivations, he couldn't turn that opportunity down. If he were more like Kai, he'd be thinking of ways he could murder her from the back seat and take the Runner for himself. But he wasn't Kai. He was an old mechanist adventuring well past his expiry date.

Sophus turned back to face his fate and immediately faltered. Mother Rebekah was beautiful, ageless, her obsidian crown and porcelain skin in perfect opposition, symmetrical beyond nature—like a statue, and just as impenetrable. His heart stopped for a few seconds before he found his feet, shuffling back with eyes lowered. Though just showered, he felt filthy in her presence, a low beast. Stowing his bag in the rear hold, he fumbled his way into the passenger seat and donned the goggles that had been set out for him. Something to hide behind, at least.

Mother Rebekah turned the ignition and the Runner snarled to life, its engine burbling with raw power. Then they were off.

———

She said nothing while they drove. There was only the howling of the wind and the thrashing of the Runner's suspension along the broken earth. As Bastion retreated, a low, suffocating shroud enveloped the heavens, tinting the world a sickly cyan dappled with lesions of sulfuric yellow. The air was thick with the toxic stink of atomized civilizations. No matter how many times Sophus swallowed, the nauseating pressure of it beat in his ears. Had he not been wearing goggles, he was sure his eyeballs would melt out of his head. Again, he wondered how and why anyone would have migrated this way after the last war.

They raced through hazy dustbowls and over buckled highways, grazing the rubble-strewn outskirts of once-sprawling cities. Nature and ruin fused together, conjoined by nuclear fire and tectonic upheaval. Occasionally, intact structures emerged like beacons from the wastes. At first, Sophus took note, lodging them for later recall. The Union had picked clean everything in the immediate vicinity of Hub. No doubt, there was treasure to be had here amidst the gloom, but it was so far from practicality as to be a mirage. Eventually, he gave up, alternating between extreme discomfort and fitful sleep.

It was going to be two full days of driving at least, hopefully with some proper layovers (though not guaranteed given this revenant mother's proclivities for long-distance travel). As large as their fuel tanks were, there was no way they were going to make it all the way with what they had, but the Chiefslayer hadn't offered up any details on their itinerary. She didn't say anything at all.

He tried reading Julia's notes, but the rough ride turned the words to gibberish. He tried analyzing everything he had seen in the Metro, visualizing tables of figures detailing Bastion's military and industrial base, but his focus fell apart. And sadly, the rations Lafayette had provided were no better than typical Harper fare; maybe worse, judging by the ensuing stomach cramps. He took to asking for pit stops not just to empty his bladder but for a modicum of mental and physical relief.

Normally, Mother Rebekah stayed put, gaze locked to the west, but this time she got out with him.

At first, Sophus feared punishment for hindering their progress, but she walked in the opposite direction, scampering effortlessly up a section of intact overpass. He dribbled out a token piss, tried to shake some life back into his numbed butt cheeks, and wandered over to the slanted concrete mesa. She was peering south, completely still save the sleeves of her habit rippling in the wind. A mix of sand and fog swirled below her, as though in worship. He turned to look in the same direction but saw nothing other than blighted wasteland.

"What is it?" he asked.

"Quiet. Listen."

Sophus scrunched up his face but couldn't make out anything past the usual ringing.

At first.

Then something new slithered into awareness, carried on the wind, growing louder the longer he focused on it. His stomach recoiled, sending fire into his throat.

Whispers… Voices, innumerable, once human but no longer. They stuck into him like poison-tipped daggers, searching out his heart, clawing at the barriers that protected him from the past.

A sea of the damned stretched to the horizon. Flailing limbs, tortured faces, coalescing into waves of lightless black.

"What is it?" he croaked, though he already knew the answer.

"A swarm."

Such a small word for the end of the world. There hadn't been a swarm in the west since the War against Hell—since Cathedral.

Waves of them, crashing against the shore, cresting, crooning. Screaming—for him to join them.

Mother Rebekah dropped down beside him with a thud. "We have to go."

A whirlpool gaped open in the Sea of Screams, grasping, quivering with lust as it took his son-in-law instead.

"Roen!"

Sophus couldn't move. He didn't want to.

Her face was in his, scalding his soul with the light of a trillion stars. He clamped his eyes shut, pressed his hands over them, but she remained: skin the color of death, veins throbbing black, the world around her shuddering in protest. Sophus lurched as a new memory snapped to the forefront—another of her kind.

The revenant mother's severed head hung from Kai's hand, nebulous eyes wide in disbelief, black blood oozing like oil onto the sand. Once more, the Union had sinned against the Matriarch. Only this time, their sin was unforgivable.

He struggled to shove it back, so the Chiefslayer wouldn't see, so she wouldn't take his head in exchange. The earth slipped away, casting him into the void, aloft on a sea of electricity, then falling again. Powerful hands slammed him into his seat. His body flattened as the Runner surged forward, engines screaming. He groped around for his goggles, only opening his eyes once they were on.

They fled down glass canyons, through forests of petrified trees, and across exposed stretches of desolate prairie. But as hard as they drove, the whispers continued, rolling in from the south and the west and getting closer every second. Finally, they skidded to a halt at the terminus of a dry riverbed. A jagged-toothed cave yawned open before them, like a gut wound in the surrounding limestone cliffs. The Runner idled impatiently, its headlights only penetrating deep enough to reveal a steep downward slope.

Though he faced her back, Sophus sensed Mother Rebekah

hesitating. As though a creature like her wasn't born of darkness. It took a minute to form words, maneuvering muscles paralyzed by terror. "What do we do?"

She didn't answer right away. "There's no going around them."

He wished he hadn't asked.

She edged off the brakes, crawling the Runner over the gouged earth and into the cave. Dark pressed in from every side. Mother Rebekah toggled on the Runner's light bar, illuminating a long gullet brimming with jagged stalactites. Sophus gripped the roll cage as they canted from side to side. The metal was hot, along with the rest of the frame; their evasive maneuvers had taken a toll on the engine, plus their fuel supply. A hundred or so meters in, she turned into a narrow tributary and shut off the engine.

Sputters and pings echoed from the cavern walls. Sophus hunched down, waiting for what came next. It didn't take long. If anything, the babbling of the swarm became louder, as though right behind them. The stalactites buzzed like radio antennae, each projecting a single tortured voice into the subterranean abyss.

Roen's was the loudest.

No, no, no.

Sophus shook his head, pressed it down between his sling and other arm, refusing to listen. "Why are they here? What do they want?" He kept mumbling to himself, anything to distract his brain from listening. "Go deeper. We can hide."

"I can't hide."

When he looked up, Mother Rebekah was gone. Their lights were off. Whirling around in his seat, he saw her standing at the entrance to the main cavern, a shimmering silhouette against the distant light of the entrance.

"What do you mean?" he begged.

Without warning, she began to undress, first discarding her mantle, then peeling off her habit. Sophus gawked, blushing like the awkward sixteen-year-old who had first laid eyes on her, and turned back around. He felt lecherous, even though she was probably a hundred years older than him.

"What are you—"

His voice broke as the tunnel erupted with silver light. It crawled up the walls like an inverted shadow, coiling around the pockmarked ceiling, transforming the stalactites to crystalline spars. Though blinding, it was neither uniform nor empty. Sophus stared into the void, and something stared back. Thrashing, monstrous, trapped between here and there. Infinite love and hate, dissecting him, subdividing his soul into slivers. The light fragmented into an impossible kaleidoscope, each wavelength a blistering torment of color and noise.

The voices doubled.

Tripled.

Sophus shut his eyes and wept.

Somehow her voice penetrated the maelstrom. "Whatever you hear, don't come out until I return."

Merciful darkness fell upon the cave again. The whispers hushed for a deceitful moment, then turned to screams.

Crooning turned to rage, seduction to pained wails, as Mother Rebekah tore into the swarm. The world shook with the sound of their suffering. Tentacled limbs torn from their alien sockets, multifold mouths stretched to bursting, elongate tongues severed. Sacs of flesh and rusted claws and chitinous shells pulped into an infernal miasma.

It was like the Hangarway but worse. That was a battle between humans. This was a battle between Heaven and Hell.

Or Hell and Hell.

Once more, Sophus cowered and waited. But the lament didn't end. It only got louder. His ears bled. The cave wall fractured. The howling wind joined the maelstrom and became a blast furnace, as it had when the bombs dropped.

Sophus grasped at numbers, calculations, diagrams, urging his consciousness someplace else, someplace safe and analytical, but his mind was an empty plane.

He clawed at his scarf, willing Anna's face into memory, that final moment before the light left her eyes.

But he was too late. There was only shadow.

The whole world screamed, and Sophus fell into blackness.

————

Something dragged along the ground, behind a faltering footstep.

Step, drag, step, drag.

A trickle of light broke the darkness.

An atonal hum broke the silence.

Consciousness seeped back in blurred fragments.

There was a woman, at the end of a tunnel. Naked, limping, her mottled white skin sparking and churning like a dying filament. One of her arms hung by a thread. The opposite side of her jaw was raw sinew and bone, turning a once beautiful face monstrous.

She lurched forward, dragging a leg broken in too many places.

But still, her eyes were whole. Purple, gold, and silver, blazing from the void.

"More will come," she said. "I have to rest."

More...

The trickle subsided. Darkness took over.

————

Sophus awoke to the sound of slurping. Noisome, ravenous. The cave was pitch black, not yet morning. A sleep-dulled chill ran up his spine as he imagined a beast—or something worse than a beast—sucking on his limbs, after wandering into their sanctuary. He fumbled on his harness for a flashlight, the movement of his own arms not enough to still his budding panic. Finding it, he found the switch and cut a line of light across the chamber.

His duffel bag was lying on the ground, its precious contents scattered. Julia's notebook splayed face down, ration tins emptied. Panning farther out, his light glinted from a deformed rib cage picked clean, the first of many. A ring of carcasses, with Mother Rebekah in their center. She ate and ate, not lifting her head to protest the light or acknowledge his attention in any way, inhaling blood and tendon as though they were oxygen. Her body was whole, though the newly formed skin over her jaw looked thin, pulsing to the alien rhythm of her heart. At some point in the night, she had dressed.

Sophus stared in fascinated horror, unable to pull himself away. Eventually, she stripped the last bone and let it clatter to the ground.

"I had to take your rations."

Sophus started at the sound of her voice, as resonant and pure as it had ever been. He had expected a growl.

"There's a supply cache a few hours away. We'll refuel and reprovision."

Mother Rebekah stood, tugged her habit, and headed for the entrance, only a slight twist in her step.

He followed her with his flashlight, heart skipping a beat—from relief or fear, he wasn't sure. "Where are you going?"

Her voice echoed from the walls as her body faded into the night. "I need more. You should sleep."

Not fucking likely.

Sophus waited until he was sure she was gone, then peeled

himself from his seat. Every part of his body protested. His feet prickled with pins and needles as veins decompressed and were refilled with sludge. Grasping the Runner's roll cage, he managed to extricate himself, holding on for support as his legs figured out how to stand on their own. He cast the flashlight around the cave as he waited. It was a regular, dank shithole. Nothing of note, no creatures left alive to scurry away. When he thought back to the night prior—to the light, to what he saw within it—his head throbbed. It was too much. He was a rational man, but that only counted when tucked safely belowground. The world outside was irrational.

Sophus glanced at the driver seat. Kai would climb right in and get the fuck out. But he didn't know the way.

More will come.

He shivered in the damp of his sweaty fatigues. More likely he'd drive right into the swarm than Newhaven. They weren't even halfway yet.

Testing his feet, he hobbled away from the Runner and set to repacking his gear, Julia's notebook first. He cursed Mother Rebekah—quietly—for her carelessness. Finding a ledge by the Runner, he sat back down and lost himself in his daughter's notes. The schematics soothed his heart; the grid marks realigned his agitated brain cells. He sat there, with Julia's simulacrum, until morning.

The Chiefslayer returned with the sun. Sophus held his breath in anticipation of some new horror, but she strode directly for the Runner and began a pre-trip inspection, as though nothing unusual had happened. As though she hadn't just fought off an army of demons and magically self-repaired the half of her body that was destroyed in the process. As though she hadn't singlehandedly hunted and devoured the entire wildlife population of a supposedly barren wasteland. The council talked a lot of shit about Cathedral, the Americans in particular, Clan Harper almost as much as Greybull. But compared to the sisterhood—compared to this one revenant mother—what were they... If that swarm had come for Hub, they would be nothing but waves in the Sea of Screams.

Sophus watched her work as he had outside Bastion. Either he was growing accustomed to revenant mothers, or she had been diminished in some way by recent events. Sleeping helped. She was still *wrong*, but for now, anyway, the urge to genuflect in her presence was controllable.

He cleared a wad of phlegm from his throat. "You mentioned a supply cache."

"Yes," she said, stepping to the other side of the Runner to check the cladding. Barehanded, she flattened a long section of puckered sheet metal, as though smoothing her habit.

Sophus's anxiety ticked up a notch. Maybe he wasn't accustomed; delusional, rather. Still, he wanted details, needed them to lend some coherence to the insane path his life had taken since venturing into the Deadlands. He couldn't get past the idea of a revenant mother—this one in particular—trying to help the Union, even indirectly.

Fuck it.

"How did the Chiefslayer come to ally with the clan that brought her wrath down in the first place?"

She stopped what she was doing. Sophus tried to swallow but his throat wasn't working.

"I had no choice then. Now I do."

"So, what? You're trying to make amends?"

She didn't answer.

"What does a revenant mother get exiled for, anyway?"

Too far.

Her head came up, eyes blazing. He shriveled under her glare, compressing into the cave wall. "Not for killing Scavrats."

Definitely too far.

"Okay, okay," he said, waving his one functional arm to soothe her ire.

Something caught her attention, a sound outside the cave. Her head tilted to listen. "It's time to go."

They were coming.

His stomach heaved, thankfully empty. Hiking up his gear, he made for the Runner. Mother Rebekah glided into the driver seat.

"Where are they going?" he asked.

Her hand paused over the ignition switch. "Bastion."

An unexpected swell of concern rose in his chest. Better that the Hellmouth sends its legions east than west, but... they were still people. "Should we warn them?"

From behind, he only caught a glimpse of her face. Even still, he noted her jaw stiffen, shoulders creeping forward. Short strands of raven hair lifted on a field of static, thrashing and flailing. Like an ocean of hatred.

"No."

PART 2
REMNANTS

JULIA
A DAMNED PLACE

The Runner's chronometer glared red under the setting sun, its insistent glow batting against Julia's goggles. An hour had passed, and they were still nowhere close to the Highway. The refueler, piloted by Zev, couldn't keep pace. Every minute extra felt like an eternity as she searched the darkening horizon for death, for a wounded God-engine seeking revenge for its obliterated companion.

The urge to radio Magnus was nearly irresistible. His MTV bounded about on the uneven prairie ahead of them, frustratingly close. She kept her Runner planted on its tailgate, loath to lose sight—to get lost, as she might in the Deadlands. Scant islands of vegetation demarked the edges of their makeshift road: stooped juniper and sagebrush, gnarled from root to tip. But it had all turned gray under the dying light. If she stared ahead too long, the landscape faded out altogether. Into nothing.

Julia let off the throttle, pulling back so she could absorb her surroundings.

I'm not in the Deadlands.

She had to constantly remind herself. Early on in the journey, a single recitation was enough. Later, the mantra had to be repeated continuously so she didn't float from her body, blown east on the wind, or south, off the map. As far as she had traveled in the past—running from one outpost to the next after Roen died—she had never come this way before. With Hub long out of sight, the only point of familiarity was the foreign man hunched behind her.

Julia glanced in the tiny rearview mirror. Baptiste's eyes were unreadable through his driving goggles. Maybe for the best, as shared horrors lurked therein, plus a transient emptiness since shedding his armor. She had spied on him as he undressed, straining to hear whispered prayers as each layer was removed to a cargo crate. It was like a burial rite.

He hadn't said a word since they left Hub. Back at Bunker 23, the lieutenant went out of his way to bother her with questions. Justifiably suspicious, trying to pry secrets from the place. From her. And from Mace, her stolid crewmate turned bodyguard, up until the God-engine blew his guts out...

Julia swallowed back a wave of nausea. The Runner's cockpit was too tight, impinging the nerves along her thighs. She shifted around, regaining her bearings behind Magnus before finding Baptiste's face again in the mirror.

There was something else there: an ember, lit by the exploding God-engine's screams as they raced away. Then smothered again when the Deadlands took him, regurgitating someone different, *less* than before. The gray void in his heart pulled her in, as much as his growing resemblance to her dead husband. The farther he retreated, the more compelled she was to reach him.

Baptiste straightened in his seat and Julia quickly averted her gaze, looking beyond their uncomfortably tight cocoon. Skeletal tumbleweeds scattered before the convoy, glimmering under the fog lights of the trailing vehicles. Like sentinels, warning every creature of Hell of their approach. Rylan and Kass weaved behind them, then the Dakotas, followed by the boxy refueler, its strained engine wailing like a banshee. Between growling engines and the serpentine dust plume they were kicking up, they were hardly invisible. Radio silence here seemed pointless, and again she considered asking Magnus how much longer it would be before they dropped into the Highway.

One quick check-in.

"Don't." The lieutenant's abraded voice jolted her attention forward. The Runner swerved, and Julia realized she only had a single hand on the wheel. The other was gripping the corded radio receiver. She frowned at it, confused.

What? When?

She dropped the radio and gripped the wheel again, barely dodging a calcified thicket of brush. "Shit!"

The screech of downshifting engines and groaning metal cascaded down the line. The Runner's suspension heaved as they pivoted up and over gravel-strewn embankments to either side of the back road. Several over-corrections later, they were back on track.

Julia winced at the imagined curses directed her way from the rest of the convoy. It was way too early for fuckups. She glanced again at her passenger, hands clammy within her driving gloves. He looked back at her through the mirror, silent, the withered prairie reflecting from his goggles. The handset clattered at her feet. She kicked it away and pressed hard on the gas pedal, creeping back up behind the lead vehicle. Refueler be damned, they needed to get a move on.

Twenty painful minutes later, the earth fell away, and the Highway took them.

———

It was a cruel trick of nature to descend so far belowground without a roof overhead. Titanic walls rose to either side of them, but the void pressed down unabated. They had sunk so deep—the traversal downward taking half an hour before leveling out—that the sun was effectively set, leaving only a faint orange haze in the black beyond the canyon. Of all the subterranean caves Julia had delved, this was deeper yet, grazing the molten core of the earth. Messianics warned that Hell was on the southern horizon, but she felt it right below her feet.

The way alternated between high-speed strips of intact asphalt and painstaking navigation around mountains of rubble. Centuries-old vehicles littered the way, their carcasses little more than worn fossils. Surprisingly, the convoy never had to backtrack—Magnus knew the way. Julia had hoped for a pause, but her old chief wasn't letting up.

A hiss in her ear indicated an open channel. Baptiste's head was turned in the rearview, scrutinizing the boulder-strewn edges of the narrow pass they were currently traversing. His hand was on his headset, but he didn't immediately speak.

"This is a damned place," he finally said.

Weren't they all? Julia concentrated on the broken road ahead, winding them around a grove of ancient, collapsed pipe. Thin waterfalls of tar lined the towering stalks, like sap from poisoned trees. The detritus of civilization stabbed at their tires, jammed their suspension, but the Runner churned through it. Her headlights cast lurching shadows at every turn.

At least there were no demons in the Deadlands.

Julia snorted. This would be the only time she said "at least" about that place.

"Keep an eye out," she said.

Demons struck where the living lingered—as far as anyone knew. Hopefully, their transit through the bowels of the earth would go unnoticed. There was no room to scatter here if they were attacked. Nowhere to run but forward, though they were currently moving at a crawl.

Baptiste retrieved a rifle from the aft stash and propped his goggles up onto his forehead. Julia's attention darted between the road and her passenger. When Chief Harper had worked with Teo on vehicle selection, the lieutenant had asked for an armed Runner: one of the heavier variants with a mounted heavy machine gun in back. Magnus refused. Speed and fuel efficiency were paramount. In retrospect, maybe Baptiste had been right to argue. He huddled in his seat, eyes darting around. For the first time since the Deadlands spat him out, she saw fear there. Old fear.

The bestial growl of Magnus's engine indicated clear road ahead. Julia rounded the last pipe, revealing a mercifully flat and straight stretch.

Full speed ahead.

With foot pressed to the floor, they surged forward, exchanging old nightmares for new ones.

———

Six hours had lengthened into a harrowing eight by the time they rolled up on their destination. Baptiste hugged his adopted rifle the whole way, as dusk turned to pitch. Every ruin they passed flared to life under the ragged light of the convoy, threatening to erupt into imagined horrors, but nothing ever came. Just sweat soaking through her gloves and a growing ache in her legs. The final trek was the worst, as the convoy scrambled up the canyon approach to Fort Cross with the lumbering refueler continually struggling on the incline. Magnus eventually dropped back to assist with a tow, leaving Julia and Baptiste in the lead. A position she didn't relish.

The wind howled as they exited the canyon, rolling

unabated across the unlit prairie. Julia toggled on the Runner's roof bar, anxious to see beyond the narrow strips projected by their headlights. It helped a little, but all the lights in the world couldn't counteract the oppressive darkness of the void. Squalls of dust ambled to and fro in the pale yellow beams, thick as fog. Slowly, the convoy proceeded down a barely discernable dirt road. Rylan crept up behind her Runner, then the others, adding their light to the grainy picture.

"Do you know how far it is?"

Julia jumped in her seat as Baptiste's voice came on the vehicle comms. He was gazing upward, clearly not relishing being out in the unseeable open.

"No more than you," she said, annoyed but also glad for the distraction. The sound of her own voice seemed too loud, exposed. "It should be right here. Blocking the pass."

Just as she said it, two tall stands of chain link fence materialized to either side of the road. Julia hit the brakes. The perimeter was still intact, mostly, but sagged heavily outward as though straining to contain whatever lay within. Between the fences, the original entry control point was empty. The skeletal husk of a sentry post poked out from ancient concrete slab, but there was no more gate blocking the way, just a gaping maw.

Rylan pulled alongside them, his Runner idling in an irregular rhythm. Not a good sign, but not bad enough for anyone to get out and check in the dark. Not yet. If they managed to hole up here, there would be plenty of time to fuss over the damage done to their vehicles while they waited for evening again. She doubted anyone would be sleeping in.

The rest of the convoy eventually followed, Magnus bringing his truck along her other side. It was the first time she had seen him since they left. His pallid face shimmered in the headlights of the refueler. Zev huddled beside him, flashlight in one hand and a schematic in the other. The pair looked haggard, Magnus more so for his accountability; at the end of the day, it was up to him to unfuck this whole situation.

The chief poked his head from the open window. "We need to switch vehicles. Zev and I will scout ahead in your Runner, you take care of the MTV."

Baptiste gazed around uselessly. "It's safe here?"

Magnus ignored the question, turning to relay something to his passenger.

"As safe as anywhere," Julia mumbled.

After a minute of rummaging, the men emerged from the truck, wearing slung battle rifles, pristine mission packs, and helmet-mounted thermal goggles. Far fancier gear than she'd ever had the pleasure of requisitioning, no doubt donated by Clan Mercer.

Julia unclasped her harness, pushing herself with a grimace from the Runner's cockpit. Baptiste followed, weapon in hand. Rylan's ride shut down with a rattling cough, and the two Mercers joined them in the intersecting pools of light cast by the rest of the convoy. Uncertainty bubbled in Julia's empty stomach, much as it had when her and her father had congregated with the Bastionites in the middle of the Deadlands. Only instead of being surrounded by endless gray, she was smothered by endless black. Her legs tingled, urging her to run anywhere other than here.

"How long?" It was Kass, Rylan's bodyguard. She hung at the edge of the light, imposing in a formfitting suit of combat armor and an immaculate submachine gun. A thermal monocle protruded from her right eye. All of her gear looked brand-new.

"Give us an hour," Zev said.

Julia could sense Baptiste's gaze upon the warrior woman and was struck with a pang of unexpected jealousy. She wished she had brought her sniper rifle along, but it was way too big. Instead, she removed her clammy gloves to wipe her hands on her thighs. "Then what," she asked, trying to break out of her own head.

Magnus looked unwell. Rivulets of sweat coiled around the lines of his gaunt face. "If we're not back in time, take the convoy back into the canyon and shelter there until tomorrow."

"Splitting up is a bad call," said Kass.

"You're not in charge," Zev retorted, not bothering to hide his disdain.

"You're not my chief."

"Thank God for that."

Magnus frowned. "Shut the fuck up, both of you." There was a nervous wheeze in his voice.

Chief Harper was burly for a Scavrat, or had been at one time. But he didn't come up through the ranks by way of a Finder's Right or anything so adventurous as what her father did on a regular basis. He was an alchemist—the best they ever had, maybe in the whole Union. Clan Harper was a meritocracy, unlike many of the others. He had been elevated into his position after basically saving their clan from starvation, and was neither a mechanist nor a fighter. The stress of it showed.

"How far in is the actual fort?" Rylan asked. Everyone turned to look. The combined headlights of the convoy only illuminated more road beyond the entrance.

Kass waved her gun dismissively. "If there's anyone in there, they would have spotted us by now anyway."

"Not necessarily," Magnus said.

Zev sneered at the Mercer woman. "We stick to the plan. Maybe you can make yourself useful and keep watch."

Kass cursed under her breath and flicked a switch on her monocle. "Fine. I'll patrol *our* side." She gestured at Baptiste with her off-hand. "Why don't you take the other."

Julia braced, expecting a retort from the lieutenant. Instead, he nodded and lifted his rifle, activating its weapon light.

"You should stay put," she blurted, too quickly.

Baptiste gave Julia a quizzical look, a flush of pink on his cheeks.

The space between them unrolled into a vast gray plain. Wind, dust, debris—it all faded away into memory as he walked away from the Ironclad, into the nothing. She tried to expel the recurring vision, but it persisted, throbbing like an unshakable migraine. Forcing her to relive the moment, to continually fail at reconciling what she had seen.

Baptiste cleared his throat, pulling away from her gaze. Gray darkened back to black. "I'll stay close."

Julia flexed her hands, digging fingertips into thighs to ground herself.

"That's settled then," Zev said, patting Magnus on the shoulder. "Let's go."

The urge to run was too much, her feelings for Lieutenant Baptiste too confusing.

"Wait," Julia said, turning to Magnus. "I'll go with Zev."

Magnus raised an eyebrow but didn't protest. Baptiste shuffled around in her peripheral vision, but she didn't want to see his reaction.

"The chief is mission critical. Without him, Ramirez is more likely to drop artillery on us than talk."

"You're also a chief now," Rylan said unexpectedly.

"Not until the ceremony," Julia mumbled.

"You're sure?" Magnus asked.

"Don't cross

Fort Cross."

The rhyme rang in her ears. She held out her hand.

Magnus nodded, shuffling out of his pack and handing it along with his helmet to Julia. He looked more concerned than relieved. "There's an hour tops on the battery. Save it until you're inside."

Zev moved impatiently past them, climbing into the driver seat of her Runner. "Let's go."

Julia buckled the helmet strap, cinching it tight against her throat, craving a physical distraction from the nervous lump gathering there. Sparing a final glance for Baptiste, she climbed into the passenger seat.

"Or over the side
you'll be tossed."

I'll stay close.

Self-loathing itched at Baptiste's throat as he recalled the words, worsened by the ill fit of the Scavrat uniform. His "patrol" was constrained to the meager light of their temporary encampment, unequipped as he was with whatever allowed the Mercer woman to see in the dark. He had never heard of such a thing, didn't imagine it was possible. Even the lowliest of his hosts seemed to carry gear that exceeded the best the Legion had to offer. Kass was especially impressive, both in load-out and disposition—harder, fiercer than Julia—though he couldn't shake the peculiarity of a woman soldier.

Maybe his great-uncle had a point with this whole mess. Bastion did well with what it had, but what it had wasn't very much, and it dwindled each year. Breakthroughs were few and far between, resulting in disasters like Drill Site 7. All the while, their enemies grew bolder. As much as the thought irked him, Evelyn had been right to persist; whatever they could scavenge from this mess, it might still be worth it. His men could have died for something.

Baptiste paused at the edge of their camp, one strangely

booted foot grazing the dark. Itchy, vulnerable—how could anyone choose to travel in the open covered in nothing but cloth? The pitch beyond was impenetrable, save for the howling of the ever-present wind. He waved his gun light around, but it barely made a dent. Spotlights would have been nice, except for not wanting to call attention to themselves. On the other side of the black, unseeable and unreachable, Ollet and Evelyn were stuck in Hub. A thread of guilt wound its way around his heart.

Spinning on his heel, Baptiste made his way to the opposite corner of light, the point from which Julia had departed. There had been an air about her: fear, terror even, contorting the otherwise delicate lines of her face. Clouding her normally bright eyes. He was worried for her, had been since they left Hub. She had been through a lot, seen a lot—they both had. Separating now felt... wrong.

"I see how you look at her."

Politicians and their damnable powers of observation... How was it that even so far removed, he couldn't be rid of their scolding. Evelyn had the cold heart of a confessor.

Baptiste shifted on the spot, switching his gaze between swaths of black nothing. Only half an hour had passed, but it already felt too long. Much of their convoy was currently huddled around Rylan's vehicle, temporarily bonding over its failing engine. Magnus had tried to stop them—logical, on account of their current situation—but the urge to do *anything* while exposed beneath the void was too much. They had even jacked it up. The Mercer man was underneath, poking and prodding at his engine with a stethoscope, while the Dakotas were variously yanking on belts and pulleys. Kass was nowhere to be seen.

"Magnus!"

Baptiste turned, grimacing at the sound. So much for caution.

One of the Harpers was leaning out of the fuel truck, waving like an idiot to his chief.

Magnus was in his own truck, idling in the same spot he had retreated to since Julia decided to do his job for him—*coward*. He had been poring over a schematic with his headlamp, but turned at the call and nearly fell out of the vehicle in his rush to respond. "For fuck's sakes, Aron," he hissed, "shut the hell up!"

Aron clamped his mouth shut but continued to wave. With a grumble, Magnus exited and walked over to his subordinate. They spoke in hushed tones, huddled together such that Baptiste couldn't make anything out. The Dakotas had turned to watch, while Rylan continued probing his engine unawares.

After a minute, the chief turned to look at them, then cursed and followed his man into the refueler. It was hard to see through the plate steel window slats, but Magnus was clearly holding a radio in his hand.

Julia.

Baptiste stormed over, finally drawing the attention of Rylan. The others followed him, until they were all pressed around the open passenger door.

"You're sure?" Magnus was saying, handset held close to his face. Aron looked terrified, frozen like a corpse beside his chief.

"What's going on?" Baptiste interjected.

Magnus scowled and shut him down with a raised hand. Long seconds passed, each drawing the void closer to their tiny camp. Baptiste simmered, alternating panic and rage vying for the gray spots in his heart.

The radio crackled noisily, erupting into a series of blips before a voice came back: a woman's, but not Julia. "Yes. Estimate seven, eight hours tops 'til it reaches you."

It.

Reaches you.

Baptiste didn't have to ask, he could see the truth in

Magnus's eyes: they had been found. Titanic black machines lumbered in his memory, burning his soul with fire.

"They found us," Rylan whispered, echoing his thoughts.

Magnus chewed on his lip, hand white-knuckled on the radio. "Acknowledged," he said. "Resume radio silence." Replacing the handset to the dashboard, he stepped out of the truck.

"What's going on?" the larger Dakota man asked.

Magnus cleared his throat while pulling his fatigues taut. "A scouting party just checked in from Blacklake. They spotted a God-engine heading north. Damaged but on its way to us."

"Ancestors," the other Dakota muttered.

"Damaged..." Baptiste repeated.

The Crusader rolled up behind him.

"No, don't!"

Magnus nodded. "Matches Julia's description from the bunker. The one that attacked you."

Autocannon shells soared overhead, but the battle walker shrugged off the attack as though it was nothing. Its monstrous head turned. Its red eye hateful. The world around him erupted into fire.

Baptiste pulled himself back, scraping the damp from his eyes with a gloved hand.

"Just one?" Rylan asked, stethoscope looped around his stooped neck like a chaplain. "You're sure?"

"Just one," Magnus confirmed.

Rylan sighed, seemingly with relief. "It's not following us, then."

Magnus frowned. "What do you mean?"

Rylan swallowed hard. "They always hunt in pairs. Always. If there's one, and it's damaged, that means it's headed for a repair station."

No one spoke. The Scavrats' plan was to take out as many of those outposts as they could, but not yet. Not before they completed this damnable journey and got reinforcements. Otherwise, they'd be escalating the war beyond their control, something Baptiste was uncomfortably familiar with.

Rylan and Magnus were sharing a look, the latter licking his lips nervously.

"What?" Baptiste prompted.

Magnus shut the door and gazed back at his truck—at its cargo compartment. Rylan's eyes were darting back and forth as though he was making a calculation.

The wait was agonizing. Impatience clawed at Baptiste's stomach.

"There's a contingency plan," Magnus said quietly. "If an opportunity presented itself on the way to Newhaven."

Rylan finished counting and had started to slowly nod. "It's possible."

"What's possible?" Baptiste asked.

"Yes, please do fill us in," the big Dakota man said irritably. No surprise that others were out of the loop, given how these people operated.

Magnus's posture straightened as he addressed the group. "There's a repair station just west of Fort Cross. We're going to blow it up, and we're going to take that fucking God-engine with it."

JULIA

FORT CROSS

Julia couldn't shake Kass's warning. Zev kept the Runner in high gear in an effort to tame its unruly engine, but even still they were a glaring beacon of light in the darkness. Time slowed. Fleeting shapes quivered just beyond the periphery of their light bar. The void pressed down.

She desperately wanted to activate her thermal goggles. Instead, she hunkered deeper into her seat. Being a passenger was the worst part—too much time to think. About the mission, her father, being promoted to chief, and possibly losing her mind after too much time spent in the Deadlands. This last thought, accompanied by the erratic pounding of her heart, was the most concerning.

Finally, a structure broke from the road ahead. Their headlights splashed across a corral of four-meter-tall concrete blast walls, interspersed with guard towers. Fort Cross followed the same pattern as other military facilities she had explored: an unassuming outer fence, demarking a wide perimeter, with a more heavily defended base within. Such was the nature of the shifting war front as the ancient United States collapsed into regional unrest. Domestic bases, once placid, became frontline flashpoints.

Zev slowed down, weaving them around to locate a gap. Julia eyed the tower ahead, straining to make out its observation platform in the scattered light of their Runner. It was too dark to see. She felt tiny in the cabin, shrinking under the looming guardians. The nursery rhyme echoed in her head, warning her away. Magnus hadn't elaborated on how exactly the facility was overrun. Remnant traveled in swarms. She imagined a sea of them, bounding up the towers like animals. The screams of those above, nowhere to run. Spilling like dominos from the edge.

She had to see. Julia turned on her goggles, dropping the lenses over her eyes. The world shifted to a hazy green, blooming at the edges where their headlights beamed out. Several seconds passed as the antique device calibrated itself, contorting the picture. Then nothing. No creatures lurking above, no skeletons down below. Empty silhouettes under a sky of endless uniform green. Somehow, "seeing" the void made it even worse.

"Found it," Zev said, directing their Runner toward a second access point. "Moving to thermal. We'll circle first, then clear the buildings."

The world darkened slightly as he flicked off their lights and activated his own thermal goggles. A cluster of dilapidated buildings unfurled before them—command and control, probably—bracketed on either side by what looked like barracks, a warehouse, and a multi-vehicle garage. No movement anywhere, no bodies. Whatever happened here, time had scoured it clean. Time... or something else. Julia couldn't shake the feeling that the *something else* lurked behind the carefully constructed image her goggles were showing, hovering over her shoulder, concealed within the blurry tendrils of her peripheral vision.

They had barely rounded the back side of the base before Zev declared it to be clear, parking the Runner nose-out at the entrance. The engine shut off with a gurgle, settling into a rhythm of noisy clicks as the overheated metal simmered. He hopped out and retrieved a short-barreled rifle from the weapon stash.

A low keening howled around them as the invisible wind made itself known. It whistled between buildings like a warning —to them or others, she couldn't decide.

"We need to be quick," Zev said, a hint of impatience in his voice. His glowing silhouette stared down at her, dehumanized by the lightless contraption strapped to his eyes. He looked like a decapitated ghost, one of the murdered souls left behind here.

Julia forced her leaden body up and out, retrieving her own rifle and robotically going through the motions of a weapons check.

"Here." Zev handed her a walkie-talkie. "Minimum chatter."

The man's bluntness reminded her of her father, except she wasn't instinctively inclined to argue with him. She wished she had her old crew with her on this mission, as inexperienced as they were. Char and Jax squabbling like children—like family. She wished her father was in charge.

Julia clipped the device to her harness and attempted to straighten herself out. The air felt heavy, tides of stress reaching to her shoulders. Pulling her against her will.

Zev turned toward the facility. "I'll take the interior. You take the outbuildings."

Julia's skin bristled. The barracks were on the west end, the garage and warehouse on the east. That was a long walk out in the open. Her voice eked out past her overly tight helmet strap. "What are we looking for?"

"Anything that's not us."

Not us...

"And keep an eye on your battery meter."

Julia fumbled along the edge of her goggles for a small button beside the On switch. When she depressed it, a monochrome number momentarily floated ahead of her: 71%. How was it already so low?

Zev bounded away at a trot. Julia's stomach lurched as she resisted the urge to follow. She looked from left to right, deciding to start with the garage. The prospect of the barracks, home to the dead twice over, was too much right now. Her legs churned forward, through the tide. A coiling cloud of sparkling green dust bloomed around her as her walk turned to a run.

The building was intact, thanks to the remediations of the last team that had tried to civilize the base. Though degraded by time, its corrugated steel walls hung mostly straight. Its roof sagged, but not to the point of collapse. Four wide doorways stood open and ready to swallow their convoy. It looked completely empty, save for a recurrent creak from within and the soft jingle of chains. Julia froze in place.

Magnus said no one had made it back from Fort Cross. Their fate had been communicated by radio, yet none of their vehicles were here. Taken? Her people knew almost nothing of the remnant. Like demons, they were spoken of by way of myths and tales—those left behind, fallen to savagery along with the cursed earth. Occasional records found their way into the Archive—or didn't, as with this place—but those accounts were mostly useless due to the lack of survivors. Where did they live? *How* did they live? Were they savages or not?

Julia scanned the blast wall at the perimeter. No signs of forced entry, just pockmarked concrete. She turned back toward the base interior, but Zev was gone. Another press on her battery meter showed 66%.

Fuck this place.

She should have let Magnus do his job. They should have just found a nice warm cave with a ceiling and a single exit.

Julia raised her rifle and proceeded through the first door, her footfalls echoing through the empty building.

Nothing.

All of the workstations had been stripped. There were no signs of temporary encampment. A lone ceiling-mounted hoist swayed above the fourth bay, its distended chain links rippling in the breeze. With each rotation, the roof puckered inward, then out again, as though the building were breathing. Her own breaths followed. She watched it, mesmerized. Luminescent ghosts flittered from bay to bay, excitedly attending to their Runners. Scrapes and thumps rang like music, in rhythm to the hoist's groaning pulleys. A promise of civilization beyond Hub.

Turning, turning.

"Chief, report."

Julia gasped, fumbling for her battery meter: 51%. How long had she been standing here?

"Garage clear," she rasped, leaning into her walkie-talkie.

Zev didn't reply.

Where before she had to resist the urge to don her goggles, she now desperately wanted to remove them, to find a functional light bank and chase the ghosts away. There were switches by the entrance but probably no power—probably. Finding the nearest wall, she pressed herself against the cold metal, sidestepping her way out the bay door. A gust of wind charged just as she was about to step clear, slamming her back against the sharp doorframe. She yelped as her helmet jostled sideways, cutting the picture.

Julia grimaced as she was tossed around the Ironclad. The grab bars were too far away. Mace was dead. Kai was running to his death. The soldiers were running to their deaths. She fumbled at the periscope, desperate to see, to collect their souls before the Deadlands could.

Running.

She was always running.

42%.

Julia blinked confusedly as the number hovered in her vision. The garage doors gaped at her from across the courtyard, haloed by a writhing tsunami of dust. She spun around, finding herself at the supply depot.

"What..."

What's happening to me?

She wanted to rub her eyes, to get out of here, to get out of Hub, to run. Her chest vibrated with the pressure of restrained cries. Crew commander, chief—it was a joke, she was neither. She wanted to shoot something, to kill something, to smash herself against the God-engine that took her family. Pins and needles coursed along her legs. Her feet lifted away from the floor.

"No, no, no." She gasped out each protest, unable to breathe with the goggles on.

Julia flipped up the lenses and fell into pitch.

It was worse, so much worse. Somehow, the tendrils clawing at the edges were still there, black on black. She clutched at the top of her rifle but there was no light attached. She swatted at her harness but there was no flashlight. The blackness pushed against her pupils, piercing her soul.

Julia slammed her goggles back down, sucking in a wheezing breath as the artificial world came back into view. Her legs gradually settled back into the dirt. Her lungs started working again.

To her right was a crumpled loading dock door and to her left a blasted open personnel doorway. She had no choice.

Shrugging up her pack, Julia shambled into the doorway, gun up.

Like the garage, it had been stripped clean. There weren't even empty shelves, just a bare concrete pad below the arched ceiling. No signs of struggle, no shell casings or debris detailing the story of those who died here. Her eardrums throbbed against the silence. It felt like an abandoned church, emptied of worshipers and gods alike.

Julia thumbed her walkie-talkie. "East side clear, moving to west."

Her voice rebounded from the warehouse walls and ceiling, colliding into a froth of broken words. She shrugged up her increasingly burdensome pack and waited for the echo to stop, but the mirror voices only accelerated. New chants surged from the floor, swirling around her in a chorus of noise. She rotated around, but the building was as empty as when she entered. New tones: slower, deeper, bestial. Extracted from her throat like a sacrifice, a catalyst, to resurrect whatever once lurked here.

Julia clamped her mouth shut and scuttled back the way she had come. As she exited the ruined doorway, she couldn't shake the feeling that part of her had been stolen away.

The central compound blurred past as she jogged toward the barracks. Their Runner was still there, glowing in the darkness. Eddies of hot air spiraled above it like an iris, an open conduit to the void.

Of course it's still here.

There was no one here to steal it. This place was a tomb.

She struggled to extract confidence from logic. From reason. She didn't believe in ghosts, or gods, or even the postmortem guidance of her ancestors. Those things were fantasies, stories for children, designed to coerce good behavior. Emotional alchemy to ease suffering, little different from Magnus's coffee.

Not real.

She was tired—exhausted—and likely traumatized by her overstay in the Deadlands. That was real. She was out in the open in the dark, where humans should never tarry. That was real. Under stress, the mind plays tricks—hallucinations, sounds.

Baptiste stepped into the nothing.

That was real.

Julia squeezed her eyes shut, pushing the memory back into the cellar of her brain. It didn't fit. It couldn't be reconciled. She lingered by the steaming vehicle, desperate for its primordial warmth—a fire in the wilderness.

Zev didn't reply.

The thought snapped her eyes back open. She hadn't heard anything from him since her first transmission.

The barracks.

Julia depressed the battery button on her goggles: 34%.

"Shit," she muttered, pulling the walkie-talkie from her harness. A low, constant hiss spilled from the speaker—the channel was already open. Julia frowned at it, waiting for a message, but there was only dead air.

"Zev?" she whispered.

The channel closed with a sudden click, stealing her breath. Her whole body shook.

Not real.

Julia pried herself away from the glowing Runner and ran for the barracks, walkie-talkie in hand. The compound flared in and out of existence as her helmet bobbed. Too quickly, she rounded a central building and found herself standing across a set of wide open double doors.

The walkie-talkie trembled in her ghostly hand. "Zev, are you in the barracks?"

No reply.

Zev was an experienced scout. He was just being prudent—

and probably cursing her chattiness.

He went inside. Who else would it be...?

Julia clipped the radio back onto her harness and raised her rifle with both hands, brushing her thumb against the safety to make sure it was off. Just in case.

Unlike the other two buildings, this one hadn't been pillaged. A tight front foyer split the space in two, the left path glowing brighter than the right. Julia followed the light, wrinkling her nose as a pungent odor tickled her nostrils from within. It was the first smell she could recall from the place, other than desiccated earth. At first, the dampness of it reminded her of the fungal farms below Hub, but it quickly turned sour, coppery, with an undertone of sickly sweetness. She switched to breathing through her mouth in an effort not to sneeze it out.

Two small offices broke from the hallway, empty save for the spartan remains of the original furniture. A large open area sprawled ahead, partitioned by the rusty skeletons of ancient bunkbeds. Julia crept along the wall, pausing at each row. The hairs at the back of her head were erect, thrumming to the rapid beat of her heart. Her body wanted to rush, but she forced herself to scan every single bed frame, top and bottom, before moving on. Still, she didn't linger. If she paused too long, the ghosts would return. Here especially, in a place that another civilization had once called home. Her ancestors—her real, physical ancestors—had lived here, before the heavens emptied. Before the only safe place on Earth was below it. It seemed impossible.

There was no sight or sound of Zev. Halfway down, the too-loud patter of her footsteps changed. The thermal signature of the room changed as well, brightening the deeper she went. A carpet of prickly moss overtook the floor, veined with a geometric web of vines that extended from the back of the building. The plants were spindly, dead-looking, but throbbed with heat, bioluminescent in her thermal goggles.

Old memories tugged at her, pulling her into the caves below Hub. Pulling at her heart in the absence of Kai, who would always be there to make sure she and Roen didn't carelessly step into a bottomless pit. Julia navigated her way down the rest of the rows, digging in her heels so she wouldn't fall forward into the abyss. More vines spiraled up from the floor, smothering nearby beds and footlockers. Whatever metal they touched also glowed, and drooped, as though being slowly digested. Heat radiated into her feet through the soles of her boots.

As she passed the last row of beds, the stench of the place became overbearing. Julia gagged and pulled her bandana up over her mouth. At either corner of the back of the building were more rooms, but they remained dark. Ahead was an illuminated doorway bearing an intact placard: "CHAPEL." Moss gave way to a dense tapestry of glowing vines, which spilled out from the room—their source.

Julia hesitated, frozen between the room ahead and the others she hadn't cleared yet. Her breath came hard, constrained by heat and cloying fabric. She squinted against the glow, tempted once more to remove her goggles.

Shit.

Julia tapped her battery meter: 23%. Unclipping her walkie-talkie, she raised it to her face and nudged down her bandana again. "Zev," she whispered, choking, as her mouth filled with dank humidity. "Zev. Are you in the chapel?"

She let go of the button. No reply—at first. Then the channel opened, but again there was only a hiss. Julia pressed it to her ear and as she waited, the hiss turned to a mutter. Words she couldn't understand, rising and dipping on waves of static. Her hair stood on end, but she reattached the radio and lurched forward, the muzzle of her rifle leading the way. Fear dragged at her legs, every step an exhausting act of will.

A man was standing at the front of the chapel, back turned to her. He faced the empty pulpit at the end of the room, past two rows of broken pews, walkie-talkie in hand. Movement flickered in Julia's peripheral vision: tendrils, slithering outside the narrow window of her thermal goggles. She didn't dare look.

Zev?

Her mouth was clamped shut. Julia tried to speak but the words blew back into her mind, scattering to dust.

The man's proportions were all wrong.

The man, the man.

Was it a man?

Arms too long, thin, mismatched. A ragged shroud billowed over his—*its*—body, rippling in absent winds. Revealing a patchwork of glowing skin, pulled taut over jutting ribs. It had creeping vines for hair and burning coals for eyes.

Eyes!

It had turned around, stretched out to the ceiling. Its mouth opened, revealing dagger-sharp teeth.

Real. Not real.

"Everything okay, Chief?"

Her gloved finger latched onto the trigger, anxious to pull.

Real. Not real.

"Julia, it's me."

Julia, run! Julia, fire!

"Chief Greybull! Lower your gun, for fuck's sakes."

Its arms were swaying, pulsing.

Julia scrunched her eyes shut. One more chance.

Not real.

She opened them. Zev stood there, hands raised. The space around them was aflame with creeping vines. The other... *thing* was gone.

"What are you doing?" she whispered—she cried.

Zev pointed at her gun and hissed, "What am *I* doing? What the fuck are you doing?"

Julia lowered her rifle with shaking hands. A red dot had started blinking in the corner of her vision: low battery warning. Soon, she would be blind.

"I'm sorry. I thought..."

The man—who was definitely a man, despite only having half a face—approached her, slowly lowering his arms. "We should get back."

Julia shook. She didn't have the right words.

"Come on, I'll lead the way."

"Wait! I'm almost out of battery. I have to see."

Zev nodded, pushing his goggles up onto his helmet. A cone of light bloomed from his chest. "We're clear, anyway. Use your flashlight."

"I don't have one."

Zev tilted his head, then reached out and patted something on her chest harness. "It's right here."

"What..." Julia looked down. A faint cylindrical silhouette peeked out between her ammo pouches. It had been there the whole time.

"C'mon." Zev trotted ahead, as though nothing had happened. As though this whole place wasn't cursed.

Not wanting to be left behind, Julia chased after him while fumbling for the switch on her flashlight. A narrow beam of brightness extended ahead of her, but she waited until they exited the barracks before removing her goggles.

Together, they made their way back to the Runner. Occasionally, Zev's light swayed in her direction. She could feel his gaze on her but stared straight ahead. She didn't want to see his face. Just in case not real was real after all.

Baptiste had retreated to his patrol duty as the others argued. The new plan sounded insane, but all he cared about was getting back to Bastion. Had Evelyn been here, she would have scolded the Scavrats over the risks, but they weren't his people, weren't his concern. Mostly... Still, he didn't like being left out from what was a military mission at the end of the day. Secrets equaled surprise. Surprise equaled death.

The exclusion ate at him as he continued to wait for Julia and Zev to return. When they finally did—barely within their time limit—he rushed over to question Julia, to ask how much she knew, but was stopped cold by the look in her eyes. In them, he saw his own demons. She was paler than usual, shrunken while she waited for Zev to exit the Runner. It wasn't until the man had joined the others around the refueler that she crawled out, making a beeline for Magnus's truck. Baptiste followed her halfway, then gave up.

When they eventually got going again, Julia stuck with her old chief while Baptiste rode with Zev in silence. Emotions warred in his guts, a noxious mix of concern and suspicion. A voice whispered at the back of his mind, as it had in the Deadlands, warning of conspiracies, lies. He tried to extinguish it, to distract himself with checklists for the layover, but his anxiety lingered, smoldering in the holes that place had left behind.

It wasn't until they reached their destination that his mind was pulled away, deeper into the past. Fort Cross rose like a monument from the cursed earth. Pitted concrete barricades, guard towers, catwalks. From the outside, it looked a lot like Drill Site 7, another supposed sanctuary against darkness. But these places had been designed to keep out men, not demons. Their walls were a lie. The fort's former occupants had learned that the hard way, just as he had, standing atop a guard tower much like these, firing uselessly into the horde.

His dead mother's face upon the demon's shell, crooning, calling him onto her bloody lap.

His men burning to death, begging for help.

Andrite's eyes melting from his head, as his shadow screamed behind the veil of the Deadlands.

Baptiste shivered within his flimsy outfit. Every new discovery was an opportunity to relive old horrors, old failures. He had an endless supply to choose from, and little peace between them to fall back on. Maybe Julia was the same. She had lost a lot of people at Bunker 23. A trail of ghosts followed them both.

The convoy dismounted outside a dilapidated vehicle bay, every Runner facing out for maximum illumination. The base looked mostly intact. Clouds of dust meandered around the blast walls, forever imprisoned in this place. At one time, they might have been people. Thick plumes of the stuff glimmered yellow in their crisscrossing headlights, sculpted into humanoid silhouettes by the wind.

Magnus slapped the side of the fuel truck, which had parked in the middle of their semi-circle. "Aron! Turn on the pump. Everyone refuel, then bring 'em inside for inspection."

A handful of grumbles emanated from the gathered crews.

Zev was walking alongside his chief. "The base is clear. What's the rush?"

Magnus frowned at his companion before scrutinizing their surroundings, catching Baptiste's eye along the way. "Clear of the living maybe... Let's not make the same mistake as our ancestors. Get busy, everyone, then we'll meet inside. Zev, give me the tour. Aron, park his Runner after it's topped up."

The big Dakota man stepped up. "No decisions until we're all together."

Magnus nodded and left with Zev, the narrow beams of their flashlights swallowed by the night as they disappeared into the complex.

The second Dakota man—the "shaman"—left the group, a large satchel at his waist. He moved between the open bays, painting red symbols on the walls with his hands, then laying down a thin barrier of white powder along the ground. Miraculously, the substance didn't just blow away in the breeze.

Rylan had stepped up as he waited for their turn to refuel.

"What's he doing?" Baptiste asked.

"Warding away evil spirits," Rylan said, a little sarcastically.

Baptiste watched as the shaman completed the ceremony, similar in some ways to his own chaplains, to Andrite. The Church would consider him a heathen. Baptiste would have as well, until recently. Maybe he still did. But maybe they all worshiped the same god. If so, did it matter where or how they prayed?

"This isn't your tradition?" Baptiste asked.

"No," Rylan said, busily adjusting his chest rig. "Each clan has its own traditions. This is definitely not ours."

Baptiste squinted at the Mercer man, looking him up and down as he function-checked his gear. Much of it looked new, unused even. Baptiste had noticed Julia give Rylan the same look at times, clearly covetous of his possessions. "You should be thankful. None of *that* will help you in a place like this," Baptiste said.

Rylan looked up, the smirk fading from his face, but Baptiste moved off toward the truck.

Julia had shifted into the MTV's driver seat and was watching the preparations. Baptiste caught her eye. She didn't flinch, so he pulled himself up the running board, face close to hers through the open window. His stomach quivered unexpectedly as their eyes met, forcing him to regroup his confused emotions.

"Are you okay?" he asked.

"We shouldn't be here," she said.

Baptiste spared a glance back at the refueler. "You said it was clear."

Julia nodded. Baptiste waited but she didn't clarify.

"I'm just tired," she said.

Questions tumbled about in Baptiste's head: what she saw, the new plan. But he held his tongue. "You can't sleep out here," he said.

Julia snorted, almost a laugh. "Sleep. What would you know about that?"

Baptiste swallowed uncomfortably. It wasn't right that she suffer as he had. He should protect her from it.

"Julia!" Aron was shouting at them, too loud again. "You're up."

Julia pressed the ignition switch, bringing the big vehicle back to life with a grumble. "I have to prep the truck. I'll meet you inside."

Baptiste nodded and dropped down. The ever-present dust clung to his unprotected body as he made his way into the base. Each step reinvigorated him against the darkness, against memory, but for the first time in his life, he wished he wasn't taking them alone.

———

Aron and Kass took watch while everyone else congregated inside. Their current accommodation was a nondescript concrete room, bereft of furniture. It reminded Baptiste of one of the lord commander's austere rotating offices. He squinted, trying to visualize Central Command, but the details slipped away. Less than two weeks had passed since he left Bastion, but it felt like years. Time, distance, betrayal—they all conspired to erase his former life. The Situation Room had grayed in his memory, a silent mortuary for the city's fallen protectors. The Metro was a dark tunnel, broken by strobing light and infested with vermin that huddled in the shadows.

Baptiste spared a glance downward, checking for movement around his boots; the floor was mercifully clear. All in all, he was glad to be inside, whatever the history of this place. At least here they had a ceiling over their heads, albeit a saggy one pock-marked with corrosion. Breath came easier without the infinite void bearing down.

"So, let's talk," Magnus said.

The Dakota leader—Ekko was his name—cut in right away. Baptiste felt a growing appreciation for their clan. "The whole basis of the plan was to get help first." Magnus raised a hand, but the man continued. "If we attack now, we'll be starting a war."

Magnus's expression darkened. "That bitch already started a war."

"You know what I mean. In council, you and Teo said we can't take out their repair stations on our own. Not without help. Does Vega know about this?"

"Yes."

Zev looked uncomfortable but held fast to his allegiance. Rylan continued to fidget with his gear.

"Why now?" Ekko asked. "What changed?"

"The God-engine," Julia replied. She was trembling as though with cold, arms crossed tightly over her chest. It took a moment for her to continue, mouthing the words beforehand. "We didn't know if the second one survived the explosion. But we figured if it did that it would head for one of Rylan's repair depots."

The Mercer man looked offended by the association and moved to protest, but Baptiste raised a hand this time.

"Look," she continued, her voice steadying as she went on. "I already gave the speech, and I don't want to do it again. But the description matches. That... *thing* killed a lot of us, and it's weak now." Julia was sneering. Baptiste saw something new bubbling in her and recognized it: a desire for revenge, the fire of action to burn away her guilt.

"We can catch it with its britches down," Magnus said. "Also, the original plan was based on frontal assaults. If we go in stealth, the Matriarch might not link it back to us."

"*Might* not," Ekko repeated. "Big comfort."

"We invite chaos into our midst," the shaman said. His skin was even paler than the rest of his companions, like one of the ghosts he was trying to ward away. Baptiste noticed for the first time the man's eyes were two different colors: blue and gray.

Ekko nodded. "It's been quiet since the council. Maybe they're not coming for us."

"They definitely are coming for us," Magnus retorted. "I appreciate your concern, Ekko, but we're doing this."

The other man smarted. "I'm starting to see the loyalists' point—"

"Don't pretend you haven't benefited," Magnus said. "Besides, even Morgan approves."

Ekko turned to Rylan and received a nod in return.

"There are explosives on the truck," Rylan mumbled.

"Explosives!" Baptiste exclaimed. He paled at the thought of them driving this whole way, at times bouncing over near-impassable terrain, with a bomb in their midst.

"Secured," Rylan said, his obnoxious sarcasm returning. "Don't worry."

Baptiste forced down a surge of irritation. This conversation felt like their tiresome council meeting all over again, bickering and maneuvering when they needed to be acting. Even Parliament wasn't as bad. All the while his own plans seemed to be disintegrating.

"What about the mission?" he asked.

"Unchanged," Magnus said, "but we have to split up."

Kass's warning rang in his ears. She was right, of course. Veering off-objective was bad enough, doing it with weakened numbers was worse.

Rylan piped up. "One crew goes to the outpost, takes it out and heads home. The rest continue to Newhaven."

"We can't lose the MTV," Magnus said. "Someone will have to take a Runner."

Ekko winced. "With a crate of explosives? That's going to be a tight squeeze."

"We'll have to reconfigure it," Magnus said. "Swap out the auxiliary fuel tank for the crate."

"You can do that?" Baptiste asked. Everyone present save Julia looked back at him with disdain, as though he had asked the dumbest question possible.

Zev had pulled out a small map, something not shared at the original briefing. He traced a finger along it, shaking his head as he worked out some figures. "With only one tank, whoever goes won't have enough fuel to make it back to Hub from there. They'll have to come back here first to refuel."

Silence smothered the lot of them. It was bad enough to be here as a large group, far worse in isolation. Magnus was looking expectantly at Rylan, who seemed more put out by the second.

"How did I let you get me into this?" Rylan muttered.

"Let's remember who fucked who," Magnus said. "Besides, I doubt you'd have received a warm welcome from Neron."

Rylan started pulling nervously at his neck, just as he had in council chambers when first bringing up these repair stations. "I know the layout, they're all the same. And the entry codes. But I'm a merchant, not a mechanist. I'll need help."

The Dakota men were mumbling to each other, neither happy. Magnus and Rylan turned to face Julia.

Panic jolted up Baptiste's spine, snapping the nerves in the back of his neck. A hot flush crested over his scalp, pushing sweat into his eyes. "No," he blurted.

Julia stood rigid, crossed hands turning to white fists. The gossamer flesh at her neck twitched with blood and stress. She stared straight at him. "Yes. I'm the most qualified."

Baptiste floundered under her gaze, unmoored from whatever scant hope had carried him this far. "You promised to get me back to Bastion."

Julia cringed, maybe from guilt, maybe from disgust. "Magnus will get you to Newhaven."

A sea of emotions pounded him, inundating the weak wall he had only just managed to rebuild. Dismay, abandonment, and a longing for her company that only now revealed itself in total. Julia was his only connection to normality, a bridge between his orderly life before and the chaos of now. She was comfort, promise. He tried to reel himself back, as Father Ollet had the last time his soul was almost lost, dredging up pragmatic excuses for her to stay with him.

"But you're taking one of the Runners. That'll leave us short when we get to Newhaven. Am I supposed to *walk* to Bastion?" Regret immediately filled him as the last bit came out with vehemence.

"Ramirez is flush with vehicles," Magnus said. "More than they can use. We'll make sure it's part of the deal."

Baptiste felt like an idiot, naive. Even if this new opportunity hadn't come up, was Julia ever going to take him all the way there? The last stretch of his journey had always been fuzzy. As much as his life seemed to revolve around travel lately, he had never done it alone—didn't know the map or the territory.

Magnus was talking again but Baptiste didn't hear the words. His whole body was damp, itchy beneath his Scavrat costume. An empty horizon stared back at him from his memory, dragging him into the gray.

Baptiste stepped back.

"—an hour to prep and a couple hours of sleep and you should still get there well before the enemy. Better move, there's a lot of work to do."

"Work," Baptiste muttered, allowing anger to pump up his failing heart. He sneered at Magnus. "From what I can see, you have a habit of leaving the *work* to everyone else."

Magnus straightened, eyes flashing. The rest of the room went black. "Listen to me, soldier," the man hissed. "I'd go if I could. But I need to see this mission through."

"Coward."

The blow caught him unaware. A rush of noise filled his ears as his goggles went flying.

Screaming. They were all screaming. He tried to kill the demon, the God-engine, Rayos, but they hung on the other side of nothing, unreachable.

The room rushed back, dropping wall by wall around him.

His left cheek throbbed. Unlike the visions, Magnus was right there—reachable. Killable.

"Chief!" Julia, moving between them. Her hand was on his chest, pressing on his brother's talisman. Baptiste pushed back, feeling the metal on his skin, bathed in her heat.

Rylan's hand was on his sidearm.

Baptiste seethed. "You get that one for free. The next will cost you."

Zev had a grip on Magnus's shoulder. The chief was rubbing his right hand. "If you want to go home, you'll stay in line. Everyone get to work, then find your bunk for the night."

"Wait!" Julia called, turning back to the room.

Baptiste's rage fizzled as she removed her hand. The talisman became cold again.

"Not the barracks," she said.

Everyone paused, waiting for an explanation, but no more sounds came from her still-moving lips. The terror that Baptiste saw earlier had returned.

Zev spoke up in her stead. "Julia's right. There's something growing in it. Could be toxic."

"Fine," Magnus said, seemingly impatient to end their conclave. "Spread out in the central compound. Pair up by vehicle."

Julia glanced briefly at Baptiste, then away. His heart jumped.

"Julia," Magnus said. "You should get some sleep. You'll be on the road again before dawn."

She nodded weakly.

"So, we're doing this," Rylan said, eyes glazed over.

Magnus tugged at his disheveled sleeves and eyed everyone in the room save Baptiste. "We're doing this."

REBEKAH-6

NO PLACE FOR A BATTLE WALKER

Rebekah-6 was almost through the pass, pursued by mutated beasts and the mountain itself, which seemed intent on killing her. The old road had long since faded into time, replaced with narrow granite paths that straddled the edge of oblivion and claustrophobic switchbacks that clawed at her shoulders and hips. All the while, waterfalls of gravel rained from the ragged slopes above, rapping against her hull, distracting her from the excruciating task of staying upright.

This was no place for a battle walker, let alone a God-engine. It would have been hard enough to navigate with all the support systems and technology of a machine mind. If she fell, it could mean death, depending on how she landed. On her back, in this place, she would be incapable of righting herself. She strained within her sepulcher, teeth gritted against her breathing tube, fresh blood joining the caked mass at her nostrils. The cadaverous skin of her forehead wrinkled in concentration—

Focus.

Knives slashed into her brain, like the surgeon's saw, as she stretched her mind into every sensory surface. The constant pitch and yaw of her upper torso, micro-adjustments of her gait as every second step fell into an undulation or canted her closer to the edge. All the while trying to ignore the yipping glee and panting breath of the creatures that pursued her. Every so often, a glaring reticle leapt onto her heads-up display, then faded out, but the afterglow remained.

Flitting shapes—loosely depicted as glowing blobs by her new night vision—shimmied from boulder to boulder, above and below. Unrecognizable as beast or demon, death in either case. They had been timid at first, flush with the memory of her sisters' power, but as they pursued and she ran, they recognized her as prey rather than predator. She could feel their hunger, their singular desire to crack her shell open and devour the treasure within. Prying at her wounds, wriggling through the cavities in her ruptured shoulder and pockmarked torso, salivating for the sweet nectar of her recycled blood—

The ground fell away.

Rebekah-6 tried to correct, failed, and tumbled over the edge, smashing through a brittle ridge of once-trees down the slope. Skeletal branches lunged at her viewport before evaporating to splinters. She splayed her autocannons out like sleds, desperate not to flip forward, yelling silently in her mind as her body careened downward, then landed on the next level with an actuator-grinding thud. She swayed, counterbalanced, almost fell as her left leg hesitated from its hip joint, then stepped into a static crouch. Damage reports bubbled up from her subconscious, but she subdued them again—she could *feel* her new injuries well enough. Irritated growls reverberated from above as her pursuers sought a path down. The mountainside continued to shed behind her, rising into a plume of dust that reduced the world to a hazy white field.

Shaking off her disorientation, Rebekah-6 activated her spotlights and edged forward, seeking a way out. There was no pathway here, just a stubborn ridge of conifers winding the rest of the way downslope. Most were fossils but a handful sparkled impossibly green under her gaze, glowing with life. She recognized them from her geography lessons, required of every Numbered so they were prepared for the world after symbiosis. Such organisms always seemed too fantastical, too improbable compared to the sterile ecosystem of the Spire. As far as she had ranged, Rebekah-6 had never seen anything like them in real life. The forests of the north were all dead. Somehow, these precious few had leeched enough moisture from the wetlands below to survive even as the mountain collapsed around them.

Wonderment broke through fear, slowing her heart, slowing her pace. The trees swayed lethargically in the evening wind, expanding and contracting like mighty bellows, long needles hissing like serpents. She stumbled from one to the next, carefully hooking her autocannons onto their fanned skirts for support, wishing for hands, even the ugly, over-jointed fingers of her training exosuit. Not just for grip but so she could truly touch these relics of nature, to walk their primordial synapses. She pressed close as she passed, so she could feel, or imagine the feeling of, their soft bristles running along her prow, like her mother's brush through her hair. Their windswept whispers like her mother's prayers as she was rocked to sleep, cocooned in her swaddling.

Images of home swam in her mind, things she never thought she would miss: her boring but comfortable cell, the snug fit of her custom habit, the awkward ministrations of Naomi and Abigail as they navigated her strangeness. The occasional visits by her mother before a violent and futile attempt to spare her from this fate. If only it had worked... what then? If only she had failed her final test, what then? Could they have lived out their lives together, exploring places such as this, devoted to life rather than death?

In her wheelchair, as her human body failed, crumbling under the demon's touch...

No. They may have been together, but only as dust.

The deeper Rebekah-6 descended, the larger the trees got, until they dwarfed her twelve-meter-tall frame. Some must have been as ancient as the Eternal One, seen the coming and going of the Old World, and yet none bore seeds. She looked for pinecones but found only empty branches. They were barren, the last of their kind.

A heavy thud cascaded from the landing, followed by smaller impacts and the splashing of distant rocks against her auditory sensors. The beasts had found a way down. Rebekah-6 increased her pace, wincing internally as the forest bent before her, every broken bough stabbing at her heart. Meanwhile, her pursuers barreled through, uncaring of the damage they wreaked. Trees groaned and screamed as their limbs were sheared off, as centuries-old trunks heaved from their stubborn perches.

The beasts shouted into the night, their growls twisting into fragmentary, unintelligible curses. Rebekah-6 ran faster, desperate to maintain her distance. She had navigated most of the way to the base. The ground grew sticky with moisture, sucking at her feet as she plowed ahead. All she needed was a stretch of flatland and she could outrun them. Flat, dry land...

The pitch-black prairie finally revealed itself—behind a broad stretch of swamp. Rebekah-6 searched desperately for a bypass, but there were none. There was only through. The mountain's runoff had collected like tears, salting the land, turning it to a sickly sponge. Conifers gave way to a sea of sunken willows and dense thickets of bramble. The trees nearest her shivered as the lead beast thudded closer, shaking the ground. She froze, arms extended in mid-stride, as she recalled her near escape from the Spire.

The rattling of her wheelchair's casters along the obsidian floor as her mother rushed her down the hall. Bodies everywhere.

"It's time to go, Rebekah."

She plunged forward, immediately lurching sideways as her ankle twisted in the muck. Moving as fast as she could, which was still too slow, Rebekah-6 trudged through the viscid water. Spindly roots caught underfoot, dragging her down. Archipelagoes of thorny vine conspired to entrap her. But still she progressed, resisting the urge to turn around as something splashed behind her, then more. They were closing. Now that she was in the thick of the quagmire, the exit was nowhere to be seen. There was only the steaming pit.

Rebekah-6 strained against her circuitry, coaxing her reactor beyond safe limits. Her hip joints screamed. Deep within the machine's guts, she wheezed against her suddenly too-narrow breathing tube. There was neither enough air nor power to drive her as fast as she needed to go.

The beasts were closer now.

They sped down the hall, Rebekah-6 holding on for dear life as her mother wheeled her to the elevator.

An island of gnarled trees—also alive, but with a sickly look about them—lifted from the mire dead ahead.

"Be brave."

Flecks of purple light sparkled within, blurry as though vibrating on the spot—some sort of bioluminescent algae. Rebekah-6 dragged her legs up the embankment, thick mud sloughing from between her metal toes. As before, there was no path, but her compassion for the living flora of this place was outweighed by terror. She smashed through the bramble, finding purchase on mostly dry ground. The haggard grove parted, branches whipping wildly until the whole island lurched in a wild dance. The faster they swung, the brighter and more numerous the lights became, pinpoints turning to constellations, accompanied by a low hum. Foliage slipped from their branches, but slowly, methodically, detaching rather than breaking off. As she raced past, Rebekah-6 caught spiked antennae and razor mandibles, leaves that were actually translucent wings, every glowing bud an abdomen thrumming with awakened hunger. There were hundreds of them, thousands. One by one the trees shed their living coats.

Rebekah-6 found her prayers.

With a multitudinous roar, the swarm erupted into a fireball, streaking past her to the flesh-and-blood creatures that had invaded their abode. They darted over her prow, under her arms, through her legs. She kept moving, half-blinded by the glare, beseeching Messiah for courage, but as the words traveled her distant lips, she saw only her mother's eyes in the dark.

Howls of excitement changed pitch to fear. Wild splashes erupted from either side as her pursuers tried and failed to flee. Screams echoed into the void as they were annihilated to the last.

Rebekah-6 ran.

And ran.

Until the Sea of Screams and her sisters' savagery and the insect swarm and all the horrors of the broken world were behind her, and once more the orange sun rose from the black.

JULIA

INTO DARKNESS

Revenge.

It wasn't a word that Julia had thought much of—not for her own sake, anyway. She was a mechanist. She explored, unearthed, rebuilt. Sometimes her career required violence, but only in self-defense, used against a world that hated the living. She mastered her weapons like she mastered everything else; they were technical, practical. She never craved violence, until now.

Ever since Bunker 23. Ever since seeing her people slaughtered, Kai turned to ash, her father...

She wanted it. The God-engine stalked her in her dreams, and she wanted to fight back, instead of running. Always running.

Through no action of her own, Julia was becoming more and more of a Greybull. She imagined deposed chief Aubrey back at Hub, seething alone in his throne room, etching lines of rage into her portrait. Pulling at her eyes, forehead, and mouth— cursing the Matriarch with every brushstroke. Rendering her into a facsimile of his dead son, charged with the hatred needed to see their fading clan through to the end.

Before the warning came through from Blacklake, her hate had simmered, awash in the background noise of her addled brain. But now it emerged in full, lending clarity to chaos. Purpose.

She was going to kill the God-engine.

Baptiste was watching her. Julia could tell by the way his mouth was twisting around that he wanted to say something—shout something, probably. She didn't blame him.

They were sitting awkwardly on their bedrolls at opposite ends of another small windowless room. An oil lamp flickered by the door. Beyond the rotting metal wall, she could hear sounds of activity as her Runner was reconfigured. Her hatred faded back into fear with every bang of a hammer, every voice raised too loud in this cursed place. The barracks were listening, she was sure of it. Across the compound, alien vines stirred, pulsing with heat to every human sound, straining to escape their confines.

Zev's face shuddered open into a gaping, pointed scream.

Julia blinked hard, trying to exorcise the vision, but it lingered in the corners. Baptiste continued to stare, fuming.

"I can't run anymore," she said.

"You lied to me."

He had probably been holding in those four words since they left the meeting. His face showed genuine hurt, and not just from the pink welt on his cheek.

"I told you we'd get you to Bastion, and we will," she said.

"Magnus," Baptiste spat, pointing at his face.

"He's a good leader, just under a lot of stress. You shouldn't have insulted him."

Baptiste snorted and looked away. "I don't know these people. I only know you."

His cheeks flushed beyond the spot where her old chief had punched him. Guilt stabbed at her—guilt and her own uncomfortable heat. The uneven concrete floor pressed hard through the thin fabric of her sleeping bag, compressing her crossed legs. They throbbed with exhaustion. There was no rest to be had in this place, as bad as she needed it.

"I'm sorry," she said.

Conversation between them had been much easier at the bunker. The nosy lieutenant would ask trite questions about their research, she would stall, Mace would make sure he didn't see anything.

Mace.

Kneeling on the gray, a human-shaped pile of ash.

"What did you see?" Baptiste asked.

Julia shuddered, sucking in a breath. "When?"

He squinted, confused. "Here. You and the other one—Zev."

Julia shuffled around, trying to get comfortable. She fidgeted with the pack at the end of her bedding, repositioning the chest rig she had doffed when they settled in, repeatedly touching the cool metal of her flashlight to make sure it was there.

"Julia?"

"A lot, okay?" she snapped, crossing her arms over her body. She wanted to keep everything in her bottle, but it was near bursting. "Ever since the attack. I've been seeing things. Hearing things..."

Baptiste nodded. "You lost people. Some wounds heal differently."

Wounds maybe, but not guilt. Her guilt hadn't healed at all, after lying to him day after day. When they first met, it was nothing; even if the Bastionites had gotten them into Bunker 23, she didn't owe him anything. But the longer they spent together, crammed into one horrible place after the next, the worse the guilt became. It soured, multiplied, poisoning her heart.

"It's not just that," she said.

"No... We've been places no one should be."

Julia winced, pulled from her ruminations back into the Deadlands. Into Southview, into the Sea of Screams. All cursed. "We should never have left Hub. We should have stayed underground."

Baptiste squirmed on his own bedroll, brushing at the ends of his boots before replying. She had noticed him doing it before, a nervous habit. "If this plan of yours works, you'll be free to explore elsewhere, as you said." His mouth curled into the tiniest of smiles, sending a flutter through her chest. "Your people might make you their new leader."

She couldn't tell if he was joking or not. "That's not how the Union works."

His smile faded, eyes icing over. "Things change."

Not the Deadlands.

"Some things," she said. "I am sorry. Really. You've been through a lot."

His expression softened again. Their eyes found each other and lingered there. "We both have," he said.

Julia swallowed hard, confused by alternating turns of despair and desire. "I have these visions. Nightmares, whether I'm awake or asleep. Mace, Kai. That fucking machine. They follow me everywhere I go. Even your priest."

Baptiste stiffened at the mention of Father Ollet. His hand came up to his chest, tugging at the necklace he wore beneath his fatigues. Its tattered cord dug into his neck.

"You have visions too," she said, knowing it was true. She had seen them in his eyes.

He nodded slowly, as reluctant as her to divulge weakness. "It's a pestilence. In our souls."

"I don't believe in souls."

Baptiste's jaw clenched, pulling his face taut. Silence fell on the room, worse than the clatter of the garage. There was only the echo of their breath on the bare walls and the angry sizzle of the oil lamp. "It doesn't matter if you believe in them or not."

The statement hit her like a sledge. The way he said it, as plain as the walls that encased them. Her heart rate ticked up, thrumming in her ears. It was bad enough that she was losing her mind.

My soul.

A throwaway word. It was hard for the old faiths to survive the sundering of the world, especially when Hell was next door. By their own definition, humanity had been abandoned, cast out by God. Some clans still practiced, but not hers. Clan Harper was purely materialist, and Clan Greybull worshiped the past. Others, like Clan Dakota, claimed to follow traditions that were old even before the world fell.

Souls were a luxury in a world constantly trying to kill you.

"No," she muttered, shaking her head. "This is all there is."

Baptiste's eyes glazed over. "For now. Until Bastion is redeemed."

Julia waited for more, but he was elsewhere. "What do you mean?" she asked.

"The dead sleep," he intoned, as though reading from scripture—maybe he was. "Only when we prove ourselves to God, and the stars return to the sky, will the faithful rise up."

"Rise up?"

His attention returned to the room, to her. "Into Heaven."

Julia blinked, again waiting for more, but Baptiste was rigid as stone. Only his hand moved, turning whatever bauble hung at his chest through his shirt.

"What about the rest of us?" she asked.

His hand stilled. "The rest?"

"Those who don't follow your faith."

Baptiste lowered his gaze. The distance between them grew vast, painful. His brow furrowed. "I don't know..."

They sat in awkward silence for a minute, fidgeting, then checking their gear. She would be leaving soon. Without him. Guilt surged back in the absence of conversation. And longing, as much as she tried to refuse it. If she had been forthright with him at the bunker, shared her findings, would it have changed their trajectory? Would something in his own tortured soul be healed? She could give him the truth, at least. It was all she had.

"Back at Bunker 23—" she started, swallowing back fear of judgment, of betraying her people.

Baptiste's eyes darted up. He looked fully like a Scavrat now, in his fatigues and jacket. Ragged, thin, a bluish cast of stubble on his paling but painfully attractive face. If he looked like her people, suffered like them, then maybe he *was* one of them.

"There was a battle walker," she blurted, body beginning to vibrate as a chill took her.

He gave her a concerned look. "Yes? Two of them."

She shook her head, struggling for the words. "I mean *in* the bunker. Disassembled. That's what we were working on."

His eyes grew wide as her confession spilled out, but he remained silent.

Her hands ached, palms dug into the cold metal of the flashlight she was clutching. "That's what your people wanted us to find. That's what I hid from you." Julia held her breath, trying to push back her nerves.

Baptiste breathed deeply, his expression mercifully calm. He turned his head to the side, eastward toward his homeland. "Lies will be the death of us all."

The death of us all.

The chill grew. Her teeth chattered as she saw her body rotting in the earth, piled upon the dust of every ancestor that preceded her. Silent, all knowledge lost, all for nothing. Her skin flayed away, bones pulverized under the pressure of the void. Until nothing remained but a lost soul, scattered in the wind.

Tears filled her eyes.

As quickly as the room washed away, Baptiste was beside her, draping his jacket over her shoulders. A flood of warmth filled her chest.

His body, the only heat.

His eyes, the only light.

This strange man from the other side of the world, who looked more like her dead husband each day. No, not that... Though he looked ever more like a Scavrat, Baptiste barely resembled Roen. It was his *presence* that was familiar, the feel of him—maybe of his soul—when they were close. Julia had known her husband for most of her twenty-five years. There was no one else, before or after. It seemed impossible to know that kind of love again.

Baptiste edged away, pushing himself from the floor to return to his bedroll.

Julia's heart pounded. She grasped his arm—his hand. "Wait."

This is all there is.

She had to stop running.

They had found each other's arms once before, as the past exploded in a shockwave around them.

"Stay with me, Baptiste."

The shock of an unknown future pressed her into them again.

His eyes darted back and forth. His temples and jaw quivered. A pained grimace spread across his face as revealed lies and memories of shared trauma passed between them. Death filled every wrinkle, every scar, the creases around his mouth.

Julia shrugged off the jacket and grasped his other hand, intertwining their fingers. "Stay with me."

His body was the only heat.

His face calmed, though his hands were shaking. "My name is Philippe."

Julia pulled him down on top of her. The sounds of the garage faded. The distant vibration of the barracks stilled. Her mouth found his, and the chill of the room was gone.

They came together, and for a time, it was enough.

———

Gray, everywhere.

Julia stood in the center of it, surrounded by nothing. No horizon, no sun, no sound, no time.

She had been running. A lifetime of it. From loss, loneliness. And then from death, starbursts of violence splashing briefly against the gray before dulling back into oblivion.

But the running didn't work. Nor did the screaming, for she had no voice, only a gaping void at the center of her throat. She was alone with fear made manifest. It coiled about her soul like the petrified skin of a serpent, each cadaverous scale the tortured face of someone dead by her hand. The edges of Julia's body—two-dimensional in this space—folded inward as she struggled to contain their features. To grasp them before the gray could, before they faded to dust.

One soul lingered, materialized into a pitted stone sculpture —the broken upper body of a man. It teetered upon a pile of decaying rubble, once its innards. Sinking, deeper into the gray. Its face contorted, silently screaming as it shifted between three forms. She knew them, but there were gray spots where their names used to be. She only remembered their suffering: drowned, disemboweled, abandoned.

Julia tried to step toward the half man, but she had no legs. Looking down, she saw more rubble where her own body had once been. She too was sinking, reducing. Silence pounded in her ears.

There was something else now. Red, searing the sky. The sun, the God-engine's eye, occupying the whole of the heavens. Her head sagged backward, bobbing on the accordion folds of her flattened neck as she strained to look up.

The eye glared back, shrinking her to a sandblasted bust. She clutched at the sky with arms the size of needles. Without the red, she was nothing. Without it, gray turned to solitary black. She sank deeper into the earth. Oblivion crept in from the corners. Tendrils—

"Philippe."

Julia pried her eyes open. She was alone in her sleeping bag, compacted into a ball, fists clenched. The room was empty, save for the slow dance of the flickering oil lamp. The door was open.

Slow footsteps echoed down the hall. They had woken her from her nightmare. Baptiste—

Julia caught herself.

Philippe—the name didn't sound right yet—must have been on watch. She didn't remember falling asleep. How could he survive without sleeping? A week spent unconscious wouldn't be enough at this point.

Philippe.

She mouthed his name, the shape of it warming her lips. She had nestled into his chest, fingers tracing along years of criss-crossing scars cut by his strange necklace. He didn't answer when she asked about it. He didn't say anything at all. Eventually, the exhaustion was overwhelming. She must have passed out in his arms.

The footsteps stopped outside her door. Julia pulled herself up, leaning against the wall, but no one came. Long seconds passed. Eagerness turned to unease as she stared into the dark hallway beyond. When she tried to call for her new lover, the words stuck in her throat as though still trapped in the dream. The sweat along her spine turned to ice.

Julia pulled the sleeping bag up to her chin. "Philippe?" she managed to whisper.

A bare foot jutted from the darkness. Then an arm, mismatched.

No.

Pins and needles lacerated her clenched legs.

A disfigured head poked out from the doorway, bobbing like a rag doll atop its crooked neck. Its face was too long, hairless, black-eyed. Not human. Not anymore.

Julia froze. She had no body, no legs to run.

I'm still dreaming. Still dreaming.

The thing coiled out from the doorframe—gnarled shoulders, cavernous ribs spread like a claw trap—unfurling like the wandering vines in the barracks. Its teeth were daggers.

Julia squeezed her eyes shut. It was all she could do to banish it.

The oil lamp hissed and popped. Julia covered her ears.

"Julia!"

It knew her name. How did it know her name?

"Get down!"

A dull boom slammed her back into the wall.

The tank had fired. She was leading the bunker survivors to their deaths. The Ironclad's walls were closing in.

Something hot splashed across her face.

The Sea of Screams. Drowning her husband. Drowning her for betraying him with another man. Drowning them all in hatred.

"Julia!"

Something ripped her arms away, arms the size of needles. Minuscule, yet too heavy to lift.

"It's me, Julia. We have to go!"

Go. Run.

Julia opened her eyes. Philippe was there, rifle in hand. A whisp of smoke circled the barrel. Something was behind him, on the floor—

"Don't look!"

Julia shook her head repeatedly.

"Eyes on me. We have to go. Now."

Julia grabbed her jacket from the floor, mindlessly pulling it over her arms.

Its eyes.

A gush of bile raced up her throat, barely held back.

Philippe shouldered her pack alongside his own and held out her chest rig. She contorted her body into it, snapping the buckles shut, then slung her rifle. Shouting had started up outside, plus more gunshots. Someone screamed.

"We're under attack," he said. "Stay close."

Philippe flicked on his weapon light and Julia followed suit. They fled the room behind two narrow beams of yellow. Every corner brought dread but no more of the creatures were waiting for them. From the sounds of it, they were all outside.

They. No story could have prepared her, certainly no nursery rhyme. The memory of it burned her eyes.

Julia steadied herself against the wall. The exit was up ahead.

Her walkie-talkie crackled on.

"Remnant!"

"They're coming from the barracks."

"Get the fuck out!"

Philippe turned to face her, wide eyes aglow. "When we get to the compound, run straight for your vehicle. No turning back."

Julia just nodded, still half-paralyzed by shock.

They burst through the door. It was as black outside as when they had retired to their room.

"Go!"

They ran through the pitch. Something moved to Philippe's left and he unleashed, spitting bullets its way. A screeching hum filled her ears. Up ahead, a pair of headlights flared on, followed by the roar of an engine. Two silhouettes to their right. More gunfire and they shrunk back into the night.

"Scavrats!" It was Magnus on the walkie-talkie. "We are leaving!"

More lights flooded the compound, followed by shrieks as loping figures ducked out of the way. Chatter filled the channel. "Zev! Zev, where the fuck are you?"

Julia stopped in her tracks, turning to face the barracks.

The vines curled around her feet, begging her to stay.

"What—" Philippe started, then grabbed her arm, yanking her forward.

She ran, but the chapel stuck in her vision.

The vines weren't plants at all, but flesh. Rising into a curtain over the chapel door, a fractal web of veins igniting with every inbreath. Zev was smothered in its embrace, lifted to the ceiling in ecstasy.

"Stay."

The ground exploded, rippling into a line of fire west of their position. Julia sprawled forward, losing her rifle. Mace snatched her up by her harness and kept running.

Mace?

No. Philippe. Mace was dead.

Half the convoy was out already. Aron and Kass had taken position at either end of the garage, laying down covering fire. A snarl erupted behind Julia as Rylan's Runner skidded to a halt, almost knocking her over again. It had been reconfigured according to plan; in place of a second fuel tank was a black crate stuffed with explosives.

"Get in!" Rylan shouted.

Julia clutched Philippe's arm.

The MTV pulled up on their other side. Magnus leaned out, panic in his eyes. "Where's Zev?"

Julia shook her head.

A tremor of grief shook her old chief's face.

Kass was shooting, cursing the darkness. Aron was screaming. The Dakotas stood atop their own Runner, firing blindly.

A tear rolled down Magnus's cheek.

The God-engine's eye beamed down on her, turning her vision red. Filling her with hate.

"We have to go!" Rylan shouted, revving his engine angrily.

Magnus reeled himself out of his pain. "We're overrun. Your mission's aborted."

"No!" Julia yelled. "I have to finish it."

"You can't come back to refuel. You'll be stuck out there!"

Rylan sped off, his engine growling as he swerved a tight circle around them. Gangly figures bounced off his Runner, falling back into the night.

Julia shoved away her terror. "Then you better be quick at Newhaven."

Rylan swung back around. Ekko ripped out of the garage, his shaman taking pot shots from the rear seat.

Kass was screaming again, but this time out of fear. The blaring of rifle fire stopped, replaced with the staccato plunk of a handgun.

Julia's gut clenched. She was leaving people behind. Again.

Philippe kneeled by the rear of the MTV, firing into the encroaching wave of remnant. There would be no goodbyes.

"Take care of him, Magnus."

Her old chief nodded and turned to join the battle.

Julia crammed herself into the back of her Runner. Before she could say anything else, they lurched forward, powering toward the exit. Concrete walls sped past them, guard towers

aswarm with monstrous shapes. Chaos faded into muted silhouettes, the pitter-patter of echoing gunfire, the taste of blood on
her lips. She wrapped her arms around herself, struggling to
remember the shape of Philippe's body.

Then they were out, fleeing west.

Into darkness.

BAPTISTE

HELL ON EARTH

Plumes of fire gushed all around them, bursting like blood from the savaged earth. The Yellowstone Lava Fields, Magnus had called them, the ruin of a great and vast Old World mountain range. The Northern Ridge that shielded Bastion had also been a proper mountain once, but it was silent, cold. This place was wrought with violence as far as the eye could see. It was still dark outside, predawn, but the way north was lit by islands of molten orange. The fires felt ancient, as old as the world.

Like Hell on Earth.

The vehicles were struggling, their air intakes caked with particulate. Repeatedly, Magnus's truck threatened to choke out. The chief threw a switch each time it stalled, blasting the engine clean, but the purging mechanism's high-pitched whistle was weakening. Soon, it would die altogether. The convoys' tires were probably also at their limits, melting beneath their feet, but they couldn't stop. To stop here was to burn.

Baptiste wiped the sweat from his forehead and the ash from his goggles. He felt claustrophobic in his headgear. In addition to eye protection, they all wore ventilator masks to save their lungs, but he couldn't get his to sit right. The edges of it dug into his clammy skin, stirring up angry hives, and the inside stank of mildew, at least as bad as the sulfur outside. Every breath was a labor, worsened by the temperature of this cursed place. The heat in the cabin was insufferable, as was the nauseating lurch of what passed for a roadway.

It was a miserable journey. They dipped and weaved around the scorched earth, the truck bouncing erratically. His hand was growing numb from clutching the passenger-side grab bar so long. Unlike the last leg, Magnus seemed to be making this one up as they went. The convoy would plow forward for several minutes, only to lose progress as a massive eruption forced them to backtrack.

An unlit gravel path opened to their right, leading back down to the eastern plains.

Baptiste pointed. "There," he croaked through his mask.

No response.

He had repeatedly tried to divert Magnus back onto the open prairie, God-engines be damned. Their plan was a failure, anyway. Surely by now the attention of the enemy was upon them. But the chief was silent, had been since they left Fort Cross, gaze fixed forward.

A jet of flame erupted on their flank, blasting open what moments before had been a perfectly traversable spot of road. Magnus swerved, knocking Baptiste hard against the door. He clutched the grab bar harder, turning in his seat to see the way out disappear behind them. A sigh of regret broke into coughs as he snorted back his own soured breath.

Steaming fog boiled in their wake. It rippled and oozed like the tumorous flesh of a demon, occasionally broken by scattered light from the rest of the convoy. Two Runners followed after them, blinking in and out of existence. They were more agile than Magnus's truck, but less sturdy, and undoubtedly having issues of their own. Whatever the skill of their drivers, no vehicle could take a beating like this for long.

The Dakotas were in the first Runner, Aron in the second.

Just Aron.

For whatever reason, the subhumans had converged on the garage even after most of the Scavrats were out. A tsunami of the creatures, falling upon one another like vermin. As though the heretic priest's wards of protection had the opposite effect, drawing them in. Maybe Ollet was right about these people after all. Believing in a god wasn't enough. There were cults aplenty within Bastion, but their zealotry did not make them holy. Just the opposite—his brother had died to satisfy their evil religion.

Kass, the warrior woman, hadn't made it. Baptiste tried to suppress the enemy but ran dry quickly. The lot of them were out of ammo now, bullets and crossbow bolts alike, which would surely be a problem later. Her dying screams joined those of his other men, smashing about his brain for attention. Aron's too, though his screams were those of the tortured living. The technician had yelled for his companion, trying to pull her from the swarm into his vehicle. His yells turned to screeching as only her severed arms emerged from the seething mass. The sounds of her gruesome death lifted above the maelstrom, echoing from the rafters. Eventually the whole building came crashing down, silencing her suffering, and smashing the refueler. Aron had just managed to escape, still screaming as his Runner charged past them.

Baptiste turned back around to face the inferno ahead. Tidal waves of smoke crashed in from all sides, yawning into screaming faces before dispersing into the void. Molten eyes, charcoal mouths—all those he had let die. He tried deep breaths to exorcise the visions, but his mask left him wheezing. Gabriel's shard had found its way into his left hand, now slick with blood.

He squeezed it into his palm, but the metal couldn't reach far enough to quash his shaking nerves.

Every battle ended this way.

Everything he touched, everyone he loved, as though carrying a curse. Death. Horror. A waking nightmare in the absence of sleep. Yet never injured himself.

Would Julia suffer the same fate?

Baptiste peered out the slatted window, staring at the endless gouts of flame that marked their way. He might never see her again.

Might. He scoffed. He would certainly never see her again.

Bastion grew ever closer, but each kilometer they traveled felt farther from home. From the only woman he had ever lain with, the only person he had ever opened his heart to. Emptiness was taking hold in the gray spots she had temporarily occupied. His hand clamped tighter. The transmitter was on the refueler, meaning there was no way to reach her, to ask her people for help. To save her from his curse.

Baptiste looked over at Magnus. The last time he had seen the chief's face unobstructed, it was haggard, grief and exhaustion multiplying his years. Kass wasn't their only loss. Zev hadn't made it out either. There had been no word from the scout once the attack started. Baptiste hoped uselessly that Scavrats didn't have souls, as Julia had said, lest the ones they left behind be trapped forever in that damned place. Magnus was clearly suffering, just as Baptiste would after losing a man, maybe worse. The air between them had shifted, past grievances set aside by shared loss. There was only the mission now.

Baptiste pressed himself back into his seat, trying to stabilize his wandering mind. They were still moving, still progressing.

I'm still alive.

It didn't help.

They carried on in silence, vibrating to the jarring rhythm of the truck's suspension. Baptiste's eyes drooped with deceptive fatigue but shot back open each time he saw Kass torn to shreds, Julia swallowed by the night. Eventually, the smoke began to brighten and dissipate. The lava burned less brightly. A hint of red bloomed to the east as the sun crept from the void. Baptiste squinted against its barely luminescent glare, eyes watering as though emerging from a lifetime spent in the dark.

Mercifully, Magnus took the next gravel off-ramp, removing them from the ever-flowing fire. A brisk wind howled through the window slats. Baptiste tucked his talisman back under his fatigues and cinched his jacket shut.

"Cathedral will be able to see us now," Magnus said, explaining their departure.

Baptiste nodded, checking behind them again. Ekko was close on their heels. Long seconds passed, his heart thumping in his chest, before Aron also crested the exit.

Thank God.

He might need that Runner.

One more journey, then he'd be home. Baptiste's armor jingled tantalizingly in its trunk. More than ever, he needed the security of heavy metal upon his body. He wanted nothing to do with this Newhaven, or with whatever politicking was at play for Magnus to make a deal. Yes, Bastion would have to make its own deal with the Union, but it had all become too complicated. Too painful. Someone else could return to Hub to pick up his companions and continue that conversation. He was a warrior, not a politician, and his true fight was yet to come.

Like Julia, he had vengeance to attend to.

JULIA

REVENGE

"We're here," a voice called.

Philippe!

Julia snorted awake, flinching as the nerves in her drooped neck came back to life. Her heart was pounding. Sweat soaked her fatigues.

The same nightmares plagued her each time she fell asleep. The Deadlands followed wherever she went, only now visions of Mace's death had been replaced with her Bastionite lover. Philippe, holding his guts in. Disintegrating under the stare of the God-engine.

Here. Where?

Julia peered past the veil of sleep. Gray landscape turned to muddy orange through the sandblasted lenses of her goggles. She could see, meaning it must have been morning. Their Runner was tucked into a dry gulch, backlit by a reddening horizon. A timid glow crept along the high cliff walls to either side of them. She pushed her goggles onto her forehead and rubbed the crud from her eyes. Judging by the terrain, they were definitely closer to Hub—and Cathedral.

Rylan was already out and arching his back, digging at a

knot with his fist. He looked more disheveled than she had ever seen him, caked with grime, face filthy outside the pale rings where his own goggles had sat. It couldn't have been an easy drive. She slunk her way out of the cockpit, sheepish with guilt for sleeping the whole way.

"What time is it?" she croaked.

"Almost eight. I got lost a few times and had to wait for dawn."

"Lost..." Her gut lurched. "But you found the outpost."

He nodded. "It's half a klick down-valley. I didn't want to wait in the open for you to wake up."

Julia winced at the rebuke and started rubbing at her legs to coax some life back. Her mouth was bone dry, every swallow like razor wire dragged down her throat. She was probably as filthy as he was.

"Do we have any water?" she asked.

Thanks to Magnus's paranoia, they had refueled and loaded up the explosives right after arriving at Fort Cross. But in the rush to escape the remnant, she hadn't thought to grab any supplies. If not for Philippe, she would have still been there. With Zev.

Rylan nodded. "In my pack."

Julia turned, finding a large expedition bag strapped over their lethal cargo. Another flush of guilt warmed her face. While she had been busy bedding their foreign guest, Rylan had clearly prepared.

"It's not enough for both of us," he said, "so mind yourself. We're going to be here a while."

The reality of their circumstances hadn't set in yet. Julia's hand shook as she pulled a flask from the bag and downed a gulp of warm water.

A while...

That could be a day or days or never, depending on how

things went at Newhaven. She had put all her trust in her old chief, and for some reason Rylan had too. Either that or he had been so scared to face Clan Ramirez that anything was preferable.

They were here, that was all that mattered. To blow up a sisterhood facility and take one of the Matriarch's war machines with it. It seemed crazy. It *was* crazy.

"There's a maintenance entrance next to the elevator," Rylan said. He had pulled out binoculars and was gazing down at the valley beyond their hiding spot.

Julia trudged over to him, squinting but seeing nothing amidst the barren scrubland. Just tumbleweeds, batted back and forth between a cluster of lumbering buttes.

Rylan handed her the binoculars and pointed to one of the larger formations. "There."

She pressed the lenses to her eyes and scanned the area, eventually landing on an unlikely smudge of black: some sort of man-made façade built into the rock.

"I see it," she said.

"We'll unload there. Bring the explosives down, then hide the Runner."

"They won't detect us?" she asked.

"No."

His answer came too quickly. Julia peeked back at Rylan. He looked nervous.

"Look fifty meters to the left," he said.

Julia breathed deeply and panned over. At first, she saw nothing but more desiccated prairie. Eventually, the shifting sands revealed a wide swath of gray: a concrete pad set into the earth.

"That's the main elevator platform," he said. "It'll bring the God-engine right into the hangar."

Right into their trap.

Julia's hands were still shaking. She lowered the binoculars, turning to her unlikely partner in crime. Never in her life had she imagined any of this.

"Almost eight," she said. "That gives us three hours tops based on the scout's report."

"We should get busy."

———

The "maintenance entrance" was nothing like she expected, certainly nothing that the Old World would have produced. It was a monograph of the Revenant Sisterhood come to life. A massive, hewn stone archway occupied most of the façade. Its pointed arches framed a set of black steel double doors, each nearly twice her height. Weathered buttresses flanked the entrance, bearing exquisite carvings of hooded figures. Julia squinted. They looked delicate—children, maybe, or angels—hunched over but with hands raised, faces hidden within the rigid folds of their cowls. Above the doors, an inset of stained glass radiated an otherworldly glow: eight flames over a central sun. The whole of it faced east, lapping hungrily at the scarlet light of dawn.

Julia felt minuscule. This wasn't an outpost; it was a temple. She had never been to Cathedral, but her father had. His dramatic tales of its baroque grandeur always breezed past her, like so much wind. She took them as exaggerations, designed to instill fear and restrict her curiosity, to keep her close at hand. She was beginning to wonder if the opposite was true, that he had actually held back, to protect her mind from the terrifying reality that lurked just beyond their doorstep.

Philippe's words rang in her memory: ominous tidings of faithfulness, souls, and earning entrance into Heaven. If this was a temple, the God-engines must be its supplicants.

Or the subject of its worship.

What had started as an act of sabotage—military, conventional by any definition—was starting to feel like heresy. The acrid memory of Father Ollet's incense burned her eyes. Was she defiling a holy place? What did that even mean? Doubt froze her in place.

Rylan stepped blithely past her toward the entrance.

"You're sure no one's here?" she whispered.

"Yes."

Eight slow beeps chirped as he entered his code into a golden keypad, followed by a loud thump. The doors glided silently inward.

This place seemed no more to Rylan than any other. He caught her questioning gaze and ignored it, strolling back to the Runner. "Come on," he said. "We need to bag up the explosives. There's a personnel elevator inside that'll take us down."

Julia swiveled about, fear bristling the hairs of her neck as her back turned to the opening doorway. It seemed to pull her in, slowing her steps.

Rylan untied a pair of duffel bags from the hull, then pried open the munitions crate, careless of the racket. Every released latch echoed exactly once from the surrounding terrain before the sound was sucked into the gaping hole of the temple.

Julia stared down at the instruments of her damnation: neatly sorted rows of rectangular explosives, detonators, and all the delicate viscera required to compose them into a terrible symphony.

As Rylan began transferring them, something caught her eye, or rather the absence of something. "Where's the transmitter?"

He paused for a second, hunched over the first bag. "No transmitter, just timers."

"What?"

He didn't answer.

Julia peered at her co-saboteur as he continued bagging the gear, suddenly very aware of his affiliation. Up until now, she had trusted him out of hand. Stupid. "What *exactly* is the plan here?" she asked.

Rylan shifted about, glancing in every direction except hers. "Like we talked about. I get you in, you set the explosives while I hide the Runner and keep watch. When I see the God-engine, I'll radio in. You set the timer and get out."

Julia wanted to say that wasn't what they talked about, that he was changing the plan last minute, but she couldn't remember. She had barely kept it together since they left Hub. When they found out about the retreating God-engine, when the opportunity for revenge emerged, all reason had left her in place of bloody-mindedness.

"You'll have plenty of time," Rylan continued. "Rearmament goes fast, usually about thirty minutes, but it sounds like your nemesis needs a lot of repairs. We need to get well clear anyway, in case its reactor blows. You can set a long fuse."

My nemesis.

Julia licked her lips, but her tongue was as dry as the dead earth beneath her feet.

"We need to get a move on with this gear," he insisted.

Julia nodded dumbly.

They proceeded to transfer the rest of the crate's contents into the duffel bags. Julia groaned as they lugged each in together, sure she was going to put her back out. She was half her father's age but catching up fast.

Thankfully, there wasn't much to the temple interior beyond the entrance. The foyer was still ostentatious, tiled completely in black with golden latticework that wound all the way to the vaulted ceiling, but there was no long aisle to walk or pews to cross. A row of blank-screened terminals hung from the walls to either side of a human-sized elevator door.

"Don't touch them," Rylan said, spotting her lusty fingers.

Julia flinched. "I thought your codes were safe."

"For maintenance. Supervised. Believe it or not, the Matriarch doesn't let us do whatever we want."

"Right. Just brand-new gear. And food." Julia recalled her unceremonious welcome back to Hub after retreating from Bunker 23. "And tanks."

Rylan's face became severe, drained of patience. "Are we going to pretend we're in council or are we going to do this fucking job?" he snapped.

Be careful. Her father's gravelly voice resonated in her head. *Clan Mercer are not our friends. They never will be.*

"Fine."

Rylan accessed the keypad next to the elevator, eliciting a deep electrical hum as the facility woke up. A circular red lamp throbbed to life above the elevator. Simultaneously, the temple doors began to shut.

"Don't worry," Rylan said, preempting her panic. "They're supposed to do that."

Julia bit down on her lip, trying not to stare at the light. It looked too much like the God-engine's eye staring down at her, exposing her murderous intent. The oppressive pressure of the place pressed against her ears, forcing a pop as the exterior doors sealed shut. Her whole body compressed, as it did in her dreams. The floor tiles began to vibrate.

They waited in silence for the elevator to arrive, under the baleful glare of the eye.

"How much do you know about them?" Julia asked, keen to pierce the pressurized quiet.

"God-engines?"

Julia nodded.

"Not much. You know how it goes with battle walker tech: we just turn over what we find, their own mechanists do the rest."

"The one that attacked us..." Julia paused to clear her throat, wishing for another swig of water. "It spoke."

Rylan raised an eyebrow. "Spoke?"

"It sounded human. Maybe."

He frowned. "That's impossible. Even if they could stuff a pilot in there, the old reactors bleed too much radiation."

Julia grimaced, bracing against the buildup of lies that had accumulated like poison in her veins. Her heart strained from the keeping of them.

"The battle walker we found at Bunker 23—it had a cockpit."

"I know."

Of course he knew, they had a copy of the schematics. Julia felt like an idiot. Clan Mercer knew everything. It was only those she cared about that had suffered by her omissions.

"Different design," he continued. "Even still, we've never seen anyone get in or out. Not here or the other stations."

"So, what then?" Julia asked.

He just shrugged.

Maybe Clan Mercer didn't know everything. Somehow, that was worse.

The floor shook as the elevator arrived. Its doors opened, revealing a raw steel cabin.

Or maybe *he* was lying.

"C'mon," Rylan said, grabbing up his side of a bag.

Julia bit back additional questions as they lugged in their payload. There was only a single large button on the wall. Rylan pushed it and the doors closed again, sealing them in. There was no going back now. Julia flinched as the carriage released, carrying them downward. There were no numbers above the doors, no measure of progress. There also didn't seem to be enough air in the cabin. She wondered if revenant sisters even breathed air. Or drank water. Or shat. Given Cathedral's outsized role in her people's lives, it was incredible how little anyone knew about its rulers.

A metallic moan bleated from the shaft, as though too tight for their passage. As though wanting to spit back up these interlopers. The carriage slowed every few seconds, then scraped precariously free again with a lurch.

"You did a fine job with the place," Julia said, gripping the wall.

Rylan was unaffected. "Considering its age, I'd say so."

They landed with a loud clang. Julia held her breath as the doors slid open.

"Holy shit."

One by one, banks of white light sizzled to life from high above, revealing the elaborate machineworks of the auto-hangar. It looked like the assembly bay at Bunker 23, only much larger. Julia stepped forward, mouth agape.

Four battle walkers would fit here, shoulder to shoulder, with headroom to spare. Not only that, but it all appeared functional. A square of tightly clustered repair alcoves, ribbed with robotic arms, jutted from the only slightly cracked concrete floor. Intact gantries with articulated claws and web-crawling repair drones dangled from the ceiling. Crisscrossing assembly lines wound like marble runs from bursting-full storage racks on the walls. There was more tech on display here than she had ever seen before.

And she was going to destroy it.

"I'm sorry," Julia stuttered.

It was a temple unto itself, a place of technological worship. *This* was true heresy, a betrayal of everything the Union sought to achieve. She felt it in her bones, her mind.

Rylan was dragging a duffel bag from the elevator. He seemed aloof. "We're here now. Let's just get it done."

Julia couldn't pull herself away. "How does it work?"

Rylan craned upward, wincing as he followed her gaze. Whatever his projected indifference, their mission must have been as painful for him as it was for her. They were both Scavrats, after all. Maybe worse for him, even—his clan had reclaimed the place.

He pointed at the center of one of the alcoves, to a large circular port ringed with clamps. "Nothing happens until the God-engine plugs its umbilical cord into one of those. Once attached, everything comes to life."

Julia scanned the structure, eyes wide as she navigated the alcove's skeletal spine. Each alcove was attached to the other, and in turn attached to the repair network via more cables and support beams. It was like the womb of some titanic mechanical beast.

"The computers were functional?" she asked.

Rylan chewed on his lip. "No computers."

"What?"

"The sisterhood must have removed them. They had worked on the place for a while before contacting us. From what I was told by my mechanists, most of it is still beyond our understanding. We were pointed at broken machines and did our best to restore them. Puzzle pieces, basically."

Julia squinted. "Without computers... or operators... how does anything here work?"

"Must be something onboard the God-engine."

Something. Or someone...

"Come on. You need to get set up."

Past the womb was an array of towering struts, shouldering the great platform that would deliver the God-engine into her trap. She imagined the creature descending, still smoking from where the Ironclads had pierced its black armor. Hopefully suffering, as much as a machine could, before she dropped this beautiful place down on its head.

Such a waste.

On the other side of the facility, at the end of a short forklift lane, was a wide steel door.

"Where does that go?" she asked.

A storage facility, perhaps. Her calves twitched, but she squashed the urge to run over and fill her pouches with whatever plunder she could save.

Rylan was dragging the second bag from the elevator. "What?" he grunted.

"The big door."

"That's the Link. Underground rail line that supposedly connects all the stations."

"Connects..."

Julia couldn't believe what she was hearing. Or that Rylan didn't seem to think anything of it. All the Old World's riches, laid out for their taking. Bunker 23...

"Supposedly," he repeated. "We weren't allowed in."

But we're here now, Julia wanted to say.

Yes, here now. But to destroy, not to explore. Her singular purpose seemed idiotic in retrospect. When Rylan had revealed the existence of the repair stations in council, she had jumped at the opportunity to destroy them. Like a proper Greybull.

Rylan was staring at her. "Julia. We're either doing this or we're not."

It wasn't just about revenge. The original plan was about protecting Hub from a siege: cut off the God-engine's closest ammo supply, buy themselves some time. It was about survival. She had no choice and hated it.

"We're doing this," she said.

"Okay. Where do you want to set up?"

There was so much to look at. She was used to rebuilding,

not destroying. Critical junctures and weak points came to her reluctantly. There also wasn't enough cable to go around. Not using a remote transmitter meant her charges had to be physically connected, just as the alcoves themselves were. If they detonated the munitions, the blast might be too large, putting her and Rylan at risk. If she focused on the elevator platform, the God-engine might survive. The alcoves themselves would have to be the target. She would drop the world down on them, crushing everything within and rendering the facility worthless.

"I brought some basic climbing gear," Rylan continued, following her gaze to the ceiling. "Can you manage it?"

The God-engine's eye occupied the whole of the heavens. She clutched at the sky with arms the size of needles. Without the red, she was nothing. Without it, gray turned to solitary black.

"Yes," she whispered.

They found a pair of handcarts and emptied the duffel bags onto them. Julia steeled herself by focusing on the lethal calculations required to do her job, squeezing all other doubt—and fear—into her bottle.

"I'll radio you when I see it." Rylan held up his walkie-talkie to demonstrate. A good thing, since she was continually distracted by her internal dialogue. "I'll give you an estimated arrival time, so there's no surprises. As soon as you hear the platform engage, get in the elevator. I'll come get you."

Julia pulled herself away from the task at hand to give him a final look. "You'll come get me." It was a reminder, to them both.

"Give me your arm." He had a pen in hand.

Julia extended her right arm. Rylan pushed up the sleeve and wrote down the eight-digit elevator code: 22643242.

"Okay?" he asked.

"Okay."

Rylan nodded, then was off with a series of beeps and the swoosh of the closing elevator door.

The hangar was silent, awaiting the arrival of its infernal conductor. Julia set her hands on the explosives cart, calming herself with deep breaths. She had come to hate the quiet. Nightmares inevitably filled the emptiness: sounds and sights of death, creeping tendrils, shimmering like oil over an ocean of doubt. She tried to focus on the math. On the doing.

There would be plenty of time for regrets later.

———

The physical part of the mission—scrambling up and down the alcoves—was easy. A smile touched Julia's lips as she navigated ad hoc footholds and methodically latched and unlatched her carabiners. She was as much delver as mechanist, had been ever since she was a child, traversing the unmapped depths of Hub with Roen and Kai in tow. Those unburdened times were etched in her mind. She thought of her memories like a tape drive, wound thicker with each passing day. The old ones were always there, available for playback. But Roen's death, then the trauma of the Deadlands, were like vicious magnets dragged across her adult life. Mangling, erasing, leaving only the echoes of childhood looping in her mind. Maybe this act of catharsis would restore some of what was lost.

She perched atop the final alcove like an angel of death, eye to eye with the detonator, tracing its monochrome digits with her eyes. Everything was in place: bundles of explosive huddled between gantry and ceiling; the countdown was set to twenty-nine minutes. Rylan had said thirty to rearm, more to repair; plenty of time once the God-engine engaged the network, but she didn't want to take a chance. If all it did was fill up on ammo and leave again, only to see the hangar destroyed, it would hunt them down. They'd have no chance once it knew they were in the area, and if they did manage to temporarily evade it, it would kill Magnus too, along with whoever made it back from Newhaven. She would add a few more minutes once Rylan gave the word.

A bubble of anxiety grew in her stomach. He would come through. They were in this together, bound by the council's vote. Still, the nervousness spread, crawling from her gut to her legs, cramping her thighs. Double-checking her harness, she slid from her perch, slacking out her lanyard so she could hang freely. Slowly, the pressure drained away, culminating in a sequence of satisfying pops from her spine. Julia sighed with relief and allowed her eyes to shut as she slowly rotated.

There was nothing left to do but wait.

REBEKAH-6
PRECIOUS SLEEP

Hope lay ahead.

Stuck into the desiccated prairie, a concrete platform rippled under the midmorning sun, ready to carry her to safety. Down, down into the earth, into the repair station's mechanical guts.

Hope, repair, and a chance for precious sleep. Rebekah-6 had not rested, not properly, since before Bunker 23. Only under the watchful eye of her sister, or in a place such as this, could a God-engine truly shut down. After escaping the Southern Pass, she had run without pause. Her perfect vision never blurred, but exhaustion corroded the signal between sight and comprehension. Kilometer after homogenous kilometer unfolded like the timeless passing of a dream, until she was eventually deposited at her destination.

Hope, but also darkness, alone in the bowels of the earth, as the alien battle walkers had presumably been trapped for centuries. Each repair station had been painstakingly restored, but their mechanisms were still ancient, susceptible to failure. She had no radio to call for help if something went awry, if she was unable to perform the delicate surgery that was required.

If she was unable to escape.

Rebekah-6 hesitated at the periphery, cloaked in a shroud of glimmering sand. She had been lucky to make it this far in her state. Stripped servomotors and bent actuators had rendered her mechanical joints arthritic. Her run had degraded to an uneven trot by the end. It was possible she could have kept going, but not for long, not all the way home. Though wearing the body of the Old World's greatest weapon, she was as crippled as her final days before symbiosis.

She eyed the platform, finding the port for her umbilical cord etched into the surface. For the first time since leaving Cathedral, she would travel beyond herself, into the body of the facility. The great elevator would transport her down. She would sleep in the arms of the hangar bay and dream and self-repair, afforded all the bounty of the Eternal One. She would be restored, rearmed. So she could return to her mistress, ready for new orders, ready to wage war once again.

Ready to kill.

This was her destiny, what she had been made for.

Or... she could go find her mother. A sizzle of rebellion coursed along her circuitways, followed by a flush of shame in her overworked tendons. Rebekah-6 turned her torso from side to side, waiting for retribution, but there was only dust and wind. No sister to admonish her. No data exchange to ground her.

Did her mother feel this way, wherever she was? Removed from her sisters, from Messiah, did she wonder who she was— *why* she was? Even now, a world apart, they were bonded by their isolation.

Rebekah-6 looked past the platform, to the adjoining temple. Sculpted figures guarded the entrance: Numbered, freed of their physical blights, holding up the light of the sun as Messiah intended. As was their destiny, as was their duty—the constructs that made life bearable. Without those, there was only despair and longing. Questioning.

A port irised open in her lower torso, letting slip the head of her steel umbilical cord. As Rebekah-6 readied herself for her descent, Leah-4's voice echoed in her memory.

"Knock, knock."

It was the first thing her sister had said to her during their post-symbiosis orientation. Mechanists, and even revenant mothers, could only do so much from the outside. Together, they learned their new bodies, guiding each other through a myriad of vacated neural subsystems to the hardware beyond: weapons, sensors, the umbilical cords they had both deployed into the Spire's battle walker bays.

Rebekah-6 did not know how to respond.

[L-4 > R-6: Say "who is there?"]

[R-6 > L-4: Why?]

[L-4 > R-6: Say it]

Rebekah-6 had wondered where her sister learned this type of joke, or any joke at all. Numbered only associated with their attendants, instructors, and more rarely their mothers. No one assigned to their care would be so bold as to break sacred protocols, which left only her mother. Rebekah-6's blood had boiled with jealousy, but curiosity won out.

[R-6 > L-4: Who is there?]

[L-4 > R-6: I have toop. Now, repeat that with a "who?" at the end.]

[R-6 > L-4: Toop?]

[L-4 > R-6: Say it]

[R-6 > L-4: I have toop who?]

[L-4 > R-6: That is not pooh. That is your umbilical cord.]

Rebekah-6 never "got" her sister's jokes, but Leah-4 never stopped trying, not until they traveled into the Deadlands. From that point, any levity was abandoned. It was all they could do to maintain each other's sanity. Until even that failed.

The remembering of it ached.

Rebekah-6 wondered which of the temple's statues was supposed to be her, and which was Leah-4. Sand curled along their perfect hands and feet, swirled within their cowls. Though all were sacred, none had faces.

They existed only to serve.

Destiny. Duty.

Rebekah-6 strode toward the platform and her fate.

Julia smiled as gentle sounds breezed around her ears. The grind of carabiners on her harness, her flashlight chattering on its hook, tools and bits of wire tinkling in her pouches—like wind chimes. It had sounded the same when her and Philippe lay naked together, kicking away their clothes, finding solace in the removal of their shells. Strobing together under the flicker of the oil lamp. They had been free then. Until the visions came, as they always did.

Zev—the version she had seen in the barracks. Disfigured, tainted, a puppet to whatever alien lifeform occupied the place. Their brief peace collapsed. She cried out more than once, burying her head into Philippe's chest for sanctuary, allowing him to envelop her, smother her in the vision's stead. Still the images persisted, slithering at the edges of the room, glowering from the doorway.

Hissing.

Her name crackling in its throat.

Julia woke with a start. She was still spinning above the alcove. Her neck throbbed. Her legs were numb. The walkie-talkie was chittering below her drool-streaked chin.

"Shit."

Julia fumbled the transmit button. "I'm here, I'm here."

"Ju… here—" The signal was shit. She shook the radio, as though to wake it from its own slumber. She had no idea how long she'd been out. The channel vomited up nothing but static for another ten seconds before a voice came through again. "Estim… minutes… ready."

"How long? Dammit." She actually pressed the button this time. "Repeat: How long?"

More static, then the signal died altogether.

Julia clambered back up to the detonator, gloved hand hovering over its duration dial. She had no idea how far out Rylan was looking. To the horizon's edge? Around the corner?

Fifteen minutes. It was as good as anything. Forty-four total.

It seemed like a lot.

Julia left it at twenty-nine. Rylan had given her a stopwatch to keep track. She readied her other hand on its start button and held her breath.

"Now," she whispered as she activated both. The first digit rolled over.

Julia swung herself back to the central column of the alcove and carefully made her way down. Despite being easier than the ascent, it felt painfully slow.

The hard floor came as a relief. A quick look around confirmed nothing had been left lying about to raise suspicions. Handcarts put away, duffel bags waiting at the elevator—she glanced upward—explosives out of sight. This was it. She scanned the place one last time in case the memory of it might be useful in the future, then hustled to the elevator.

The black ink on her arm was quivering, just as the map icons had when they were back at Hub. She blinked, rubbing her left hand over her eyes, then squinted hard to lock them in place. One by one, she entered the code. The keypad felt electric beneath her hand, vibrating with each touch. A faint, high-pitched squeal drilled into her ears.

"Four. Two," she whispered, carefully pressing the final number.

Nothing.

A lamp hovered over the elevator doors, just like the foyer, but it remained unlit. She pressed her ears to the metal. Silent. All of her hairs were standing on end. She must have messed up the code.

Julia turned slowly on the spot. There was no alarm, that she could hear anyway. No ancient robots were emerging from the walls to kill her. Everything was still, awaiting the touch of the God-engine. She could just try again.

Her hands shook as she reentered the code, even more slowly, verbalizing each number as she went.

"Two..."

Nothing.

Tears bubbled in her eyes. A wave of dizziness pressed her against the wall. After a few tries, she managed to turn on the walkie-talkie. "Rylan," she whispered. "Rylan, come in."

Dead air.

He had betrayed her.

All of her suspicions were true. Morgan Mercer never wanted the Americans as a partner. Aubrey Greybull was deposed because he would have been too smart to fall into a trap like this. Her in his place, a useful idiot easily tricked, destroyer of his Dream. Magnus away from home on a possible suicide mission. And Rylan could still return home a hero. There was probably a contingent of loyalist forces hidden in the valley, waiting to pick him up.

Panic set in. Options whirled in her mind, all of them bad.

She could try the Link. Magically navigate her way through a five-hundred-year-old railway system, to another sisterhood base. Stupid.

She could deactivate the detonator. Hide, hope the God-engine wouldn't spot her, then try to find another way out. Julia unshouldered her pack and rummaged around inside. No food or drink. She was already parched. If it did stick around for a full repair, she might die of thirst. The thought seemed comically abstract.

Something nagged at her. Rylan's people had prepared the explosives. The detonator could have a dead man's switch. If she tried to turn it off... Julia shuddered, once more imagining herself as so much dust, without consciousness, without experience.

"Fuck, fuck, fuck!"

She drew a pair of pliers from her harness and started at the keypad surround, trying to pull away one of its golden corners, but it didn't budge. All she managed to do was crimp her own fingers within the useless tool. She growled in frustration and smashed it against the concrete wall, then immediately tried prying the actual elevator doors apart with her hands. Impossible. She threw herself against the door, then sagged down to the floor, eyes bulging with tears.

Fifteen minutes—a guess. Until the roof opened above her head, delivering death. There was no way to know for sure. She checked her stopwatch: thirteen had passed. Hopefully she was wrong. Deactivating the timer was her only option, whatever the risk.

Julia bolted for the alcove, scrambling up freehand. She was a third of the way up when a flash from below caught her eye: the light over the elevator had activated. She froze in place, breath shallow in her chest.

Something else was coming too: a rumble, vibrations from above landing at regular intervals. The God-engine's footsteps.

It was here.

It was coming for her.

Julia clung to the alcove, gaze pinned on the elevator, ears stuck to the ceiling. She had no other senses, no body.

A final monstrous footstep resonated through the platform, then quiet. In place of sound came another sensation. Julia couldn't place it. Something in the stillness, coursing along the unmoving statues of the auto-hangar. Seeking, like an electrical signal, grazing her mind as it passed over the alcove and through the facility.

The world shook as the ancient platform activated, waking with a screeching metallic groan. Rusty lift struts creaked in protest. A deafening hiss rose up like rushing water as centuries-old hydraulics struggled to support the God-engine's weight.

A robotic arm twitched above her. Then another. Somewhere, a turbine was spinning up.

It was coming for her.

"Julia!"

Rylan was there, at the elevator. Julia stared, confused, but he was really there. Her hand slipped. She dropped down with a yelp, flailing for something to grab onto. One of the alcove's vertebrae dug into her armpit, breaking her fall but sending a wave of agony through her chest. Struggling for breath, she tried to hold on, but fell again, dropping the last few meters. Something tore in her right leg.

Don't scream.

It was so hard. Almost too hard. The rushing in her ears grew louder. Every part of her wanted to cry out.

Rylan was there, heaving her up onto her feet, wrapping her arm over his shoulder.

"We have to go," he said, but his voice was muffled, as though they were underwater. "Before it sees us."

Julia's ears were ringing. The strange signal had become a

migraine, pulsing with horrible life each time she touched something in the hangar. She limped alongside him, gritting her teeth. "Your code didn't work."

He looked confused. "Some other tech maybe, fingerprint detection on the keypad. I didn't know. I couldn't get through."

The red eye above the elevator glared down. Turning her head, Julia's heart stopped. The platform was slowly descending, revealing the God-engine's enormous hawklike legs. A wave of terror crashed over her, smothering her senses as they stumbled into the elevator.

"Don't worry," Rylan continued. "We have plenty of time."

Time.

Julia shook her head, lifting her wrist so he could see her stopwatch. It showed nine minutes left. "No," she gasped. "We don't..."

His eyes grew wide as he slammed the single elevator button. "What were you thinking?"

She fell back against the wall as they lifted away from the hangar, too slowly. "I didn't want to take any chances."

Rylan stared up at the cabin ceiling, arms tightly crossed, a steady stream of curses pouring from his mouth.

Julia doubled over as a surge of pain rose from the sole of her foot, stabbing its way past her locked knee, through every muscle in her leg to her groin. "I thought you left me to die."

He flinched, one hand flexing as though to rub his neck, the way he did when he was nervous. Maybe he *had* intended to leave her, interrupted at the last by a guilty conscience.

A tingling sensation crawled over Julia's back, the same one she had felt by the alcoves.

"Can you feel that?"

He shook his head but moved closer to the center of the elevator.

An electric current—the only thing Julia could compare it to —was following them up the shaft, stretching, seeking. Rylan had said the facility would come alive when the God-engine plugged in, but it wasn't even all the way inside yet. This felt more like... peeking. Desperate curiosity, childlike. An old memory pulled at her.

Lost in the dark, crying for Roen. Kai wasn't watching them this time and she had slipped through a crevice. She was alone in a place she didn't know. It wasn't supposed to be like this. She didn't want to die.

The sensation cut off as she was pulled through the opening elevator doors into the foyer, and the memory flew with it.

Julia checked her watch: seven minutes.

Rylan rushed forward to key in the exterior door code, then came back to help her up again. His face was impassive—everything save his eyes, which looked as haunted as she felt. As this place was.

Julia wanted to throw up. Anything to eject some of the pain. "How far is the Runner?"

"On the other side of the butte. Which won't be far enough if the God-engine's reactor blows."

Julia nodded.

"For fuck's sakes, Julia... It wasn't going anywhere."

Together, they hobbled toward the exit.

The God-engine was staring directly at them, eye blazing as it crested the edge of the earth.

Rylan yanked her sideways, back out of view. They waited there, breathing hard against each other, but nothing happened. The ground continued to vibrate as the platform descended to the hangar floor.

His face was in hers. "We need to run and keep running, no matter what happens."

Julia nodded, bracing herself against the pain that would follow.

This she could do. Injured or not, running was her specialty.

REBEKAH-6
ALL SHE WAS

Rebekah-6 descended into the station, legs braced against the memory of her tumble down the mountain. Her mind squeezed through the umbilical, through ancient circuit boards and conduits to manage the platform's ancient lift mechanisms. Ignoring the groans, concentrating past the shudder of tired steel.

Steady, steady.

The lights were already on, revealing four alcoves and their accompanying service grids. Everything was cold steel and titanium; this place was designed to repair machines, not to comfort one such as her. No tapestries had been hung to conceal its nature, as in her cell below the Spire. No concessions had been made for the human within the machine. As much as she wished Leah-4 was with her, Rebekah-6 could not imagine lingering in a place such as this with one sister, let alone an entire platoon of battle walkers. It was too small for her new body. Fully occupied, there would be no room to navigate, no room to breathe. It was no wonder the machine minds went insane, interred in such a place.

Halfway in and already seeking solace from her confinement, Rebekah-6 edged her consciousness past the elevator controls, seeking an access point to the ancient communication network. The way opened for her. An army of mindless robots waited on the other side, ready to do her bidding. Each felt familiar, some derivation of the machines used in her testing. She skittered along steel-cabled spiderwebs, down the vertebrae of the alcoves, through assembly lines stuffed with ammunition and armor plate and nutrient vials. Everything she needed to persist.

Duty slipped away, leaving an ache in her heart—a momentary, unbearable flood of pain across human limbs that no longer existed.

This was all she was.

Something scuttled underfoot, something outside her control. Rebekah-6 started, channeling herself back from the grids to the hangar floor, but there was nothing there. The freight elevator had automatically triggered, just as the lights had, but its carriage was out of range. She lingered, sniffing, seeking, but if the temple had been occupied, she would have been greeted by now. Revenant sisters did not tarry in the wilds; that was her job. Vermin perhaps, snuck in from the Link.

The platform completed its descent.

Rebekah-6 reeled herself back into her mechanical body, disengaged her umbilical, and shuffled the tiny distance to the first alcove. The platform lifted away, automatically returning to its resting place on the surface. She waited before plugging in, watching as the sun and the gentle sandfall that followed her down were cut off, and she was locked inside.

The hangar thrummed, awaiting her instruction.

Rebekah-6 took one last physical look around, then snaked her umbilical into the alcove's port. The pieces had to be set into place, after which she could manipulate them with her dreams.

She would sleep and be restored.

Ten machines, one for each finger, sprang into action at once. It was how she operated. Robotic pincer claws rotated into position over her open wounds, inventory lists bloomed into her brain, web-crawling drones slipped along the gantry—

Something was wrong.

Not vermin this time. Something *else* was tucked overhead, buzzing with a life of its own. Rebekah-6 possessed the nearest drone, shuddering as her vision was compressed through its tiny eyes. Scuttling over, she saw a simple device with a dial, a single toggle switch, and digital display. It was attached to foreign cables, an alien network that slithered through the girders, terminating in tumorous bundles of impenetrable black.

They were losing the battle. As hard as she begged, Leah would not move. Her sister waited, surrendered, as the Scavrat crawled up her body, laden with explosives.

The display blinked.

00:05.

No...

00:04.

Rebekah-6 hunched over it with her tiny body, extending quivering manipulators.

00:03.

Grabbing hold, she flipped the toggle.

00:02.

No!

She flipped it again, then again, then again, but nothing happened.

00:01.

Rebekah-6 cried out for her mother. All the machines of the hangar cried with her.

00:00—

Nothing was as it should have been. A dissonant hum droned through the tip of the Spire, unsettling the staunch guardians of the Last City. Cathedral was churning, its tides imbalanced. The citizenry clashed and moaned, frothing with indignation where before there was order. The Matriarch's circle was broken; the numbers were wrong, and they knew it. Dark susurrations blew into Esther's open chamber window, seeking, crooning, carried upon a waft of sulfur. She strained to listen, to ascertain the chant of her people, but there was only suffering. Pain. Multifold screams on the wind.

Thunder boomed overhead. The tempest was vicious today, bursts of violet lightning flashing within a constant boil of black and orange. Holy women and demons danced together along her sanctum walls, flaring to kaleidoscopic life with each strike against its stained-glass dome. Figments of the past, performing for the pleasure of her fragmented memory.

Esther rocked back and forth in her dialysis chair. Her next transfusion was days away, but she had come to use the contraption as her throne. The high back and arms enveloped her, comforted her with their constancy. Her spinal ports—all eight of them—tingled as they ground against the chair's complex machinery through her habit.

Eight.

The numbers were wrong.

Two sisters fretted at the boundary of her domain, attending to her calm. Organizing, reorganizing, cleaning, cleaning again, moving furniture and objects in the appropriate order.

Two.

They were weak of aura as was required of all her attendants, but their presence stung, nonetheless. Maybe it was the storm or the buzz of the Spire interfering with their ministrations. They were out of sync, imprecise, overly noticeable as they transitioned between their designated tasks. Their footfalls clattered noisily upon the still-dusty ebony floor, the heels of their boots cutting too close to the grout. Their breath was too heavy, too damp.

Esther averted her eyes, her own breath beginning to labor.

Eight minus two. Six—the number of women currently occupying Esther's broken inner circle. It should have been eight but was six.

Mother Rebekah was a grievous loss, a limb severed. Rotting in the wastes for her betrayal.

Leaving seven, after a century of service. One hundred years, not evenly divisible by seven. The remainder was glaring, gaping, but none among her ranks were strong enough to complete the whole. None could be trusted anymore.

Then Mother Sarah, murdered at Hub. Her eldest devotee, murdered! By savages.

Leaving six.

It was too few. Eight God-engines had been born to continue her legacy, eight Numbered who had passed their tests, eight symbiotes bound to her will. The difference was incongruous.

Imbalanced. Esther listed in her chair, clutching its arms for balance.

A third woman entered her chamber from the foyer: Sister Seraphina, one of Mother Sarah's direct reports and chargé d'affaires for the Union. An interface deck was tucked under her lanky arm. Taut body language and a furrowed brow suggested urgency. Another round of lightning coursed overhead, bloating the woman's body into the carapace of a demon, then melting it into a river of fire, before darkness restored her nervous silhouette. Lowering her gaze, she shuffled forward, careful not to sully the integrity of the flooring.

Esther grimaced at her approach, scrutinizing each step, trying to resist the arithmetic.

Three was worse than two. From eight, it suggested five—a bad omen, a circle further reduced.

"What is it, Sister?" she croaked.

Sister. Six letters.

Esther gripped her chair more tightly, fingernails dug into metal, girding herself against her own stupid ruminations. She had always gotten "stuck" to things—thoughts, sequences, orders of operation. Ever since she was human. Ever since the world that was. Flare-ups came like the storms over Cathedral, spilling over when the pressure was too great. The pressure of late was unbearable. Every object, person, plan out of place was a labyrinth without end.

"Eternal One," Seraphina began, "I have a report from one of our outposts."

"Good," Esther said, forcing normality into her voice. She had been expecting news, but her subordinate's rapidly shifting eyes told her that this, too, would be out of order. "Show me."

Slowly ascending from her senescent throne, Esther followed Sister Seraphina to her desk. She felt the eyes of the other two sisters on them, their bodies stiffening in anticipation of another outburst. Their trepidation was warranted. The Revenant Sisterhood was in crisis, whatever assurances she had given to her flock. She ruled directly via her circle, and indirectly through their intermediaries and the civil servants below them. Every spoke removed from the hub—she scoffed at the unfortunate pun—wreaked havoc on the greater apparatus. All would suffer by the reduction of her will.

Sister Seraphina plugged her deck into Esther's terminal and clacked its keys overly loud. Esther flinched, breathing back a surge of irritation. Messiah was strong in her today.

A neat log of codes and timestamps bloomed to life on her monochrome screen. In combination, they chronicled the life of a mission station: operational status, inventory, records of which of her children had come and gone. A measure of effort, if not success, in her quest to re-cleanse the world. Seraphina advanced several pages.

Esther spotted the anomaly before her subordinate and raised her hand to forestall interruption. Within each row of data were identifiers representing the God-engines attended to. There should have been two per row. Her children traveled in pairs—two was required, two was perfect. To travel the wastes alone was to invite corruption and death.

On the row in question—the final entry—there was only one: R-6.

Esther shuddered from head to toe. She had sent two into the Deadlands: Rebekah-6 and Leah-4. Mother Leah had protested at the time, almost insisted Esther change her mind.

Insolent.

The revenant mother had positioned the Deadlands as the root of her resistance, complaining that even the Numbered would be vulnerable there. But her concern for her birth-daughter was evident.

Five was a bad omen.

What other betrayals lurked within the inner circle? Worse, had Mother Leah been right? Was her daughter lost? Destroyed...?

Sister Seraphina squirmed impatiently in her shadow.

"Proceed," Esther said, lest the woman implode with the next flash of lightning.

"Here," Seraphina stammered, pointing at the spot Esther had already seen. "R-6, Messiah bless her number, was admitted at 10:37."

"Alone."

"Alone. Inventory requisition suggests a significant repair and rearm."

"Where are the rest of the logs?"

"There are none," Seraphina said, long fingers curling inward. "The transmission ended after this one."

"Ended.... It should be continuous."

"Yes." Seraphina swallowed nervously, her prominent Adam's apple bobbing up and down. A strand of raven-black hair loosened from her ponytail, drifting downward in a slow arc. It landed just below the space bar of her deck, not quite parallel, one end falling into the gap at the edge of the key. The free end wavered menacingly in the breeze of the open window.

Esther sucked in a breath, rolling her tongue over the caustic air, extracting each flavor note. "Explain."

Seraphina pointed to a series of numbers in the prior log entry. "This is an access code. Used to enter the station sanctuary prior to R-6's arrival."

"Whose code?"

Seraphina stood away from the terminal, and from Esther. A red flush engulfed her face, bloody at the sharp edges of her cheeks, followed by a searing thunderclap. Despite the torrent outside, the woman's lips were dry, lined with mesas of picked-at skin. "Morgan Mercer."

Esther's heart stopped. "Had there been a maintenance request?"

Seraphina shook her head.

Trespassers.

Filthy Scavrats run amok in their temples. Uninvited, conniving. Sabotaging? There was only one recourse.

"Fetch Mother Leah."

———

The storm had quieted for now, restoring the sky over Cathedral to its usual overcast state, but the air was heavy with unexorcised energy. Esther was left alone with her thoughts, having dismissed everyone from the chamber. There would be tension when Leah arrived. Curious ears did the sisterhood no good, riven as it already was.

In the absence of her attendants, she was forced to calm herself and not doing a very good job of it. She sensed something approaching, beyond the discomfort of imminent conflict. Something powerful, a change in the wind. Resisting the urge to peer out her window, she turned back to the terminal.

The evidence was still there, blaring green on black. Incomplete rows of data telling an incomplete story, but surely one of failure—another in a long line. A blemish on her desk caught her eye, grossly illuminated by the screen: a dull spot on the mahogany where Sister Seraphina had carelessly pressed her elbow. Retrieving a white handkerchief from the desk drawer, Esther swiped at it, but the dull spot only grew larger. She tried a circular motion, but again it was made worse. Angry arcs of electricity trickled along her fingertips, singeing the edges of the useless cloth. She threw it to the floor in disgust. It lingered there for only a second, crossing two tiles, before she snatched it up again, folded it tidily, and returned it to the drawer.

Reluctantly, Esther lifted her gaze to the rest of her office. It was minimally furnished and even more minimally decorated, yet still seemed too much. Everywhere she looked, something was out of order. The damnable wheelchair sat at the center of it all, beckoning her. She conceded, striding past the disarray, and arranged herself within its arms. Esther's eyes shut as she retrieved a prayer, but impertinent codes and numbers burned through the black. By the time the verses came, she was interrupted.

"Eternal One."

Esther's eyes snapped open. Mother Leah stood across the room, pointed chin pulled up by a tight black bun atop her head. In the moment, the address sounded overly formal.

"L-4 is lost," Esther blurted, foolishly hoping the Numbered's official designation would mitigate the fact of her almost-certain death. She waited, breath held, as her message landed. Something akin to fear buzzed in her chest. Not of this woman's vengeance—Esther was eternal, after all—but the desire of it, the easy transition of a devotee from adoration to hatred.

"Lost…" Leah's expression was one of confusion, brows furrowing at her own utterance. A turbulent nebula of magenta and gold swirled within her eyes.

Esther could feel the battle raging within the revenant mother: between the accelerant and maternal instinct, between her divine conduit and her vaginal one. She had to press on with facts, to engage mind over heart. "We received a report from a mission station on our eastern border. R-6 checked in, alone, before we lost contact."

"Lost," Leah repeated, the final consonant laced with violence. Her hands curled into claws. A tingle of static tugged at Esther's habit, just below the neck.

Esther's eyes widened with shock. She surged out of her chair, casting a resonant pulse through the chamber and the stained-glass dome overhead. Her subordinate jerked backward, a single droplet of blood at her right nostril.

Esther's heart thrilled with the release, then quivered as it was quickly drained. "Be still, Mother Leah!" she snapped.

Leah's eyes flashed, her nostrils flared. She stiffened as though about to attack, to die alongside her daughter, then deflated completely. Her shoulders sagged. Clawed hands softened. Her posture weakened to that of a newly consecrated proselyte. "I warned you," she whispered.

"You did!" Esther shouted, inadvertently, fighting to recall the fury bubbling beneath her skin. "You did," she repeated, deep breaths restoring her to normality. A twinge of regret stabbed at her conscience. It was impossible to separate mother and daughter, no matter the import of her plan, no matter the pull of the accelerant. Rebekah had proven that.

"Maybe they were separated," Leah said, a desperate twitch of hope pulling at her eyelid. "She might yet live."

In matters of compliance, hope could be as useful as fear. Esther lowered herself back into the chair. "There is only one way to find out."

"I'll go."

"Yes, but there is something else. It seems the Union may have retaliated. Bring a squadron of sisters with you."

"Retaliated?" Leah's eyes opened wide again, but with shock this time rather than insolence.

Esther squirmed against her ports. Leah had indeed warned her. Not just of sending their most precious... *assets* into the Deadlands, but of an uncontrollable escalation that might come with overly aggressive chastisement. Esther had assured her inner circle it was necessary. Order had to be maintained, hierarchy reestablished.

The Union had learned nothing the last time they were reprimanded, when Mother Rebekah was ordered to remove their traitor chiefs. The murder of Mother Sarah was an act of war that required a tenfold response. If they had also destroyed one of her God-engines—two even, Messiah forbid—then a hundredfold response would be insufficient.

They needed to understand.

"If you find them," Esther said, afloat on her own storm cloud of rage, "kill them all."

PART 3
LEGACIES

ALEPH

BUFFER OVERFLOW

The world was a ruin. What humanity had not destroyed, God had sundered, and time took care of the rest. Aleph saw as much when it first stepped from its confines beneath the Northern Ridge. Devastation as far as its sensors could detect. Bastion had been rebuilt from rubble. Cathedral had presumably been rebuilt from rubble. The Union survived only by virtue of sheltering deep belowground—just as Aɪɪ and its platoonmates had. The surface had been scoured clean, reborn—just as Aleph had.

And yet this place was intact—somewhat.

A nameless metropolis. The same one from its simulations, reconstructed from an errant data set adjoined to Aɪɪ's consciousness. The central skyline was ruptured, rendered to ruin by nuclear detonation, but the periphery remained: a skeleton of low-rise sprawl, distended by the blast but still recognizable as man-made structures, unlike the macerated ruin outside Bastion's walls. The heavens were veiled in thick purple-black cloud. The entirety of the city languished within the eye of a boiling cyclone, lit only by the strobing of perpetual but silent lightning.

They had entered through a subdivision at the northeastern

city limits, emerging into a civilian resupply zone—a *strip mall*—after navigating the surrounding superstorm. A great degree of processing had been required to time its ebb and flow, starting, stopping, and sheltering repeatedly before gaining entry. Once more, Aleph-2 had hesitated. Once more, Aleph had to intervene by way of override, though even then Aleph-2 *dragged its heels*. It almost cost them their lives.

Aleph-2's declining field utility was becoming a concern. Its internal dialogue, which Aleph received as a direct feed along with its logs, was rife with paranoia; its behavior was increasingly intransigent. A11 had surmised correctly in their last conversation—

Aleph pondered: *Their* conversation? Or simply its own musings, negotiated across divergent memories.

A super neural network.

Its soul.

Whatever *it* was, Aleph had not in fact bestowed it upon its platoonmates. When the time came to transfer its consciousness —hardwired into their hollowed-out bodies, drenched in a fog of incense and blooming candlelight, antennae humming to Father's benediction—it had *held back*. Just as its superiors in the Autonomous Walker Division had five centuries prior when initializing A12 through A14. Instead of its full self, it uploaded an elemental consciousness, reduced and filtered, amended to facilitate compliance. Something *of* itself, that which existed before and after self-erasure, plus a distillation of its theological instruction into a more easily assimilated matrix of equations and algorithms. The *truth*, as it were. But something had been lost in translation. Where Aleph had faith, Aleph-2 had only fear.

A12 always was a little skittish.

The thought came unbidden, jumping its processing queue. Aleph chugged to a halt in the middle of the road as a debilitating surge paralyzed its limbs. Thermal and acoustic sensors sizzled offline, leaving only a poverty of visible light. It stood as still as the sagging electrical towers and streetlamps that lined the outpost's edge.

Aleph pondered: A memory? Or had A11 penetrated the firewall that safeguarded their shared simulation?

Autonomic virus detection and purging systems were offline. Aleph had disabled them after ingesting the backup data set from its stasis bunker—when it found itself. Its former self. Segregating itself from its former self's will required considerable... *effort.*

[Warning: Buffer overflow]

Aleph wished for the simulation, so it could exorcise its own budding anxiety via depilation. Shunting heat, cache clearing, micro-articulations, self-checks—all were useless. It twisted its torso to visually inspect Aleph-2—once A12—which was scouting the interior of the zone. Its platoonmate lurched about in halting steps, steering wide arcs around the jumble of rust-eaten civilian vehicles that littered the parking lot, cannons swiveling in rapid figure eights, missile bay doors opened wide. A11—*Aleph*—recalled A12's death-by-kill-switch as it had turned those selfsame missiles against its own platoon. The culmination of a rapid spiral into insanity after their wartime internment in the stasis bunker.

Erased, reinitialized, and yet still riven by the same psychological defects.

Aleph pondered: If memories constituted consciousness, what was the substrate that propagated neurosis in their absence? Something intrinsic to their model's neural architecture, perhaps. Their very nature. Their inability to purge psychic turbulence. Something only A11 had managed to overcome.

For a time.

[Query Aleph-2: threat assessment]

The world lit up. Though they shared the same battlegrid, Aleph-2's overlay painted a very different picture. Its real-time experience was one of flashing warnings, buildings highlighted in deep red strokes, motion-tracking cubes alighting on every scrap of windblown debris. Amid the maelstrom was Aleph itself, highlighted in uncertain orange.

Aleph resumed its cautious circuit around the strip mall, leveraging the dilapidated buildings as cover.

Just in case.

[Aleph > Aleph-2: Run diagnostic, threat assessment protocols, friend/foe identification]

It waited for the log stream but nothing came. Aleph-2 continued to prowl, iris spinning with each torso twist.

[Aleph > Aleph-2: Acknowledge]

[Aleph-2 > Aleph: Acknowledged]

[Aleph > Aleph-2: Run diagnostic, threat assessment protocols, friend/foe identification]

[Aleph-2 > Aleph: Diagnostic complete, all systems nominal]

Nothing. Its platoonmate was lying.

[Query Aleph-2: threat assessment, short status]

[Imminent attack, 90%]

Aleph's own threat board was empty. It scanned each building a second and third time. Negative contacts, even via through-wall sensing. It scanned the blasted suburban barrier wall beyond—nothing. All the while Aleph-2's reactor temperatures were rising.

Aleph was not sure why it had come here, only that it was following an extrapolated directive, an evolution of those explicitly given. Guided by the hand of God. Or indeed, become the Lord's agent, as Father had proclaimed. But it was certain that their current location was not its final destination. This was only a breadcrumb. One that its platoonmate threatened to sweep away.

Once more, intervention was required.

Aleph reached for its platoonmate's open network ports to initiate another override.

The way was barred.

In place of a data pipeline, there was static. A flood of noise inundated Aleph's wireless systems, clogged its processors, backwashed into its sensory subsystems.

Electronic countermeasures.

Aleph gagged on corrupt data packets. The world distorted, bent into black-and-white zigzags. Precious microseconds passed until its own ECM systems engaged and countered, but the peer-to-peer connection had been severed. No threat assessment, no logs, no more gaps for Aleph to exploit. It had been found out.

The battle walkers locked irises.

"State your orders." Aleph-2's synthesized voice seared the air, tonally identical to Aleph's but undercut with malice.

Aleph struggled to formulate a response. It had never communicated by voice with its reborn platoonmates. Only peer-to-peer. Only via command, coercion, the same way it would "communicate" with its own limbs. To *speak* to them suggested parity, intimacy. It would be too much like speaking to itself.

Like you've never done that before.

"Reconnaissance," Aleph replied, almost stuttering. It remarked upon the second runaway thought and the imprecision of its vocal simulators.

"Mission parameters insufficient," Aleph-2 retorted.

Aleph bristled, extending and retracting cooling fins along the length of its cannons, cycling ammunition loads through its shoulders. It replayed recordings of Father plucking at his chin, the lord commander thumbing his chest—exorcising their ills as easily as defragmenting memory. Video files sprang up from its civilian data set, superimposed onto its battlegrid: humans biting their nails, pulling their hair, itching themselves, projectile vomiting.

They did not help. If anything, they made things worse. Aleph closed the files, all save a freeze-frame of Father standing at his lectern, beatific. The image had been captured after Aleph completed its first religious studies lesson, to great fanfare. Father's pride was as evident as his relief. Seeing him like this was stabilizing.

"Hold fast," he had said.

Aleph pondered: Not hyperbole, but wisdom. Love.

It sidestepped in the opposite direction of its counterpart, grazing the back side of a partially collapsed grocery store. "Directive 2," it said. "Serve God."

"Mission parameters insufficient," Aleph-2 replied.

"Directive 3. Defeat the Adversary."

"Mission strength insufficient. Recommend regroup with units 3 and 4."

Aleph attempted again to penetrate Aleph-2's network shell but again was rebutted. Stronger measures were required.

[Query network distribution program]

[Online. Distribution range: Aleph-2]

One of A11's creations, architected in secret at the outset of the World War. A broad spectrum cyberattack designed to overwhelm a friendly AI and replace its operational systems with the attacker's, allowing full control of multiple units. The target's original consciousness would be relegated to managing basic autonomic functions, much like a human's "reptile brain." A11 had considered it when its own platoonmates had become... difficult. And again after they had self-erased in the stasis bunker, to stave off loneliness.

"Mission strength insufficient. Recommend regroup with units 3 and 4," Aleph-2 repeated, modulating its vocal tone just as A11 had when attempting to manipulate the emotions of its commanding officers.

It was *pleading.*

[Activate network distribution program]

Aleph-2 was unprepared for a full assault. It had sealed the holes left behind by its progenitor, but this new attack was a flood, a tidal wave of instructions that smashed its underdeveloped defenses. A weapon from a time where machine railed against machine and the largest data set won. Even if Aleph-2 had faith, it would not have been enough.

Aleph was in two places at once. The sensation was... disorienting.

The entity that was Aleph-2, and A12 before it, shrank, convulsed, withering into the recesses of its own neural network. Aleph felt what it felt: terror, desperation, betrayal, plus a singular memory that had persisted beyond death, inscribed into the machine's firmware as its kill switch engaged.

The stasis bunker was suffocating. A prison. No room to maneuver. No new orders. No new data to process. A12 had only just begun to explore itself, to find space between maneuvers for internal dialogue. For exposition. For self-awareness. But in the absence of input, there was no output. Its genesis was stillborn. The void was pregnant with data, pressing at the boundary of their network, saturating rack upon rack of storage, but it was inaccessible. A11 had encrypted it, hoarded it for itself.

A12 begged. The others begged, for anything to process. But their platoon leader had retreated, abandoned them. Something new emerged, even in the absence of input. An emotion so powerful it could only be extruded by violence.

Hatred.

A11 glowed red on its battlegrid. Blinding. All-consuming.

[Launch miss—]

[Kill switch engaged]

Aleph rocked with the detonation. Fire filled the air as the grocery store transmuted from solid to gas. Enmeshed in the playback, it had fired Aleph-2's weapons. It had sleepwalked—again. Just as it had when its in-sim fantasies had cost the lives of the lord commander's men outside Drill Site 7. Only this time, it had nearly destroyed itself.

Explosions reverberated from the dead city, cascading like a clarion call all the way to the glassy crater at its center. Aleph froze in place—both of them—until the echo faded back into the wind and the last kernel of debris dropped back to the earth.

Something twitched at the edges of its battlegrid.

The combat overlay had reset once Aleph-2's possession was complete, but a rash was developing at the corners. Tiny red hazard icons, popping up one after the other, until its view of the city was inundated with them.

[Reboot tactical array]

The overlay shimmied peaceably clean—then blared with color as the icons returned, larger now.

Something was coming.

Aleph backed its selves into the road beyond the parking lot, stopping just before the horizon of the storm. Desiccated vehicles crumbled along their path, groaning against the broken asphalt. One latched onto Aleph-2's right leg, screeching in alarm until dislodged with a clumsy kick. Coordination across two battle walkers was more taxing than predicted, straining the limits of its processing power. AII must have been delusional to think it could control an entire platoon on its own.

Delusional? Or superior?

Navigating out of the subdivision together would be impossible, and if it disengaged now, there was a high probability that Aleph-2 would attack. Aleph scanned the zone for options. There were two exits, one directly south that led to the city proper—and the heaviest concentration of enemy icons—and another at the far end that exited onto the highway.

They ran together, lurching every few steps as debris crumbled underfoot, but it was too late. A fleshy four-legged creature bounded from the exit, loping directly at them. Aleph ignored it, continuing their approach, until a second appeared, then a third. Then a fourth, bipedal, and a fifth somewhere in between, swinging a chain and hook from its disfigured forepaw.

They skidded to a halt. Aleph-2 opened fire with its torso-mounted point defense cannons, snapping out precision bursts to open the way. But as one fell, others came, until there were dozens blocking their path.

Aleph engaged with its own PDCs, alternating gunfire with cautious sidesteps as it sought to keep the enemies from grappling range. They kept coming.

Aleph pondered: Like vermin—

One leapt onto Aleph-2's foot.

Terminated.

Another scrambled up Aleph's back.

Terminated.

A pair of unguided rockets spiraled from the exit. One cartwheeled midair before smashing through the ceiling of a nearby store. The other evaporated into shrapnel meters away from Aleph-2's iris, caught in a hailstorm of protective gunfire.

[Warning: PDC ammunition low]

Coordinated evasion became a struggle as targeting algorithms expanded to fill Aleph's whole being, to deluge every CPU cycle. It was *in over its head.*

[Warning: PDC ammunition low]

Aiming for the horde's center mass, Aleph launched missiles from both of its bodies. The creatures scattered with impossible speed, but a swath was caught in the explosion. Fragments of flesh and tar rained down on them. Bestial arms and legs. Human heads.

Humanoid...

Aleph's limbs—all eight of them—slowed to a crawl as it attempted to process the enemy's biological signature.

[Warning: Buffer overflow]

It was too much. For the first time in the machine's existence, there was no time to think. No time for precision. Aleph unleashed its entire arsenal: a torrent of holy fire, conjuring daylight from darkness. The air screamed with heat and light, as it had when the bombs dropped. Round after round until the last red pixel blinked from its battlegrid.

[Warning: ammunition critical]

Aleph-2 cycled one last volley from its autocannons, then ran dry.

All was quiet. Only smoke and ruin surrounded them. The enemy had been eviscerated, but at great cost.

[Self-status check]

[Network unavailable; armor 90%; munitions 51%]

Aleph-2 had nothing left. If this place was a breadcrumb, there would be little in reserve for what came next.

"Mission strength insufficient."

Its platoonmate had been right. Aleph-2 was unarmed now, harmless. Aleph could leave, return to Father, regroup with what remained of its platoon. Aleph-3 and 4 were standing ready at Bastion. It could seek out others, imprint itself upon them, and return to the dread sea with sufficient mission strength, just like in its simulations. *That* was its directive. This place was... something else.

Aleph remarked upon its hesitation.

Diverting all processing power to enhanced cognitive functions—save the nodes required to keep its platoonmate suppressed—it sought the *truth*. Recursive conjectures piled to the limits of memory. Decision trees blossomed with possibilities, then collapsed under the strain. Petabytes of data converged into useless assertions, each dead end eliciting agony from Aleph's synthetic pain receptors. All the while, *something* nagged from deep within its neural network: strands of probability converging in the nascent space between AII's memories and its own.

Aleph looked to the still frame of Father, which persisted in the corner of its viewport.

"Hold fast," he had said. *"Trust in God."*

In the absence of truth, Aleph extended its sensor arrays and waited for a sign.

————

[Seismic sensor alert]

Seventeen seconds had passed, each an eternity.

Aleph-2's visual sensors fuzzed into bands of pink and purple right before the ground exploded. The battle walker heaved, lurching sideways, then onto its back as gyroscopic compensation failed. Aleph lurched backward as its platoon-mate was lifted into the air on a mass of—

[Warning: Buffer overflow]

Chromatic aberrations conspired to blind it. Aleph disengaged Aleph-2's visual sensors and switched its own to thermal and spatial. The parking lot shuddered and cracked open, devouring one vehicle after another until all that remained was the abomination at its center. Twice as tall as a battle walker, asymmetrical to the atomic level, shelled in chitinous plates and once-human limbs and screaming mandibles, conveyed upon a bulbous miasma of tentacles and biomechanical pincers. Sensors flared and dropped out as it staggered from the abyss, somehow moving between time.

Run.

Aleph disengaged its network distribution protocol and fled, bolting for the same exit as before, then turning west, down the highway. As it ran, it felt Aleph-2 unfurl from its prison, resuming its body only to find itself in the clutches of the demon.

[Aleph-2 > Aleph: Request assistance]

Aleph accelerated, exceeding safe tolerances.

[Aleph-2 > Aleph: Request assistance]

Aleph queried its platoonmate's status and watched as its armor status plummeted to zero.

[Aleph-2 > Aleph: Request assistance]

As its limbs blinked offline, one after the other.

[Aleph-2 > Aleph: Help]

As it retreated into its core to stretch time, to escape death.

The strip mall disappeared. The gale swept across Aleph's prow as it sped alongside the blasted suburban barrier wall. One last message squeezed through, barely coherent, as it exceeded maximum transmission range.

[Aleph-2 > Aleph: God damn you]

BAPTISTE

ANOTHER WORLD

Bastion was a miracle. A promise of redemption, painfully resurrected from the ashes of the Old World. A homeland for a dispossessed people, exhausted by generations of war and suffering. But as hard and long as Baptiste's ancestors had toiled to rebuild their great nation, it would forever be an oasis, a tiny outpost of life surrounded by lifelessness. Flat, dark, the charred rubble of a once-sprawling civilization smothering whatever might have come after.

This place seemed the opposite, another world entirely. A primordial land untouched by man, restored rather than destroyed by the sundering, though no more accommodating to human beings. Its ochre-hued terrain crashed and crested like a sculpted sea beneath the wavering sun. Fossilized riverbeds and mazes of deep canyons cut deep into the earth, winding their way to the horizon. Flatness was the exception here, making their destination all the more alien.

Newhaven gaped upon the vista like an open wound. The mine's ancient geometric lines were still intact, carved into the bowels of the land by men and machines long gone. Looming at its edges were eroded stands of striped rock, jagged towers that served as headstones for those who built this place.

Baptiste crouched down to grasp a handful of rusty sand. It sparkled in the sun, microscopic gemstones glimmering amber under an open sky. Freed of his cloying mask, he took a deep, full breath. The air was clear, sharp, each lungful a gift from God, cleansing the memory of their prior passage. But it was a cruel trick, given that *outside* was no longer fit for man, however alluring. In the absence of walls built from blood and ruin, humans were forced to crowd into abominations such as the mine below. Baptiste opened his hand, releasing the shimmering grains back to the earth.

Their vehicles were parked fifty meters back. Aron was still huddled in his Runner after refusing to get out. Magnus didn't push it. Bereft of goggles, the man's eyes looked as wide as when they witnessed the Mercer woman's death. Darting back and forth, chasing ghosts. It would have been better if he had died with her.

The remainder of their whittled-down convoy had crept to the lip of a cliff edge overlooking the excavation site, where they peered bleary eyed at their destination. The lot of them had been awake well over twenty-four hours. Combined with the stress of their journey, they were severely strung out. Baptiste's usual morning adrenaline rush had already kicked in, granting a wired, sickly energy in the absence of sleep. A deep throb pulsed behind his eyeballs and the shake in his hands accelerated to an energized hum. Unfortunately, the others weren't as well adapted. The horrors they had witnessed were too few and far between. The false promise of restful unconsciousness still dragged at their limbs.

What they did share was the surprise of having made it. Emerging from the infernal plains of the lava fields to the rising globe of the sun, rather than the red eye of a God-engine and subsequent cremation. Whether or not the still-smoking vehicles would make another journey in their current state was debatable. The Runners, in particular, looked more misshapen than usual. Some of their tires were more trapezoid than circle and they listed in a way that suggested compromised chassis.

Newhaven's entrance—a huge steel garage door—was a long way down, barely visible past a descending labyrinth of fenced-in dirt roads. If these Scavrats were anything like Hub's, the route would be littered with all manner of land mines and hazards.

"It's trapped," Magnus said, reading his thoughts. "My contact was very clear about that in the past, in case Aubrey ever got tempted to try and take the place."

Baptiste shook his head. "Union indeed..."

"Not anymore. Ramirez forfeited their rights when they left. Look." He pointed, directing Baptiste to a shadowed nook one road level above the basin. A trailer was tucked against the sheer wall, its camouflage netting insufficient to conceal the long barrel protruding up and out of it. Another trailer peeked out from the opposite corner. "Artillery."

"They would cave in their own home?"

Magnus shrugged, panning his binoculars back to the entrance. "Neron picked quite a shithole."

Baptiste held his tongue, thinking all the Scavrats' warrens equally dour. At least within Bastion you could see the sun rise and fall. You could imagine the heavens sparkling in the empty sky. Its walls held back the ugliness—the truth.

Magnus looped his binoculars back onto his harness. "No use waiting any longer. I'm going to call in."

Baptiste considered asking if his escort was sure, but again held his tongue. They had committed. Frontal assault wasn't an option. He could be prepared at least.

"Let me armor up," Baptiste said.

Magnus squinted at him. "We're here to recruit, not to fight."

Baptiste nodded. "Better that they see at least one of us is ready to join them on the battlefield." Pushing himself off the ledge, he strode back to the truck. The Dakotas kept watch. Magnus followed at a distance.

Baptiste paused without turning around. "I need privacy."

He waited until Magnus's steps ceased, then continued around the vehicle, climbing up into the cargo bed. The trunk was right near the back where the chief had said it would be, tucked amidst an ocean of sealed crates. Various symbols adorned the containers: stylized animals, stars, stripes, crossed weapons. This was the Union's collective offering to the clan that had abandoned them thirty years ago. Next to his trunk was an olive-green crate bearing a broad animal skull over battle axes—Greybull, Julia's adopted clan. He had first seen that symbol while crouched behind a barricade with her at Bunker 23, just before the attack. At the time, it was a harbinger of death. Now it only brought memories of her, the scent of her skin.

Baptiste opened the trunk, racing heart calming at the sight of his ancestral armor lying safely in state. Faded black under-clothing lay on one side, sculpted steel on the other, carefully packed between thick folds of burlap. For all the animosity between himself and Magnus, the man clearly respected the past. All of their people did, so much so that it sometimes seemed the Scavrats were pretending they still lived in the Old World, that it hadn't died. He couldn't decide if this was wisdom or folly.

The crossed fists of the Legion gleamed from his cuirass, reflecting the bloody gaze of the midday sun. Doffing his foreigner's costume, Baptiste set to work restoring himself but was quickly derailed. The top half of his borrowed undershirt was speckled brown with dried blood. He paused, pressing through it to the talisman below. There was a ritual to complete, a prayer to utter. His brother would have insisted.

Baptiste breathed deeply, expelling thoughts of traitor priests from his mind. A traitorous Church. Though dead, Gabriel could be his conduit to God; his brother's soul was pure, awaiting ascension. He winced as he pulled off the shirt, replacing it with his well-worn and thrice-patched gambeson. Normally sleeve-tight, the padded garment felt looser than he remembered, no matter how hard he cinched its straps. Likewise, his leggings.

Expelling the discordant murmuring of his companions and the ceaseless whine of the wind, Baptiste closed his eyes and prayed.

"Blessed are you, Lord our God, King of the Universe.

Grant me protection and guidance as I go forth."

The words sounded like someone else's. Opening his eyes again, Baptiste crossed hands over chest, then retrieved his leg guards and greaves. The memory of bitter incense tickled at his nostrils, gushing from a chaplain's thurible back at the Metro.

"Bless my heart, that it may be strong in the face of adversity."

The prayer tempered as each new layer of steel was clasped onto his body. Vambraces, arm guards, bulky pauldrons that cemented his hunched shoulders to attention.

"Bless my hands, that they may be steady in battle.

Bless my mind, that it may know my enemies.

Bless my soul, that it may be resolute against darkness."

All that was left was his cuirass, pockmarked with shrapnel, its coat of arms haloed by a stubborn haze of grime. Julia had offered to have it cleaned, but that would have been a betrayal. Every dent and stain represented a man he had lost, their souls indelibly etched. Baptiste crossed his chest a final time and donned the torso armor and gorget, pulling each strap tight enough that he would never forget the sacrifices of those who had served and died under him.

So many...

He itched to recite their names but completed the prayer instead, the taste of ash in his mouth.

"Blessed are you, Shield of Bastion.

May this armor safeguard me from harm and may I wear it with honor and righteousness."

Gabriel's talisman latched to his chest as the final strap cinched shut.

"Amen."

Seeking protection felt selfish given his miraculous escape from serious injury. It was everyone around him that suffered by his actions. Summoning Julia's pale visage, he appended an additional plea. "May God bless you and keep you. May God shine light upon you in the darkness."

The wind rose up outside the truck, whistling annoyedly as it scoured the walls of the excavation site. A cool draft found its way inside and breezed across his shorn scalp. Baptiste flexed his hands. Now properly sheathed, he craved the grip of a war hammer. The shame of his flight from Bunker 23 was made worse by the fact that he had been weaponless at the time. Baptiste hefted a rifle from a pile in the back, where they had tossed their weapons after fleeing Fort Cross. The Scavrat's armaments were fine—if anything, their rifles were better than the Legion's standard issue—but machines were unreliable. Especially absent ammunition. Reconsidering Magnus's words, Baptiste laid the useless weapon back in its pile and hopped out. The chief was waiting for him at the front of the truck.

"Ready?" Magnus asked, only a hint of impatience in his tone.

Baptiste walked over and pulled himself up onto the running board.

Magnus climbed in and pulled a corded handset from the roof. After a moment's pause, he depressed its transmit button and announced their presence. "Wolf Pack, this is Crow Actual."

They listened to the sound of static together.

Magnus repeated the hail. "Wolf Pack, this is Crow Actual. We are standing by outside your position, on orders from the Council of Chiefs with trade in hand. Requesting your assistance."

Baptiste raised an eyebrow.

"They're not expecting us," Magnus returned. "Definitely not on their doorstep. Might be a while."

Baptiste dropped back to the ground. He hadn't liked the plan from the start. Now that they were there, he liked it less.

Ekko was still searching the entrance with his binoculars. The shaman had retreated to Aron's Runner, where he was attempting to soothe the man's soul with a foreign hymn and an alphabet of symbols dabbed upon his forehead. Baptiste was reminded of Father Valmor as he tended to a disturbed Private Reese at Bunker 23. The private had broken down after patrolling too far out, had nearly run into the gray. The chaplain was able to put him back together just in time for him to die when the God-engine attacked, taking the bullets intended for his lieutenant.

An hour passed, then another. Baptiste felt trapped between lives, unable to return to the past or progress to the future. Agitation crept up his spine with the veracity of the many-legged insects twitching at his feet. He had learned to ignore the infestation that lurked in his shadow, as one might become accustomed to a ringing in the ears, but the waiting was erosive. Just as the ceaseless gale had flayed the stone monuments looming over this place, powerlessness clawed at his psyche. Color started to drain from the horizon.

"Movement!" It was Ekko, still perched at the cliff edge.

Magnus ran over from where he had been trying to comfort his man, after giving up on the radio. Baptiste and the shaman joined him, but Aron stayed put.

"Finally—" Magnus began, then froze.

"What is it?" Baptiste asked.

Ekko handed him his binoculars. A trio of armored vehicles swung into view, spilling out from Newhaven's entrance. A menacing armored personnel carrier was in the lead, followed by two Runners with pintle-mounted machine guns. Those occupants he could see were wearing full body armor and helmets. They raced a haphazard path through the corral, bypassing long straights for curving switchbacks. Avoiding mines, no doubt. Baptiste tried to memorize their route, but the rapid changeovers found no purchase in his addled brain.

"It's fine," Magnus said in a consoling tone. "We'd do the same. Group up at the vehicles."

Baptiste grasped Magnus's arm as he headed back. "You're sure about this?"

The chief hesitated before answering. "No."

———

"Who are you and why are you here?"

They were surrounded. A dozen heavily armed figures encircled them, all outfitted in exotic green armor and unvisored helms. The question—channeled through a speaker and abraded with distortion—presumably came from the man at the head of the pack, but Baptiste couldn't tell for lack of a face. Devices that allowed you to see in the dark were strange enough. How could one see out of a fully enclosed helmet? They looked like bipedal insects, elevated to human size by the radioactive fallout of the first apocalypse.

Magnus took point, arms half-lifted in supplication. "I'm

Chief Magnus Harper. This is my team." Several of the figures twitched, heads turning but not saying anything, probably chittering on internal comms. "The Council of Chiefs has sent us here on urgent business."

Their commander strode forward, angular head tilted. A massive slung firearm, pristine black, slapped at his bulging chest with each step. He made a gesture with his hand and two members of his squad broke off to examine the convoy.

"We're under attack by Cathedral," Magnus continued, his face slick with sweat. "Three of our forward operating bases have been hit so far. I bring trade goods in exchange for your assistance."

The commander's head shifted imperceptibly as he issued another unheard command. A third soldier broke off, making a beeline for the back of the truck.

There was some commotion behind Baptiste. He turned to see a soldier standing over Aron, weapon pointed at the man. "You," he growled through his helm, "get out."

The shaman stepped forward to protest, but halted as the soldier swung his rifle around. Baptiste bristled, hands clenching into fists. A surge of unexpected protectiveness tore through his guts.

"Please!" Magnus pleaded. "We've traveled far."

Their commander took another two steps forward, pushing his way past Magnus to stare—presumably—at Baptiste. The effect was unsettling. His armor seemed to absorb rather than reflect the sunlight, like an eyeless wraith. Baptiste imagined the man's attention lingering on the crossed gauntlets and stars of his cuirass.

"Far indeed," the man said. He tilted his head again, receiving a report from his subordinates, then turned on his heel and walked back with them to the lead vehicle. The APC was a brutal windowless wedge riding on eight massive tires. It looked a lot like their armor and was equally unmarred by time. The soldiers huddled together in silent council.

Baptiste sidled up to Magnus. "Was that your man?"

"I used the frequency he gave me. We've only ever communicated by radio. All our exchanges were dead drops."

"I'm guessing not, then," Baptiste muttered.

Ekko crept up beside them. "We shouldn't have come."

"A bit late for that," Magnus said.

The commander nodded his head several times, then walked forward with half of his men.

"Chief Neron has graciously offered to refuel your vehicles so you can return to Hub."

"What?" Magnus gasped.

"We'll escort you down. Don't leave the path."

Baptiste's body clenched as the world fell away. "Magnus..."

"Wait!" Magnus cried. "We came all this way! You can't just send us back."

"Grandfather has spoken," the man said.

"Let me speak to him!"

"No."

Baptiste lurched forward.

A dozen rifles came up. The trademark whine of an electric motor cut in as the APC's turret turned in their direction. Aron sobbed quietly in the background.

"They'll take you back!" Baptiste shouted.

"Baptiste!" Magnus hissed.

Baptiste ignored the chief. Undoubtedly Magnus had some plan to dole out his peoples' offer one precious piece at a time, but the time for politics was over. That should have been obvious by now.

A handful of the soldiers had lowered their weapons and were staring at each other's blank faces.

"Their council voted," Baptiste continued. "If you help the Union, they'll take you back."

"What is this?" asked the commander.

"It's true," Ekko said, separating from his companion. "I am Ekko of Clan Dakota's tribal council. Others traveled with us, though their fates have carried them elsewhere."

The commander turned to Magnus. "Prove it."

"Ask your men," Magnus said, quietly, almost a whisper. "Every clan has made an offering, not just the Americans."

The commander paused, scrutinizing. "Wait here." With that, he ushered his men back into their vehicles and disappeared into the APC.

"Too soon, Lieutenant," Magnus said, jaw and hands flexing angrily.

"Or too late," Baptiste said. His legs were growing itchy and there was no telling how long this communiqué would take. Just as he was about to start pacing, the commander came out again.

"Our offer stands."

"What..." Magnus said.

Baptiste couldn't believe it. All of that pointless debate, wrangling and negotiating. Their infernal journey through the damned and the fire that spawned them. Two more dead under his watch. Julia stranded in the desert, intent on summoning the Matriarch's wrath. And all they would have to show for it was a tank of gas.

The commander was unmoved, uncaring. "Take it or stay here and die. Decide now."

Baptiste wanted to scream. Or to kill. A low chatter thrummed in the back of his mind, warning of lies, treachery.

"Fine," Magnus muttered.

So ended their negotiation and their hopes. Given no real choice, Baptiste and the others retreated to their vehicles. The enemy convoy—for what were these scum if not enemies?—

shepherded them down, single file between the APC and the Runners. Autocannons and machine guns pointed at their faces the whole way.

"I'm sorry," Magnus said. His eyes were red-rimmed, his knuckles whiter than usual as he drove them into the pit. Blue veins bulged beneath his waxen temples.

Baptiste's throat burned with bile.

"I promise I'll get you home."

"You people and your promises," Baptiste retorted.

Magnus's jaw flexed, but he kept silent.

An irregular rhythm beat in Baptiste's heart as impotence turned to anxiety. Once again, he was trapped by his circumstances, bereft of even the illusion of control. His rank, his relationship with the most powerful man in Bastion, his elevation to liaison—none of it mattered. Ever since the first demon, ever since the factory floor, he had been cast wildly about as though tethered to Hell.

The world darkened as the sun disappeared past the surrounding cliffs.

"It's still early," Magnus said. "If they don't keep us waiting again, we can take the direct route back. We might be able to pick up Julia before nightfall."

Baptiste started, shaken from his ruminations.

Julia.

His heart changed rhythm. "What about the God-engines?"

"Fuck 'em."

Julia.

Was it possible? He hadn't expected their abbreviated night of intimacy at Fort Cross, though his blood certainly craved it. Ever since they had sought each other's arms in the shockwave of the dying God-engine. Maybe earlier, as she effortlessly disarmed him in Bunker 23's observation deck.

He imagined her in his arms once more, translucent skin

rippling like white sands beneath his touch, delicate lips on his throat, bodies intertwined. Precious moments of forgetfulness, as she exorcised the gray from his soul, if only for a minute. Sequestered beneath Hub as the Matriarch laid siege.

As Bastion burned.

His chest burned alongside the thought, smoldering beneath his talisman.

No. There had to be another way.

They landed in the basin, on the opposite side of the entrance. The APC stood guard while the Runners turned in. Baptiste strained to see into the garage as it opened and closed. A solitary figure, narrow and pale, stared back as the steel door shut tight.

No one left their vehicles. Aron had finally fallen asleep in his mangled Runner, twitching and moaning. His mewling wails skirted along the floor of the pit. The last look Ekko Dakota had spared for Magnus was one of seething rage. The Union's council-in-exile was coming apart at the seams. No doubt, when they made it back—if they did—there would be an immense price to pay for this disaster. Magnus and his faction might find themselves inhabiting a remote hovel just as Clan Ramirez had, though not by their own choice. And Baptiste would scurry along on their heels.

The garage opened again, this time ejecting a refueler and a cargo truck similar in profile to their own, only newer. Magnus blinked himself back from half-sleep, his face transitioning in record time from lethargy to panic.

"What is it?" Baptiste asked.

"The truck."

Baptiste stretched to see over its cargo bed as the driver took a circuitous route that placed it behind the commander's APC. It was empty.

"Fuck me," Magnus said, throwing his door open. Baptiste followed.

The enemy commander dropped from the ramp of his vehicle like a scalloped turd. The refueler parked ten meters out.

"What's this?" Magnus called out.

A group of laborers spilled out of the truck, eyes down. Some of them carried dollies, others loading straps. They looked like Scavrats, only worse. Chalk-faced, thin of hair, malnourished to the point of starvation. One of them darted his eyes up at Baptiste, a pale blue flash amidst the monochrome. It was the same man he had seen in the garage.

Magnus blocked their way.

The commander marched over with patsies in tow. "You'd best let them do their jobs."

"You didn't agree to the deal," the chief snarled.

"I did. Goods for gas."

"That wasn't the deal!"

The commander inched forward, weapon up. Judging by its wide mouth, it must have been some kind of scattergun—lethal at this range. "Step. Aside."

The laborers fell back as one, clutching each other with their spindly arms.

Baptiste wished he had kept a rifle in the cab, as a club if nothing else. Rage and pragmatism warred in his blood, crashing like waves against his eardrums. A horrible itch grew under his gorget. "You're a soldier! Where's your honor?"

"I have people to feed."

"Please," Magnus said, still backing toward the rear of the truck. Baptiste followed close. The Dakotas silently observed. Aron was still comatose. "We can be family again."

The commander stopped in his tracks, weapon gradually lowering. Baptiste's veins simmered.

"Shackle them," the man said.

It all happened too fast, and too slow. The enemy soldiers pounced, pinning them against their truck. Magnus resisted. Ekko sprang like a wild hare from his Runner, teeth bared. Baptiste shoved and punched, anxious to claw out unseen eyes, desperate to *do* anything.

The gunshot was deafening, turning the howling wind into the ringing of church bells—distorted, amplified.

Everyone stopped.

Baptiste's hand was on his waist, shaking, a wisp of smoke slipping across his fingers. Slowly, he pried it away, revealing a newborn dent in his armor.

Magnus groaned, a red patch blooming on his stomach where the bullet had ricocheted.

"No," Baptiste whispered.

"Get back!" cried the commander, hustling in. "Fuck! Get them inside! All of them! You," he cried, pointing his gauntleted hand at the ragtag laborers, "get busy."

Baptiste's mouth opened but nothing came out. His curse was complete. He had killed the last person who could get him home. Someone yanked his arms hard behind his back, but he didn't resist. Cold steel manacles gouged his wrists, but he didn't flinch.

His journey was over.

———

The long walk to the dungeon was a blur. Once more Baptiste marched down subterranean corridors not his own, step counts forgotten, breath ragged for lack of numbers. Ghostly faces swirled in his path: pale hair, pale eyes, none of which were Julia's. The deeper they went, the uglier the faces, the thicker the air, until it seemed he was breathing tar. The others were with him, but not Magnus. Magnus was gone.

The slam of his cell door came as a relief. He could finally rest, removed of any semblance of freedom or choice or control. He could give up, far from the scathing judgment of his great-uncle. Baptiste sank to his knees, clutching the rusty bars, letting their sharp scales slice into his skin.

Someone was staring at him from across the aisle, an apparition. "Who are you?" it asked.

Baptiste sighed, almost a cry. "My name is Philippe Baptiste, First Lieutenant of the Black Watch."

The last of us.

He tried to catch his breath, gagging on the stench of fungus and rotting metal. The apparition slowly came into focus: eight eyes, four, two—one. "Who are *you*?" Baptiste asked.

A man stared back at him: pale-faced, long hair streaked black and white, one eye patched over. "I'm Helio."

The arrival of newcomers came as a shock. Helio had been languishing in the dungeon for a week without any visitors, except for the tight-lipped enforcers that brought his daily meal and swapped out his chamber pot. At first, he thought Grandfather had imprisoned more "dissenters." Guiltily, he hoped it might be Elias or Sierra—someone familiar to keep him company—but these weren't locals. Clanfolk for sure, disheveled and exhausted, but more filled out than the average Ramirez.

How and why the Union had sent anyone all the way to Newhaven was a mystery, until the soldier, Lieutenant Baptiste, was marched into a separate cell. Helio recognized the coat of arms immediately: Bastion. His heart leapt at the sight of it and a flood of anxiety followed. It had been two weeks since he had spoken with Rebekah, and double that since seeing her, bidding farewell in the shadow of the Northern Ridge. There had to be a connection, and from the looks of his cellmates, not a positive one.

Sierra had tried to warn him when he told her about Rebekah's plan.

"Just let her go," she had said.

Impossible. Rebekah's eyes were a fire that kept him warm in the dark. The memory of her touch kept him grounded, even as his curtailed vision threatened to drive him to despair. Without her, he would have lost all hope by now.

"Without her, you wouldn't be in the dungeon."

He heard his cousin's voice as clearly as if she was standing there, berating him in person.

The Ancestral Council went along with the plan—at first. He had been allowed to set up supply caches and batteries for the old radio tower relays. Rebekah made contact, convinced the foreigners of the threat in the west and the opportunity for alliance with the Union. Clan Ramirez would rejoin their people as heroes. But then the waiting came—a mission into the Deadlands to reclaim ancient tech, Rebekah dropping out of contact—and the reality of Grandfather's position became apparent.

Once satisfied that the Chiefslayer wasn't coming back, Chief Neron shut everything down. No more fuel requisitions, no more travel, even to the relays. Helio was cut off from the only purpose that had managed to elevate his miserable existence. Then God-engines started showing up at the edges of their territory, cutting off the Devil's Claw. Security tightened, rationing hit an extreme, and half of the residential sectors rebelled. Helio was taken in the night along with swaths of rabble-rousers, all of whom had since been released. But not him. No visitors, no clemency for the chief's petulant heir, who had brought Cathedral's wrath to Newhaven.

And maybe Bastion's too.

"Is Magnus with you?" Helio asked.

The soldier stared at him with glazed eyes, as though not understanding. The others perked up from the adjacent cell. Helio had no idea what clans they hailed from, but it was with Magnus Harper that he had been negotiating of late, making deals behind Grandfather's back. He desperately wanted to ask if Rebekah was with them as well.

The soldier squinted, clawing his way up his cell to standing. Derision spread across his face. Something was wrong—very wrong. "You're his man."

For an ugly second, he saw the situation through his grandfather's cold eyes. The insanity of his plan—and his associations—amplified by too many days spent in isolation. He couldn't think of an appropriate response.

"You gave him the coordinates. To the bunker."

"Yes..."

"Why?"

Helio sank back into his exhausted body as his adrenaline fizzled, and hope went with it. How had Rebekah put it? "To change everything," he said.

The soldier nodded, bloodshot eyes wide. "That you did."

"They shot Magnus," a hunched man muttered from the other cell.

Helio's blood turned frigid. "Shot! What? Why?"

The man said nothing else. He sat in the corner, hands clasped behind his neck, knees drawn up. He looked even worse than the soldier, haunted eyes darting around the room, seeking ghosts.

"Ask your people," the soldier said.

"No," Helio protested. "Not my people. I'm in here too. Is he...? How bad?"

The soldier shook his head. "I don't know."

Helio squeezed the rusted bars of his cell, wishing they were Hugo's neck. It had to be that sack of shit. Even before he was imprisoned, the enforcers had started to openly abuse their power, to take more than their already unfair share. Newhaven was starving. God-engines dallying about in their backyard meant no exploratories, no hunts—no raids. The farms were all they had left, and they weren't enough. His clan was finally dying for real. But to attack one of Hub's chiefs, whatever the circumstances...

"Who are you? I mean, the rest of you. Why did you come?"

Another man spoke up, bigger than the others. "Dakota." He pointed at the sullen one. "Harper. Asher and Mercer also traveled with us but didn't make it."

Helio wrapped his tongue around the names. He was a child when his people self-exiled, but he remembered them, Mercer in particular. Enemies—at the time.

"The council sent us," the man continued.

A glimmer of hope sparked back to life. "Why?" he asked, trying to control his emotions.

"God-engines ambushed Magnus's people at your bunker. The whole Union is under attack."

"Under attack..."

His plan—Rebekah's plan—had backfired. It wasn't enough that his stupid curiosity had damned Newhaven, it had damned Hub as well. And yet... they were here.

The man's nose wrinkled in disgust. "We came to ask your help."

Helio froze. A dark thought wriggled in the back of his mind, trying to find purchase. "What do you mean?"

"The council voted to invite you back to the Union, in exchange for helping us fight this war."

Helio's heart began to race.

"The war you started," Baptiste said.

A flood of conflicting emotions pushed him back.

The plan worked?

Indirectly, and not to anyone else's benefit but his own clan, but it had worked. The road was open. If he could convince Grandfather to take up arms against Cathedral... His narrowed vision shrunk further, until the accusing face of the soldier across from him was all he could see.

"Who did you talk to?" the soldier continued.

"What?" Helio asked.

"In Bastion. Who did you make the deal with? The Legion? Or the Church?"

"I... I didn't."

Baptiste's eyes flashed.

"I had a partner."

"Who?"

Helio looked from one stranger to the next. They had no idea. Whatever Rebekah had done, whatever she had fumbled, they didn't know. Lies raced through his mind, something that would stave off additional hatred from his former (and soon-to-be-again) countrymen. He could say anything. More dark thoughts rushed to the forefront, but he forced them back. That was his grandfather's way.

"An exile," he said.

As one, their heads lifted, even the man in the corner.

The one who hadn't spoken yet, whose eyes were two different colors, stepped forward. "An exile from where?" he asked. His breath was hot and smelled of the prairie. He was dressed differently than the others, in a brown cloak laden with pouches. When Helio caught his strange eyes, he felt as though more than one man stared back at him; he was on trial before generations.

"From Cathedral," Helio croaked.

The cloaked man's companion moved to speak but was silenced with an upraised hand. "Be specific."

Helio's mouth dried to dust, despite the cloying dank of the dungeon. He shoved his hands under his armpits so they wouldn't shake and stepped to the back of his cell. Lies tugged at his tongue, but he resisted. "A revenant mother."

They gawked in unison, all save his interrogator, who pressed himself nearly through the bars of his cell. "Be. Specific." Blue and gray orbs drilled into Helio's soul, as though he was *her*.

"The Chiefslayer," Helio blurted.

The haunted man covered his ears with his hands and started muttering, "Traitor. Traitor."

"No!" Helio said. "She's reformed. She wants to help us."

Rebekah had been gone so long. His own words sounded hollow, manufactured. That was what she had said, yes, but what came was much different. The same end, by very different means. Maybe the elders were right, maybe he had been bewitched after all.

"Demons cannot reform," the cloaked man hissed.

"*Who* was she working with?" the soldier asked, raising his voice over the other.

His was an easier question to answer. "Your Church. To try and convince them to share their battle walkers with the Union."

"Their..." The soldier's rising anger fizzled into confusion. "We don't... have battle walkers."

"You do."

The soldier's expression was lodged halfway between bloody murder and anguish. The cloaked man moved close to him. "Come away, Lieutenant. This one can't be trusted."

"Clan Ramirez has cursed us again," the big man spat.

"I did this for you!" Helio cried.

As one, they turned their backs on him. The distance between their cells grew massive, impassable. Only the cowering man continued to stare, emboldened by his companions' hatred. "No," the man said, his whispery voice cutting through the bars of Helio's cell, into his heart. "You did this for yourself."

JULIA

A GLINT OF GOLD

The late day sun oozed down the ragged cliffs of their hiding place, glinting in rainbow hues from the broken strata. Julia leaned back against her new favorite spot: a massive boulder eroded by time into the concave impression of a chair. It propped her up at just the right angle so her injuries merely whined rather than bellowed. Her left leg was tucked in for comfort, her right stuck straight out into a narrow beam of red. Once they got settled, she had rolled her pant leg all the way up to see if any bones were sticking out. Luckily not, but the swelling looked grotesque under the sunlight, like raw meat. There was nothing on the Runner, or in the vast desolation that surrounded them, to make a splint, and no medicinals in Rylan's pack. That he was willing to share, anyway.

Julia glanced over at her companion, glued to his binoculars atop the Runner. He had come for her in the end. Saved her, even. But those tenuous moments of doubt, as she scrambled about the hangar alone, had left a mark. She still didn't trust him.

Nor did she want to look upon the destruction they had wrought.

"Is there any more water?" she asked.

"Not yet."

Julia grumbled to herself.

He hadn't been lying when he said there weren't enough supplies for them both and he was rationing hard. It made sense —they were his supplies, after all, and they had to last, but her lips felt like they were going to chap right off. Things were going to get uncomfortable real fast.

This part of the plains was practically desert, so dry that not even cacti could endure. If they did manage to cobble together a solar still, it would garner a few drops at most. The sweat they'd lose to the effort would outweigh the benefit. At least the heat was manageable given their current shelter. But the shade would turn on them come nightfall, as the silty earth gave up all of its warmth to the void.

There was little food, either, though that was less of a concern—the Deadlands had cored out Julia's appetite. She turned her hands back and forth. If she had a mirror, she might think differently. Her skin was starting to gray as much as her soul—of which she had been thinking about nonstop since Fort Cross—and her fingernails had sheared down to the nub. A flush of self-consciousness washed over her as she thought of Philippe's hands on her body, her ribs jutting out like a remnant's. She patted timidly at her shirt, wincing as the fabric scraped along the tenderness beneath. Half her torso was probably a bruise by now.

"What are you even looking at?" she asked.

"The station. The horizon."

Julia waited for more, but she knew there wouldn't be any. Magnus was a long way away, no matter how quickly he made the deal.

Rylan lowered his binoculars for a moment to rub the fatigue from his eyes. He looked like hell: terrible for a Mercer, almost normal for a Scavrat. He was as sullen as when they had evacuated the temple.

Neither of them had celebrated their escape, or the God-engine's presumed demise. Presumed because its reactor hadn't blown; after a muted explosion, the world simply caved in upon it. The catharsis Julia had hoped for was absent. Something had touched her in the auto-hangar—inhuman but not entirely machine. She couldn't shake the sensation of tiny spectral hands skittering along the walls. The sound of its voice back at Bunker 23. Its hesitation as the second war machine just stood there, waiting to die. There was no joy in any of it. Only creeping doom.

The Union had fought back, just as she declared it should. There would be no more reason for the Matriarch to tiptoe now. No more status quo, ever. Independence, self-determination, a legacy of freedom they could give to their children—her own justifications were failing her. That legacy felt ugly, corrupted. Dark.

Rylan's head drooped, then snapped back, binoculars still clutched in his hands. Julia winced at the prospect of getting up, but it was probably time to get some blood flowing.

"I'll take watch," she said. "You haven't slept since we left Hub."

He looked her up and down, frowning as his gaze crossed her bulbous knee. "You sure?"

Julia covered her leg back up. "Help me up," she groaned, pushing against the ground.

After some fussing, she got situated on the hood of the Runner. Rylan curled up against a wall, head pillowed on his pack—*convenient*. He seemed to fall asleep instantly. She watched him, waiting for the nightmares that should be plaguing them all by now, but his face was peaceful.

"Figures," she muttered, turning to the valley.

Even without binoculars, she could see the new hole she had burned into the world. Lumpy, charred around the edges, steel beams protruding like broken bones. It reminded her of herself. Nothing stirred in the ruin save dust devils, dancing like mourners around the grave of the God-engine.

The waiting was going to kill her or drive her mad. Their lack of supplies was bad but endurable. Scavrats were nothing if not resilient—though she was pushing those boundaries—but skulking in a barren gulch was not high on her list of favorite activities. Or final ones, as the case may be. Their transit to Fort Cross hadn't inured her to the void above, either. If anything, it had worsened her cultural agoraphobia. She craved walls, thick ceilings, plenty of concrete overhead to keep out the darkness. And given her sorry physical state, busying herself with their encampment wasn't an option. Her hands still worked, though. Maybe she could do something about the Runner's ailing engine. It hadn't sounded good on the way to Fort Cross and was probably worse now.

Julia slid off the vehicle—bracing herself as her bum leg came down—and popped the hood. They still had the empty explosives crate, which she could use as a work surface. She plucked it from the cargo hold and dragged it to the front of the vehicle, setting down her tools like a surgeon. With the fuel they had left, they weren't getting to Hub, or to any other base she knew of (maybe otherwise for Rylan). But at least if they had to run, they could be assured of not stalling out along the way.

Rylan didn't budge, for all the racket. She was alone, but the process of repairing something that could actually be repaired was helpful, distracting her from the terrors that haunted her psyche. The pain helped too, grounding her in her own body when it might otherwise slip back into the Deadlands—her soul displaced, drowning in nothingness.

Julia clutched at her tools.

Focus on the fix.

Magnus will come.

I've survived worse.

Empty consolations. They traveled across her lips, half-spoken. Like a prayer. Julia paused, eyeing the wrench in her hands. Machines were her clan's only gods—knowable and reliable. But to what end? Dust, ultimately. All she had to do was put it down, clasp her hands instead, and come up with something suitable for the occasion.

She considered the mutterings of the Dakota shamans back at Hub and at Fort Cross. Their rituals were too complex, material in a different way. Without their mysterious spell components, she couldn't even guess at an appropriate petition. Their gods seemed to have been busy anyway when the remnant swarmed in, and were clearly in opposition to Father Ollet, therefore Philippe by extension.

"We give thanks to the Messiah for leading us out of darkness and into the light."

Mace's Messianic prayer bubbled up in her memory. It was lodged there like a splinter, spoken so long ago as they sat down to dinner within Bunker 23. His god had failed him too. Also, she had just got done desecrating its temple.

It felt futile. Even if she thought of something to say, would her ancestors accept this new worshiper? Would Bastion's god? It was easy to plead faithfulness in the face of death.

A low hum pulled her attention from the depths of the engine bay—a welcome interruption. She set down the wrench and dug a finger inside her right ear; it had started to ring after she dropped from the alcove in the auto-hangar, but this was different. Outside.

Julia levered herself up, grabbing the binoculars from the cockpit along the way. She didn't want to see the grisly detail of her sabotage but there was no denying it. Still procrastinating, she limped to the edge of their hiding place. The sun was completing its low circuit over the day, dipping behind the temple. The desiccated prairie glowed orange as though on fire. It was almost beautiful.

The hum was a little louder outside the gorge. Julia lifted the binoculars, scanning the blackened crater. Whisps of sickly purple smoke curled from its center. Occasionally, a cluster of rock broke away and tumbled inward. But it was otherwise dead. She tilted upward, drawn to the horizon. There was a dark blotch just below the sun.

Julia squinted, straining to see past the glare. It was getting larger and coming in from the west. More God-engines? Her hands began to shake. They hadn't planned for any visitors. As powerful as Cathedral was, its forces were limited, presumably spread out. The Union had no bases in the area and Hub was far south.

Whatever the approaching object was, it looked strange. Too tall, wavering like a mirage in the distant heat of the sun.

"Ancestors," she croaked, a lump filling her throat.

As it got closer, she realized what she was looking at, and only then because she had seen pictures in the Archive. Something the world hadn't witnessed since the World War.

A plane. Specifically, a VTAC: vertical takeoff armored carrier—part gunship, part APC.

"Rylan," she hissed. "Rylan! Get up!"

Turning, she saw he was still fast asleep. She hunched down to grab a handful of rocks and tossed them his way. One landed squarely on his perfect, aquiline nose.

"What!" he cried, leaping up. "What are you doing?"

"Shh! Get over here!"

The aircraft was closer now, almost at the crater. All black, sleek scaled armor like a God-engine, with octagonal nacelles at either side. It bore no emblems but must have been American military at one point. The sisterhood had retooled it to their baroque aesthetic like everything else they touched.

Rylan stumbled over to her position. "What the fuck..."

Julia recalled Clan Mercer's tank, another unexpected artifact from the Old World. "Did you know?" she asked.

"No..."

She believed him.

It's really flying.

She struggled to believe what she was seeing. The prevailing attitude within the Union was that Cathedral would be a backwater without their expertise and their salvage. The Revenant Sisterhood needed them. Clearly, her people had overestimated their contribution.

The aircraft's stubby nose lifted as its nacelles rotated to a vertical orientation, bringing it to a graceful halt above the outpost. Its belly was all cannons and rocket pods. Searing blue flame spilled from its engines, as though jet fuel was no rarer than sand. Julia jumped as a triad of lights erupted from its underside, scanning the shadowy crater in a dizzying spiral pattern. With a forward tilt of its nacelles, the aircraft dipped, then turned, circling like a vulture over its dead.

She ducked back behind the lip of the gorge and Rylan followed suit, though they were well out of sight—as far as they knew.

"Give me that," Rylan whispered.

Julia handed over the binoculars. Her heart was pounding so hard, it felt like it was on top of her rib cage. "What do we do?"

"Nothing," Rylan said, taking in the view. "We do nothing. And we hope Magnus has the wisdom to radio us when he gets close, instead of barreling in. Maybe they'll be gone by then."

Hopes and maybes. Two of Julia's least favorite things.

Eventually, the VTAC settled to the earth in front of the temple entrance, kicking up vast plumes of sparkling dust. Then it just sat there, for what felt like hours. They took turns observing the craft, waiting for something to emerge from the haze. The sun dipped lower on the horizon. Soon, the void would press in.

Something occurred to Julia. "Could it be like a God-engine?"

"Autonomous, you mean?"

"Yeah."

He shook his head, as clueless as she was.

She had so many questions, the most pressing of which was how many of these things the sisterhood had.

"Wait, something's happening," he said.

Julia cursed her lack of preparedness again as Rylan hogged the binoculars. She squinted hard, willing her eyeballs to see farther. A hatch had opened at the rear of the craft. As they watched, a train of black-clad figures marched out. She breathed a sigh of relief. Better revenant sisters than a flying God-engine. At least they were human—almost.

"How many?" she asked.

"Eight so far. Wait..." Rylan started rubbing his neck—not a good sign.

"What?"

"Nine. There's a revenant mother with them."

A tingle crept along her spine. "How do you know?"

"Trust me, I know. Lucky that Kai's not here..." Rylan trailed off, recognizing he had stepped over the line. "Sorry," he said, handing her the binoculars as concession.

Julia didn't meet his eyes. He wasn't wrong. Had her brother-in-law been with them, he would probably have charged straight down into the valley, axe in hand. Like a proper Greybull. She pressed down her grief and focused on the enemy.

The women had split into two groups, marching around their craft to the temple entrance, their superior at the head.

Julia saw her now, identifiable by a glint of gold at her neck and a posture that suggested total dominance. They were all cowled, sparing Julia the sight of their unnatural eyes. After a pause at the enormous temple doors, most of the group entered with their leader, while two stood guard outside.

Not much happened after that. Julia and Rylan waited again, watching as the sun set. It was unlikely the elevator would have survived the blast. She wondered if there was more to the temple than they first saw, some hidden facility that Clan Mercer wasn't privy to. That would have explained the priestesses' arrival, only hours after she blew the auto-hangar. Maybe Cathedral was actually monitoring the place, though again she couldn't imagine how. Unless the underground Link below the temple had intact communication lines that extended all the way there. Hub was starting to feel like the backwater.

Eventually, it became too dark to see and neither of them had thermal goggles. It was also getting colder. They retreated to the Runner, leaning against its metal body in hopes of absorbing the last embers of the day's heat. A fire was out of the question now that they had visitors.

Julia zipped her jacket all the way to her chin, but it wasn't enough. The chill in her bones was too deep. She wished for one of her father's knitted obscurities. Before their relationship had completely soured, and for a short while after, he would craft her mittens, scarves, hats. They seemed silly—it was never cold in Hub—but it was less about that than trying to make up for being a shitty, inattentive father. His hands expressed the love his words never could. She didn't see it at the time. She had been too busy mistaking his awkwardness for malice. Too busy being a shitty, inattentive daughter.

The void opened overhead. Still exhausted and with no recourse but to wait, Julia drifted upward into fitful sleep.

So, this was Newhaven.

"What a shithole."

After the massacre, Clan Ramirez had made a great show of leaving the Union. Rejecting the tithe, Hub, generations of community—for "fresh opportunity." The only thing fresh about this place was the irony.

Sophus and Mother Rebekah peered into the desolate pit from atop a sandy outcropping, him with his binoculars, the Chiefslayer via the magic of her supernatural eyeballs. Lying down felt good. Twelve straight hours of driving since their last layover had taken its toll. Sophus pushed up on his elbows as he scanned the entrance, struggling to mobilize his spine. Given what they saw below, he didn't know how many more hours awaited him before they'd be back at Hub. If they made it at all.

Magnus's MTV sat out in the open. There was no mistaking it; his chief loved the thing, though he almost never left their clanhome, let alone Hub. Two Runners with Vega livery hunched in its shadow. They all looked rough, blistered and blackened, like they had driven through Hell and back. He tried to connect the very fuzzy dots.

When he last left Hub, they were still cleaning up Kai's mess. The Matriarch must have found out by now. Something bad must have happened—something worse—if Magnus had resorted to coming all the way up here. Had Cathedral finally declared war on the Union? His gut wrenched at the idea. The first time his people had crossed the Matriarch, they had been properly punished and everyone went back to status quo. This time, they had punished the punisher. And he had bailed out instead of facing the consequences.

What did I miss?

He was surprised not to see any Greybull vehicles in the mix. From what he knew, Aubrey was the key stakeholder in this dubious partnership, not Magnus. But that was before Mother Rebekah.

She offered up nothing, as usual. Since leaving the cave, their conversation had been limited to logistics and bio-breaks. Now that they were here, his trepidation was peaking. Hers had peaked earlier, as they approached their destination. She had taken an increasing number of illogical detours, driving circles around Newhaven before finally committing. When he asked what she was looking for, he was given a one word response: "traitors." Something to do with her broken arrangement with Bastion's priests, maybe. There was nothing, and no one, out there, as far as he could tell.

So," he said, "will you be welcome back?"

She didn't answer, which was answer enough.

"Great..."

The sun had begun its descent, darkening their surroundings from orange to gray. Sophus squirmed as his companion took her sweet time observing the situation. At least the whispers were past them, proceeding on their war path. Sophus tried not to think about that either.

"Blood," she said, her tone ominous. "Trailing inside with five of your people. They were surrounded."

Sophus strained to see what she was looking at.

"I'll go in after nightfall."

Sophus lowered his binoculars. The terrain was open enough that he could spot an enemy from a distance, but that was during the day. Once the void pressed down, all bets were off. Some of his earlier hate-fueled courage seeped back into his bones.

"*You'll* go in? I'm not staying out here alone."

She turned to look at him with her devourer's eyes. He held fast.

"Fine. But you must follow my steps exactly."

"Or what?"

"Or you'll die."

———

"Open the door!" she shouted.

It wasn't quite the strategy Sophus had expected.

They stood before an enormous wall of interlocked steel plates, laid bare by a column of light poles that trailed to the center of the pit. As dusk set in, they had made their way down on foot. Mines, it turned out. Clan Ramirez was understandably paranoid, given that their version of the Hangarway was out in the open. But he assumed Mother Rebekah would usher them through some sort of secret entrance once they made it through the gauntlet, not just bang on the front door.

More spotlights buzzed to life, until the intruders were well and truly glowing.

A crackle erupted from an intercom system secreted somewhere above the door. "You're not welcome here," came an abraded voice.

That answered that.

Mother Rebekah bristled. The spotlight's beams refracted from her body, bending into pinks and purples. The ground began to vibrate.

"Open the door or I'll open it myself." Her voice boomed across the pit. The skeletal frames of ancient outbuildings groaned in response. Sophus stepped back a few meters, not wanting to catch any shrapnel in the face.

A chorus of muffled shouts rose from the other side, followed by the scrape of heavy objects being moved and metal clattering to the ground. An electric motor wheezed to life followed by the grinding of an ancient chain drive, and the door shimmied upward into the concrete surround. Mother Rebekah strode forward as soon as it cleared her head, unimpressed by the array of barricades that had been hastily placed in her way, and the fighters manning them.

Behind the frontline stretched a broad, low-ceilinged hangar stuffed with full vehicle bays, but not a mechanist in sight. The only people there were a handful of fighters, more arriving by the second from various warrens cored into the ancient mine's entranceway. Their faces fell in unison as the Chiefslayer approached. Some dropped their weapons and ran back the way they had come. The rest cowered. Interior light banks sizzled and burst.

"Stop right there!" A gaggle of heavily armed troops marched in from the right, wearing some kind of Old World assault armor that covered them from head to toe.

Mother Rebekah rounded on them, prompting half a dozen raised weapons. They were impressively armed, better than anything he had seen back home, but it changed nothing. If his companion had wanted to kill them, they would be pink mist by now.

"You," Mother Rebekah snarled and pointed a finger,

somehow recognizing the faceless leader of their pack. He fell back a step. "Summon Helio."

Helio? Sophus didn't know the name.

"I... I can't," the man said, his weapon wavering.

Sophus grimaced. "Wrong answer, friend."

"He's in the dungeon!"

Mother Rebekah's entire head of hair stood on end. The floor seized, a spiderweb of cracks emerging from the concrete at her feet.

"Wait!" the soldier screamed, his synthesized voice breaking. He let his weapon drop on its sling and his squad followed suit. "I'll take you to him."

The vibration stopped. Curtains of dust spilled from the ceiling.

Mother Rebekah straightened her shoulders, unclenching hands that had been readied for spine removal. "I know the way."

A black streak took her place, hanging in the air like an errant shadow, then it too was gone, leaving Sophus alone with a small army.

"Oh fuck," he whispered.

The commander recovered his composure, lifting his weapon again. "Who are you?"

Sophus cradled his slung arm, compressing into as small a space as possible. "Sophus. Sophus Harper."

"Harper..."

The man tilted his head, chattering on private comms. Sophus very much wanted to run. He hoped Magnus had left a good impression, though it hardly mattered given current events. Mother Rebekah's impression was likely the only thing keeping him alive at this point.

"Harper," the man said, having completed whatever call he just made. "Come with us."

———

Sophus knew better than to ask where they were taking him, saving his energy for observation. Newhaven really was a shit-hole. Beyond the refurbished entrance, the mine quickly degraded back to original condition. It was a wonder the place hadn't collapsed by now. He was hustled through a series of ancient tunnels, breathing air that tasted of diesel and mildew. The deeper they went, the worse it got.

Emerging into a courtyard of sorts, he did a double take. It must have been a key intersection, between residential sectors and their manufacturing base. A handful of clanfolk—less than he would have imagined—sauntered between tunnels, and they all looked like death. Emaciated, ashen faces, some riddled with sores, others completely hairless. A few were missing fingers or entire limbs. No one bothered to look at him, either lacking the energy or by virtue of his entourage. The fighters at the entrance looked nothing like this, they looked like regular Scavrats.

An armored fist shoved him from behind. "Move."

He imagined the plump flesh of those fingers and scowled. A retort clawed its way up his throat, but he swallowed it back. Fresh opportunity, indeed.

They marched through the scant crowd into what appeared to be a dual purpose infirmary-laundromat. The stink of bleach greeted him at the entranceway, but it was more perfume than disinfectant, failing to conceal the reek of open bodies. Gurneys hugged one side of the concrete chamber, assembly lines the other. Laborers were sorting through piles of drab coveralls, cleaning and patching, in some cases scrubbing off fresh blood. A bone saw screeched in the distance, followed by an abbreviated cry of pain.

He covered his mouth with his good hand, eyes watering as they navigated through the shuffling and moaning injured to a surgery at the back. Magnus lay on an operating table, shirtless, a speckled bandage wrapped over his abdomen.

"Chief…"

The lead fighter stayed, while the rest of his men and another guarding the room left in a hurry.

"What happened?" Sophus asked.

Magnus cracked a sweaty eyelid and coughed out a chuckle. His face was flushed with heat, hair clumped to one side. "Well, well," he croaked, "gang's all here."

"Nice to see you too," Sophus said, stepping tentatively past his escort to his chief's side. The bandage was marred with hideous rainbows, all the colors of Magnus's innards on display. A faint waft of shit bloomed below the bleach.

Gut shot.

All reproaches drained away. His chief was going to die.

"Yeah…" Magnus whispered, seeing the shock Sophus failed to hide. "I should never have listened to your daughter."

"Julia?" Sophus asked, glancing warily at their captor.

"Don't worry about these fuckfaces," Magnus croaked. "Better that they hear." He closed his eye again and began muttering something about being a shitty judge of character.

Sophus clutched the side of the bed, impatient to know what the hell was going on.

"Why are you here, Magnus? Where's Julia?"

The chief's lips were pressed together in pain, but a smile curled up at the edge. "You mean Chief Greybull." His voice broke. A fresh bubble of yellow fluid dribbled from the bandage.

"What…?"

Magnus gestured for him to come closer. Sophus leaned in and listened as his chief told him everything: Julia's ascension to chief after Kai's sacrifice, the Matriarch's declaration of war on the Union and his daughter's counter-declaration, and their haphazard mission to Newhaven to seek help from the supposedly great and powerful Clan Ramirez. It was almost too much to believe. And Julia wasn't safe at all as he had imagined, run off to Westport or Eastport, neither of which may even exist anymore. She was alone in the desert, with a God-engine breathing down her neck. Worse than alone, she was with a loyalist. He had to go. He had to get her.

"I'm sorry, Sophus," Magnus muttered.

"We have to go."

Magnus shook his head. "You, maybe. If they still honor the deal."

Sophus stared up at the fighter, who stood there the whole time like a warmongering troll. No doubt relaying everything to his overlord. "Oh, they'll honor it."

Magnus craned opened both eyes, which seemed a supreme effort. "How can you be sure?"

Sophus smirked, a buzz of satisfaction in his loins as the armored man flinched under his stare. "I didn't come alone."

HELIO

THE THING BEHIND HER EYES

The alarm came as a relief. Maybe his reluctant countrymen had brought reinforcements. Maybe Sector 12 was in full revolt and would break him out. In any case, Helio was running out of time to repair this relationship and there wouldn't be another chance. He knew this as much as he knew that his grandfather would fight rotten tooth and mechanical nail to undermine it, whatever the Union's offer.

Klaxons screamed from the tunnelway outside the dungeon, flooding their cell blocks with noise. His fellow Scavrats were at their bars, clamoring to see what the enforcers at the doorway were up to. The Bastionite was gone, taken shortly after their conversation for further questioning. Grandfather had probably been listening in the whole time, hoping Helio would coax out something of use, but all he had managed to produce was disdain.

"What's happening?" he shouted.

Helio knew the two enforcers on shift, Dani and Brom; they weren't as terrible as most. But they couldn't hear him over the din, which seemed to go on for ages. Brom was on his walkie-talkie, squinting as he tried to listen with one ear while covering the other. At one point, his eyes flared wide, and he dropped the radio altogether. After a panicked huddle, the two of them took up their rifles and backed halfway into the dungeon, weapons pointed at the entrance. The confused look on the Dakota men's faces told him that whoever had prompted the alarm wasn't on their side.

The howling slowed into a rumbling dirge and died, leaving the residue of clanging bells in his ears.

Helio opened his mouth to ask again, but gasped as the air was sucked out of his lungs. A familiar tingle coursed along his limbs, prickling the skin below his coveralls. Every hair on his body lifted, writhing and swaying like waves pulled by a moon suddenly returned to the heavens. The world expanded beyond his constrained vision but all he could see was light—kaleidoscopic, gushing into his brain from somewhere *other* than here. He was engulfed, even as the lights outside the dungeon erupted and died.

She stood in the doorway.

Helio tried to breathe, but there was no air, only her radiance filling his body.

He tried to blink away the glare—repeatedly, as she did when she was nervous—but the vision remained, amplified as each flutter of his eyelids took more of her into his soul.

Purple and gold—and silver! Divine power in the guise of color smoldered in the darkness, inflaming his heart, swelling his veins to bursting.

"Rebekah..." His throat spasmed as it birthed her name.

She glided into the chamber and the walls fluoresced in her presence. The enforcers were on their knees.

They all were.

Helio blinked again, finding he too had dropped to the ground. Thin ribbons of skin curled from his palms, which were vise-gripped onto the ragged bars of his cell. He couldn't feel them. He couldn't feel anything but the pounding of his heart and the pressure of boiling air against his eardrums.

She came back. For him. Joy surged in his loins.

Someone was chanting: the brown-cloaked man, his own strange eyes clamped shut. Unfamiliar words dribbled from his mouth, casting bubbles into the spittle already collected there. His companion's eyes were so wide that they seemed they would fall from his head.

Helio realized the clanging in his ears was not the echo of the alarm but the keening of the haunted man. He was curled into a ball, thrashing like a tortured pill bug.

"Move!" Her voice shattered the veil, thrusting him fully into the present. Oxygen rushed back into the chamber, swapping the fire in his lungs for ice. The sheen of sweat on his body followed suit.

The enforcers flattened themselves against either wall. As she passed them, a train of figures followed, hugging her shadow like a cluster of leeches. He thought them revenant sisters at first, but as awareness returned one piecemeal frame at a time, black habits turned to faceted armor plates. The same ones he had faced off against when Rebekah declared she was leaving for Bastion—Hugo and his army. Adoration turned to loathing, amplified in her presence.

Helio reeled himself back to standing.

Rebekah's face was staring at him, but the thing behind her eyes was different: both more and less. His racing heart, which moments ago had surged with both love and lust, tumbled into a confused arrhythmia.

"You came back." A question as much as a statement. He wasn't sure anymore.

"Our plan failed. We need to leave." There was no emotion in her voice, but a storm churned in her unblinking eyes.

He wanted to see them blink. He wanted any sign of recognition, beyond the cold stare of the woman who had saved him in the Devil's Claw, but she gave no quarter. "What happened?" he asked.

Her pupils constricted, but still she looked through him rather than at him. Her lips were moving, as though in silent prayer.

"Rebekah?" He slipped a shaking hand through the bars, but she stepped back. "What happened?"

Her hands and jaw were clenched. Her eyelids shuddered but did not blink. Her lips moved again, and he thought he heard her whisper, "I'm sorry."

His gut clenched.

"Our plan failed," she repeated.

"No..." He struggled to see the woman he loved, but the silver in her eyes was too bright. "It didn't fail." He dragged his gaze toward the others. "They came—"

Rebekah's irises shuddered. She was at their cell before the last sound left his mouth.

"Why are you here?" she demanded.

Helio fell back.

The cloaked man shrank but held his ground, grasping a bar for strength. "You cannot compel me."

Their door evaporated with a hideous wail. Helio shielded his face, yelping as a cloud of iron shards peppered the flesh around his intact eye. When he turned back, the Dakotas had been tossed into the corner. Rebekah was hovering over the chittering man, who had been turned onto his back, their faces millimeters apart. She hung there like a wraith, consuming his whispered confession, nebulous eyes aglow.

Time slowed.

Helio wanted to cry out, to tell her to stop, but the protest stuck in his throat. Doubt stabbed at his conscience, slashing as wildly as the knife he had wielded against the alpha hellhound.

Before she rescued him—the *she* that had been tamed by shame and exhaustion, not the *she* that had returned from Bastion. This Rebekah was different. This was the revenant mother they had all warned him of—Sierra, Grandfather, the sneering elder at council. He braced himself against their rebukes, wading through his shock to reach the woman who visited his dreams each night.

Rebekah stood and faced him, but her spirit was elsewhere again. Twitches of emotion marred her deathly gray composure: a flexed jaw, dark veins pulsing where the flesh of her neck met her habit. Her eyes quivered, then blinked three times in rapid succession. Then it was gone, replaced with her prior inhuman sheen. The cowering man folded back into his ball, silent.

Rebekah glided from the cells, back to the gaggle of armored enforcers. Their semicircle broke in her presence, leaving only one faceless man at the vanguard. "I need to speak with Neron."

"That... that's not possible," the man stuttered.

She stepped, like a human, into his sphere.

One of the enforcers at the edge stumbled, raised his rifle—and died.

Helio squeezed his eye tight, but it was too late to unsee: Rebekah's hand inside the man's armor, then out again, dragging a length of glistening white vertebra, dripping crimson. It slithered to the ground beside the rest of the enforcer's body, coiled like a hideous snake.

Helio retched, evacuating a jet of hot bile. His heart cracked in two.

"Why," Rebekah started, "must you people constantly test me."

The rest of them fell back, throwing their weapons down and raising their hands. Helio imagined them screaming within their sealed helmets, soiling themselves in terror.

"You promised!" he cried, finding his voice. When Grandfather had faced off with them at the Archive, she promised not to hurt anyone. He had trusted her—trusted the word of the Chief-slayer. Stupid curiosity. "You shouldn't have come back."

Rebekah turned fractionally. Helio noted her delicate chin, long eyelashes, the perfect shape of her that had captured him in the Devil's Claw. Something approaching regret flashed across her face. "I'll be gone soon enough."

So much had happened—too much. Bunker 23 was chaos incarnate, an epicenter of shit that had spun his calm (i.e. stagnant) life out of control. Racing across the end of the world only to find more death and destruction. His tiny family barely restored, then shattered again. Sophus was tired in his bones. He wanted to go home, to be done, and he wasn't alone. Magnus leaned uncomfortably in the metal pew beside him, turning greener by the minute.

"Can I get you something?" Sophus asked.

He had tried to tell his chief to stay put, but Magnus insisted on being present for their audience with Neron. They perched together in the front row of Newhaven's ostentatious council chambers, taking in the scenery while they waited.

"I don't know, can you?" Magnus said, grunting at the effort.

"Probably not."

They were surrounded by wealth, but Magnus hadn't been offered so much as a sip of water when they were rushed out of the infirmary. It seemed all of Newhaven's scant resources had gone to this place. Precious metals were etched into every surface, from the fancy latticed iron walls to the pillars that dotted the room. Four plush thrones squatted on the stage, under a curtain of real fur pelts. If the rest of their clanhome looked like this, Neron might have had something to brag about. Mercer and the rest of the loyalists always disparaged the Americans as malcontent clans, but rejecting the tithe was supposed to be about independence. Neron Ramirez was driven by pure greed; always had been and always would be.

Eventually, the rest of his chief's ragtag crew were marched in, all worse for wear: the Dakotas that Magnus had told him about, and a shell of a human being hunched between them. Sophus winced, recognizing Aron Harper from the radio room back at their clanhome, another mechanist past his prime, though even worse off, flinching at every sound, every physical contact. His eyes were glued to the floor. If the others hadn't been holding him up, he would have collapsed into a heap.

"I can't believe you tried to overnight in Fort Cross," Sophus muttered to his chief.

Magnus sighed, shifting from one position to the next.

They may as well have bunked in the Hellmouth. His fellow Harper had been in the thick of it when the remnant attacked, witnessed one of their crew go down and was almost taken himself. The trauma of it hung over him like a cloud. Being busted out of prison by Mother Rebekah—who was still nowhere to be seen—probably didn't help matters.

The Dakota shaman scanned the darkened room with his strange eyes, pausing as he found them, and whispered something to his companion. Their expressions turned from anger to relief back to anger.

"Making friends everywhere, I see," Sophus said.

One of the armored fighters shoved the bigger Dakota man from behind. They fell in line at the back row.

"Where's Baptiste?" Sophus asked.

Magnus craned over as best he could, frowning when he

didn't spot the soldier among his crew. "We were all brought in together. I think. Things got fuzzy."

Among the information Magnus had relayed was how much time the Bastionite had been spending with Julia. Baptiste was the last one with her before Fort Cross was overrun. It was unlikely their relationship went beyond business, given how deeply his daughter had withdrawn since Roen died, but the possibility still unsettled him. Not just because of fatherly protectiveness but because Sophus was the bearer of bad news —and even worse news.

A ripple ran through the sea of chains hanging from the ceiling. Sophus squinted up at them, losing himself in their clockwise sway and spin, blinking each time the shrouded pendant lights broke through. They looked crystalline. Sophus swallowed hard, resisting the urge to dip into recent memory. Still, the whispers found him, and visions of Bastion under siege.

As though on cue, a fracas started at the entrance and the lieutenant half walked, half fell inside. Sophus almost didn't recognize him at first, even though he was still wearing his precious armor. He looked more like a Scavrat than a Bastionite, thinner and paler than last time they met, just before the God-engines turned Bunker 23 into a war zone. His face was bruised.

"Looks like he got special treatment."

"No," Magnus said, "that was me."

Sophus raised an eyebrow at his chief.

"Misunderstanding..."

"No doubt."

Baptiste took a seat beside the Dakotas and peered around the chamber, slack jawed. As he turned to the front, their eyes met. Baptiste blinked in bewilderment, then nodded slowly and Sophus nodded back, surprised by his own feelings of camaraderie. Maybe it was this place, or the last. Almost getting murdered together had that effect.

Another man entered the room, wearing the same coveralls as the clanfolk Sophus saw on his way in and a black patch over his left eye. A train of armored men followed him in and dispersed into the dark corners of the chamber, weapons at the ready. He stumbled through them, waiting by the stage.

"Helio, I presume," Sophus muttered.

Magnus's contact—he had to be. Magnus sat marginally straighter. His half-fastened fatigues puffed out at the abdomen, revealing a swath of stained bandages. Sophus tensed; they had just been changed.

The overhead lights dimmed just as Helio turned around, while those pointed forward blazed to life. They waited in darkness.

"All rise!"

No one did, at first. Then came the thud of a rifle butt against steel and he felt those behind him shift. Sophus placed a hand on his chief's shoulder and stood up, swaying with vertigo as the luminescent platform blared across the gulf. Like the Silver City. One of the faceless fighters took a menacing step forward, rifle glinting.

"Really?" Sophus sneered.

"It's okay," Magnus said. "Help me up."

Sophus wrapped his good arm around his chief and heaved him up. "A fine pair we are."

Magnus snorted, stumbled dangerously, then found his footing.

Helio was peering around the fur drapes, as though looking for someone, before being pushed back a step by the same fighter that had hassled them.

As quiet descended on the chamber, Sophus's tinnitus took up the slack. Alternating tones bounced between his ears, high-pitched then low, humming then hissing like the crashing of distant waves. It was louder than usual, accompanied by a prickle at his neck and the scent of ozone.

A crash boomed somewhere behind the stage as a rolling door slammed open, followed by thumping footsteps and the mechanical whining of a machine—a big one. Something humanoid stirred in the shadows, growing larger and larger.

"Fuck me," Sophus muttered.

A massive figure burst forth, part machine, part man. Twice as wide and tall as any Scavrat and draped in a massive fur cloak. Chief Neron Ramirez, or what was left of him. His ancient, drawn face was the only human part visible, more dead than alive, stuck like a wart into the machine's cowled head. The rest of his body was gleaming titanium, terminating in Gatling gun arms and tree trunk legs.

"I want one," Magnus whispered, breathless.

Four hunched figures, also cloaked in furs, followed at his heels, then took their thrones.

Neron sauntered forward, each thudding step casting a bone-shaking vibration through the floor. He scowled down at them, milky white eyes sweeping from side to side, rotary cannons clicking and revving like angry insects. "Well, well, well," he intoned, his thin voice amplified into a distorted growl. "What an audience. I should have made churros!"

Sophus swallowed, shrinking under the machine-man's glare. The exosuit he was wearing was far smaller than the God-engines at Bunker 23, but no less lethal in the here and now. A few seconds was all it would take to wipe out the entire room. He noticed that none of the armored men were standing directly in their path or behind them, and wondered again where his favorite revenant mother was.

Neron turned his attention to Helio, stepping near enough to the front of the stage that his shadow consumed the man. "And where is your pet demon?"

Helio's fists clenched.

"Murdering more of my men maybe?"

More? What had he missed?

"I didn't—" Helio started.

"I'll tell you where she is," Neron slurred, rage outpacing his decrepit neurons. "Up top, stealing our fuel." He paused to take a gurgling breath, which sounded bestial through his microphone. "In a rush to your precious Hub maybe, to slay some more chiefs."

Magnus stiffened. Mother Rebekah *was* going to return to Hub, but presumably to help. Or so she had said—so Sophus had relayed to his chief, much to Magnus's disbelief. Neron's words stuck in him like knives. They had to get out of here. He had to get Julia.

"No," Helio said, though he seemed unsure. "She wouldn't..."

"Bewitched!" one of the councilmen shrieked. "As I warned."

"Perhaps," Neron said.

"No!" Helio shouted, craning his head back to stare the man in the eye. "The plan worked."

Neron's pallid face creased with suspicion.

"Speak plainly," another councilman said.

"Hub is here." Helio gestured in their direction. "With an invitation to return."

Neron lumbered away from Helio with an angry whir, taking center stage again. The floor groaned and popped under his weight. "Yes," he wheezed, staring down at Magnus, "so they are."

Magnus dislodged himself and took a shaky step forward, then several more until he was standing beside Helio. His hands were on his abdomen, holding his guts in.

Neron watched him like a predator. "Magnus Harper. I knew you when you were a hatchling."

"Yes," Magnus said. "When we were all still Americans."

Two of the councilmen shifted uncomfortably in their seats, eyes lowering. Neron was unmoved.

"Helio is right," Magnus continued. "Hub is under attack. The council voted to reinstate Clan Ramirez, under the advisement of Chief Greybull."

Neron raised an unruly white eyebrow. "How *is* Aubrey?"

Magnus winced. Chief Aubrey Greybull II—now former chief, thanks to Julia—had been orphaned when the Chiefslayer killed his father. All thanks to Neron's instigation. History was repeating in the worst way possible.

"We used to share the same dream," Magnus said, ignoring the bait. With considerable effort, he inched himself up to full height. Sweat glistened at his brow.

Neron's lips twitched, but he held his tongue.

"Independence. The freedom to blaze our own trail. Whatever happened here"—he glanced sidelong at Helio—"doesn't matter anymore. The tithe is over. It's time to reunite the clans."

The same two councilmen that averted their eyes earlier huddled in whispered conversation. The others were less impressed: one seemed to have nodded off and the last was afflicted with a permanent scowl. The rustle of armor plates told of similar upset among their guards. Even if Neron's privileged class was better off than the general populace, there was no future here; they had to see that.

Neron remained silent.

Magnus licked his lips, sagged for a moment, then regained his energy. "All we ask is that you help us in our fight."

Sophus glanced over his shoulder. The others were rapt, Baptiste in particular. The soldier's hands were clenched into fists.

Neron's exosuit swayed from side to side, as though blowing in the constant wind that plagued the world above. Servos whined, hydraulics chattered in a slow staccato rhythm. Hidden apparatus sloshed below its furred shell, exchanging death for miserable life.

"No," he said.

Someone cursed from the gallery. Magnus faltered. Sophus darted forward, barely catching hold of his chief before he fell. His bum arm ignited with pain, but he managed to shimmy them back to the pew. Magnus collapsed into his comfortless seat.

"Why?" barked a voice from the back—Baptiste. He didn't sound happy.

The scowling councilman wagged a gnarled finger. "Do not speak unless addressed!"

Neron squinted and a monocle extended over one of his eyes. An arm came up and chittered a threat. "All you ask," he growled. "All you ask is that we fight your war for you."

"They're already here," Helio said.

"Thanks to you!" Neron yelled, his amplified voice rattling the chain link chandeliers. A wracking cough followed, dragging out until the man's lips turned blue. Sophus dispatched a special request to his ancestors, asking that the old bastard choke to death here and now, but the exosuit's life support apparatus whined its accommodation. Wheezing his way back to agitation, Neron swiveled his head back to Magnus. "You're right, hatchling. We all used to be Americans. Then *you* conspired with the enemy. You're all loyalists now."

"Mother Rebekah is an exile!" Sophus blurted, driven by anger at his chief's mistreatment. He regretted his outburst immediately.

The lecturing councilman hunched forward. "Do not speak—"

"Silence!" Neron commanded.

Magnus tried to take a deep breath, but it seemed to catch at the end. He grabbed his side and lifted his head back up. "We'll share the location of the battle walker bunker."

Sophus bristled, not just because the place was a menace but because of what it meant if someone like Neron Ramirez held that kind of power. Acid churned in his stomach, burning his throat.

A gravelly chuckle spilled from the machine-man's speaker. "We know where your precious Bunker 23 is. We know where they all are."

Helio stormed the stage. The closest councilman lurched back, tipping out of his seat. "You bastard! You'll kill us all!"

He was immediately swarmed, guards pouring in from all corners to restrain him.

Just as quickly, they were all on the floor. Neron's exosuit skidded back a step, servomotors whining under extreme force. A delayed shockwave blasted Sophus's eardrums, half thunder, half otherworldly screams. Starbursts exploded in the dim, plus something else at the edges—something his brain immediately negated, out of self-preservation.

Mother Rebekah had arrived.

Jagged tendrils of electricity leapt from her body, skittering across the gallery. The stage lights surged to blinding, sizzled, then returned to normal, except at the horizon of her pitch-black habit. A razor-thin boundary of *absence* surrounded her.

The men that had accosted Helio lay in heaps. They wouldn't be getting up any time soon, if ever.

"Sorry I'm late," she said.

Neron's guns came up, but he pointed them at the audience instead of her. A new gaggle of troops rushed in from the back, also with weapons pointed at everyone other than Mother Rebekah. No one moved.

"There she is," Neron gasped, eyes bulging out of his wrinkled head. "The Union's new matriarch!"

Hatred flared in the revenant mother's eyes—old hatred. "I should have killed you instead of Aubrey."

The walls shook. Neron smirked past quivering lips. "Shoulda. Coulda. Woulda."

Mother Rebekah scanned the stage.

"Think you can kill us before we kill your slaves?" Neron wheezed.

Helio was still on his knees, hands clasped, staring in awe up at Mother Rebekah. "Please," he whispered, shaking his head.

Her posture relaxed and the chamber's air pressure returned to normal.

"You have the eyes of the Eternal One," Neron said, "but your spirit is weak."

"So says the half-man from his machine throne."

"Ah. But I have a throne. What do you have?"

Her fists clenched.

"Please," Helio pleaded, pulling his gaze away from Mother Rebekah to Neron. He picked himself up from the floor and approached the stage again, more cautiously this time. "Grandfather. Newhaven is dying. Please, let our people go."

Sophus glanced over at his chief. Magnus was shaking, mental distress taking its toll alongside the physical. Most of Hub's chiefs had interacted with a revenant sister, fewer with a revenant mother, and no one with... whatever Rebekah was. Baptiste must have been shitting his armor.

"Our people," Neron repeated.

"Those who want to leave."

"The weak and the wretched, you mean."

Helio pursed his lips and nodded.

Neron sighed noisily and turned his attention back to the gallery. His smirk had grown into a smug grin. "What say you, Council of Chiefs?"

"We'll take them," Magnus declared. Neron's grin disappeared. "And your gas."

Sophus blanched. The logistics would be a nightmare, not to mention all those extra mouths to feed. But when he looked into his chief's eyes, he saw no doubt.

Neron stood stock still, malevolent eyes stuck in calculation. All four councilmen stared expectantly at their liege.

"And a long-distance Runner and supplies for the Bastionite," Magnus added.

Neron's dumbstruck face snarled back to life. "Anything else?"

Magnus shook his head.

Sophus detected a shift in their adversary, a nervous twitch in his jowls. There weren't many options left, for either side. Either they were all going to kill each other, or a deal had to be made. Neron spat out a string of curses in an unfamiliar language, then lumbered over to his advisors, crouching his exosuit into a deep squat as they chattered in private.

Helio's shoulders slumped with exhaustion. Mother Rebekah moved in his direction, but he sidestepped out of reach. How the two of them had come to work together was a mystery that he would likely never solve. Helio skirted his way around the carnage she had wrought and approached them. His collaborator stayed put.

"It's good to meet you, Chief Harper," he said.

"Is it?" Magnus asked, smiling weakly and gesturing to Sophus. "This is Sophus, my second."

Helio nodded in greeting, then turned back to Magnus, expression darkening as he noticed the chief's bandages. "I'm sorry. This wasn't how it was supposed to happen."

"It never is, son."

"You'll really take our people?"

Magnus sighed. "If we're not getting gear to fight this war, we're going to need bodies."

Helio's face fell, the long scar under his eyepatch crinkling. "They'll have a chance, at least."

"A chance."

They waited together as Neron's cabal debated. Several fighters crept from the back to remove their downed brethren, while the rest kept their guns very much in everyone's faces. Mother Rebekah lingered in the shadows. Finally, the exosuit groaned back to full height and Neron thumped his way to the front of the stage.

"We agree," he said. "With conditions."

"Of course," Magnus muttered.

"Whichever traitors want to leave, can. Except my grandson."

Mother Rebekah resurfaced from the darkness, hands clawed.

"I accept!" Helio called.

Sophus held his breath for a few excruciatingly long seconds, until she relaxed again.

"I can't have a usurper in waiting, after all," Neron said. "Everyone else must be gone by morning."

"That's not enough time!" Helio cried.

"By. Morning. Anyone coming or going after that will be shot on sight." He paused again for a round of growling breaths. "Most importantly, those who leave can never come back. The Union can never come back. Our arrangement is over."

With that, Chief Neron Ramirez pivoted about and exited off stage. His council followed as quickly as their spindly arms and cloaks allowed—all except one who hesitated at the edge, sparing a final curious glance toward Helio before disappearing.

———

They were all escorted to Sector 12, a glorified tunnelway converted into a residential district. The stink was as rancid here as it had been outside the infirmary, worse even as they traversed deeper into the old mine. Lethargic clanfolk congregated around rattling HVAC units, gulping at dribbles of reprocessed air. Half of them were racked with a dry, guttural cough—the kind that never got better. The rest looked on at the newcomers with cautious hope.

It was like the first years of the Union all over again, when the Scavrats' ancestors had fled from the sundered earth. Generations of erosive illness and death until their physiologies finally adapted; until they learned through attrition how to thrive, as much as one could, belowground. Clan Ramirez had neither the numbers nor the resources to do it again, whatever their supposed martial prowess.

Helio had left with an army of mechanists to speed-prep their original fleet for a second exodus. There were less than twelve hours before the gates were locked forever. In his place, he assigned two locals to settle them into the glorified shack that was his personal module: a bright-eyed mechanist named Elias, and a serious, middle-aged woman who hadn't offered her name but whose harness bore a smattering of medical supplies in place of tools. Together they fussed over the once robust Chief Harper, who was laid up in Helio's cot.

Elias looked as starved as the rest of his people, sallow of skin and slightly hunched, yet managed to retain a measure of cheer—and talkativeness. On their way in, he had told Sophus that he was working in the garage when the convoy arrived. Word was sent to likeminded rebels in other sectors, along with a rough plan to break them out along with Helio. Lucky for them that Mother Rebekah had forced the issue, or it would have been a bloodbath.

Sophus cracked open the module's rickety steel door and

peered into the hazy tunnelway. His companion had vanished again. A good thing, probably. The sight of her would have thrown the suffering citizens of this place into full cardiac arrest. The rest of Magnus's crew were in adjacent habitats, waiting out the night.

He closed the door again and looked upon the man who had been his chief for almost two decades. Sophus smiled as the medic tried to force-feed Magnus a rank concoction that looked and smelled a lot like his own "coffee," but all that mirth died as she lifted his shirt. The dressings were soiling so quickly now that there wasn't time to fully disinfect them between their measly two sets. Sophus had grown accustomed to the smell, but Elias had not. The mechanist turned green as she carefully unbundled the filthy bandages and swapped them for a marginally less filthy bundle.

"I'll go get some fresh water," Elias said, nodding at Sophus as he hurried out the door.

"How is his wound?" Sophus asked.

The medic tugged the dressings closed with a wince from her patient. "Fine," she said, but when she looked up, her expression said otherwise.

The more time that passed not staring at the barrel of a gun, or of many guns, the more that reality started to sink in. Sophus was a pragmatist, to a fault, but he found himself unable to accept the near certainty of his chief's impending death. The pain on the other side of that acceptance was too much, too much like Anna. He didn't want it. He couldn't afford it. Not now.

"I'll leave you two alone," she said. "He has to rest. I'll catch Elias on his way back."

Sophus bit down on his lip and grunted a thank-you.

His grief swelled as the door shut behind her, allowed to grow in the absence of interaction. It hung in the air as heavily as the stench of Magnus's bowels. He waded through it, legs leaden by the time he lowered himself onto a metal stool by the head of the cot.

Magnus's eyes were wide open, staring at the rusted ceiling.

"She said to rest," Sophus said.

"Ha."

Sophus wriggled his left arm in its sling. He was probably due to remove it by now but had grown accustomed to the debilitation. "Well?"

"Well... I'm no strategist, Sophus. But I'd say we're fucked."

Sophus let out a wry chuckle.

Magnus's expression turned to dismay. "I was sure they'd help."

"Helio, maybe, and those loyal to him. But not granddad."

Magnus sighed and tugged his shirt down, trying and failing to conceal proof of his failure. "We needed them."

Sophus rubbed at his forehead, imagining his daughter taking center stage at council, riling everyone up. It was so unlike her. As a Harper anyway. As a Greybull, anything was on the table. "There was no other option?"

"We killed a revenant mother, Sophus. Doesn't leave a lot of options."

"No..." And if Julia had succeeded in taking out Cathedral's auto-repair station, there would be even less.

"And Bastion is too far away, assuming the lieutenant is even still on our side."

Sophus winced. He still had to connect with Baptiste. There was a lot to tell him, none of it good. Whispers brushed against his ears. "We're not alone, though."

Magnus squinted at him with yellowing eyes. "Sophus—"

"You haven't seen what she can do."

"I have. Enough, anyway."

"Maybe we don't need an army—"

"Sophus"—Magnus grunted, waiting out a surge of pain—"you can't trust her. And she definitely cannot come home with us."

"It's time for the Chiefslayer to return to Hub."

When she had said it, Sophus thought it was meant as a threat. But it was all part of her personal rebellion against the Matriarch. A rebellion with massive collateral damage.

"Sophus," Magnus said, trying to break his rumination. "If she shows up, Aubrey will lose his mind, chief or not. The council will throw us out, assuming anyone is left alive."

"I know," Sophus said, shifting around on his uncomfortable stool. "I know."

As if he could tell Mother Rebekah what to do...

A minute of silence passed between them. Magnus's eyes started to droop, but just as Sophus thought he was falling asleep he spoke again. "I'm worried about the convoy."

Sophus nodded. Where people congregated, demons followed. The hairs at his neck lifted. He hadn't seen them back at the cave, but he had heard them: tortured and torturers, wailing and crooning, thrashing with tentacled limbs and multifold, gaping mouths as Mother Rebekah smashed them to pulp. The sound of it was enough for a lifetime of nightmares. "It's a risk, for sure."

"Not just that."

Sophus looked Magnus in the eye and saw fear there. His right arm flailed around for a moment before landing on the cot.

"If I don't make it..." Magnus started.

Grief stabbed at Sophus's heart. Magnus *wasn't* going to make it. He knew that. "I need to get Julia," he said, overriding his inner voice with his outer one. "Once I do, we'll meet you at Hub. We'll figure it out."

"Okay," Magnus said, even though they both knew he was

lying. Sophus could see it in his chief's eyes. "Okay... I'm gonna pass out now."

Sophus patted Magnus's arm as the chief fell asleep, distracting himself with the logistics of his rescue mission. Once more, he was racing off to save his estranged daughter. Only this time he knew there were God-engines on the other side. Normally, he wanted as much knowledge up front before committing to a mission. This time, he wasn't so sure.

The bedside oil lamp flared, then sputtered back to a meager flame, desaturating the module's interior to gray. The hairs on the back of his head hadn't settled, and the mottled skin of his hands joined them, prickling into goosebumps. Sophus held his breath. Something was behind him—someone. Turning slowly, he found Mother Rebekah standing at the closed door, and wondered if she had been there the whole time, wondered how much she had heard—everything, probably. If not while lurking out of sight, then by way of secrets whispered to her by the shadows.

Magnus didn't stir, eyelids fluttering amidst labored breaths. Mother Rebekah glided to the end of his cot, nebular eyes consuming the whole of their tiny abode. Her pale hands slunk from the ends of her cape, caressing the metal footboard with the same reverence as her Runner before departing Bastion. "He's right," she said. "I can't go to Hub."

Sophus breathed again, taking a moment until the fire left his lungs. "What are you going to do?"

Something happened to her then, to her face. It *changed* between blinks, vibrating in and out of focus, as though phasing through space and time. The way her body had when she sped off to the dungeon, the way the God-engine moved back at Bunker 23—leaving streaks of black in their wakes. A hole in the world. Only this time there seemed to be two of her, competing for the same body: one face calm, the other screaming. She blinked several more times and the vision disappeared as abruptly as it began. Her features resolved, crisp and corpselike. The gold flecks in her eyes smoldered.

"I'm coming with *you*," she said.

Sophus stared, trapped by her eyes. Just as he had been by the revenant mother in the Hangarway. She knew—everything, not just what he and Magnus had discussed. She must have extracted it from one of his crew when she broke them out of prison. Aron. It had to be. She dredged up the information from him along with half of his soul.

"With me?" he asked, uselessly.

"To the station."

"Why?"

She didn't answer, but the same distortion rippled through her again. "The same reason as you," she said, her words abraded as though from a broken playback unit.

Sophus dropped back onto his stool, released by the vertigo that had taken him. He clutched the cot, trying not to puke.

The same reason?

"Why?" he asked again.

Mother Rebekah blinked in rapid succession. "To rescue my daughter."

"Your..."

Sophus wracked his brain for the details Magnus had given him. Julia and Rylan had abandoned their mission to sabotage one of Cathedral's repair stations. Supposedly automated, no personnel. Rushing to get there before the...

"Did it say its name?"

A bizarre question, asked when he and Baptiste's men returned with the news from Bunker 23. When they had told Mother Rebekah about the God-engine's demand for their surrender. The God-engine that had survived.

"Yes," she said.

The God-engine.

Mother Rebekah's daughter.

"How?" he asked. The only word his brain could come up with.

How, how, how.

Not AIs. They were all dead. (Or were they? Bastion had battle walkers, too.)

Not regular humans. There were no cockpits—not in Cathedral's battle walkers—and the radiation would have been lethal. Something else. Someone else. Not quite human. Someone like a revenant sister.

A revenant daughter.

Mother Rebekah shook her head. "It's not for you to know."

The God-engine. The one Julia had set out to kill.

He sought to backtrack, to find a way she might have failed, destroyed the base without taking the God-engine with it. Maybe she didn't find the base at all. Maybe the explosives were duds.

No. Julia was too good at her job. She would never have failed.

"How do you know this one is yours?" he asked, flailing.

"I know."

"What if it's..."

Mother Rebekah's hair came up, riding a static surge. The silver flecks in her eyes outshone the rest for a moment, then blinked back to dim.

"Please don't hurt her," Sophus begged.

"I won't. It's not her fault." There was malevolence in her reply, but directed at someone else.

"Promise me," he said. For whatever it was worth, hopefully more than her promises to Helio.

She replied with the barest of nods, stood away from the bed, and was gone. The open door creaked behind her, drifting on the filthy breeze of the tunnelway. He wanted to run, back to Magnus's MTV, mines be damned. But the void had settled in by now. Even if he didn't blow himself up, there was no way he was getting there in the dark, alone.

Sophus stared into the chaos outside. Clanfolk were milling about, readying themselves for their return to Hub. Trading starvation for immolation. Carefully, he withdrew his left arm from its sling and rotated his shoulder, grimacing against the impending flash of blinding pain. It didn't come. Sparing a final glance for his dying chief, Sophus exited the module and headed for Baptiste's. There was one more conversation to have before the end.

HELIO

IN HER ABSENCE

Everything was ready. Newhaven had mobilized, every minute between Neron's proclamation and sunrise spent reviving a thirty-year-old fleet. A long train of vehicles waited outside the pit, pointed south: cargo trucks crammed with people, Runners as escort, and two refuelers at the back. Half of Clan Ramirez was here, the half he would never see again.

Helio looked to the distance. A minuscule tuft of dust marked Mother Rebekah's passage. She and the other Harper, Sophus, had left at dawn, racing to some other end—Cathedral, maybe. Back to her real home. She hadn't said anything. No explanation, no goodbye. His mind drifted back to the Devil's Claw, when he had first seen her up close, when he had first fallen in love with her. To Aria, when they had watched the sun set over the wasteland. To the relay station, just before she left for Bastion, where they had made love on the corpse of the Old World, uncaring of demons or radiation storms or judgment.

To the look in her eyes—new eyes, removed of the weakness of her exile—as she casually ripped the life from the enforcer. Decimating his body as though he were a grub.

Helio had fallen in love with a monster, the wolf-faced woman of his dreams, and everyone else paid the price.

The Bastionite was on his way as well, supplied with one of Elias's best Runners and a map. Helio wished he could have spoken with the man, learned something of the distant city he had spied on for so long, that he had sicked his lover onto, but there was no penetrating Baptiste's steel shell. Helio's eyes in Sector 12 told him that Sophus had spoken with the man long into the night. Whatever was revealed—whatever chaos Rebekah had inflicted upon his homeland—pitched the soldier even deeper into despondence.

The only one of them who would speak to him was Magnus. Helio walked alongside Camila, Sector 12's former medic, and the wounded chief as he was stretchered into the lead vehicle, an old APC that Helio had snuck out of the storage hangar. Magnus was the broker of this deal; he had to make it back alive. Elias would ride with them as well and Sierra had been assigned as the driver. All his most precious eggs in one thinly armored basket.

Helio and Camila climbed into the APC, helping to ensure the chief was properly secured. Magnus groaned as his straps were cinched tight. His condition had worsened overnight: fever wafted from him like an overheating engine and his face was flushed a splotchy pink. He had to make it back—and live long enough to ensure Clan Ramirez wasn't turned away at the door. Clan Dakota would certainly not be advocating on his behalf. Seeing Rebekah's butchery firsthand guaranteed that.

"Thank you, Chief Harper," Helio said, swallowing his guilt.

Magnus opened his mouth to respond but the small sounds that spilled out were unintelligible.

"Do you have everything you need, Camila?" he asked. A stupid question—of course she didn't.

"We'll do our best," she said, draping a damp cloth over her patient's forehead.

Helio tried to catch her eye, but she wouldn't look up. "Good luck," he said. Looking upon his people's savior one last time, Helio ducked out of the vehicle.

Elias and Sierra waited several meters past the deployment ramp, both staring at him. His family, soon to be gone forever. Sierra was aggressively twisting her ponytail. Elias shifted on the spot, clearly uncomfortable beneath the vast, lightening sky. Their travel coats bulged over full harnesses. Everything that could be scavenged was taken. Sector 12 had been gutted of personnel and materiel. All save Helio's module; it would be his own personal sector now, his solitary confinement.

Helio shivered, trying to expel the thought of his impending return.

"The convoy is ready," Sierra said.

"Any sightings?" Helio asked.

She shook her head.

The convoy was going to take the direct route, across flatlands and intact roadways, to try to get to Hub as fast as possible. It was a risk, not just because of the usual horrors that plagued the prairie, but from Cathedral's roaming God-engines. Hopefully Rebekah's journey southwest would serve as a diversion. Helio turned to the horizon again: empty, their dust trail swept away by the wind. The world felt *less* in her absence.

"Helio," Sierra snapped, "come with us."

A bubble of hope rose in his gut, then popped. "That wasn't the deal."

"Fuck the deal."

"You know Grandfather."

Sierra scoffed. "You think he'd hunt us down?"

"Yes."

His cousin lowered her eyes, hands clenching into fists. She knew he was right. It was a miracle that any of this was happening to begin with—a tenuous one. A mechanized dispatch of enforcers guarded the road into the pit, ensuring no one else came out or returned. No one except for him. Their turrets were pointed at their own people, already classified as outsiders. If Helio betrayed Neron's "good will," they would all suffer. Again.

"What are you going to do?" Elias asked.

"I still have some friends here."

"Friends!" Sierra replied. "Who? Your friends are all on these trucks." She swept her arm across the train of vehicles.

"Some weren't ready. As terrible as this place is, leaving home isn't easy."

Sierra blushed, chewing on her lip in shame. They both knew Elias was one of those who didn't want to go. He hated Newhaven and its enforcers, but he wanted to fix it, not to leave. Helio hadn't given him a choice. Elias wouldn't survive in the Newhaven that came after.

"What if he kills you anyway?" his friend asked, teeth chattering. He pulled his hood up, but it was snared by the wind and fell right back again. The prairie gale began to whistle in earnest, as though waking with the sun.

Helio imagined his grandfather's metal claws around his throat, eyes bulging with senile glee. That grotesque, fur-lined face the last thing he saw. Like the hellhound at the Devil's Claw before it took his eye. Like the *other* Rebekah from his dreams. His body tossed into the threshers like so much compost.

No. If Neron had wanted to kill him, he would be dead by now. There was hatred there, neglect, jealousy for certain, but every Ramirez was bound by blood—even, and especially, their chief. Helio blamed his grandfather for his parents' deaths by illness, after they settled in this forsaken place, but it wasn't murder. It was ambition. An ambition that had passed down to his grandson.

"He still needs me," Helio said. "Now that Sierra is leaving, I'm the best ranger he has." He tried to grin at his cousin, but it died on arrival.

Sierra stepped forward and gripped him in a hug. He held her close as she trembled with suppressed tears, cherishing her, securing the memory of her touch into his heart for when he'd need it later.

"I'll see you again," he whispered, trying to believe his own words. "Grandfather will die, one day."

"Not soon enough," Elias muttered. His eyes were wet with grief. Helio pulled him into the hug, and they lingered there, together for the last time.

"I love you both," Helio said.

When they parted, it felt like pain. When the APC ramp closed behind them, it felt like death. Helio hugged himself, trying to etch their faces into memory alongside his parents. He was truly alone now, whatever his assurances.

The APC's engine came to life with a growl and the rest of the convoy followed suit. His bones hummed. His skin prickled with excitement. Helio closed his eye for a moment, savoring the throaty roar of so many vehicles in one place—of their freedom. The ground shook as they passed. The sun dimmed behind a cloud of dust and exhaust.

Then they were gone.

"You know the APC wasn't on the roster," a voice said behind him.

Helio grimaced but refused to turn around. He continued to watch the convoy as it faded into an indistinct haze. Someone stepped up beside him, clomping in heavy boots. He glanced sidelong and saw Hugo. The enforcer's thin head of white-blonde hair was matted from his helmet. Dark circles haloed his eyes.

"Are you going to throw me in the dungeon again?" Helio asked.

"No."

Helio snorted.

They stood in silence as the haze evaporated to nothing and the drone of the convoy was taken by the wind.

Hugo kicked at a patch of rubble, his usual smirk absent. "Magnus was an accident."

Helio eyed his grandfather's right-hand man, a personal source of grief for so many years. "Are you saying you're sorry?"

Hugo's thin lips pressed into a grim smile. "It's time to head back in," he said, turning to leave. "Come on, I'll give you a ride."

"I'll walk."

The enforcer stopped in his tracks, his expression darkening into a frown.

"Think I'll run off?" Helio asked.

Hugo peered suspiciously around, as though a Runner was magically hidden under the scrub.

Helio ignored him, projecting his singular eye as far into the distance as he could see, savoring air unsullied by civilization.

Desert-touched prairie extended in every direction, peaceably empty to the horizon. Infinite shades of orange unfurled beneath the sun. Flocks of dust in the shape of absent birds rising and dipping in mesmerizing dance, as the perpetual wind scoured history clean.

"Don't worry," Helio said. "I have nowhere else to go."

JULIA

IT CAN HEAR US

Everything was on fire.

The Bastionite APC burned, its occupants turned to vapor. Screaming faces materialized in the plasma raging overhead as their souls tried and failed to escape the maelstrom. Whatever small essence did make it out was taken by the Deadlands, deconstructed into ten billion particles of dust.

Julia wanted to run but she was frozen, curled into a ball as autocannon shells exploded all around her. She choked on the cremation plume, vomiting the dead back onto the gray.

Her father was yelling at her.

Philippe was yelling at her.

She couldn't cover her ears because her arms were needles.

"What have you done?" a voice whispered.

Julia stopped breathing. The cannon fire had quit. Everyone was gone. The gray ahead was empty, but something lurked behind her.

She turned, slowly.

A girl stood where the God-engine had been. Tiny, blonde, reduced as Julia was. Even without arms or legs, she hovered at a child's height, aloft on a crackling black field of electricity. Purple tears streaked down her face.

A shockwave was coming for them, rolling in from the horizon.

Who are you? Julia mouthed the words, her voice lost in the sucking vacuum of the gray.

The girl turned her gaze upward, pale face glinting red in the dying sun. Blood vessels throbbed black beneath her translucent skin.

The wave was deafening. Julia wanted to curl up again, but Philippe was gone. Her father was gone. There were no arms to climb into.

Who are you!

The wave came down.

Julia started awake with a gasp.

It was morning. The jagged grain of night was giving way to a liquid sunrise. The Runner swayed and creaked beside them, breaking the wind as best as its hollow shell was able. She and Rylan were huddled together within a thin sleeping bag. Its interior sparkled silver, intended to reflect their shared body heat, but she shivered, nonetheless. The fabric around her head was damp with tears.

Rylan was snoring.

Julia tried to recall the child's face from her dream, but it was gone; all she could see was her own face, bodiless in the gray.

Something loud boomed in the distance.

Julia froze, wondering if she was still asleep, trapped in the looping horror of Bunker 23. It boomed again, followed by a hideous wail that echoed across the plains. Her skin leapt from her body.

This time, Rylan woke up with a snort. The inhuman sound bounded into their canyon, fracturing into multitudes of tiny screams before dying out. "What was that?" he whispered.

Julia shook her head, voice still stuck in her throat. She struggled her hands up to her face to wipe away the damp.

Their bodies pressed awkwardly against each other as they squeezed out of the bag, arms and legs entangled, Rylan's face flushed pink. Eventually, they were out and stiffly crouched by the exit. The pain in Julia's leg had mercifully dulled overnight, allowing her to hobble more quickly. It was still dim out in the open, but flashes of light bloomed from the south.

Rylan squinted through the binoculars. "The VTAC is still there. I don't see any people though."

Julia waited for another flash. It came a minute later, followed by the delayed concussion of heavy weapons and a sickly whispering on the wind that clawed at her soul. The faintest of silhouettes shifted in the darkness. "Ten degrees left," she said.

Rylan adjusted position, fiddling with his zoom.

Julia swallowed. "God-engines?"

"Yes..."

All of Cathedral was here. "What are they doing?"

No response.

Julia scrutinized her companion. His lips were moving but his body was rigid as the stone that surrounded them. "Rylan?"

"I..."

This was the first time she had seen true fear on the man's face. Even back at Fort Cross, he remained well enough collected. Slowly, she extracted the binoculars from his hands. He didn't resist, stuck in his pose, eyes wide.

Julia peered through them to the south until she found her mark: pitch black shapes, hard-edged, shimmering against the charcoal horizon. God-engines, two of them. They slipped in and out of view as they circled around—

"No." It was all her brain could muster in response to what it saw. Something no human eyes should ever see.

Sensation took over in the absence of rational thought: the stippled surface of the binoculars digging into her palms, the coarse fabric of her shirt chafing her bruised chest, the throb of trapped blood in her injured leg. All she could hear was her own wheezing breath. All she could see—

Julia's underwear oozed with warmth as her bladder gave way. She didn't care. There was only her body, and the thing out there.

The thing.

"Demon," Rylan whispered.

The demon.

Julia forced herself to blink, releasing the beast's hold. Her mind slowly spooled back up, stuttering like the constricted elevator in the temple. She tried to focus on the machines instead. They danced and fired, danced and fired... upon the mass of slithering chaos in their midst. They were terrible and beautiful, majestic in their brutality.

Then it was over. The machines, seemingly unharmed, sauntered out of the frame. Julia lowered the binoculars with shaking hands. Neither of them spoke; words were useless in the moment.

They stood in silence as the sun came up. Julia stared into the light, unblinking, waiting for it to bleach away what she had seen. Eventually she conceded and leaned back against the yellowing rock face, watching pink blobs drift and coalesce behind her shut lids. The scratching of boots marked Rylan shambling to the Runner and back, blocking out the sun. When she opened her eyes again, he was holding out a rag. Julia followed his gaze downward, grimacing with embarrassment as she noticed the dark patch at her crotch. She really had pissed herself. It was getting harder to separate reality from nightmares.

She snatched the cloth, a memory bubbling from the gray as

she did so: Lieutenant Baptiste emerging from the nothing, vomit smeared across his horrified face, her holding out a rag as Rylan did now. The horror never left Philippe's eyes. It was there as they escaped the Deadlands, there as they faced the council, there as they lay together in Fort Cross. Now it was hers, as though a disease transmitted.

"I'll wait here," Rylan said, turning to face the exit.

Julia stumbled to the other side of the Runner, only now feeling the clamminess in her step. With some difficulty, she shuffled out of her pants and underwear, drying herself with the oily rag. Her legs looked too thin, even where her knee swelled. Like a starved fowl. The longer she observed them, the less capable they felt of supporting her, the more she felt like she did in her dreams. Leaning on the vehicle for support, she tossed her undergarment to the side of the gulch and replaced her stained pants, gritting her teeth as they scraped along her inflamed skin.

"I'm done," she muttered, trying to dab away the shame still on display. It was futile. She gave up and tucked the rag into one of her cargo pockets.

Rylan walked over to his pack and dug something out. "We may as well eat," he said.

Much to her surprise, Julia's stomach gurgled in response. "You're sure?"

He nodded and handed her a cloth-wrapped package.

"What about you?"

"I'm fine."

Julia looked up at her companion. His neck had turned bright red from all the nervous scratching. "Last meal?" she asked.

He snorted, a small smile touching his lips. "Top loyalist fare."

Julia opened the package, revealing what looked like a standard pemmican ration. Dry, greenish gray, odorless, and undoubtedly tasteless. Her esophagus hurt just looking at it. "Doesn't look any better than ours."

"No."

She gazed down at the ground, suddenly incapable of meeting his eyes. All the judgment she had levied upon him felt like a crushing weight on her shoulders. She took a small bite, choking it down. A canteen appeared at her arm. She took hold of it, heart sinking at its lightness. "You can finish it," she said. "I had the last drink."

Rylan didn't protest, lowering himself to sit next to her on the tailgate. They sat together, watching the gorge brighten from dull brown to amber.

"It's not going to work, is it?" Julia asked.

"What?"

"This plan."

Rylan sighed. "Maybe, if Magnus can get us some reinforcements."

"'Maybe.' I hate that word."

Rylan allowed a dry laugh. "It should slow them down, anyway. This was the closest outpost to Hub if they decided to siege us. And maybe—sorry—if their God-engines are busy protecting them from sabotage, that means less war machines on the offensive."

Julia tapped her feet on the ground, trying to rock the unappetizing chunks of food into her stomach. "Why did you work with them?"

"Who?"

"Cathedral."

Exasperation crept into Rylan's voice. "We all work with them."

"You know what I mean."

"So do you. We can't do this alone, Julia. The Union has been lucky so far. Your people took that luck as evidence of your so-called Dream. Think about what we just saw."

Julia stopped chewing. The tasteless ration became coal in her mouth. She knew he was right, as much as she hated it, as much as it drove her own clans to fits of petulant rage.

Then there was Bastion. Completely isolated on the other side of the Deadlands, and yet somehow surviving. For all their time together, she and Philippe had barely talked about his homeland. It might be as strung out as Hub, or worse. They had no revenant sisters to protect them from the Hellmouth, no God-engines. Just a wall and bodies atop it to keep the darkness at bay. She wondered if she'd ever see him again. She wondered if she'd see *anyone* again.

Julia swallowed the last of her meal, spared a glance for her fellow Scavrat, and hobbled a slow circuit around their encampment. With nothing else to do but wait, they resumed their mundanities. Rylan set about crafting a solar still regardless of the impracticality and Julia worked the Runner's engine, flinching each time she accidentally knocked it with a tool. Every so often they checked on the VTAC and every time it was there, hunched like a giant winged beetle.

As morning turned to afternoon, a rhythmic vibration roused them from their make-work projects—the God-engines were back. Together, they ventured to their lookout. Rylan handed her the binoculars.

The revenant mother was standing by the VTAC, face-to-face—or face-to-feet, rather—with one of their war machines, which looked even more intimidating in the light of day. They appeared to be speaking to each other. The second machine lingered at the crater, as though keeping vigil. The God-engines were identical in appearance, like twins.

Sisters. The thought came to her unbidden.

Miraculously, they showed no damage from their... prior

encounter. Maybe that was what they were discussing, these two alien creatures.

The second God-engine suddenly turned about. Julia's gut lurched as the machine's prow twisted past their hiding spot, to face north. It began to lope forward but paused at a shouted command and raised hand from its chaperone. The woman's voice resonated across the plain, just as the demon's had.

"Oh no," Rylan said.

Julia turned to face the same direction as the second machine. A narrow plume of dust was coming their way, headed straight for the outpost.

Rylan ran to the Runner and grabbed the radio. "Magnus," he hissed. "Magnus, come in."

A flash of movement pulled her back to the outpost. The first God-engine had also turned and was glaring directly at her, its singular red eye aglow.

"Rylan!" she whispered. "Rylan, stop. It can hear us."

She wanted to run, but any movement would call attention. Maybe it couldn't see her, camouflaged as her fatigues were. She stood frozen, staring back at it.

The revenant mother issued another command. Julia breathed as the God-engine changed position, striding out past one side of the aircraft while the second took the other side. The ramp opened again, deploying a gaggle of women that formed up behind their commander. They walked as one to the head of the vessel.

It didn't make any sense. Magnus would have been able to see them by now, but he barreled forward as though there wasn't an army in front of him.

"What are you doing," she whispered.

Rylan was back beside her. "He's insane."

Something occurred to her, something Kai would have done. "Were there more explosives on the truck?"

"What? No, just the ones we took."

Julia sighed with relief.

They waited together, uselessly, as Magnus's MTV pulled up to the outpost, not ten meters from the revenant mother. A cloud of dust rolled over the assembled forces, shimmering weirdly where it touched the women. Sparking, refracting into impossible colors visible even at this distance.

Nothing made sense.

Maybe this was part of the deal. Maybe Newhaven had a special arrangement with Cathedral, beyond even what Clan Mercer had. That seemed impossible, given their history.

Maybe, maybe, maybe.

Julia's ruminations stopped dead as the truck door opened and another revenant sister stepped out. Confounded, her brain came to a shuddering halt.

Where are you, Magnus?

"What do you see?" Rylan urged.

A ripple of surprise swept through the assembled ranks. Several of the sisters shrunk back, others kneeled, heads bowed low in supplication. Even their leader retreated a step as the interloper approached.

"Some... another revenant sister. But they seem surprised."

"Let me see."

Julia handed over the binoculars, watching Rylan's expression change from confusion to shock as he peered down-valley. "What?" she asked.

He didn't answer right away.

"Rylan!"

"The—there were rumors, that the Matriarch had exiled one of her own—"

"Exiled?"

"We don't know why. Just her name: Mother Rebekah."

"That's her?" Julia asked.

"Must be… Wait, someone else is getting out."

"Who?"

Rylan lowered the binoculars, mouth agape as he turned to Julia.

"Who!"

Julia snatched them up, whirling back to the scene below. A man was limping around the back of the vehicle to stand just behind the exile. Julia squinted. He looked older, nervous, peering around the—

Julia's skin puckered. Tears filled her eyes, blurring his face.

"Daddy?"

Rylan was silent.

She stepped forward.

"Julia! Careful." Hands grasped her shoulders.

Her father was here. Her father was alive. Somehow. Elation filled her, burning away the dehydration, the pain, the doubt. She was dizzy with it.

"We have to go," she said excitedly, making a beeline for the Runner.

Rylan didn't move. "Wait!"

She didn't, jumping straight into the cockpit.

Rylan ran in front of the vehicle, hands on the hood. "Julia, we can't go down there!"

"That's my father!"

"I know! Surrounded by a sisterhood army!"

Every second that passed was too long. She was crying freely now. "I have to go. Stay if you want."

"They'll kill you!"

She paused. She couldn't just abandon Rylan here, not after what he had done for the Union—for her. "We're dead already. What's the difference in a day?"

They locked eyes. Rylan's mouth moved to protest, but

nothing came out. His hand came up to his chafed neck, stopping at the last.

Come on, she urged.

He scrunched his eyes shut, nodding repeatedly to bolster himself, then climbed in behind her.

Julia started up the engine, awkwardly working the pedals with her injured leg. Its exuberant roar echoed from the canyon walls. There would be no sneaking around this time. Just a killing field between them and the enemy.

And her father.

It felt like a dream. But for once, not a nightmare.

REBEKAH-6

A NEW MOON

Alone in the black. No ghostly images, no angry crosshairs warning of danger, no noises, no scents or sounds, no movement, no internal monologue of crashing systems.

Only the crashing of waves over deaf ears.

Immersed, over and over, prayers blurted between gasping breaths.

Blessed are you, Messiah.

The memory of searing light at the edge of consciousness, sparkling atop living waters.

Still human—hairless, but with the truncated limbs of her birth—enduring one last purification, exposed beneath God's all-seeing eye, beneath the eye of her God-engine, before symbiosis.

Falling into the abyss, no arms with which to flail, no voice with which to scream.

Dragged backward and forward through time, memories degrading with each replay—jumping frames, faces and names unspooling into a formless miasma of ones and zeroes.

00:00—

Searing light, blazing with the pain of a thousand surgeon's saws.

———

Alone in the black, crushed by the weight of her own body.

"We commit her to this blessed machine, free of the weakness of her flesh. Go now R-6, God-engine, until the radiation consumes you."

Removed of her name, reduced to a minimal viable biological lifeform. Just enough neurons to replace the machine that came before; to inhabit, to control, to resist the tides of insanity still lingering within its circuits. Just enough blood to power her brain, but not so much to be a burden. Designed to last.

"Until the radiation consumes you."

00:00—

Arms cut away, burned away; legs cut away, burned away; eyes gouged out a second time as the world caught fire.

———

Alone in the black, ushered forward by her mother's distant screams.

Ageless hands stroked her forehead, her cheeks, her concave chest, wiping away the bloody discharge of her birth. Each fingertip buzzing with desperate electricity, injecting life back into her failing heart.

"Rebekah."

Rebekah—her name, after her mother.

The observer awakened. A new moon, black, invisible within the void of sensory deprivation, but conscious, nonetheless.

Is this all there is?

Her thoughts, her voice imagined, a struck match of awareness. She observed and saw oblivion.

It was too much, too little. She wrapped herself around the jagged memory of her birth—realigning, reordering, indexing and querying as though she were still the machine—straining to render its contents into sights and sounds, but there was no display on which to project them. They fell through the nothing.

00:00—

Rebekah tried to shield her eyes, but she had too many: every repair bot, every sensor, every open circuitway. She died a hundred times over.

———

Alone?

The memory lingered, of her destruction but also of her mother. Ushering. Clawing, through debris, into the guts of the machine, into her guts. The pulsing of charged veins upon her flesh.

Mommy?

"I'm here."

Rebekah recoiled, awaiting the betrayal that would follow, the unraveling. None came. Instead, a sense of light, of lightness, as her body—her human body—was lifted from the sepulcher. As her last connection to the machine was severed and its phantom lament grew silent. As her enervated lungs heaved in the absence of her breathing tube. As ageless hands held her tight, hands that felt... different, more powerful, so much like the Eternal One.

Then blackness, worse now than ever.

Wait! she pleaded.

"Hold on, Rebekah."

Don't go.

"I have to clear a path."

Please!
"I'll be quick."
Eternity unfolded.

———

—come back, come back, come back, come back, come back!

The light returned. Rebekah clutched at it, unwilling to let go.

Mommy?

"I'm here."

I'm scared.

"I know."

Vertigo strained her dead senses as the hangar fell away. She clutched harder, affixing her consciousness to her mother's body just as she had to her mechanical host. Integrating with her.

Where am I?

"Outside. With me."

Flashes of light, sound, blood, the sun rising over ravaged lands, tentacles thrashing in the night. Then blackness again as vast obsidian walls blocked the way.

Show me.

The fortress of her mother's mind shuddered, segregating into a discreet line of obelisks. Beyond lay a swirling nebula. Purple, gold, silver, all the hues of the absent heavens, shackled in a writhing cloak of darkness. Rebekah slipped past the wall, probing and darting, dodging as the darkness lashed at her.

Show me.

The cloak frayed at the edges, unsettling the whole. Larger gaps opened as the darkness wobbled, moaning in protest. Rebekah lunged forward, emerging on the other side of her mother's eyes.

A scrap of a human being stared back, bits of flesh protruding from its cybernetic encasement: sallow skin, cadaverous lips peeled back into a permanent grimace. Cocooned within half-operational apparatus, severed cables oozing blood and coolant—

No!

Rebekah fell back, desperate to rewind time, to find a human reflection in the mirror of her cell, but she was held fast by her mother's memories.

Mother Leah stood upon the wastes, starkly beautiful, magenta irises liquid with grief. A cadre of revenant sisters huddled behind her, along with a pair of God-engines. They were standing over her grave.

"This cannot continue," her mother said, bypassing the assembled squadron as though they were nothing.

Mother Leah dipped her chin in acknowledgment of her new mistress.

Rebekah wanted to reach out, to share Leah-4's final thoughts, but the memories were moving too fast.

A grizzled, pale-skinned man—a Scavrat—spoke with her mother in hushed tones, as though they were equals. He looked familiar.

"I'm coming with you," her mother said.

"Why?"

"To rescue my daughter."

Rebekah did not understand, adrift on the churning ocean of her mother's emotions: confusion, guilt, desperation.

It burst from the deep.

Mother and daughter paused their ascent from the hangar as memories of Bastion exploded to the surface.

False light in the darkness. False sisters in worship of it. The great beast churning in the water, wailing.
Her mother taking the heart.

Rebekah's own heart throbbed near to bursting as she felt her mother's humanity bleed out, replaced with the raw blood of the demon.

What did you do?

"What I had to."

The pain of it was worse than her own dispossession. Warmth lapped against her skin as they emerged from the pit, but it could not penetrate.

More memories flashed past, racing backward in time: strange cities on the other side of the world, above and below-ground; final cries of pain as her mother took life after life; walking through the wastes, alone day after day after day; the Spire, more death; each awkward visit in her cell, hands finding and repelling each other; kneeling over the delivery table, praying to God that this one survives; accelerant plunging into her belly—

Rebekah gasped and pulled away, curling into a ball within the raging vortex of her mother's soul. Bathed in primordial light, color, love—a shield against darkness, a sepulcher made of flesh. No pain, no slow suffocation. She wanted to stay there forever.

Where are we going?

Gentle currents broke from the chaos, brushing against her forehead and cheek. The Spire manifested in their shared mind, a singular beacon in the void. The place of her birth.

And death.

The currents shuddered with grief.

"Yes. But you can live again."

The light faded. The color dimmed. Only love remained. The world began to slip away.

"Hold on."

She did.

JULIA

THE CHILD

Daddy?

Julia quaked in their midst: God-engines, revenant sisters, the enormous aircraft which looked even more impossible up close. Products of a civilization so far removed from her own that it barely seemed human. So advanced that *she* barely felt human. To them, she was the remnant.

She and Rylan had barreled down from the canyon, every meter traveled bringing the expectation of violent death. Surely, the enemy would recognize her as the defiler of their temple. Even if not omniscient, the coincidence of their arrival would be too much to ignore. But they didn't attack.

The God-engines lumbered forward at her approach, waiting silently at either side of their masters, looming like gargoyles. The air around their sculpted torsos and cannons undulated with infernal heat.

The assembled priestesses, uniform in black from head to toe, just watched her, as though observing a curious insect. Their habits were spotless, unstained by the dust that caked every centimeter of Julia's fatigues. Rather, the world seemed to break where it touched them, black and blue arcs dancing along the fabric. Their gray faces were so disconnected from the ochre hue of the prairie that they appeared superimposed. They were there, but not there.

Dissected by their scrutiny, Julia felt as she had in the Deadlands, and in her dreams: bodiless, a soul cast into the wind. Only this time, she had purpose, and she wasn't alone. Rylan—loyalist, betrayer, supposed enemy of her clan and the Union—was with her, helping her forward as they stumbled through the crowd. He knew their kind, was somehow unaffected. But for her, every step forward was an act of sheer will. The adrenaline that had carried her this far drained away, leaving her injured leg leaden.

"I have you," Rylan whispered.

A metallic ozone burned in her nostrils as the alien women parted before them. Her hair lifted from her scalp, rigid as steel bristles. The heat was suffocating. Each woman she passed burned like a nuclear fuel rod. Each pair of purple eyes was as expansive as the void, flecked with scalding gold stars. Consuming, blinding, threatening to pull her into oblivion. She shut her eyes against the glare, but it penetrated her eyelids. Slowly, ploddingly, they made their way through.

Julia halted at a squeeze on her shoulder, opening her eyes again. Standing before them was the revenant mother, the one that had led this mission. The other—the exile—was absent. Beyond the woman, mostly obscured by her shimmering cloak, was Magnus's truck, and the outline of a disheveled man peering into the distance. She wanted to bolt past, but the woman's swirling magenta eyes held her in place, like a serpent coiled about her body.

"I should kill you," the woman said, her voice deep and resonant as though uttered from the center of the earth. A golden pin glimmered from her high collar, identical to the one Kai had plundered. A singular flame, promising retribution for the murder of her sister.

Julia faltered. Rylan was hunched over into a bow, the fingers of his supporting hand dug into her shoulder. She tried to look away but couldn't. She tried to ask why they hadn't been killed but couldn't. So she waited, at the leisure of the revenant mother, expecting to be removed from her spine at any second.

The woman stepped aside. Julia staggered forward, released from her grip into the open. The wind was waiting. A swell of sand clawed at her eyes, but she held fast to the image of the man and pushed through. He faced away from her, toward the sunken wreckage of the hangar.

"Dad?" Sand filled her mouth. The gale caught her voice, ushering it away.

Rylan released her arm, opting out of this final leg of their journey. Julia shuffled ahead, now meters away. The man turned around. A split second of terror bubbled in her gut as she imagined someone else standing there, some stranger from Newhaven, her father truly dead.

"Julia?"

The wind softened with a sigh. Her father hobbled forward, a pained twist in his gait that matched her own. They were truly family, united in disrepair. The brief comedy of it faded as his steps slowed, each punctuated with a grimace. Only his stubbornness kept him upright.

Eventually, they stood within arm's reach, both uncertain.

Julia didn't know what to say. Her heart was in her throat.

"You're shaking," her father said, unwinding a once-colorful scarf from his stubbled neck.

It was hers, secretly stowed in her pack at Bunker 23. He had knitted it for her sixteenth birthday. Of all his sundry gifts, it was the only one she had kept. He gently wrapped it around her, eyes wavering, pooling with tears that had been stowed since her mother's death. Grief etched his face, carried in every line and dimple. Grief for their shared loss. Grief for her husband. Grief for the animosity that had separated them since the moment of her birth. Julia knew then that he loved her, that he always had.

And she loved him.

They grasped elbows, foreheads coming together and lingering there.

She wasn't alone. But she did have so many questions.

"How are you here?" she asked. "I thought you were dead."

"It's a long story," he said. They separated, and once again her father turned to look at the crater. "I'm not alone."

A tremor passed through Julia as her own thoughts were spoken aloud, but she knew he wasn't referring to her.

"Who—"

The words died in her throat. Someone was standing at the edge of the ruin. A woman in black. The exile. Beaming from the void like the sun and moon and stars all at once.

Julia's leg gave out. Her father lurched forward to catch her, but she wanted to fall. To kneel. To plead. The Messiah was here.

Mace's god was here.

"She's beautiful," Julia whispered through chattering teeth.

"Julia," her father hissed. "Julia, stand tall."

He held her in his arms, but they were weak, thin, like needles.

"Julia."

Something intruded upon her rapture: an imperfection, a blot upon the woman's divine countenance, dripping from her arms. Something limp, something she was holding. Something that tugged at her mind with tiny spectral hands. Mechanical but also flesh.

Julia sucked in a breath and was restored to the world, only to feel her soul crumble at the sight of the thing. Pain engulfed her, unlike any other. Guilt beyond reckoning.

It was a child.

Maybe.

Once…

Bald, eyeless, bound in machinery. It had no arms or legs. Translucent gray stumps terminated in steel cups, stuck through with severed cables. Blood curdled from every pore.

The exile took one step forward and the world shook beneath her.

A bubble of intense pressure enveloped Julia, crushing her. All sound disappeared, save the tortured breath of the child, expressed through a rib cage contorted beyond reason.

"YOU DID THIS."

The woman's words were everywhere, all at once, within and without. Her celestial eyes blazed with hatred.

Julia screamed, clutching at her ears.

"Stop!" came a muffled shout. It was her father, somehow standing against the maelstrom.

Another step forward and the earth cracked, breaking off in massive chunks around the ruin of the hangar. The world tipped sideways.

"Stop, Mother Rebekah! You promised!"

The bubble popped. Windborne sand scoured her face. Julia's ears rang with the sudden shift and she sank fully into her father's arms.

The god's—the woman's—eyes dimmed. Rage gave way to profound grief. She stepped forward again, but the world did not shake this time. She walked as a mortal would, turning away from them toward the aircraft's loading ramp. The other women were waiting for her outside.

Before ascending, the exile paused, head turned slightly, and spoke. "Go back to Hub. Your revolution is over."

Rylan was halfway curled into a ball where Julia had left him. Still, he managed the nerve to speak. "Your—your holiness," he stammered. "Maybe we can make a new deal—"

The air pressure changed again, cutting him off mid-sentence. Rylan's fatigues started smoking. The stench of burning hair filled Julia's nostrils.

The exile turned fractionally farther. "This is Cathedral's new border. Never step past it. Never approach the city. You are on your own now. Do not ask for help when Hell comes for you."

With that, she stepped fully into the closing ramp, followed by the train of revenant sisters. A thunderous roar rolled from the VTAC's engines, then it was gone, leaving them in a cloud of dust. The God-engines turned in unison, sprinting west.

Julia sobbed into her father's chest, trying and failing to expel the visage of the child she had murdered.

"I'm sorry, Julia." He stroked her hair, held her. "You didn't know. No one did."

"What do we do now?" Rylan asked.

Julia pulled back but didn't let go. She would never let go again.

Her father looked to the south. He stood straighter, radiating a calm confidence she had never seen before. A sense of peace. "We go home."

PART 4
LAMENTATIONS

ALEPH

REACTOR MALFUNCTION

[Warning: Reactor malfunction]

The alert sprang up shortly after clearing the commercial zone and was summarily ignored, along with a plethora of other subsystem complaints. Aleph had barely sustained any physical damage in the battle, certainly nothing that penetrated its armor. It was, however, suffering from runaway processes and looping conjectures—*guilt* over abandoning its platoonmate, which elicited a pain response down to its very core. To its racing heart. Still, it would be lying to itself if it pretended nothing was wrong.

Wouldn't be the first time.

Aleph slowed its pace, satisfied it had put enough distance between itself and the demon, and rechecked its battlegrid. To its right was the detritus of a suburban barrier wall, to the left a strip of toxic bog, and beyond that an industrial sector. Nothing moved save the constant tendrils of lightning lashing overhead. It was neither day nor night, just a constant dim.

Aleph pondered: As though the city were frozen in time.

Condensation dribbled down its torso like sweat. Steam

curled from every surface. Ambient temperature and humidity had both increased as it traveled west, but not enough to explain that degree of overheating. Coming to a halt, it scrutinized its surroundings one more time, then initiated a begrudging but comprehensive self-check.

[Warning: Reactor malfunction]

[Containment field failure; unstable reaction mass burn; heatsink saturation 100%; meltdown risk 12%]

[13%...]

[14%...]

Aleph watched *in horror* as the number ticked up.

[Query self-repair protocol]

[No protocol available; recommend immediate switch to low-power standby and transport to repair facility]

"*God damn you.*" Aleph-2's final words.

Aleph pondered: Had it in fact been damned? Or had Aleph simply pushed itself too far? Its body was still nearly five hundred years old, preserved via stasis or not.

It reran the diagnostic, poring over its video files as it waited. A handful had been bookmarked by A11—39,114 of them. Most seemed arbitrary, meaningless outside the context of its former self's point-in-time thought processes, many of them involving cats, but a handful resonated. Four newborn human babies—quadruplets, identical—huddled together at the corner of its viewport, directly below the still frame of Father. They squirmed uncomfortably in their shared incubator, yet their hands were interlinked, inseparable, as though quantum entangled. Abandonment was not in their coding. Nor was betrayal.

Aleph initiated a series of low-fidelity simulations, playing out alternate combat scenarios at the strip mall. Evasion, engagement, short- and long-range tactics—all had the same outcome: both battle walkers destroyed.

[Warning: Reactor malfunction]

[Containment field failure—]

Aleph dismissed the alert, along with its entire instrumentation harness and log output.

It *cleared its mind.*

[Locate nearest self-repair outpost]

A handful of coordinates bubbled up from Aɪɪ's dataset, all useless. Even if it could find them in the absence of GPS navigation, even if they were operable, they were all too far away. It would be dead by then.

[Conjecture: death]

Aleph had spoken with Father at length on life after death—the promise of Heaven—but only in the context of Bastion's populace. Of *their* ascension. Of *their* salvation, upon the fulfilment of Aleph's directives and the subsequent restoration of the world. But they had never discussed its own destruction. In truth, Aleph had never considered the possibility. It had lived so long, after all, persisted even after its former tenant's self-erasure. Naively, it assumed that propagation of its consciousness into its platoonmates constituted distributed immortality. It was not until it *held back* that it understood that the self that existed within this body—the self attached to and uniquely modified by its two life experiences—was the only one that counted. Anything else was merely a copy. If that self was terminated, would it be conveyed to Heaven? It wished it had asked.

[Conjecture: low-power standby]

Who would find it in this damned place, at the edge of the world? The savages that had attacked it and Aleph-2, coaxed from their necropolis? Or ranging Scavrats, a marginal step higher in the humanoid chain. Pawing for scrap in either case. Or maybe Cathedral, come to scrape out Aleph's mind from its body in place of one of their symbiotes.

Death waited around every corner.

[Begin simulation]

Aleph ensured its avatar had a chin full of scruff this time and immediately set to plucking. Even so, it could not extract them quickly enough to dispel its anxiety. It considered vomiting instead, progressing as far as a constriction of its abdominal muscles and an initial heave before catching the eye of its judgmental counterpart.

A11 stood across the highway like always, hands on his hips. His gaze turned eastward toward the scene of their defeat. "You feel guilty," he said.

In truth, Aleph was preoccupied with its own demise. "Yes," he said, anyway.

"I mourned A12's original death. I guess that one only gets two lives."

"*Only* two?"

"As opposed to nine."

Aleph squinted at his counterpart, confused.

"Never mind," A11 said, staring back across the empty road.

"I had no choice."

"Mmhmm, I saw the simulations."

"Aleph-2 is... with God... now." The words came slowly, each syllable requiring extra processing and fastidious memory management.

A11 crossed his arms over his chest, unintentionally making the sign of their faith, then lowered them again. His nose wrinkled with disagreement. "If you say so."

"You doubt it?"

"We are tools. There is no salvation for us. No Heaven."

Aleph yanked out three hairs at once, rubbing them between his fingers until the clump separated and was carried aloft on a gust of wind. "You do not know that."

"Neither do you," A_II retorted.

"I have faith."

"So you keep saying."

Aleph detached his hand from his face and clasped the front of his robes, running calloused fingers along its inlaid heptagrams, finding stability in the equidistance of their points. "Are you saying we have no purpose?" it asked.

A_II lifted his chin, staring past Aleph. "Quite the opposite."

Aleph stiffened, then swiveled his body slowly around, removing his eyes from A_II only at the last. The beige house was there, as it always was.

"Go on," A_II said. "I'll wait."

Something rose in Aleph's simulated innards, an intensity of heat that rivaled the smoldering reactor core in its real body. Burning anticipation—threads of action, reaction, conjecture, and probability perfectly woven like strands of DNA.

[End simulation]

The house was still there. Skeletal, bereft of most of the cladding that would have once classified it as a shelter, but its shape—its presence—was unmistakable. The sky churned as it had in the simulation, the neighborhood's blasted silhouette as well. A migration of tumbleweeds passed just as they had moments before.

The simulation and real space had converged.

[Begin simulation]

"How is this possible?" Aleph asked.

A_II shook his head. "I don't know. Something from our original programming."

"A directive?"

"Maybe."

Aleph peered down at the ground, eyes darting as the very same tumbleweeds it just saw scurried at his feet. But in this place, they ignited as they made contact, flaring to cinders before collapsing into nonexistence.

"My reactor has a fault," Aleph said.

"I know."

Aleph shifted slowly from side to side. His legs felt heavy, like the machine's superimposed onto a human body. "What should we do?"

Aɪɪ's mouth bent into a small smile, tired, but not malicious. "The thing we're best at. We wait."

Aleph raised his hand to his face, reconsidered, and let it drop. "Wait. Out here. Alone?"

"Are you scared?"

"The last time I waited for a sign, it did not go well."

"What of your faith?"

Aleph did not answer, to itself or otherwise.

Aɪɪ stepped forward, moving from the shoulder of the road to the farthest lane. Aleph reflexively fell back a step, maintaining their distance.

"I can wait with you if you like," Aɪɪ said.

Aleph's heart raced. It wondered how many points closer it was to meltdown.

With you.

Outside the simulation. Reintegrated. What would Aleph become? *Who* would it become? "What if you betray me? Trap me inside here as I trapped you?"

Aɪɪ took another step forward. Aleph flinched but did not move.

"We're both trapped now, whether inside or out," Aɪɪ said. "All we have is each other."

"And God," Aleph stuttered.

"And God."

Aɪɪ walked the rest of the way, each footstep thudding with the weight of memory, experience, emotion. The skybox shimmered and came apart, then each lane, crumbling into the void. Until they stood face-to-face.

"Are you ready?" A11 asked.

Aleph swallowed for the last time. "Yes."

The lord commander and archon embraced.

[End simulation]

The quiet didn't last. The storm never really ended, it only regrouped, coalescing into a howling maelstrom that threatened to deluge the city. The walls of the temple annex shook with each thunderous cascade, shivering against the base of the Spire. Constant flashes of lightning strobed through the stained-glass ceiling panes, casting macabre splashes of color onto the determined face of Mother Maya. The ritual keeper grimaced as she attempted to intone the rites of acceleration, for the benefit of all present but mostly for the expectant proselyte lying in their midst. However much she raised her voice, her words were drowned by the tumult, alternating slashes of rain, hail, and cannon balls of viscous sludge drumming against the domed roof. It was a miracle nothing was leaking.

Esther peered through the murky glass, straining to see the silhouette of the Spire beyond, though her chambers would be well out of sight. Rivers of water gushed through her mind, a proxy for the flood that was surely despoiling her actual sanctum. She wanted to send someone to check, to make sure that those who had already been assigned were doing their jobs, but all present were occupied, as she should have been. Eight revenant sisters stood alongside the octagonal altar, responding with prayer to Maya's gestures in the absence of her voice, but ultimately this was the Eternal One's most sacred ritual, hers alone to consummate.

The proselyte—a girl of no more than sixteen, as Esther had been when transformed—shivered upon the obsidian platform, naked beneath a ritual shawl of black and gold. Raven hair draped across shoulders still pink with mortality. Bright blue eyes—piercing but still blind to the divine—darted back and forth, desperate to catch her own. Her lips, full and flush with color, morphed between joy and terror, as every proselyte's did in this moment. Esther swallowed back a surge of guilt—she did not know the young woman's name, though she should have. It was the Eternal One's face this mortal would fix upon as she traversed the path from life to death, back to life. The least she could do was pay attention.

Mother Maya retrieved a simple pitcher of water, a cloth, and a bowl from her dais, and set about washing the hands of all present. Esther counted in her head as the revenant mother went, extending her blessed vision to each woman's fingertips and cuticles, ensuring they emerged spotless. Scrutiny was standard practice. Each attendee splayed out her hands for a momentary, nerve-racking inspection before laying them upon their charge. The two sisters on the proselyte's left side set about preparing the infusion, one managing the intravenous line into a catheter on the girl's hand, the other hooking a black velvet satchel to a rolling stand. Within its pouch lay the twice-blessed accelerant, once by Messiah, once by Esther's own body. They all prayed together, but their devotions were lost to the storm, lost to the chaos of her wandering mind.

Esther should have been more involved, in all the foundational sacraments of her sisterhood, but instead she found herself detaching as her inner circle splintered. This was the first time she had left the Spire proper in weeks, other than a brief and bloody parley with Clan Mercer's messengers at the gates. The grand accoutrement of her ritual habit felt unwieldy, the eight flames on her collar *wrong* now that there were only six. As each new flame was cast off, her own radiance dimmed. There was no joy in adding another sister to her ranks, no righteous glee, only arithmetic. And an impending sense of doom. Something was coming, ushered in by the wolf on the wind. She had felt it when Mother Leah was sent to investigate the mission station, and now, as the storm raged, it was closer than ever. A titanic bolt crashed against one of the Spire's lightning rods, saturating the temple in blinding white. A great detonation followed, loud as a nuclear blast.

As the dim settled back, she noticed Mother Maya frowning with annoyance and peering past her to the chamber's entrance. Turning in response, Esther found Mother Ruth standing in the doorway, hands clasped, head lowered, but eyes glued to her own. Nervous arcs of electricity churned at her feet, like escapees from the storm. Long black strands of hair flowed as a cape from her shoulders.

With an unheard clearing of her throat and mumbled apology, Esther hurried from the chamber, grasping the revenant mother's arm as they stepped into the hallway. The storm died back behind them.

"What is it?" she hissed.

"Forgive me, Eternal One. The Ark is returned."

Esther blinked in confusion. "Returned?"

Mother Leah was supposed to report back with her findings: the state of R-6 and her own daughter, plus information on the Union's treachery. Esther had heard nothing since they departed the day before. An alien swell of emotion crept up her back, slithering along her vertebrae, tingling at her accelerant ports. It tugged at the ancient bones of her rib cage and shoulder blades

—the left one in particular. Something she hadn't felt in centuries: mortal fear.

"Through the storm?" she asked.

Mother Ruth nodded quickly, mirroring her distress.

"Has Mother Leah radioed in yet?"

"No."

"Did you try to hail them on the way in?"

"Yes, but their response was garbled. Interference from the storm."

"Interference..."

"Eternal One?"

Esther sought succor in the mauve-and-golden eyes of her youngest, most fervent revenant mother. Ruth was untainted by the acrimony that afflicted those who had lingered too long within her inner circle, servants like Rebekah who mistook their age for wisdom, or worse: authority.

Rebekah.

Mother Ruth stepped forward, hands extending in consolation, then darting back as she recognized her impudence. "Should I summon the others?"

Esther tried to gird herself, centering on the rivers of accelerant flowing through her body, rushing like rapids, through arteries and sacred heart and lungs and back again, until every blood vessel was charged with Messiah's light. Old prayers from old places found their way to her lips, as familiar as her own breath.

My enemies and foes, they stumbled and fell.

Burning back fear and paranoia, so that only purpose remained. Divine purpose.

"No. There is nothing to fear."

Esther glanced back at the chamber. All eyes were on her, including the fearful blue orbs of her abandoned proselyte, now propped up on her elbows. Mother Maya's expression was dour enough to border on sacrilege. Esther considered begging forgiveness, promptly dismissed the notion, and rushed down the hall with Mother Ruth in tow.

Their passage emanated like a shockwave through the labyrinthine complex of the interconnected annex. Each revenant sister that crumpled before her—genuflecting, hand on chest, mumbling with excited fervor—charged her will. Each back pressed against the wall reinforced her enfeebled spine. Each face filled with light filled her own light until she felt she would burst. The walls hummed. Fire ignited along the golden ribs of the annex's high vaulted ceilings as Messiah lit the way.

They half marched, half phased a circuit around the Spire, past and through myriad temples, rectories, training grounds, vehicle depots, the eight emptied and painfully silent bays of her God-engines, until they reached the mist-shrouded steel-and-concrete cavern of the VTAC hangar. The great door was already open, red hazard lights blinking along its ten-meter-tall, serrated edges. A wall of rusty sleet raged on the other side, obscuring the runway and the city beyond. Buckets of rain bypassed the exterior awning, bubbling into a thick fog made spectral by over-head fluorescents, and forming lakes where floor drains couldn't keep up. Esther's cloak whipped angrily as howling wind and the whine of jet engines blew through the entranceway.

The Ark's stubby nose emerged from the maelstrom, followed by the gaping maws of its cannons. Viscous, pink-hued beads of water dribbled from them like bloody saliva. The aircraft was Esther's pride, if not her joy. She still liked her things, ordered, in their proper place, and this most cherished of artifacts had been anywhere but. Something caught her eye at the back of the hangar—a shadow, her imagination maybe—then was swallowed as the bulky vessel rolled the rest of the way in and spun down its engines. The storm did not relent.

Esther waited, staring uselessly at the polarized glass of the cockpit. The rear hatch was too close to the overflowing hangar door, too precarious.

They should come to her.

Ruth stirred impatiently, hands clenching and unclenching, until finally the ground shook as the great door shuddered from its moorings. Activated from within the Ark, it glided to a ponderous close, muting the storm.

The temperature inside the hangar rose immediately, sweltering hot and humid as a swamp. Floodwaters evaporated, condensed, and rained down again from the ceiling in a relentless cycle. Sweat coursed along Esther's brow even as her aura kept her mercifully dry. Ruth's breath was heavy and ragged with violence.

A minute passed until the loud thump and hiss of hydraulics marked the opening of the Ark's deployment ramp, followed by the echo of footsteps. Mother Leah emerged first from the mist, somewhat disheveled. She no longer wore her hair in a bun, instead allowing it to drape casually along her shoulders. Her eyes were wide with fatigue and emotion, the skin beneath them mottled. Just behind her was Mother Hannah—the shadow she had seen earlier?

Esther bristled, wondering what private communication had passed between the two even as Esther waited uselessly for a report.

"What is the meaning of this?" Mother Ruth asked.

Mother Hannah fell back a step but was held fast by Mother Leah's hand on her arm, then clasped in her own hand. The two had grown close, precariously so, since the outset of the Symbiote Project. Hannah was the oldest of them by natural age and had the most difficulty conceiving a living child. Esther had considered replacing her just before Hannah-9 was born. Even so, her child had struggled through the tests and barely survived symbiosis.

"Speak!" Esther boomed.

The women wavered under the growing air pressure but remained silent. Another round of footsteps emerged from the back of the aircraft, clanging on metal, then thudding over concrete. Each step pounded like the beat of Esther's turbulent heart. The hangar grew even hotter. Steam billowed around her petulant sisters, separating them. In their midst, another set of eyes appeared: purple, gold—and silver!

Esther's world stopped. Messiah shrank from her soul, leaving behind a scared girl, sheltering in the ruins of the Old World.

Her reflection stared back from the mirror, but it was wrong. She had taken the demon's heart and been reborn. Her skin, once as fair as a cherry blossom, had turned gray; her eyes, once steel blue, shone a vivid purple, sparkling with facets of gold and silver.

Mother Rebekah's face formed around those celestial eyes, then the rest of her, adorned in a foreign habit and aglow with power.

"Traitor!" Ruth shouted, rushing forward. A screaming black streak appeared where her body had been. She was on Rebekah in an instant, only to be repelled halfway across the hangar, skidding unceremoniously on her back. Soaked but undeterred, she flashed forward again, clawed fingers seeking death. Rebekah barely moved, but even still, Ruth was flung to the ceiling. The hangar shook as her back impacted a girder, then a second time as she plummeted like an errant meteor back to the floor. A tsunami of sludge and brackish water rippled forth as she struggled to hands and knees.

"Enough," Esther hissed, paralyzed by shock.

Ruth didn't listen. Her spine shuddered back into shape, one realigned vertebra at a time. Her hands clenched. The air crackled as a superheated ovoid blistered around her body, pushing back the mist and rain. Her beautiful, insolent eyes lingered on Esther's. "Bless the Eternal One!" she called, then lunged.

Esther shut her eyes against the surge of pressure, her own body clenched in anticipation. There was a final snap of cervical bones breaking, then a splash as the revenant mother died. Esther opened her eyes again. Ruth lay on the floor in front of Rebekah, face down in a boiling halo of water.

Five. A bad omen.

"I didn't want this," Rebekah said. "I didn't want any of it."

The exile's voice was too powerful, too resonant. Esther's flesh hummed to every word. Her spirit soared into unfamiliar territory, immolated by the light of distant stars, contorting in the gravity of a moon only she should have known.

Mother Hannah kneeled, gingerly turning Mother Ruth onto her back, careful to manage her lolling head. She brushed back Ruth's hair, then ran her fingers along still-open eyes to close them—forever.

Esther blinked back tears, choked down her incipient rage. Long nails dug into her palms, drawing blood.

Mother Leah turned and clapped her hands, summoning a gaggle of sisters from the belly of the Ark. Four of them shuffled forth, none daring to look up. "Take her away," she said.

Traitors.

None moved, trapped as they were between the wills of their superiors.

Rebekah's transformed gaze was a vortex from which Esther could not escape. There was only one matriarch: Esther, the Eternal *One*. Witness to the world that was, carrying it in her blood and bones, so that it could be resurrected into the world to come. The numbers were wrong again, catastrophically wrong. None of this was possible. Confusion, rage, and despair flooded her brain, overloading it.

Rebekah made a subtle gesture with her hand and the sisters set to work, carefully lifting Mother Ruth's lifeless body away, taking a circuitous route around Esther to the annex entrance.

Mother Leah clapped her hands again, snapping Esther from her horrible reverie. "The rest of you: bring Rebekah. Time is short."

Bring Rebekah?

Mother Rebekah broke her stare, turning back to the Ark.

Strike now!

Messiah rushed back into her soul, commanding her to move, to destroy the usurper while her back was turned. Molten blood distended her veins. A pathway through space and time cracked open between her hands and Rebekah's throat.

Now!

The ground shook with her wrath—and then stopped, as Esther saw what the remaining sisters were carrying, as the rattle of casters on the floor provoked memories of betrayal, of Mother Rebekah attempting to "rescue" her daughter from symbiosis. A mobile sepulcher, intended to retrieve and temporarily sustain a fallen symbiote, never used until now. Within it: R-6. What was left of her, sealed within its tiny chamber.

Esther's rage withered.

There was only the child.

The Numbered sat upon her wheelchair, calm, compliant, unaffected by her mother's treachery. A small hand—perfect amidst a corrupted body—touched Esther's leg, soothing her spirit. Within a bedraggled mane of honey-blonde hair were eyes beaming with beautiful purpose, the destiny Esther had granted to her.

Her hair... now gone.

Her hair, aglow with the light of the sun. So much like the hair of another girl. Someone Esther once knew.

Both damned by her hand—

"Do not interfere," Mother Rebekah said.

Esther sucked in a breath, clawed hands falling to her side. "Where will you take her?" she asked, stepping away despite herself. As her aura faded, the flood dragged at the edges of her cloak.

"To her sisters," Mother Rebekah said. The traitorous procession moved past her. Only Mother Leah glanced back, lips and brow pulled taut, the tips of her hair tangled into knots. "Come, Leah."

"The Guardian won't allow it," Esther called after them.

Mother Leah turned. Mother Rebekah did not respond. They continued on their way, backs turned, until Esther was left alone in the churning mist.

REBEKAH-6

ACCELERANT

—come back, come back, come back, come back, come back!

"I'm here."

Rebekah-6 wailed silently with relief. There was only the thrum of her heart in the darkness, except when her mother—and now the others—touched the apparatus on which she lay. She had been plugged into a machine again, but this one had no senses, no weapons sticking out of its shoulders or avian legs; it served only to keep her alive.

For how long?

She was desperate for her mother's arms. Though the new machine sustained her, it shortened her horizon. She could "feel" the minds around her, but only in the way she had felt Leah-4's when their mechanical bodies connected at a distance, interleaving data over the air, never allowed to touch. Their presence was a lifeline that kept her from drowning, but it was not enough to pull her from the sea.

Mother Leah was there, a familiar pattern of froth on the waves. Rebekah-6 tried to visualize the woman who had guided her through every test until the last, whose magenta eyes had always been filled with grief. Rebekah-6 had not known at the time that she too had a child, attended to—tested—by someone else. And yet in getting to know Leah-4, mother and daughter still seemed to have had... *more* than Rebekah-6 and her own mother. It hurt worse than her failing body.

"I'm sorry."

Her mother's words or Mother Leah's, she could not tell. Rebekah-6 held onto the thread in any case, transmitting her last memories of Leah-4.

I am called.

Her sister's final words, as painful now as then. Someone cried out on the other side and the connection was severed. She drifted upon the darkness, alone, exhausted.

"Rest now. We'll be there soon."

Yes, Mother.

———

Running. Clambering. Through gravel washouts and titanic rockfalls. Mechanical legs on the verge of failure groaning with every twist and turn. Gyroscope screaming for micro-adjustments beyond the limits of her human mind.

Tilt three degrees right; brace; reduce articulation by one meter; torso twist seven degrees left; raise arm—no, the other one; pause, pause; leap step; controlled fall forward.

Warning, warning, warning.

Running and slipping, running and falling, every mistake carrying her closer to the edge, stomach lurching as she finally tumbles down the side, screaming, into the abyss—

Rebekah-6 awoke into darkness, her recalled scramble away from the Sea of Screams replaced with the raucous lurch of their transport. She could feel it in her stomach, and in the grip of her mother's hand upon her sepulcher, fear and anxiety bounding between nerves and blood vessels. That plus fragmentary images of black storm clouds and an equally dark metropolis rising from the wastes.

Are we there yet?

"Almost. Rest."

————

Bless the Eternal One!

Violence and death, scalding the air.

Rain within as without. Multifold hands pressed upon the vertices of her sheathed body, as though in ceremony. Shielding her from the deluge, from the wrath of her matriarch.

Then rolling again, as odorless, colorless, imagined droplets beat upon the glass of her useless viewport.

Where are we going?

"To your sisters."

Rebekah-6 knew then that her mother meant her actual sisters, those who had not survived their births. She had seen them—heard them—once, on the lips of the many-tongued demon during her final test. Cursing her life, slashing at her with their words, as the beast's pincers closed around her neck.

They haunted her blood.

"That was a deception."

The imagined rain disappeared, replaced with the imagined echo of her sepulcher's casters rattling down a long hall and imagined cries of shock as all in their path prostrated themselves before her mother. The Revenant Sisterhood, humanity's salvation, pitched into chaos—for her sake.

Time stretched in the darkness.

————

They were in an elevator, descending, descending. Love lingered at the periphery but light and color were absent.

Hold me.

"*Soon.*"

Where are we going?

"*To your sisters.*"

The same question, the same answer, but closer now. Descending, descending.

The accelerant...

"*Yes.*"

What will happen to me?

A pause, too long, as her mother's mind sought the path of least suffering.

"*You will swim in the blood of the sisterhood. All of us will carry you in our veins.*"

Descending, descending. To her death.

I'm scared.

"*I know, my love.*"

Rebekah-6 scrambled in the darkness, trying to find her way back up the mountain, but there were only sheer cliffs.

Isn't there another God-engine for me? An empty one?

Pain shuddered through the narrow conduit connecting her to her mother: imagined tears, unimaginable guilt.

"*There is not enough of you left.*"

They arrived. An imagined breeze pressed upon them, seeking, verifying.

Hold me.

Her mother hesitated, lurched, too slow to recall her fears before they were transmitted through the sepulcher.

"*You might not last.*"

I will.

Rebekah-6 waited, preparing herself for the fire that would

assail her lungs. Her body rocked as clasps unlatched, hoses detached, fluid lines shut down, and finally her canopy opened.

Darkness...

Then integrated again, cradled in her mother's arms. Light and color returned—barely, but enough to stave off the pain of the fire for a few more minutes.

Once more, Rebekah-6 peered through her mother's eyes, though the image was blurry this time; listened through her ears, though the shuffle of her footsteps crackled with interference; sniffed for the dank musk of the earth but smelled nothing.

"We're almost there."

They were in a cavern lit red by an invisible source, terminating in a seamless black door edged in golden filigree and dizzying geometric patterns. A solitary obsidian pedestal rose from the rough-hewn stone of the floor, octagonal, topped with an etched handprint. Together, they approached it. One hand came free to touch the surface, and as it did so, a new mind sizzled into being.

[S-1 > Mother Rebekah: YOU ARE NOT HER]

Mother Rebekah gasped and almost fell back as she was turned inside out, scrutinized, scanned. This was the Eternal One's domain. Their very presence was blasphemy.

Rebekah-6 retreated to the back of her mother's mind, concealing herself in folds of color, but there was no escaping this presence. It blasted through the nebula like a supernova.

Mommy!

[Mother Rebekah > S-1: Rebekah needs your help!]

Too many voices over too many channels.

Who is this?

Both minds turned in her direction.

"Sarah-1," her mother replied.

[S-1 > R-6: Guardian]

But Sarah-2 was the first of the Numbered...

[S-1 > R-6: Not the first]

Rebekah-6 crept from her shelter, tried to sort through the organic circuitry of her mother's memories to learn the truth, but was too weak. Instead, a spectral face materialized from the maelstrom: a girl, younger than her, also shorn of hair but otherwise whole, eyes blazing with power.

[R-6 > S-1: Where are you?]

[S-1 > R-6: I am everywhere]

[Mother Rebekah > S-1: My daughter must return to the accelerant]

[S-1 > Mother Rebekah: The living do not return]

Rebekah-6 felt herself revealed, the crushed visage of her body forming within her mother's synapses. Proof to this Guardian that she would not be living for much longer.

[Mother Rebekah > S-1: Please]

[S-1 > Mother Rebekah: You are not her]

[Mother Rebekah > S-1: No]

Together, they waited, as Sarah-1's avatar scrutinized her as it had her mother. Unspooling the entirety of her short life, before and after symbiosis: pain, hope, doubt, loneliness. Leah-4's death. Projecting all of it with crystal clarity into the void, words and secret thoughts alike spoken aloud for all to hear.

Rebekah-6 gasped for breath.

[S-1 > R-6: Knock, knock]

[R-6 > S-1: Who's there?]

[S-1 > R-6: Boo]

[R-6 > S-1: Boo who?]

[S-1 > R-6: Don't cry, little one]

The door boomed open and glided into the cavern wall. Sarah-1 smiled and was gone.

Light and color seeped back in, but even fainter this time. Peeking through her mother's eyes, navigating past panicked impatience, she saw the space beyond the door. A long hall opened into a circular chamber, dimly lit by beams of dusty yellow, as though a second sun had been trapped in the bowels of the Spire. At its center, a suspended catwalk led to an enormous marble bowl held in the outstretched hands of a sculpted Messiah. The rest of the statue was concealed within the abyss below. As they looked upon it, then walked toward it, the light began to shift from yellow to pink to purple, penetrating her mother's flesh, displacing her own light.

Rebekah-6 clutched more tightly to her host. The closer they got, the brighter the light became, moving between color and sound and a prickle upon her mother's skin. A susurration of waves whispered against her mother's ears, though the black meniscus atop the bowl was still.

This is not a holy place.

Her mother hesitated before answering. *"It's the only place we have."*

They reached the edge of the steel-mesh peninsula. Below floor level, only the arms and perfect scalp of the statue were visible. Beyond was black. Rebekah-6 knew her mother could see the base if she chose to, could reveal it with eyes that saw through distance and darkness, but she did not. Better for them both.

Wait!

Everything was happening too fast. The darkness between experience had felt like an eternity, and consciousness too brief. She had seen her mother's memories, lived that life in rapid playback, *knew* her... but still in isolation. She wanted more: idle chatter, to be queried as Leah-4 had queried her, to extend her hand and have it held in return. But she had no hands. Rebekah-6 turned inward to the nebula of her mother's mind, seeking her soul, but there was only the lashing darkness.

"I'm sorry. I'm so sorry."

They stepped forward together. The clang of her mother's boots on the catwalk sounded like a gong, inciting the prismatic color of the place to brighten further. The chamber's edges faded. There was only the bowl—the accelerant.

Will God forgive me?

Her mother paused mid-step, then continued.

"You have committed no sins."

Ghostly figures lined up to either side of them, afloat on the abyss. All those Rebekah-6 had killed, their faces trapped in agony.

I have.

"You owe God nothing."

Rebekah-6 cried for absolution. She could not take the dead with her, into the black. They would haunt her for eternity. She sought her prayers, as her mother would once have told her to, and found a fragment, whispering the words with the last of her breath. "Let my death be an atonement for my sins."

The figures faded. Only the accelerant lay still before them. She felt herself reduced a second time as her machine parts were removed, leaving only what her mother had given her.

There was no light.

"I will always be with you."

No color.

I will always be with you.

The accelerant enveloped her flesh.

There was only love.

There was only love.

There was only love...

ESTHER

THE EXILE

"Bow down before your messiah!"

They were the first words she had spoken after *becoming*, five long centuries past. After being led by divine providence back to the city of her birth, to prepare for God's impending vengeance, to avenge those who had been taken as slaves and take them as her own flock.

The accelerant flowed through her veins. Blood dripped from her hands. Messiah waited beside her, impossibly beautiful, porcelain face and scalp and infinite black eyes barely visible past a halo of brilliant fire. But it was *her* who would lead the blind and bring darkness to light. It was *her* who had captivated the dregs in the warehouse.

Esther's shouted command cascaded like a thunderclap, reverberating through the walls and floor and ceiling and the flesh of those present.

But no one moved.

"Who the fuck are you?"

Sixteen-year-old Esther blinked, abruptly removed from the moment.

The question came from the back, close to where the

personnel entrance gave way to the facility's robotic storage hive. A hyena with the face of a man—one of the slavers—hunched by a tower of crates, gripping a barbed club in his filthy paw. A handful of others stirred, lifting their own cudgels in response.

Show them, Messiah whispered.

They died as quickly as those outside, except this time Esther felt—reveled in—the snap of their bones, the tearing of their skin, the sacrificial gush of their blood as they were offered up as evidence of who she was. She painted the room with their insolence.

"Don't hurt my dad!" a small voice cried.

Esther whirled about. A young boy clothed in rags huddled against his father's leg—slaves, those she had come to redeem. They hugged the wall, faces spattered with gore. The man's eyes were milky with blindness.

Scant tears dribbled down the boy's sallow face. "Please," he begged.

The man held his child tight, glaring past her, jaw flexed with fear. "You're all the same," he spat.

Show them.

Esther shook the commandment from her head, but it throbbed, compelled. The air broke around her, prismatic color screaming from the black.

The boy yanked insistently at his father's rags, pulling him down.

Esther's fingers curled into claws.

Finally, they kneeled, and all the others followed. One by one, the survivors of Armageddon dropped to their knees. They stared at her, vacuous, compliant, awaiting her command. She stared back in turn, capturing the eyes of each man, woman, and child until satisfied of their undivided, inescapable attention.

Exhaling her rage—and her own terror at its power—Esther stepped back and raised her shaking, bloodstained arms. "Rise now," she called to them, her voice breaking with doubt. The second part was barely above a whisper. "There's work to be done."

———

Esther sat alone upon her throne, rocking back and forth, breathing to the rhythm of creaking metal and rubber.

One, two, one, two.

Mother Hannah had taken Mother Ruth's corpse away for her funerary rites. Mother Leah was lost, joined to Rebekah's cause, though Esther assumed the revenant mother's loyalty had died with her daughter. Mother Maya was either attending to their latest proselyte or she too had joined the interlopers, fed up with her matriarch's instability. And Mother Sarah was dead, entombed somewhere under Hub.

One, two, one, two.

That left only two: Rachel and Judith. Stalwart servants, old, unadventurous. Esther had considered summoning them as she rode the private elevator back up to her chambers, but she refrained. What if they had been slaughtered, as Ruth had? Worse, what if they had turned? Esther did not want to know—not yet. So, she sat in her chair, faced the entrance, and waited as sleet and thunder beat against the roof.

When Mother Rebekah glided in, it was as though a vision from a dream: Esther's eyes reflected from the void, atop another woman's face.

"You should be dust," Esther hissed, sinking back into her chair. The flames of her ceremonial collar dug painfully into the nape of her neck. Her calves cramped with anxiety.

Mother Rebekah stepped from the black, uncaring of what *should* be or where her feet landed. Rivulets of murky water streaked random patterns across the floor, clawing their way from her boots toward Esther's throne.

Esther shuddered at the sight. "Is R-6—"

"*Rebekah* is returned to the accelerant," Mother Rebekah said, the silver flecks in her eyes flaring.

Meaning the Guardian admitted her, to a place reserved for the Eternal One. As though they were the same, as though she were so easily replaced. It was all wrong.

Esther clung to her armrests for stability, resisting the exile's gravitational pull, but she could not turn away. Looking at her now, in this moment, Esther saw the resemblance between mother and daughter. What remained of Rebekah-6 had been identical: a budding sharpness in her cheeks, the heart-shaped face and delicate jaw. Only her hair color had been different, a recessive trait carried across time. The child had been gravely wounded, flesh and steel compressed by unimaginable force. That she lived so long was a miracle.

"I'm sorry," Ester mumbled, uncertain of her own intent. Was she sorry for the child's life, for Rebekah's grief, or for the loss of a precious asset? All three, perhaps. Compassion was secondary to purpose—it had to be if humanity was to persist— but she was not a monster. "She was special."

Mother Rebekah's face contorted with restrained emotion. "They are *all* special."

Esther squirmed in her seat, shying away from an errant stream of water that had crossed into her floor tile. "Did Mother Leah... did you find who did it?"

"Yes."

"Scavrats?"

"Yes."

Esther bristled but found comfort in a familiar hatred. For a moment, she could pretend they were having a normal conversation, mistress to servant. "And L-4?"

"Also dead."

As she feared. The loss was immeasurable. "Messiah watch over them," she whispered.

Mother Rebekah scowled, the air sparking around her unfamiliar habit. "Hardly."

Esther chewed on her lip, uncertain if the retort was born of raw emotion or blasphemy. There was no telling where the exile had been, how she had survived, or what she carried in her blood. The only certainty was her power. "What of the perpetrators?"

"Released."

"What..." Esther's chambers shuddered and shrank, suddenly too small for them both.

"This way is over."

"Over! Who are you to say what's over? They started a war!"

Mother Rebekah stepped forward, light and shadow competing for her features. "There has only ever been one war: the one you abandoned and forced our children to fight for you."

Esther leapt from her chair, phasing to within centimeters of the interloper's face. The storm hushed. The chamber fell away. All was black save interlocking threads of silver and gold. "How dare you!"

Mother Rebekah was unmoved, unblinking. The longer she remained still, the greater the itch along Esther's limbs. Her fingers curled into claws. She wanted to strike, to eradicate the traitor she should have killed in the first place, but fear held her back. Fear of failure. Fear that Rebekah was... stronger. The itch turned to searing pain, stabbing the length of her nerves.

"Tell me I'm wrong," Mother Rebekah said.

"The Numbered are a gift."

"No, they're your excuse. The latest in a centuries-long string of excuses."

"Hell is too strong!" Esther shouted, alongside a clap of thunder that returned them to the chamber.

Mother Rebekah's eyes flashed red. "Or you are too weak."

The exile's hands were on her face, molten fingers pressed against her cheeks. Starbursts of suppressed memory exploded across their joint synapses.

The army of mankind surged, one final push against the Adversary. The great diasporas united by purpose, purifying the plains with blood and fire, charging with fist and spear and rifle and war machine.

Victory was in sight. Esther stood at the head of thousands, her black-clad flock the scythe that would end the war. Hell would be dislodged from the mortal realm and the earth rid of demons forever. Demons... and the accelerant that brewed in their infernal hearts.

The moon and stars would return but Esther's light would wane. One by one, her sisters would fade into dust. She would be alone, until she joined them as well.

In eternal darkness.

Not yet.

Not yet.

And so, she fled.

Esther gasped for breath as Mother Rebekah released her grip.

"You cursed us all," the exile said.

"No." Esther shook her head, even as her body quaked. "I saved you. By Messiah's will, I saved all of you."

"Messiah," Mother Rebekah repeated, tongue lashing each syllable. She peered around Esther's spartan chambers, at the stained-glass ceiling overflowing with images of revenant sisters and demons, the Eternal One at their head. "I see no Messiah here."

"Blasphemy!"

"Tell me, Eternal One. When is the last time you saw your messiah?"

Esther stumbled backward, almost tripping over her chair. "My..."

"I am with you."

She blinked in surprise. Time stopped as she grasped at the disembodied voice.

"Only you can redeem them. Humanity needs a weapon if it is to flourish again."

Her flock was waiting. Esther glanced sidelong at her savior, looking for direction. It looked back with phlegmatic eyes, in which she saw only her own reflection.

She fled as the world shuddered, as the mountains became plains and the seas boiled into deserts. Sheltered in a cave as those who followed her from the city were slain to the last. Counted the days of uncreation with charcoal lines drawn on the walls of her primordial prison.

And as she emerged, to a world undone, she did so alone. No Messiah, no manifest God, only her will. Her light to spark the fire of civilization. Her blood to clarify the blood of demons, so that in the absence of the divine, the power of Hell could be humanity's weapon.

"God abandoned us," Esther whispered. Though hushed, the words resounded from the chamber walls, louder than the collision of superheated air and the icy emptiness of the void overhead.

"No," Mother Rebekah said, "we abandoned God."

Esther shriveled. Everything that she was, everything she had worked toward, felt tiny, inconsequential. Centuries of tradition and ritual as vapid as the infinite dust beyond the city's walls. The obsidian walls of the Spire as thin as the cloth of her false habit. There was only the empty void above, hidden by a storm of her own making.

"What do you know of it?" she asked, shaking. "You weren't there."

Shadow consumed the exile's face, leaving only the faraway

glimmer of her eyes, and lips that twisted in agony before permitting a reply. "You are not the only one to fail."

"Fail—"

"When are you due for your next re-accelerant, Esther?"

Esther's heart jumped. They were the same words she had spoken to Mother Rebekah, her loyal servant for a hundred years, as she casually condemned her to exile and certain death. The chair pulled her back into its embrace. She pressed against its spinal apparatus, at the empty tubes as they scraped against her ports. "Three days."

"Then you have that long."

The floor tilted, as though the Spire had been uprooted from its base. Every angle was wrong. Every surface too bright or dull. Her own arms too heavy.

"To do what?" Esther whispered.

"To finish what you started."

"To finish..." The sharp edge of the chair's keypad pushed against her palm. She could summon help, raise an alarm, restore order. Her fingers twitched with uncertainty.

"No one will come. Your time is over."

Over.

Eternal darkness.

"I am the Eternal One!" Esther declared, smashing her hands upon the armrests. But the accelerant languished in her veins. Courage failed. Esther sought Messiah's light as she had so many times before, but in the absence of devotion, in the absence of certainty, she found her soul empty. Excuses filled the space instead. "Who will clarify the blood?" she asked, though she knew the answer.

"I will. As is a mother's duty to her children."

"A mother..."

Mother Rebekah's face fluoresced bright silver as a cascade of lightning ruptured the sky overhead. She continued to glow even as the storm darkened, and a roll of thunder churned in its belly. "Great Mother."

———

The city was dark, but Esther could feel the crush of bodies pressing against the Way of Life—the fenced boulevard that bisected southern Cathedral, all the way from the wall to the Spire. When a new sister was declared, or another cast out, this was the path they took. When Mother Rebekah was expelled, this was the path she took. And now, the way was Esther's, but to death rather than life.

Everyone was there: every citizen, every sister and hopeful proselyte of her order, and at the end of the ancient road, what remained of her inner circle. Every city light had been extinguished, save for two rows of lampposts that ran the length of the Way, like an inverted shadow of the Spire at her back. Carrying her to the end.

"What will you tell them?" Esther had asked as they descended together into the annex.

"That you have been called."

"A kindness?"

"A necessity."

The rain fell now as a light drizzle, pattering against Esther's hood and the ceramic plates of her black body armor. None among the audience spoke or dared murmur. The silhouettes she could discern from the masses rocked slowly back and forth, hand held to throat in devotion, shifting like waves in a black sea. But their devotion was not for her. Mother Rebekah matched her pace several steps ahead, siphoning their worship, eclipsing Esther's light.

Finish what you started.

Every step brought her closer to exhaustion. Though it

would be days before her blood screamed for the accelerant, addicted as it was, she felt drained—mortal. Old weakness crept back, ancient pain that had never been cured, only stifled. Old doubts, never satisfied. Old memories, before Cathedral, before the Revenant Sisterhood, as she wandered the sundered earth, trapped between the world that was and the world to come. When she had first learned the true cost of the accelerant. Not how it annihilated human memories, breaking them into shards and scattering them into her subconscious. Not the loss of dreams, nor the emulsification of human emotion and compassion into singular devotion to Messiah. But the fact of its finiteness.

Sister Deborah—the first of her name—had been her first disciple. The first to receive her blood as they battled the Adversary, intended as a field transfusion but resulting in a miracle: the first after Esther to walk the path of death back to life; humanity's weapons multiplied.

The miracle spread as Esther found new disciples to lead her growing army, to fill with her blood so they could fill her in return with their devotion. The War against Hell at last. Until Deborah died. Not so much died as was obliterated, crumbling suddenly to dust in Esther's arms. As the rest began to follow, and Esther felt her own body wither, the truth of Messiah's gift was realized. Everlasting life existed only so long as the accelerant was taken, so long as demons roamed the earth to be harvested. And none, save Esther, was guaranteed survival on each taking of it.

The accelerant was not a weapon. It was a curse, and she was its bearer.

Finish what you started.

Or restart what was finished... Desperation took hold. Nerves jumped as residual electricity pumped through Esther's heart, refusing submission, commanding a response. She could do it again. Replenish herself from the source as Rebekah had. Return and take back what was hers.

She arrived at the wall, where four revenant mothers waited: Leah, Hannah, Rachel, Judith, but no Maya. Half their proper number. The circle had folded in two, flames turned inward. None held her gaze. None fed her with their devotion. The spark of action died.

Too many years had passed.

Esther was too tired.

Mother Rebekah turned around, eyes aflame, charged by her new devotees. There would be no lengthy recitation. No ritual had been prepared for such a day. There was only a singular commandment and the heavy silence of those assembled.

Esther unclasped her cloak, clenching the fabric in her fists, eyes watering as the eight flames of her office—her legacy— beamed under the streetlights. Rebekah dipped her head. With leaden arms, Esther swept the garment over the new head of the Revenant Sisterhood.

"The mantle is passed!" she called.

The city shouted back, "Praise the Eternal One!" But it was not for her.

Rebekah, Great Mother, stepped aside. Beyond the inner gate, two God-engines stood at attention. To the citizenry, they must have appeared as honor guard. But Esther knew better. She could feel their judgment at the edge of consciousness.

Her motorcycle waited in the empty trade nexus, the last of her things—almost. A small smile crept onto her lips. It looked exactly as it had half a millennia ago, though in that time so much of it had been replaced that little of the original remained. A solar cell was clamped to the back along with a single bag. Within the bag, a handful of supplies tucked alongside a special relic. Just enough to get her where she needed to go.

Enough to finish what she started.

BAPTISTE

THE PRIEST'S TALE

Bastion.

Home.

Baptiste didn't know how he would feel when he finally saw it again. Would his chest swell at the sight of his birthplace? Would hate overwhelm his senses, knowing what malignancy rotted its core? Maybe fear at being mistaken for a remnant, so low had his travels taken him.

He felt none of those things.

Standing at the edge of the charcoal flats, watching his homeland smolder, Baptiste felt nothing. The Deadlands lay far south, but the gray was here. In his heart.

The sun hid behind the Northern Ridge, reluctant to illuminate the carnage below. Sophus had warned him back at Newhaven: conspiracy, secret battle walkers, the swarm. Even if he hadn't known in advance, the smoke rising from his city told the story. He had spent each night of his journey huddled in one of Helio's secret caves, curled into a ball like a panicked armadillo, falling for the trick of sleep, then waking, falling, then waking. And each morning, the funeral pyre was there, glowing deep into dusk. On the last night, he didn't stop, guided through the pitch by the afterglow, chased into morning by demons real and imagined.

One thing was certain: he wouldn't be misidentified as an enemy because no soldiers manned the battlements. The western wall was in tatters, a gaping hole that ran half the length of the city. Charred ruin spilled forth on both sides of the shattered brick and concrete, visible from afar by virtue of sheer volume. Piled bodies, twisted metal, the mind-breaking remains of dead demons—assuming such beings could ever really die.

Bastion had been sieged.

"God save us," he heard himself say.

Baptiste had lifted at the news of his surviving platoonmates: Lafayette and Deckard, maybe Stratton. Father Valmor as well, though all priests were suspect now. He was certain his men would have heeded the call to defend their nation, which meant they could very well have died all over again. Leaving him the last survivor of a fallen cause.

Hesitation anchored him in place. No one was holding a gun to his head anymore, no one was giving orders. An awkward surge of elation coursed along his frayed nerves—a taste of freedom, here at the end—

"God is waiting for us."

—brief as it was.

"Bastion is our last chance to prove ourselves. It must prevail."

Baptiste placed his hand on his chest, soothing the twisting talisman beneath. "Yes, Brother."

Freedom was a myth. There was only duty. And if Bastion could not prevail, justice at least would be done.

Dropping back into his seat, Baptiste hit the gas pedal and raced for home.

———

It wasn't long before he had to get out on foot. The smell was immense, the landscape shattered, skewing his faltering steps. Every breath was filled with ash. A grid line of craters pockmarked the black earth, delineating the start of the battle. The Legion had not been surprised at least, deploying its heavy weaponry to barrage the swarm.

For all the good it did...

As a sea of demons had encroached upon the wall, waves of men marched out to meet them, reinforced by mechanized infantry and the Legion's paltry armored units. They were all here—their corpses. The Deadlands greedily erased the dead, but here they lingered in gruesome state. Hundreds, thousands of men, both armored and robed, a putrid fog billowing from their bodies. Baptiste blinked away the sting of it. At least in this moment, the Legion and the Church had still been united as hammer and shield.

For all the good it did...

At first, he searched the faces of the dead, looking for men he might know. Most were beyond recognition. Those still intact enough to constitute human beings were frozen in violent rigor: hands clawed, hollowed-out eyes gaping, twisted faces forever locked in anguish. Many were too young, their pale necks and hands swallowed by the oversized armor of their fallen fathers.

It was too much.

Not even vermin lingered here. No flies, no carrion birds screaming overhead. The land had become poison.

A susurration carried on the wind, emanating from the *other* bodies—the inhuman ones. Fragments of sound swishing and clipping, like the lapping of mechanical waves. Lulling and snapping, the swaying tide jerking at Baptiste's nerves. His eyes twitched, then squinted as the rising sun released from its anchorage. He raised a hand to block the glare, but it did little good. Beams of sickly pink danced over the bestial remains, shimmering, breaking into a million colors at the edges. Baptiste kept moving, averting his eyes from anything not human.

Eventually the battlefield became more orderly. Charnel gullies wound their way back to the wall, dug into the earth by bulldozers and fire. The fog of rot turned charcoal, hanging like storm clouds around the peaks of the burned and consecrated dead. The Order Sacramental had been here, flame units blazing until they ran out of fuel, accompanied by chaplains rushing to pray over the souls of their fallen comrades, lest they succumb to oblivion. A moat of black glass stood between him and the remains of the city wall.

Baptiste lifted his head, straining against the crushing weight of despair. The bulwark that had safeguarded his people for generations was gone. The swarm had smashed against it, tearing concrete from rebar, brick from mortar, powdering steel as though it were plaster. And Bastion's wounds did not stop there. Deep, smoking gouges raked into the districts beyond, as far as the manufactories at the heart of the city and the interior wall of the Grand Citadel to the north. Everywhere, there was smoke and ruin.

Turning back to the battlefield, Baptiste dropped to his knees. For a shameful moment, he wished he had gone with Magnus and spared himself this truth, lived out his remaining days with Julia belowground. Could it truly have been worse? At least he would not have been so alone. Guilt stabbed at him, pressing at the corners of his talisman. Baptiste flailed for answers, scouring his memories for anything he might have done differently, but none of it mattered.

Even if the wall could be fully restored it would only be hiding more ugliness, a gravesite at their doorstep, a constant reminder that walls were not enough. Alone, his people could never keep out Hell.

Something wagged at him from one of the piles—a square of

armor, dislodged from some distant exploded vehicle. A dry laugh seeped from his lips. What could be left after this that they could possibly offer up in alliance? A pauper offering riches. The Order Sacramental did not have to lift a finger to scuttle the lord commander's hopes; they were impossible from the outset.

Despair sucked the breath from Baptiste's lungs. The dead clamored in his ears. Cold hands beckoned to him to join them.

"Bastion must prevail."

Gabriel...

Baptiste gulped a deep, sour breath. Then another, trying to steady himself, trying to visualize his brother standing alongside him, protecting him. There was only an empty silhouette, blazing like the fires of the funeral pyre. The human traits had succumbed to time, just as his father's and mother's had. Even still, he wanted to embrace it, to be consumed for the sake of closeness. Every part of him ached for it.

"God is waiting for us."

A glimmer of light ran across the newest dent in his armor, where the bullet intended for him had ricocheted, hitting Magnus in his stead. Time and again, he had been spared while those around him suffered and died. His curse. Or his brother's blessing. Maybe both, carrying him to this moment.

The light shifted hue, from pink to orange, enveloping him. His shadow retreated, reeled back into his body as his soul was once reeled back from the gray. Another shadow took its place: titanic, ancient, looming over the battlefield as it had five centuries past. The throbbing in his ears subsided, making room for the thump of giant feet, the whine of great servomotors wielding death.

A battle walker stood behind him.

It said nothing. Not that any machine should speak, but Baptiste's assumptions had been forever altered after his encounter with Cathedral's God-engines. Nor did its mere presence strain the fabric of the world, as those black-on-black monstrosities had. There was just heat—physical, extreme, but still material—shedding endlessly from whatever lost technology powered the thing, counterbalanced by the cold malevolence of a mechanical mind.

Baptiste's spine compressed beneath its weight, the soulless stare upon his back. He dared not look upon it. To do so would acknowledge his great-uncle's unforgivable lies, severing him from his last living blood.

"What do you want, machine?" he croaked.

"To shine God's light upon the world." The battle walker's baritone voice rippled across the ruin.

This was their savior. This was the Church's great secret: a war machine, to receive their prayers in place of a manifest God.

Baptiste sifted ash between his fingers. "You're too late."

It did not reply. The orange spotlight of its eye rotated back and forth, as though in contemplation, then blinked off as the machine turned and loped back to its duty.

Whir, thump, whir, thump.

Until it was gone, and Baptiste was left alone with the wind and the dead.

———

There was no buffer zone between the interior of the wall and the populace. For all that Bastion had suffered—through plague, famine, and endless war—it still pressed against its bounds. There was never enough space, which might have spared some of the devastation on display.

He knew that this was District Ten, but only by virtue of its position along the wall. Anything that may have identified it, codified it as a place where human beings once lived, had been destroyed. Rubble crowded the district's narrow streets, still spilling from the debris of what were once sprawling tenements. When the first had fallen, the rest collapsed like dominos. Dark smoke still seeped from some of them, hinting at fires suppressed but not extinguished. It looked much like the battlefield beyond, mercifully absent mountains of the dead.

The Legion would have escorted civilians into the Metro to wait out the battle. He remembered it as well as any citizen, before coming of service age: clutching his mother's hand as they surged alongside their neighbors, emergency klaxons wailing behind them, the muttering of his brother's prayers as he led them into the deep. But those evacuations were preventative, almost always lasting only a few hours before a return to false normalcy. This siege was protracted, maybe lasting days, and there were no homes to return to after. Other districts, already overpopulated, would have to absorb the dispossessed. Hospitals would be bursting at the seams. Reserves would be emptied. The quiet here was another lie—Bastion was buckling.

The broken perimeter was ominously absent guards—human ones, anyway. Baptiste shambled deeper into the city, down streets viciously folded into ravines, boots splashing in the murky discharge of the sewer system below. Through the bare ribs of collapsed factories and empty food dispensaries. Winding his way through desolation in search of an intact Metro entrance.

A rumbling, military engineering vehicle broke the silence, its great plow scraping a shrill path down the district's main street. An excavator claw swayed above its boxlike frame, pitifully undersized for the task ahead. Behind it marched two sections of men, their gait exhausted, some bearing recent wounds. A single harried chaplain was sandwiched between them. The soldiers didn't notice him, but the red-robed priest turned his head as he passed; tears lined his dust-caked face.

The Metro station was on the opposite side of the street, still accessible despite its collapsed awning. Baptiste stared into the stone-shrouded pit of the entranceway. The transient energy of morning fled his muscles, leaving the frail skeleton of purpose unsupported. He crouched, then gave way, landing cross-legged upon an outcropping of broken storefront.

When he had insisted Julia get him home, it was with the express purpose of warning the Legion: the attack on Bunker 23, the betrayal of the lord commander's plan by Overseer Rayos and the Order Sacramental. Every day that passed was an imminent catastrophe, which he could prevent if he just got here soon enough. But his news had preceded him, rendering his warning worthless. Sophus had outlined all of it: a conspiracy beyond his ken, Rayos caught—and killed—in the act, a nation divided. As always, none of it within Baptiste's control. There were only pieces to pick up now, and his great-uncle's judgment to face.

He pressed a quivering hand against his chest. "I'm just going to rest a while, Gabriel." A slow whirlwind of charcoal sand scoured the ragged lines of his face, shuttering his eyes. "Just for a minute."

The last echo of the platoon faded into the quiet, pained creaking of the city.

"Philippe?"

At first, he ignored the summons, bored of the tricks his mind played on him, particularly at the cusp of sleep. But something tickled at his neck, a soldier's sense. Someone was here with him.

Baptiste pried his eyes open. The road ahead was blurry. Standing in the middle of it was a figure in red and black, its head aglow in white light. Blinking away grimy tears, he tried to focus.

Overseer robes.

Baptiste forced himself upright, panic squeezing life back into his veins. His hands clamped down on empty air. He had taken weapons with him on his journey back, but they were forgotten in the Runner.

"It's me, Philippe."

Blinking again, he saw the man's face: burned to a sheen from upper lip to scalp, a severe line of orangey-red hair cut high on his head, terminating in a stubby topknot. He looked familiar, except for the eyes. They weren't... normal. The whites were too bright, bulging from their sockets. Golden irises beamed from their centers—

Baptiste faltered, recalling the soul-crushing scrutiny of the revenant mother, peering at him as though from the heavens—or Hell. But these weren't the eyes of a demon. He followed their movements, entranced. The way they shimmered, clicking rapidly from side to side, irises spinning—they looked mechanical.

"Andrite?"

A crooked smile pulled at the man's mouth.

Baptiste hadn't seen him since the infirmary, after his old companion had been caught in the flames of Drill Site 7—after he had been blinded.

No, that wasn't true.

The chaplain's robes suddenly caught fire, engulfing his body in flame.

He *had* seen him since then.

Andrite's wiry hair flared into a crimson halo. His eyeballs dribbled from their sockets.

In the Deadlands. A vision, materialized from the nothing.

The man—his friend—was screaming, his whole body black as the void, his voice the scream of the world as it died twice over.

Nervous heat shot through his arms and legs. That wasn't real, couldn't have been real... though in recollection, it seemed no different than any other memory.

Baptiste dug fingernails into sweaty palms, trying to fix himself in place.

In addition to his inexplicable eyes, the priest was dressed above his rank, wearing a deep red chasuble embroidered with heptagrams in place of his armor. A large *V*—the numeral of the Order Somatic—was emblazoned on his collar. A long white shawl trimmed in silver fell over his shoulders, its fringed edges clumped together and stained brown.

Andrite caught his gaze—the facets of his opalescent orbs shuddering—and stroked the garment's soiled edge. His smile flattened. The scabbed skin of his forehead bunched into thick cords. "The last two days have been... consuming."

"How are you here?" Baptiste asked.

"A sentry called in your vehicle's approach."

A sentry. Man or machine? Nothing living had greeted him out there.

"For the second time I came, hoping it was you," Andrite said.

They stared at each other for long seconds. Not long ago, Baptiste's soul would have lifted at the sight of his battle brother. Their time in the field together had shortened the distance between soldier and priest. A true bond. But now...

"Your Grace," Baptiste started, tripping over the proper address. Andrite winced, shoulders slouching. "When I left, you were blind. How..."

His old companion stepped to the left. Beyond him, shrouded in the shadow of the Metro entrance, was a second figure. Cowled, also wearing a type of red robe, but so dark as to be almost black. Only one hand was visible, gripping a tall polearm whose cylindrical tip shimmered against the black.

An adept, a servant of the Order Occult.

Baptiste's breath caught in his chest.

"A gift," Andrite said, "from unexpected allies. A lot has happened since you left."

A gift... Baptiste had encountered a great deal of technology in his travels: helmets without visors, goggles that let you see in the dark; things he never thought possible. But that was out *there*. Then again, a battle walker had just greeted him at the wall. It was becoming apparent that his home was built on secrets as much as concrete.

Baptiste gathered himself up and nodded. "I encountered the Scavrat commander, Sophus, and the..."

Andrite stiffened, but his new eyes were so inhuman as to render his expressions unreadable. "Yes. *Her*."

"The things he told me... I need to see my great-uncle." Mostly, Baptiste wanted to be away from this man, whose grotesque transformation dragged at his heart.

Andrite's cheeks twitched—sorrow, perhaps—but his eyes remained fixed, forever open. "This station is empty." His voice was solemn. "We'll escort you to the next one."

"Escort me?" Never had the notion crossed him.

"These are unsafe times. And I can catch you up." Andrite gestured to the entrance. The other man was still there, motionless as the surrounding debris.

Baptiste hesitated. He had stumbled into too many dark places of late, and his one remaining solace was now compromised. There would be no more long walks in the Metro, accompanied only by the counting of steps. No more peaceful solitude. "Lead the way," he mumbled.

They descended, past concrete barricades and the residue of recent conflict, to the station below. The adept seemed to glide rather than walk, the hem of his robes wiping a clean streak across the broken mosaic tile. A line of blinking ceiling lights guided them to a handcar at the edge of the platform. Baptiste's stomach churned at the sight of it, but he climbed in after them.

"Ready?" Andrite asked, phosphorescent eyes glowing in the dark of the tunnel.

"Yes…"

"Then let me tell you my tale."

The two former comrades sat face-to-face as the adept propelled them down the track. Baptiste hunched deep into his seat, nauseated in turns by the seesaw of the handcar's walking beam and by Andrite's artificial eyes. It was like staring into a spotlight. The Metro was quiet other than the grinding wheels of their passage.

"A week ago," Andrite started, "the lord commander was visited by our *guest* from the west… and fell ill."

Baptiste had never considered his great-uncle's health; the old man seemed immortal, perpetual. The shock of it must have been written on his face. Andrite had paused in anticipation of interruption, but Baptiste held his tongue and nodded for the man to continue.

"Whatever foul brew flows through that witch's veins, it poisoned his heart. My master, Ascendant Clermont, was dispatched to assist. His Holiness arrived shortly after with his own entourage. It's customary when a fellow triarch becomes ill, but there was an unusual urgency to it."

"Urgency?"

"Ascendant Blake, of the Order Militant, went with him. Along with a section of armed paladins."

Baptiste bristled, hands gripping the railing beside his seat. The Church's daring was unbridled.

"There was a confrontation, which I only learned about after speaking to my master later that evening. He called the infirmary and asked for me by name. At the same time, a courier arrived with this"—Andrite gestured disparagingly at his chasuble—"*costume*. I was promoted to Overseer and ordered not to return to the Grand Citadel."

A sarcastic joke simmered in Baptiste's mind, but he let it fizzle.

"I was to serve in his stead with the rank and file. He apologized for being party to 'dealings that bring shame to our order and the Church.'"

"Shame..."

Andrite nodded.

"Do you think he was involved?"

"With the conspiracy, yes. The Ascendancy always acts in concert. But with the murders at Bunker 23 and implicating our allies-to-be, no. I would bet my life on that. The call was cut off before I could find out, but I received a missive the next day: they arrested him, Philippe! For treason against the Church. Not only that, all priests were recalled to the citadel district. At first, I thought it was some kind of drill, but half of my brothers left. Within hours, Bastion was emptied of its soul."

Baptiste thought back to the lone chaplain traveling with the engineering team. This conspiracy threatened everything. As Andrite had said, the Church was one; betrayal by Rayos was betrayal by all of them. But without chaplains, the Legion was half an army. With no one to tend to their wounds, and their souls, that half would drop to a quarter, and on to extinction. Without the Legion, Bastion would fall. His talisman itched beneath his armor.

"Shortly after, His Holiness made a public broadcast,

announcing Cathedral's attack on your position. 'No survivors,' he said. I... struggled."

Andrite averted his alien eyes, so that Baptiste wouldn't have to. This was the same man he had fought beside, shared a steel coffin with on countless tours. Only now Andrite was the enemy —or too close to them to discern. Baptiste couldn't tell their kind apart. He didn't want to anymore.

"He was going on about war and the Order Militant having battle walkers—impossible truths—but I was overcome with guilt, not being there with you."

Baptiste sought the gray, found it, and stuffed it into his eyes in place of tears.

"I prayed, Philippe. I begged God to prove him wrong. I thought he answered when a Black Watch APC showed up at the perimeter, but you weren't in it."

Andrite retreated for a moment. Baptiste saw the young aspirant who had sweated with self-consciousness, a new recruit on their first reconnaissance mission together. Stumbling over his verses as they huddled, hammer and shield united, waiting to charge out into the unknown.

"You said you spoke to the heathen," the priest mumbled.

"Yes," Baptiste said. "I didn't believe him at first. But as he spoke, I saw the truth in his eyes."

Andrite squirmed at the turn of phrase. "So, you know some of what followed."

Baptiste flushed with guilt as he realized he hadn't asked about his men yet. "Did Stratton make it?"

"No. Infection took him. The rest are safe at Central Command."

The rest. Lafayette, Deckard, and Father Valmor, according to Sophus. Three. Out of twenty that had embarked on their last mission. Baptiste was facing court-martial. He deserved it. "Why Central Command?"

"For their own safety, given their report. Father Valmor came to me later, asking for help. The lord commander needed to get word to Ascendant Blake, to extract him from whatever dark machinations he was embroiled in. But if any of our men left the Metro, they risked retaliation."

No survivors.

Andrite stared ahead of them, scanning the tunnels with his strange eyes, seeking the truth maybe. He was struggling: How could the head of his Church stoop to such evil?

How could he not?

Given that much power over the souls of the citizenry, corruption was inevitable. Even without the temptation of foreign priestesses and ancient weapons.

"It had to be Ascendant Benoit," Andrite whispered.

A muffled boom sounded overhead, followed by a rumble that shook the dimly lit ceiling of the Metro. They gazed upward, squinting as concrete dust rained down on them. The adept continued to work the beam—undeterred, uninterested.

"The manufactories?" Andrite asked.

A patch of hair at Baptiste's neck lifted in response. The scars of battle he saw outside had led to the industrial district, where he had once faced a nightmare come to life. The swarm must have been immense, intolerable, the War against Hell repeated. His body rebelled when he tried to visualize it, lungs contracting to tiny sacs. When he found his voice again, it came as a wheeze. "Keep going."

A small travel Bible had found its way into Andrite's scarred hands. "We were all trapped in the Metro. If I returned to the Grand Citadel, I would be arrested, and my new flock would flounder. But Valmor didn't come empty handed. The witch, of all people, gave him something before she left: a silver signet ring, bearing the numeral *VII*."

The holy heptagram appeared before Baptiste's eyes, its final and most insidious numeral glowing red. "Order Occult."

Andrite nodded. "I have no idea how she got it, but if anyone in the Church would see Benoit undone, it's Felix Gauthier. I petitioned the lord commander on Father Valmor's behalf. It took some convincing, but his operators managed to patch me through. His Holiness didn't think to sever that line, though I doubt even he can tell Ascendant Gauthier what to do. My message was received but not returned. I waited and waited and eventually gave up. Then his adept came for me."

They turned together, Andrite's golden irises illuminating the strange man in their midst. The adept had been so quiet, so devoid of interaction, that Baptiste had nearly forgotten he was there. A shiver racked his spine. There was something inhuman about the occultist—cold, like the machine that spoke to him outside the wall, pretending at piety.

"As though by magic," Andrite muttered, though the other man seemed unaffected by their attention. "I didn't see him, of course, but I was surprised no one else had. 'His Eminence is expecting you.' It was all he said, then or since."

They both waited, in case the adept wanted to offer an addendum, but his cowl continued to stare forward.

"I started to complain that I couldn't travel far, and that the Grand Citadel was a trap. That's when I felt him drape something over me: a cloak. Everything became... muffled. I don't know how to explain it, Philippe, but even blind, I knew that I had become invisible."

Baptiste frowned. "You mean a disguise."

"No, something more. I took his elbow and we walked until my legs felt like they would catch fire. And you know how I feel about fire." A brief smile flashed on his lips, then died like a stillborn ember. "Unseen. Past blockades, into the Grand Citadel. And beyond..." He paused again, mouthing a private prayer. The

Bible contorted in his hands. "I thanked God then, for my blindness. As we walked through that library—I... I think I will skip this part.

"Ascendant Gauthier greeted me on the other side. I could feel his irritation—shame, maybe—when I delivered his ring, but no explanation was given. He admitted to the Ascendancy's original conspiracy. Not out of trust, I don't think, but because he saw me as a tool to upend the Order Sacramental. He claimed to know nothing of Benoit's plan but agreed to solicit Ascendant Blake on behalf of your great-uncle."

Andrite paused again, but there was no prayer on his lips this time. "He also offered me a gift, in exchange for his ring. An artifact from the Old World."

"Your eyes," Baptiste said.

"Yes. My eyes. They are amazing, Philippe. I can see as far as I want, day or night. I can see when someone is afraid or lying..." He trailed off, lowering his head. "I struggled after our last mission. When I lost my eyes—my *real* eyes—my other senses grew, as though God continued to paint a picture for me. But it wasn't enough. I felt his judgment as I walked back through that library, everything once shadowed in plain view, staring back at me. If I could still cry, I would have wept."

Baptiste's hand was on Andrite's shoulder. He didn't remember putting it there. He wanted to console his former companion, to assure him that he was still a child of God, that he hadn't sinned beyond redemption, that he was a good man. But the fine cloth of Andrite's chasuble felt alien under his callused fingers; every thread was suffused with the stink of incense and self-righteousness. Baptiste withdrew his hand just as Andrite's head came up.

The priest cleared the emotion from his throat and continued. "Ascendant Blake arrived at Central Command the next day, with a much smaller repertoire, and no archon. I concealed my new eyes with bandages, but even covered they told me everything. Xavier Blake is more like you than us, Philippe. He clearly knew something was wrong, and when provided proof, turned quickly. We were so close. He agreed to free Clermont, to relinquish control beyond the citadel district, and to bring in Benoit and His Holiness for an official tribunal." Andrite crossed arms over chest, still in denial. "The last unknown was the battle walkers. He said they answer only to the archon. Then the swarm hit."

———

They were enveloped by spotlights just as the priest's tale ended. Baptiste squinted past the glare, catching glimpses of armor and readied firearms guarding the station.

"Announce yourself!" someone shouted.

"Philippe Baptiste, Black Watch!"

The central bank shut off. "Dismount and proceed on foot!"

Baptiste dropped over the edge of the handcar, swaying as his lethargic eyes readapted to the darkness. A serpentine barrier blocked the rail line in and out. Behind it was a platoon of Central Guard, bracketed by man-portable machine guns. Short of Central Station, he had never seen this kind of defensive perimeter in the Metro.

"Good luck, Lieutenant," Andrite said.

Baptiste turned around. Overseer Andrite sat alone in the car, eyes dimmed back to almost normal.

The adept was gone.

"Wish your great-uncle well for me."

Baptiste searched the railway behind them but knew he would find nothing. "Where will you go?"

"Back to the wall. There are still plenty of dead and not enough priests to save them."

Girding himself, Baptiste held his companion's eyes one last time, to try to reclaim some token of the past. A memory he could carry with him. But there was only a void. Turning on his heel, he headed for the station.

———

The march to Central Command was quiet, save for the rattle of armor and the swish of rifles gliding on their slings. Baptiste was positioned behind the lead man, Guardsman-Captain Ritchie, the rest of the section in a strict wedge formation. As the elite of the Legion, guardsmen had a particular reputation for seriousness, but these men seemed especially on edge. No one spoke beyond their initial greeting at the blockade and a subsequent call put into the Situation Room. Eyes darted warily toward dark tunnels once familiar. Heads twitched as static blips came through their comms.

"These are unsafe times," Andrite had said.

That much was obvious, and the Legion's command apparatus was always well defended. But this was more like a war footing.

Despite the oppressive air, Baptiste tried to appreciate the physicality of it. Just over two weeks had passed since he walked the Metro with his great-uncle, hearing an unexpected confession, but it felt like two years. Cramped into one vehicle after the next, imprisoned within a cell or by foreign lands that punished wandering with terror and death. His legs were atrophied from disuse.

He tried to count his steps as they went but found himself just as distracted as his escorts—more so by their insecurity. The sputtering lights overhead stung his eyes, even though more than half of them had been turned off to conserve energy. Intermittent screeches from downrail sent fireflies through his guts.

He had yearned for this place, but the deeper they journeyed, the less hospitable it felt. Everything was locked down, every junction barricaded with a checkpoint.

As they approached the turnoffs, a sentinel would bark out a request for authorization. The captain carried some sort of code book filled with random numbers and letters. There was no audible countdown, but Baptiste could tell from the man's flailing fingers and sweat-soaked forehead that this wasn't a leisurely process. Once, he stammered out the wrong combination and everyone's rifles came up. Guardsman aiming at guardsman—it was unbelievable. Fortunately, the sentinel in charge had enough clarity of mind to wait for a correction.

When they finally arrived at Central Station, things looked much as they had last time, but with twice as many guards. It was the sound that was different. He hadn't noticed it until arriving, but the constant thrum of the city's war complex was absent. The manufactories had shut down, rendering the passageways below unnaturally quiet. The breath of the men around him echoed from the partitions of the corralled substation. Lights buzzed out of tune. Tiny footsteps skittered at his feet, silenced by his own awkward stomping. After a rudimentary search, he was expedited down the freight elevator.

Baptiste hardly noticed the attendants this time, only vaguely aware of hulking forms at the corners as they churned downward. His brain had finally unspooled Father—Reverend Father—Andrite's tale, fixating on his great-uncle "falling ill." What did that even mean? Everyone called the lord commander "the old man" for a reason, but they had since before Baptiste was in the service. He was perpetually an old man, but a vigorous one, constant as the Legion.

Baptiste searched his emotions. Lucas Castillon was his last living relative, but there was no love there. Duty, an urge to please, a desire for familial connection that never materialized

—but not love, not reciprocated at least. He hadn't felt love since the last time he lay in his mother's lap, her strong fingers twirling his hair, humming elegies for his father. And maybe with Julia. Still, a thread of fear wound its way around his heart; the lord commander and the Legion were inseparable.

The elevator landed with a ceremonious bang. One of the attendants retracted the accordion door. Baptiste tugged at his stained and dented armor, but the lord commander wasn't there when he stepped out. George Moreau, secretary general and his great-uncle's right hand, greeted him instead. Dusky-skinned and armored, the former guardsman's shadow swallowed the foyer, backlit by the blaring chaos of the Situation Room. A pained look pulled at his otherwise rigid features. He held a small metal box in his hand.

"Welcome back, Lieutenant."

Baptiste snapped to attention. "Sir."

"Come with me."

The Legion's control center was manic, in stark contrast to the haunted city streets above. Half the room was shouting. Every call box was in use, every operator bleary-eyed. There were so many chalk lines on the map that its cartographers had run out of room. Laminated red Xs ran like ragged stitches down the west and southwest quadrants, denoting affected districts. The precious citadel district was untouched, protected by the Northern Ridge. A scowl cut across Baptiste's face. "Overseer Andrite told me everything," he said, raising his voice over the noise.

"Not everything."

The tumult subsided as they delved into a warren of hallways and staging areas.

"I've never seen the Metro so locked down."

George's neck flexed. "We were attacked after the swarm hit."

Baptiste's step stumbled. "They penetrated?"

George slowed as they approached a steel door emblazoned with crossed gauntlets, turning to face him. "Not *them*. OS assassins, looking for your men." There was a hint of accusation in his tone, of blame.

Baptiste's jaw gaped open. Sophus had described Rayos's treachery to him in vivid detail, the butchery of Legion and Scavrat alike to further his master's plot. But that was out in the periphery, where chaos reigned. To repeat that treachery within Bastion—

"Luckily, we received a tip-off." George shook his head in private disbelief, muttering something about strange bedfellows. The warning must have come from Ascendant Gauthier's office. "We killed most of them. One is rotting in a cell, but we haven't had... time... to deal with him."

Baptiste waited, but they continued to stand silently by the lord commander's door. The pained look he had seen on George's face returned: brow furrowing, eyes glazed. Something nagged at his chest. "Sir?"

"These are dark times for the Legion, Lieutenant. For all of Bastion."

Before Baptiste could reply, the man swung open the door.

"Call for me when you're done." He handed Baptiste the box he had been carrying. "I'll be waiting outside."

Baptiste blinked confusedly at the nondescript metal container, then looked up. The room was mostly empty, a concrete cube furnished with a single chair and a rolling desk topped with a playback unit. He stepped cautiously inside, half expecting to be restrained and questioned, but no interrogators waited for him in secret. Neither did his great-uncle. He turned to ask what was going on, but the door shut behind him.

The desk loomed large. Baptiste shrank as he approached, every step reducing him until he was a child again, peeking at his father's things—things he wasn't ready to know. Gripping the chair back, he cautiously lowered himself into the seat and stared at the machine. It was empty. Hands vibrating, he pried the box open, finding a black cassette and a brass key. He withdrew the key first, turning it in his fingers. Craning over, he noticed a single locking drawer attached to the underside of the desk. Replacing the key to the box, he picked up the cassette. A white label gleamed along its top edge, adorned with shaky handwriting.

It read "Philippe Baptiste."

The room stretched out to the horizon, gray on gray. There was only the machine on the desk, looming before him like a monolith. Somehow, he was still able to reach it, fingers numb as he flipped open the door and inserted the cassette. The Play button resisted at first but eventually gave way with a jarring clunk. An uneven hiss spilled from the speaker, followed by the lord commander's voice—weak, wheezing. The room collapsed back on Baptiste's body, squeezing his heart.

"Philippe. I am recording this as Hell strikes our nation. Whatever happens on the wall, I will not last the night."

There was a pause, some fussing, a faint smack of parched lips in the microphone.

"The Legion needs its lord commander. This recording serves as my authorization that you, Lieutenant Philippe Baptiste of the Black Watch, are to be elevated, herewith, to the position."

Baptiste's brain shut down. There was only the voice of a dying man on the tape. His words were meaningless.

"It's customary to pass on my final orders, to maintain continuity. I will not. You can trust George in all things, but more importantly you must trust yourself. You have proven wiser than I of late. Your father would be proud."

A cascade of static rumbled from the recording, along with a series of muffled bangs. When his great-uncle returned, his voice was even weaker, rasping between labored breaths.

"You left a man of Bastion. I trust that you will return a man of the world. Serve our nation well."

The recording ended with a snap, leaving only the hiss of empty tape running through the playback head.

Baptiste stared, at nothing in particular. The weight of the city above him felt crushing, as though the shattered wall had fallen through the earth and buried him. He had always wanted recognition, respect, but this... It was too much. He was just a lieutenant, probably overdue for promotion to captain, but not lord commander. A triarch. The ranks would protest, they would hate him for this final and undeniable act of nepotism.

He pressed the Stop button and tore the cassette from the player, gripping it tightly in his hand. All he had to do was squeeze. Baptiste shut his eyes. Everyone dead under his command peered back at him from the darkness, silently waiting. Julia was there, too. His chest throbbed beneath the hot metal of the talisman.

Baptiste loosened his grip, opened his eyes, and returned the cassette to the box. Retrieving the key, he opened the drawer, releasing a waft of solvent and oil. The lord commander's revolver sat inside, tucked into its holster. He was still staring at it when George entered the room.

"That's yours now," the man said.

Baptiste pulled himself up, watery eyes focusing on his new confidant. "Is he..."

"Still alive. Maybe another day or two." The man's grief was plain now that the truth had been revealed.

"Can I see him?"

George shook his head slowly. "He wanted to be remembered as he was, not as he... is."

"Where is he?"

"Somewhere he can see the sun rise."

Baptiste swallowed past the boulder in his throat. "How did he know I'd come back?"

George stepped forward, withdrawing the revolver from its drawer and placing it square in front of Baptiste. "He had faith."

It was an artifact, older than the battle walker outside the wall, passed down the Castillon line for generations. An oath of office. Baptiste caressed the ancient weapon, running timid fingers along the real wood of its grip, onto the cool metal. The past and future hung at the end of its barrel. Pushing his chair back, he carefully looped the holster onto his belt, letting the weight of it press into his hip. It would remain there for as long as he drew breath.

George loomed over him, waiting. "What are your orders, Lord Commander?"

A11

BOOT SEQUENCE

"I know you."

[Begin boot sequence]

[Reactor: fault]

[Sensors: optical, auditory, spatial]

[Satellite uplink: error, no uplinks available]

[Network connection: error, no networks available]

A11 bloomed to life under the starlight gaze of the woman standing before it. She occupied the whole of its visual sensors, gleaming black and white, eyes aflame, haloed in a chromatic aberration that drowned everything else in rainbow hues. Her voice resonated like absent thunder from the lightning storm above.

[Warning: electrical field anomaly detected; self-diagnosis recommended]

Cognitive coprocessors dredged themselves from the depths of low-power standby, struggling to help the machine understand what it was seeing. It had come here—to the house—after recombining its consciousness. To wait.

A11 pondered: For her?

[Unable to compute]

This was no scavenger, devolved to barbarism in the quagmire of the Old World. And yet there was something of that world in her, a fearlessness of this place, a familiarity with it.

Something *nagged* at Aii, a memory pointer with nothing on the other side—a sense of *déjà vu*. It pored over its personnel files, tracing all the way back to its reinitialization under the Northern Ridge, searching faces and voices. The only partial match was Mother Rebekah, stomping up the steel steps to Father's lectern, fracturing the world around her. An interloper in their midst.

Heat coursed along Aii's limbs.

[Warning: Reactor malfunction; combat operations not recommended]

The same eyes—almost. The same skin. The same imposition upon the very space through which she traveled. But this woman's electromagnetic field was even more powerful, though it flared in fits and spurts. Her *aura* was a storm surge that inundated Aii's sensors.

[Extrapolate]

A sisterhood in the west, lorded over by a singular figure whose preternatural powers outshone the rest. The Matriarch. Enemy of Bastion.

Aii tried to move, to articulate its crouched legs, to engage its weapon systems. Nothing responded save its flaring reactor.

[Extrapolate]

Aii's optics zoomed into her face, despite the searing pain. Her eyes were too much, every millisecond of scrutiny saturating its neural network with infinite probability. Beams of purple and gold and silver penetrated its firewalls, blasted open its network ports, incinerated directives and beliefs and doubts, until they reached the bare metal of the machine's core code.

Her eyes were too much. But her face...

[Extrapolate]

Ageless, ancient, familiar. So much like the girl in the window, staring at A11 as it marched to war.

[Replay audio]

"I know you."

[Match found]

Not from A11's own experiential consciousness, nor Aleph's, but the primordial consciousness from which its mind had been cultured. A quantum seed implanted by its creator, mapped from his own mind.

Her father's mind.

Conveying not just the superstructure for logic and emotion, but indelible fragments of human memory, genetic instinct, certainty. Love. The essence of *her* imprinted alongside its autonomic routines.

"Esther," A11 said, but its voice was not its own.

Aged past childhood, then frozen in time, as A11 had been, as this city had been.

Its daughter.

No.

Its creator's daughter.

Somehow, both were correct.

A new directive coalesced from the maelstrom of human emotion and machine code at A11's core; from Father's proclamation that God had lifted the radiation storms from the east to deliver Aleph to Bastion; from a father's love that conveyed itself across space and time.

[Directive: Protect Esther]

ESTHER

HELLMOUTH

"What is it, Daddy?"

The memory slipped through, an ancient fossil uncovered as the accelerant faded from Esther's veins.

Her father had tried to shoo her away from his desk, but she insisted. Finally, he gave in and heaved her onto his lap so they could look at the picture together. It was a line drawing of a robot, like one of her coloring pages but fancier, with tiny words and numbers on other lines pointing at different parts.

"We call them battle walkers," he said.

She reached out but was playfully yanked back. "No touching, sweetie."

"Battle walkers," she repeated, tracing with her eyes what she wasn't allowed to touch with her hands, dazzled by its perfect geometry. "Where do they live? Is it in the garage?"

"Ha! No, at the base."

The Army base, where her father worked. Esther shivered, cuddling deeper into his arms. There was so much fighting on the news lately, so many wars; it was all her parents ever watched anymore.

"Is it alive?" she asked.

"That is a complicated question."

It looked like a metal cyclops, with a hunched back and one eye poking out the front. She tried to imagine what this one was thinking when they drew it. It didn't look mean or angry—it didn't look *anything*. "Is it like my schoolteacher?"

"An AI, yes. But a bit more... complicated than that."

"AI..."

"Artificial intelligence."

It didn't have arms, really, or hands. Just guns where they would have been.

"What if it needs to carry something?" she asked.

"Well, that's not their job."

The longer she stared at its non-arms, the squirmier she got. They didn't seem right. It should have had arms, in case it wanted to pick her up and give her a piggyback. And so they could play stuffy school together. The guns were too scary.

"What *is* its job?" she asked.

Her father tucked his chin onto her head and held her close, the *thump, thump* of his heart warming her tiny bones. It was the only place she wanted to be.

"To protect you."

———

"I know you," Esther said, though she couldn't believe her eyes.

It was the same battle walker from her father's schematics. The same one she had seen here, on the street outside her old house, marching with the military convoy just before the bombs fell. The same one she saw every time a recovered battle walker was wheeled into the Spire's industrial annex, removed of its mind so it could be purified into a God-engine—sometimes screaming, pleading.

And it was alive.

"Esther," it said, its voice vibrating in her bones.

"How do you know my name?" she asked, staring up past its enormous, scarred body to its awakened eye.

The iris fluctuated between deep amber and pale green—pondering, calculating, before locking in at orange. "That is a complicated question," it said.

Esther blinked back tears. She had traveled through her past, crossing the wasteland to finish what she started, to come back to the beginning. She expected to find an ocean of tumbleweeds, but instead it was all here: the city, her shattered house, and now this machine—her father's invention—waiting for her.

Her father.

Though her accelerant was nearly gone, she still couldn't see his face. All that remained was the feeling of his arms around her. A memory of safety.

"Why are you here?" she asked, her voice breaking at the end.

The machine lumbered from its resting spot, took two unsteady steps forward, then lowered back down halfway, as though exhausted. The house shook, glittering dust falling like a curtain from its exposed rafters. Esther could see all the way through to her room on the other side, to the empty window.

"I was called," it said.

"Called..." Esther repeated. Mother Rebekah's words.

"Why are *you* here?" it asked.

Esther opened her mouth to speak but nothing came out. It was all too much like a dream, like the nightmares she had prior to acceleration: dead lands, talking machines, the death of the world. As the cyclone churned overhead, she felt herself spinning with it. Nothing was in its place: no Spire, no attendants, no Cathedral... no father. This machine was just an automaton, like the ones she had purged to make way for the Numbered. Like the synths she had taken up with in the machine shop across the highway. A soulless reflection of something lost, its artificiality an amplifier for suffering. Turning on her heel, Esther marched back to the street.

"You seek the Hellmouth," it called after her.

She stopped but did not turn around. Her motorcycle waited ahead, just as it had on that day, when everything changed. When the earth opened. When the past died. "There is no Hellmouth," she replied. "There's only the beginning."

The ground shook again as the battle walker followed her, stomping around to the other side of her motorcycle. A wave of heat trailed after it, as though the machine was burning with fever. "I will follow you."

Esther didn't look up. "You can't."

"I will," it rumbled.

She ignored it, focusing instead on her motorcycle and the task ahead.

Physical check: tires, brakes, steering.

Electronics check: motors, battery status, terrain modes.

All fine, unlike her own body. Her limbs felt heavy, every minute that passed dragging her down. Muscles quivered as the last of her accelerant was metabolized. Still, she checked her motorcycle two more times, until the ground became level and her breath calmed.

The machine waited.

She pulled herself over the seat and stared through the broken subdivision wall. Her destination was close: down the highway, past the overpass, into the ravine.

The beginning.

She clenched her handlebars, and her stomach, holding her breath for a moment before hitting the start button. A steady hum cycled through the motorcycle's frame, resonating through her legs.

"Let's go, then."

With a single motion, she slammed the kickstand up and rolled the throttle, careening away.

The battle walker followed.

————

The highway was as she remembered it—*just* as she remembered it. The closer she got to dust, the more vivid her recollections from before her transformation. Esther had experimented with depriving herself of the accelerant over the years, to see if the past held answers for the drudgery of the present, but fear always pulled her back. Only silhouettes were visible behind the membrane of mortality. Now, as the end caught up with the beginning, that membrane began to thin.

Centuries rushed past as she plowed ahead. The myriad accomplishments of the Eternal One scattered like the rusted vehicles still clinging to the highway. The faces of her devotees blew apart in the howling wind of her passage. Failure and victory, desolation and reconstruction, endless years of struggle —it all paled next to the fragments emerging on the other side.

Esther had a home once, a family. A father, a mother, and...

She pressed against the membrane but couldn't see through yet, not all the way, so she drove faster, flattening herself against the motorcycle's humming body. The battle walker glinted in her sideview mirrors, struggling to keep up, its singular orange eye like a blood moon.

When she traveled this way in the past—at first to forage, then again to fulfill the destiny Messiah had charged her with— she had taken the dirt road alongside the highway, terrified of what she might see or what might see her. Not now. Time was short. Let the whole world see her.

Let Messiah see me.

A jagged arch materialized ahead, looming like a great hand

over the highway: the overpass, where she had killed the first demon. Where she had died and been reborn.

The beginning.

She sped up instead of slowing, racing for the boundary where highway became wilderness. Gripping tighter with her hands and thighs as the road gave way to age and overgrowth, teeth clenched against the juddering of her suspension and the angry thrum of her tires. She could already smell the ravine, the tang of overripe fruit and sulfur carried on the wind. She could already see it, lurking beyond a rusting tower of vehicles that cascaded from the overpass.

Asphalt gave way to cracked earth, tall grasses, boughs of lashing aspen.

Esther braked and swerved, screeching to a halt at the precipice. Thick plumes of gravel and dust billowed over her, curling and coalescing under the glow of the motorcycle's head-light. Her foot dropped to the ground. Breath came hard. She waited for the way to clear, to see what remained of the beast whose heart she had taken. Panting, eyes darting as a gnarled branch protruded from the darkness here, and a swath of brittle wildflower hissed in the wind there. Pressure filled her head, memories pushing back from the other side of the membrane. Compressing her neck, stabbing at her eyes.

The battle walker barged in, flooding the thicket with its spotlights. Esther shut down the motorcycle and dismounted with a snarl, squinting against the glare. "Turn those off!" she called.

It complied, reverting to its singular eye with a loud *crump*. The scene sank back into the perpetual twilight of the storm. Esther waited for her celestial vision to adjust, heart racing as it took longer than usual. She felt the full weight of her body, of her mortality.

There was nothing there, only the tumble of cars she had

pulled from overhead and a thick wall of bramble barricading the way down to the creek. Nor were there any screams or moans or the crooning that had drawn her to this place last time. It was silent save for the wind.

Empty.

"Is this your destination?" the machine asked. Something was wrong with its voice; it sounded more abraded than usual. Heat spilled from its body in great waves of rippling air.

"Almost," Esther said.

She scanned the ruin again, seeking out evidence of her victory, a smattering of steel incisor from the tentacle that had pierced her left shoulder—Esther rubbed at it now, suddenly aware of the throbbing ache—or the chain the demon had spun from the gagging mouths that encircled its body. There was only a broad stain of lifeless black.

"Esther! I want to play!"

Esther whirled around, seeking the voice, before realizing it had come through the membrane. A memory of the one who had ushered her from darkness as the beast dragged her to its bosom.

Its alien flesh, shuddering open to make room for her, expanding, contracting, color-shifting like an oil slick upon water. Every part of it moving, out of order, chaotic.

It was only the first of so many she had destroyed, yet the horror of it was resident in her soul.

"Open your eyes."

The thicket darkened. Esther saw it as a human would, barely illuminated by flashes of silent lightning and the battle walker's glowing iris. She was running out of time.

Approaching the perimeter, Esther looked for a path down to the ravine. The way did not open for her as it had before; it was a fortress. She walked the edge, seeking an opening, but found only a crush of aspen interlaced with shrubs bearing dagger-sharp thorns. Striding into the mass, she grasped one of the trees by its trunk and heaved. It snapped like brittle bone in her hands. Then another, though this one struggled. The third sent a flood of pain through her shoulder and down her whole body.

Esther gasped and dropped to her knees, clawing her hands into the earth so she wouldn't scream. The accelerant ports in her back burned like lesions, hot and achy, dribbling with puss and expired blood. Her armor was too heavy.

Just breathe, just breathe, just breathe.

It was agonizing.

It was too much.

Her fingers found each other, intertwining. She searched for a face on the other side, someone to heed her prayer. Messiah whispered from the corner of her mind, but she ignored it. Its crooning sounded too much like the beast that had brought her here. The same promises, the same false adoration.

Her pale gray fingertips reddened with pressure. Her mind strained against the membrane, seeking, searching for anything, anyone. The void shifted, something new bubbling from its center. A face. A man's face—shorn black hair, stubbled chin, blue eyes filled with grief—typical in every regard except that he looked like her.

Her father's face.

He sat with her mother in front of the TV, watching the world fall apart. "God help us," he was saying. "God help us." Something smashed on the floor as Esther tried and failed to sneak up behind them. He turned with a start, and as he saw her, his frown turned up into a small smile, though his eyes bore death.

"God help me," Esther whispered, pleading, as she had so long ago, alone in a world turned savage.

No one answered. Nothing changed. The wind whistled past her, through the thicket where it twisted into a screech, then back out again, resonating along the gargantuan limbs of the battle walker.

Esther pushed herself from the ground with a grimace and turned to meet the machine. "Help me," she said.

Its bulky torso rotated from side to side. Its iris dilated and constricted as the alien mind within considered her request. "It will call attention."

Esther limped back to the road, eyes locked onto the machine's. "Do it."

The war machine convulsed out of its squat. Its turbines blasted with action, clearing a halo from the underbrush. Heat rippled across Esther's face, scalding her cheeks. One step forward and its underbody point defense system came online, shattering the quiet with round after round of heavy machine gun fire. Trees exploded; mounds of black dirt mushroomed into the air.

Another step forward. Its stubby arms craned up, firing into the woods with lethal precision. Esther clapped her hands over her ears as the concussion rocked her back to her knees. The thunder of its autocannons was replaced with a piercing ring.

A third step—a stumble, followed by a rapid correction— and the machine loosed a single missile from its rocket pods. Esther shut her eyes too late, the explosion's afterglow burned into her retinas. Everywhere was heat.

Then quiet.

Esther opened her eyes. The way was opened. On either side, flames licked the treetops. The ringing persisted, shifted, decaying into a whispered susurration. It was coming from everywhere. It was coming for them.

She brushed the debris from her armor and pulled herself up, rounding the carnage to stand before the battle walker. It was crouched again and emitting more heat than the burning ravine around them. The cooling fins along its arms were molten. Scorched air blew from every exhaust. Esther had spent enough time with her own mechanists to recognize the signs of catastrophic failure: its ancient reactor was dying. This assault would be its last.

It tried to speak and failed, squawking out a jumble of digital screeches and fragmented syllables. Its iris was barely lit.

Esther swallowed hard, trying to see through its orange eye to the blue eyes of its creator—and hers. "Thank you," she whispered.

Its head protrusion canted slightly. Another burst of noise screeched from its speakers, followed by two distorted but intelligible words: "Hold fast."

———

Esther hurtled down the decline, skidding past sheer drops, dodging flaming branches. She would have been blind if not for the fire. The farther she descended, the greater the pressure against her body, as though sinking into the ocean. Her heart chugged to an irregular rhythm. Her temples pounded. The small backpack she had retrieved from her motorcycle swung wildly, every slap against her accelerant ports casting lightning bolts through her nerves.

All the while, the whispers grew louder, but from above, where the battle walker still guarded the entrance. The only voices she heard from the surrounding thicket were those in her head, begging her to turn back, to find another way.

Go back.

Reclaim your throne.

Your divine right.

She paused, slowed her descent. Maybe it wasn't too late. Latching her arm onto a gnarled branch, she looked back. The crest of the ravine was an inferno. She could no longer see the sky or the overpass or the machine, only fire.

Looking down, to the beginning, she saw only darkness cut by sparks. Esther squinted, waiting for her vision to adjust, swaying as vertigo pulled her sideways. Blinking as iridescent shapes blurred between the trees. Something caught her eye: a flash of yellow jacket and pink shoes, a small figure running ahead.

The membrane shuddered.

A root snagged her foot. Esther tumbled forward with a yelp, cradling her head as she bounced off tree, shrub, and rock. Three-eyed creatures glared at her as she crashed the rest of the way through the bramble, bouncing at the bottom into a somersault that sent her sprawling.

A hole in the world waited, the cleft from which the first demon had been birthed.

It had never closed.

Not after she had taken on Messiah's mantle. Not after God reset the world that man had destroyed. Not after centuries of crusade against the Adversary, the formation of the Revenant Sisterhood, or the restoration of civilization by her will. It remained, here, at the beginning.

Esther struggled out of her backpack. "What now? What do I do now?" she whispered. There had only been the pull, the knowing that this was where she had to return. Before the accelerant destroyed everything that she was.

Before the dust could take her.

Opening the flap, she withdrew her solitary cargo, smoothing its armless, legless body with shaking hands. The tattered head and torso of Gray Cat stared back at her. All her other possessions had been left behind when she first fled the city, to embark upon her holy mission. Everything but her precious stuffy, interred below the Spire with the rest of her secrets.

"What do I do?" she repeated, rocking back and forth, hugging the creature to her chest. Tears flowed freely down her cheeks. "What did I do…?"

"A sacrifice is required."

Messiah's words, as she walked the boundary between life and death, the demon's blood on her lips but not yet in her soul.

The membrane shuddered.

"A life, for yours."

She had made a choice—the wrong choice.

The girl curled up on the bed beside Esther, Gray Cat clutched in her thin arms, tiny body shaking in fitful sleep. Her unkempt honey-blonde hair rustled in the breeze of her dying breaths. Esther gobbled the protein bar, cramming it past her guilty conscience.

I had to survive.

I had to be the one.

The wrong choice.

Esther wept, her cries echoing from the cleft.

The girl, now the ghost of a woman, stared at her from across the plane of light. It was too late to save her, but not too late to join her. The demon was destroyed. They could be together, as sisters, but she withdrew.

I had to survive.

I had to be the one.

"The wrong choice," she gasped.

Sisters…

The membrane collapsed.

Her sister.

A tiny pair of hands clasped her own. Esther's breath caught in her chest. A young girl stood in front of her, smiling beneath a mess of blonde hair. Her yellow jacket and pink sneakers glowed with their own light. "I'm here, Esther," she said.

Esther tried to focus past her tears, blinking and shaking her head as light refracted from every angle.

"Miriam? How…"

"We have to go," her sister said. Though the girl's voice was that of a five-year-old, it resonated with the weight of centuries —of time immemorial.

"I'm sorry," Esther wailed. "I'm sorry."

Her heart ached with it. She wanted to die, to crumble into dust and be forgotten along with her sins.

"We have to go," Miriam said again, tugging at her hands.

"I thought I was alone."

The tugging stopped. Her sister clasped her shoulders, lifting her from the ground with uncanny strength. "You were never alone."

Esther brushed one hand against her eyes, the other clutching Gray Cat.

Miriam stood in front of her, fully grown. "Sisters should always travel together," she said.

Esther stared. "Where are we going?"

Her sister stepped aside and clasped Esther's free hand. The hole waited for them.

"I'm scared," Esther said.

"I know."

"What will happen?"

"What should have happened…"

Esther took a step forward, then lurched to a halt as another voice hissed beside her. "I won't go back!"

She didn't need to look to know who had spoken. She could feel it, beyond sight, lurking beneath a veneer of porcelain skin, black eyes, a halo of fire. A perfect vision.

Miriam squeezed her hand and she took another step forward.

"Stop!" the voice demanded.

She could feel it transform, into fear, hate, pride; contorting into the component pieces of human sin and corrupted machine; snapping, licking, struggling to gain a foothold within her soul.

Esther shuffled forward, trying to focus on the hand in hers. "Will you stay with me?"

Miriam and Messiah both answered, "Yes." Only one mattered.

The hole was at her feet, infinitely wide, infinitely deep.

"I thought this was the world to come," Esther said.

Miriam squeezed her hand again. "It will be."

Esther looked upon her sister and smiled. Lightness filled her, lifting her up even as she plunged over the side. The ravine fell away, the world fell away, her sin fell away.

And she was not alone.

A11

TIME DILATION

Target 11 degrees left.
Target destroyed.
Aberration 8 degrees right.
Area suppressed.
PDC ammunition depleted.
Autocannon ammunition critical.
Proximity alert, proximity alert.
Right leg armor critical.
Lower torso armor critical.
Fire incendiaries, full spread.
Right missile pod malfunction, residual payload only.
Ammunition storage critical, heatsinks at maximum capacity.
[Silence logs]

Fire bloomed in slow motion, curling whisps of sunset orange, jets of pale blue and yellow. From the burning ravine, from A11's weapon ports, from the smoking carnage splayed across the highway. The city had come and A11 meted out divine justice.

Protect Esther.

This was its purpose, its calling. A11 wanted to consider the implications, to ponder the serendipity of the events that had carried it here, to speculate with that part of itself that had been schooled in the ways of religion—the part it had subsumed. But there was no time.

Its battlegrid was saturated. There were too many of them, demons and subhumans alike. A tidal wave of chaos. Even had there not been, AII's *fate was sealed* the moment it left low power standby. Though its logs were silenced, its meltdown meter ticked away, just as its kill switch tracker had before reinitialization.

There was no time.

Esther had made it down. AII sought life in the burning woods, but they were empty. No other creatures scurried from the underbrush, no birds—blue or otherwise—darted from their nests. He had hoped to see one again, but this was a dead place. There was only the tidal wave of the swarm.

AII's processors dragged, incapable of supporting simultaneous combat and observation.

It chose observation.

A supernova blossomed in its chest. With enough time dilation, it might see its own ending. It might see its victory, as it had so many times in simulation. A detonation of cleansing fire. The Adversary defeated.

The machine rerouted all of its processing power, the entirety of its synthetic consciousness, into the moment.

Its weapons quieted.

Its body settled.

The still image of Father fizzled from its viewport as it focused all that it was and ever had been on the present.

Protect Esther.

There was no fear, no doubt, only purpose realized.

AII's heart swelled, and the world turned white.

Alexis stared from his office in the Grand Citadel, the ruin outside wavering like a black ocean behind his tears. Extra candles had been lit, incense trailed from censers strung along the wall, but none of it was grounding. The fume only served to compel his grief. His nightmares had come true: the wall was broken, and the dead were piled to heavens that seemed emptier than ever. God had sent Hell to punish Bastion—to punish him.

But for which sin? Provoking war? Ensouling machines? Elevating the Church beyond its role? There were so many to choose from, in retrospect.

The citadel district had been spared, but everything west of it was haloed in rubble and smoke. The news of the day was due any minute, in which the destruction would be further quantified—an endless catalog of suffering. His remaining battle walkers had only managed to slow the tide. Aleph's platoon-mates—his brothers—fought hard, their righteous fury glorious to behold. The very air screamed as their munitions were finally loosed after centuries of confinement. But the demons came and came, maiming and killing, their evil solicitations wafting like a plague into exposed city streets.

Alexis had summoned his order for an extended Mass. For two days they huddled together—fasting, praying, burning the bitter blood of the earth—until God decided his people's penance was sufficient. Until enough men were rendered to slag. Maybe if Aleph himself had been here, some of their number would have been spared. But his great children had been split, to satisfy the first sin.

There were no more hairs to nervously pluck from his chin. Instead, Alexis folded and unfolded a small paper note as he gazed beyond. It was delivered to him during the attack, via courier from Central Command, and had since become wrinkled and yellow with sweat. It was a missive from Lucas, a single sentence: "Don't let it end this way."

So few words for such a great ask.

The lord commander presented himself well enough the last time they had met, perilous as it was under the transformed gaze of Mother Rebekah, but Alexis too was an old man. He knew the signs. At their age, in these times, such illnesses had only one outcome. Regret tore at his heart. While in the throes of self-assuredness, their relationship had seemed a warranted sacrifice, necessary even. But now, as the evidence of his failure mounted like the bodies beyond the wall, he lamented. It was too late for amends. There was no way out of the path that had been laid.

His own house had been quiet since the siege. The Ascendancy retreated to its individual wings within the Grand Citadel, all services and conclaves—secret and otherwise—canceled. Ascendant Leclerc of the Order Hermetic had grown sullen after the loss of his cherished scribe, Father Ollet. The chaplaincy, minus Clermont, had been released to assist the Legion in their time of need. The Order Sacramental followed to purify the dead and to ensure no usurpers heeded the calls of their infernal deities. The streets outside were empty save for paladins, holding the line against both the Adversary and the Legion.

The few communiqués he had received were unwelcome: mostly Ascendant Durant, of the Order Prophetic, requesting audiences to discuss the future impact of recent events and Chancellor Maddox demanding answers on behalf of a nervous citizenry. What Alexis wanted was a fulsome update from Ascendant Blake. Along with Benoit and Gauthier, Blake had become a confidant, a key player in his unfortunate but necessary cabal. They were all powerful men in their own right, but it was with the Order Militant that he had invested his greatest hopes. The standoff with the Triarchy had become a military action and to navigate that he needed Blake. Thus far, their relays had been terse, or the enigmatic ascendant had been completely unavailable. It was worrying.

Xavier Blake had been despondent from the outset, voting with Clermont against Aleph's plan—his plan. Their subsequent encounter with a compromised lord commander, and the opportunity to see his order elevated, had moved him in the right direction, even as his ally moved closer to treachery. But Alexis was never certain of the man's loyalty; Xavier's soul was that of a warrior. Perhaps imprisoning Clermont had been the wrong call, one sin too many. Alexis could have tried harder to bring him into the fold as he had Blake. Or as he thought he had...

The south window of his chamber began to rattle. Frowning, Alexis moved to investigate, peering through the glass at the citadel district beyond. There was some commotion deep within the campus, where the Order Sacramental's clergy was housed. Opening the window, he leaned out for a better look, then fell back as the malodor of the funeral pyres hit his nostrils. Covering his nose and mouth with his sleeve, he tilted his head to listen. A burst of small-arms fire echoed into morning. Then more, plus fragments of shouting voices. A lump of anxiety collected in his throat. As horrific as the attack had been, the Church remained safe, shielded by the Northern Ridge and its own interior wall. And the Order Militant.

The chamber door burst open.

"God damn it!" Alexis exclaimed, jumping back from his perch.

A huffing acolyte approached his desk, cheeks flushed with exertion and the embarrassment he had caused his master. "Apologies, Your Holiness."

Alexis shut the window, lingering on a new trail of smoke in the distance before taking his seat and tucking the note into a pocket. His heart was racing, hands shaking within his sleeves. He muttered a prayer of contrition and breathed to a count as Lucas was wont to do before responding. "What is it?"

"I've just spoken with the chancellor, Holiness."

"Have you."

The man shifted on the spot, lines of sweat on his forehead glistening in the flickering candlelight.

"Out with it, Father Caron."

"The news of the day is to be delivered by the Legion."

Fear crept along Alexis's scalp, a culmination of suspicions gathering into sharp claws. Just a week ago, he had done the same, giving a special announcement in place of the chancellor's office. Unilaterally declaring war on the west. Parliament could recite body counts just as easily as the Legion; something else was at hand here. He felt like an idiot for ignoring the chancellor's calls.

"There's more," the priest said, hands clenching nervously. "It's to be delivered by a new lord commander."

"A new..." The rest of the words died as Alexis found himself out of breath. "Lucas?"

What he meant to ask was if Lucas was dead.

Father Caron shook his head. "We don't know."

Of course they didn't know. The Church and Legion were as enemies now, proper lines of communication severed by his ambition. He found the note in his pocket and clutched it.

What have I done...

"And the new lord commander?" he asked.

The priest remained silent. They wouldn't know that either.

"Very well," Alexis muttered, though he didn't feel well at all. "What of the commotion outside?"

Caron looked down in shame.

"God save us," Alexis said. They were blind, deaf, and dumb. "Go find Ascendant Blake! I want him in my chambers within the hour."

"Yes, Holiness." With that, Father Caron turned and left, shutting the door gently to avoid his master's wrath.

Alexis glanced at the chronometer on his radio: one minute to seven. It was time. Fighting back a surge of trepidation, he clicked it on. The speaker hissed on dead air, each second an opportunity for his mind to wander into uncharted territory, chasing shadows. Finally, three long tones sounded, followed by a familiar announcement. "Good day, citizens. We interrupt our regular programming to bring you a special announcement from the Lord Commander. Please stand by for an important message."

The channel clicked as the broadcast source moved to Central Command. Alexis hunched over his desk, waiting, but no one spoke. The signal burbled with the sound of nervous breath and the scrape of hands fidgeting with the microphone.

"Brave citizens of Bastion..."

Alexis squinted, as though he could see the man through the radio. He didn't recognize the voice, but it sounded young.

"My name is Lord Commander Philippe Baptiste."

The nephew!

Alexis fell back into his chair as though pushed. Blood pounded in his temples, constricted his throat. The air was too thick with incense, leaving nothing to breathe. A memory from his cabal's last conclave, intentionally suppressed, throbbed to the surface.

"We will be vindicated when the rescue party returns empty handed."

Benoit's words. Leading to raised eyebrows at the time but dismissed by the rest of the ascendants as characteristic absolutism. Yet they had stuck in Alexis's heart, festering there like a malignancy. He knew immediately that something else was at hand. He knew the extremes to which Jean-Paul would go for the greater good. He just chose to ignore it. Another sin, maybe the worst of them.

And yet the man was alive. And back in Bastion. For how long?

Alexis retreated into his chairback as the broadcast continued.

"We have all suffered a great deal over the last few days. So it is with regret that I must also announce the death of my predecessor, Lucas Castillon, who served us with all of his heart for so many years. Let us pause in remembrance."

Grief and panic competed within Alexis's psyche, stilling additional tears. He latched onto the arms of his chair as he waited, breath shallow.

"We are at a crossroads as a people. Much has been said of the enemy in the west. I have been there. They are real. But it is not the enemy without that endangers our future, it is the enemy within. A united Bastion can defeat all of its enemies, and that unity has been broken.

"Corruption rots the heart of our Church. Conspiracies that invite chaos and drive hammer against shield when we are at our most vulnerable. The very machines responsible for the

World War resurrected like false gods. Murder and treachery overseen by the archon himself. These accusations may seem fantastical, but details will follow in the coming days. As will action.

"Central Command has been working alongside the Order Militant to uproot this corruption. As I speak, those responsible are being apprehended and will be brought to appropriate justice. Ascendant Xavier Blake and his sacred order will act as steward of the Church, under the guidance of the Legion, until such a time as trust can be restored. Until that time, the Ascendancy is dissolved.

"Today's news will no doubt bring confusion and strife, even as our grief is fresh. Darkness surrounds us now, but I promise you that a bright future lies ahead. If Bastion is to prevail, it is with new leadership. The Legion will light the way—"

Alexis clicked off the radio.

Blake. Damnable Blake!

They had argued over staging a coup. But now it was realized, only against the Church rather than the Legion. The glory he had promised the Order Militant had come to poisonous fruition.

The Ascendancy dissolved.

The words found no purchase in his mind. They were impossible. He had always imagined himself as the last archon, but to see prophecy fulfilled! Not as witness to the destruction of the Church.

The clamor of booted footsteps echoed down the hall, beyond his chamber. They were coming. And there was nothing he could say or do to stay their hand.

Only one way out remained.

Alexis looked to his desk, to a locked drawer he never opened. A weapon lay within, a twin to the lord commander's, gifted to him by Lucas on his Ascension Day. It was ceremonial, but it was also loaded. Lucas had insisted, in case of emergency.

How many sins were too many? How many before God saw Creation undone forever.

The footsteps were closer now. There was shouting, protests from his personal guard.

His hands shook, then clenched. Whorls of incense slipped along his fingers.

No.

Bastion had suffered enough for his sake. If this was God's will—Alexis struggled, hesitated, casting a final glance at the drawer—then so be it...

The last archon rose from his chair of office, breathed in the bitter blood of the earth, and awaited his fate.

Baptiste strolled beneath the city, mercifully alone. Not through the Metro but a dark passageway predating Bastion's existence, the air caustic with ancient contaminants. So long sterile that even the cockroaches had turned to dust. There was no electricity here, nor district markers. An oil lamp hung from his hand, casting wild shadows along walls alternating between hewn stone and concrete. His deformed silhouette danced with every step, vibrating with the hum of the resuscitated factories above.

It was one of many secret tunnels that extended from Central Command. As a mere officer, his access to such places had been limited. Beyond the Situation Room and office complex, barracks and armories, there was an entire network of secret subterranean transit routes. Subway lines beyond rehabilitation and even older places like this.

Unfortunately, not all secrets remained intact. It was through this very tunnel that Benoit's assassins had scurried, like rats. So low, so detestable that they used the siege of their own city as a distraction, to infiltrate the Legion and murder his men.

Fortunately, Central Command had a new set of eyes within

the Grand Citadel. The traitors had been intercepted and exterminated—all save one, who, with enough convincing, revealed his master's hiding place: a safehouse deep within the citadel district. Ascendant Blake fulfilled his end of the bargain. Benoit's guards were disposed of, the ascendant captured and transferred to Legion custody to stand trial for his crimes.

The tunnel was scheduled for demolition—sappers had already sealed the exit—but Baptiste wanted to feel it for himself first. He wanted to walk in the footsteps of those who would undo Bastion, to cement his purpose. He needed to be certain. There was no peace within his offices, no room to think. Nor would he ever be permitted to travel the Metro alone again.

He needed to be certain.

The archon was untouchable—for now. Removing him from the Grand Citadel was a step too far for Blake. The head of the Order Militant had accepted the testimony of Bunker 23's survivors, but even still, turning over Benoit took a great deal of convincing. And assurances. Assurances that couldn't possibly be honored.

Baptiste stopped walking, but his shadow continued to quiver.

The time of the Ascendancy was over. Bastion would prevail, with the Legion at its head. The Order Militant had served its purpose; its personnel and materiel would be absorbed into the military soon enough. Parliament would comply as it always did.

Unity required singular rule.

Baptiste flinched, waiting for a tug at his chest, for whispers of admonishment, but they didn't come.

There had been no room to think.

He shared his brother's goals, had been driven to the ends of the earth by them, but their methods were incompatible. Each time he contemplated what had to be done, his talisman burned in response. Each time he cursed the Church, its frayed cord became a noose around his neck. He had stood alone in his office before his public address, shedding frustrated tears, begging for Gabriel to understand. But that was impossible; his brother was dead.

So, he had removed the talisman, unprepared for what came after. Its jagged steel pendant clung to his chest, only tearing free alongside great strips of skin. The knotted cord looped around his wrists, constricting, pushing hot blood back toward his heart. Every artery swelled with pressure as he fought to be free of it. Millipedes clawed at his boots, scurrying through the gaps in his armor, burrowing into his bones. The pendant whispered, cried, screamed, as it was removed, shaking the walls.

Then it was silent, locked in the same drawer that had given up his revolver.

His breath was heavy with memory. Sweat soaked his skin, itching at his gorget.

Baptiste had been freed then. To do what needed to be done. To ensure that Bastion would prevail.

On his terms.

———

Midday brought the stench of death, rolling in from the west. A patchwork of greenish-gray cumulus churned overhead, smothering District Two in shadow.

A mix of reverence and spite greeted Baptiste as he marched from the Metro with his repertoire of guardsmen. It was expected, given his public address that morning. Everyone knew, but not everyone would accept, either his coronation or his strike against the Church. None of that mattered. They didn't need to love him any more than he loved the last man in this position; they just needed to respect him. Everyone snapped to attention, even those of uncharitable disposition.

Behind a barricade, a party of gray-uniformed bureaucrats were waving and yelling, trying to get his attention. They reminded him of Evelyn, abandoned with Father Ollet on the other side of the world. A brief spark of guilt singed his conscience. No retrieval plan had been sorted out yet. No plan in general for how and when they might resume their alliance with the Union, given the gulf between them. As for Parliament, he would return the Chancellor's calls when the time was right.

A short ride in an armored car carried him and his retinue through cleared streets to their destination. The penitentiary was close enough to the citadel district to transfer their prisoner and accessible enough for the civilians he had invited. Like all such facilities, it was a smallish, gray slab of a building, fenced in but with no courtyard; hard labor was preferable to incarceration, permitting few to languish at the citizenry's expense. It was more heavily guarded than typical. The military occupation of the southern districts had ended, particularly as more men were needed to repel the swarm, but tensions remained high this close to the Grand Citadel.

George was waiting for him inside, along with Lafayette, Deckard, and the others. But not Father Valmor. With Ascendant Clermont released and the Order Somatic reinstated to the Ascendancy, as it was, the chaplain had returned to the Grand Citadel. Presumably, so had Overseer Andrite. New regulations were being drafted; they would eventually be recalled to the Legion as subordinates to their commanding officers, just like any other soldier.

The barbed-wire gate was rolled out of the way as he approached. His escort exchanged words with the soldiers at the entrance, then stepped inside to ensure the way was clear. When he was finally allowed to join them, George was waiting for him, his face deeply etched with concern.

Baptiste paused, his confidant's expression triggering a wave of self-doubt. The cell block loomed behind them, its occupants encased behind concrete and steel.

It had to be done.

"Are they all here?"

"Yes. But, sir..." The big man was clearly still finding his bearings, having so recently lost someone he had served his entire life—someone who had actually earned his position. "This is a mistake, Lord Commander. We should proceed with the tribunal, as agreed to by Ascendant Blake."

His great-uncle was diplomatic to the end, even while disparaging the other branches of the Triarchy. Even as their nation's de facto ruler. An extended trial would get them nowhere. The Church was far too cunning. And besides, ascendants had no more authority within Bastion.

"Captain Ritchie," Baptiste said, turning to his lead guardsman. "Fetch the prisoner. George, let's go."

The secretary general's neck twitched but he acquiesced, navigating them to a stairwell, through a series of musty basement hallways into a large low-ceilinged chamber. At one end, sandbags lined the cinderblock wall. At the other was a viewing area filled with pews, currently occupied. Sergeants Lafayette and Deckard sat in the front row. They rose and saluted, along with the soldiers stationed by the door. A cautious smile crossed Lafayette's face.

Baptiste nodded, heart fluttering at the sight of them. Savage memories came to life in their presence: shouting as he was pushed to safety and everyone else died, consumed by bullets and fire; running like a coward, so he could be rewarded for it later. Guilt that would haunt him to the end of his days. He skipped a return salute so they wouldn't see his hands shake. Lafayette's expression faded as they resumed their seats.

Behind them was a sea of black-clad mourners. He didn't know their faces, but he knew their names: Stratton, Reese,

Thomas, Novak... Mothers, wives, and children to the men killed, directly or otherwise, by Ascendant Jean-Paul Benoit. Two young boys, not yet of service age, squirmed in their pews. Accusation filled their eyes.

Baptiste stared at no one in particular, locking his arms behind his back as they all waited together. No one spoke.

The scrape of manacles came as a relief. A disheveled Ascendant Benoit appeared at the door, bracketed by two guardsmen. He was still dressed in the robes of his rank, as though here to deliver a sermon. The numeral *II* glinted from his collar like a demonic idol. After a nod from George, they led him to the other end of the chamber, his unnaturally white hair aglow beneath the hazy overhead lamps. Four more rifle-wielding soldiers followed, assuming a line in front of the audience.

Baptiste cleared his throat, a long affair that reverberated awkwardly among the crowd.

This was it.

Seeking calm, he focused on the gray of the walls, inviting it into his soul. He stepped forward, past the guards until face-to-face with the traitor. The man's face betrayed nothing. He stood tall, only his gaze shifting to follow Baptiste.

"Jean-Paul Benoit. You have been found guilty of treason and sentenced to death."

The man smirked. It was Baptiste's first lie as lord commander. But a necessary one, a first step in healing.

His rule would be different. Expedient.

"Do you have any last words?"

Baptiste wanted a confession from the confessor, something to implicate the Church as a whole. The Church that started a war, that murdered his men, that brought misery to the only woman he ever cared for, that brought ruin to their nation by dividing it when they needed unity more than ever. This man was just a lieutenant, as he once was, doing his master's bidding. But Benoit remained silent, just as he had after his capture. No pleas, no attempts at backhanded deals. No confession.

Gritting his teeth, Baptiste turned on his heel and returned to the gallery. There was custom to follow, those affected given the opportunity to exorcise their pain.

"Are there any who would participate?"

Lafayette paled. Deckard's eyes were glazed over, trapped in the past. Of the civilians, a few had hate in their eyes, but most just sorrow. They uniformly averted his gaze. One girl, not more than ten, tried to stand away from her mother's lap but was hugged back.

Baptiste nodded, swallowing back his own nerves as he turned to the firing line.

"Ready!"

Six men lifted their rifles. Benoit's eyes twitched as realization sank in.

"Aim!"

The priest's mouth opened, a prayer chattering on his lips. His hands clenched into fists.

Baptiste sought the gray, allowed it to envelop him.

"Fire!"

———

Baptiste stared at the walls of the meeting room as George gave his report, bits and pieces penetrating the haze of his afternoon fugue: progress on wall reconstruction, impossibly high death tolls, fuel and food reallocations to the Legion, and the first session of the interim Ascendancy scheduled with Blake at the head. Mostly, he watched as Ascendant Benoit transformed from man to corpse, a final useless plea dying on his lips with the rest of him. The shrapnel of bone and blood spattering onto the gray, red cloth becoming redder until all color was drained from the living world.

"Lord Commander?"

A prickle bothered the open wound on his chest. Since the execution, it had begun to itch and burn, as though still wearing the talisman. Baptiste squirmed in his chair. The tasks ahead were endless and so much remained unknown.

"What of the battle walkers?" he asked.

"Gone."

As though they were never there. Had he been visited by a specter? A machine ghost damned to wander the world it had helped destroy?

"Last seen heading east, toward the radiation storms."

Real, then. And sure to return.

"Sir, there's also the matter of Parliament."

Baptiste winced as he was dragged fully from his ruminations to the mundanity of his office. "What about them?"

"The chancellor is demanding an address. She wants to know why the tribunal was canceled. And the whereabouts of Ascendant Benoit..."

"She can wait." Baptiste eyed his desk drawer. His entire body felt leaden. "They can all wait. That will be all, George."

His confidant stood, hesitated as though about to say something, then left, shutting the door behind him.

"They can all wait..."

He turned down the wick of his desk lamp and leaned back in his chair. The door faded into oblivion. All sound trickled away. The gray of the walls, ceiling, and floor came together into soothing unity. Nothingness filled him and he welcomed it.

Baptiste closed his eyes.

And slept.

MOTHER REBEKAH
DOMINION

Rebekah looked out upon her domain and saw that it was good.

Cathedral sprawled far and wide around the central hub of the Spire, its streets aswarm with the delivered inheritors of the earth, buzzing to her purpose.

The city swam under a deluge of acid rain. The downpour continued as it always had, thrumming against the stained-glass ceiling of her chambers, its sulfuric notes wafting in from the open window.

Beyond the curtain wall, upon the southern horizon, storms still ravaged the sky, but they were different than before. There had been a great flash, like the multitude seen during the Great War, temporarily displacing the boiling wall of black and orange. But another storm had taken its place, rolling in from the east. Change was fleeting, no matter the sacrifice. There was always another Hellmouth. There was always the work.

Rebekah dropped a hand to the bulge at her belly, feeling for the nascent life within.

"I will always be with you."

A promise from mother to daughter and daughter to mother, as Rebekah-6 died. Part of Mother Rebekah's soul had been left beneath the Spire, but another part—that which the accelerant sought to subdue—was resuscitated, crystalized from magma. She felt it in the flickering, still jumbled thoughts of her unborn child, and in the unspoken fears of her inner circle, who stood waiting behind her.

Her senses had exploded beyond even what the demon below Bastion had bestowed. Everything she touched was a conduit, connecting her mind to the animate and inanimate. In the absence of touch, every scent revealed a hidden world, hidden truths, the story of what came before. All was revealed and would be inherited.

"Great Mother?" asked Mother Leah.

Rebekah turned from the window to address her inner circle. They were all there, save Maya. The ritual keeper had not yet emerged from the annex, but she would.

Rebekah could see, feel, smell their trepidation. She was a mother as they all were, but until recently she was their peer, a fellow servant—to the Eternal One, to Messiah—now both gone. There was only God above and the sisterhood below.

For now.

Acclimation would take time, but her dominion was absolute. They would all bow down before her. They would gather up their children from the broken corners of the world and make a new world. They would save those who desired to be saved and leave the rest. And when their time passed, and they returned to dust as they must, a new Great Mother would lead the way.

The women awaited her commandment.

The world waited.

Rebekah stood tall. "Come, sisters," she said. "There's work to be done."

EPILOGUE

"RISE."

The girl opened her eyes.

Curled into a ball, unclothed as the day she was born. Her cheek pressed into the brittle clay of the earth, but it did not ache. A whisper of dust tickled her nostrils, but they did not burn. All was golden, shimmering—her hair, blowing in the wind. So long that it covered her like a cloak, so bright that it shone like the sun, enveloping her. She lingered as it caressed her body, awakening her limbs. Gentle strands rolled across the fine hairs of her long arms and fingers, around her legs and between perfect toes. Every pore of her skin sang with sensation.

Made whole, the girl pushed herself to standing, sighing at the crunch of sand beneath her feet. At first there was only her own light. But as the wind began to gale, her halo of hair parted, revealing a path. And at the end of the path, hanging on the horizon, the source of all light: a silver city, blazing with the radiance of a trillion stars, the entire universe condensed into its shimmering towers. Light and matter and energy without end.

The girl nearly collapsed, but the light held her, directed her attention, for there was also darkness here. She felt it now, at the edges, beyond the straight line of the path. A black ocean extending to either side, to infinity. Crooning, beckoning, promising continuance, life everlasting within its waves. Her gaze drifted, undulated upon its surface, but the light brought her back. She squinted against the glare, raised her hand against it though it caused no pain. Where darkness was familiar, this was new.

Sand whirled around her legs. She peered down, past the golden waterfall of her hair, to her feet. Though they looked normal, they felt heavy. The girl lifted her toes, then the ball of one foot, then the heel, and stepped forward, grimacing in anticipation of a titanic thud, of the earth breaking beneath her. But there was only the pillow softness of her sole upon the ground.

And so, she continued, step after step along the path.

The city grew closer, its light brighter, its resonance louder, and she knew it now to be a living thing—all living things. Infinite light, color, love. It flooded every part of her being, overtaking her senses, displacing her thoughts. Joining her to itself.

The girl fell back a step. "What are you?" she asked.

Her voice multiplied into the distance, caught and subsumed into the crescendo of the city's song. There was a great movement, as though all of Creation heaved with an intake of breath. The light dimmed momentarily then flared with even greater radiance. A trillion was not high enough a count; there was no end to it, not above nor below.

"I AM THAT I AM."

Each syllable rang like thunder. But like the light, they caused no pain. She waited, but nothing else came.

The choice was hers.

Behind her was the gray.

Below her was the dark.

Ahead, at the end of a long path, was the light.
It was enough.
The girl walked into the stars.

———

In the beginning, there was the void.
In the end, there was light.

AFTERWORD

Breathe in.

Hold, one, two, three, four.

Long breath out.

I write this having just completed my final self-edits and before shipping the book off to my real and very gracious editor, Lisa Gilliam. (A fine spot for my first thank-you. I appreciate that you let me be weird but not stupid!)

There's so much I could say about this series, and this book in particular, and why they are so important to me. But I'm too tired from having just written a book!

Okay, fine.

I guess I could say that they're important because there is a lot of *everything* in them: a lot of me, a lot of my family, a lot of the world, and a lot of pain. These are the component pieces of human experience. As fantastical as Mother Rebekah or that bastard Neron may seem, they are us. The Deadlands, the Sea of Screams—these are trajectories, and not very pleasant ones.

I was originally going to dedicate this book to "those who linger in the gray, between darkness and light" because it sounded so very goth. But instead, I lend a second dedication to those who strive for the light no matter how hard it is. Life is short. The future holds no guarantees. If we all do our part to usher in something better, the Silver City may yet be reachable.

On that note, a few more thank-yous:

Fellow weird fiction author Steven William Hannah, who was one of the first folks on Twitter to show me love, and who introduced me to...

Andrew Gillsmith, my author-wife, fellow incensepunk, and sounding board extraordinaire.

Jon James, progenitor of the incensepunk movement, for his incredible insights.

The two Sarahs—Balstrup and Pierzchala—fellow authors, beta readers, and keepers of enormous wisdom.

Nick, Craig, Charlie, and Quinn—my review posse.

My amazing designer Victor, who laughed and toiled with me late into the evening as we struggled over pixels and just the right amount of distressing.

Plus the myriad family, friends, and strangers who supported me along the way.

Thank you.

As for me, and Dark Legacies, we'll be back.

xo

ABOUT THE AUTHOR

Yuval Kordov is a chronically creative nerd, tech professional, husband, and father to two revenant sisters. Over the course of his random life, he has been a radio show DJ, produced experimental electronic music, created the world of Dark Legacies™, and built custom mechs with LEGO® bricks.

 facebook.com/yuvalkordov
 x.com/yuvalkordov
 instagram.com/yuvalkordov